Amy's Love

William A. Clifford

authorHOUSE®

AuthorHouse™
1663 Liberty Drive
Bloomington, IN 47403
www.authorhouse.com
Phone: 1-800-839-8640

This is a work of fiction. All of the characters, names, incidents, organizations, and dialogue in this novel are either the products of the author's imagination or are used fictitiously.

Published by AuthorHouse 07/17/2014

ISBN: 978-1-4969-2627-2 (sc)
ISBN: 978-1-4969-2626-5 (e)

Library of Congress Control Number: 2014912502

Prologue

When we left Amy, she had just been adopted, and was revelling in the novelty of it. She had gone through the search for her nonexistent parents, without success of course. She had waited for two years, for this moment. The Children's Aid Society has finished with her as of our adopting our daughter. She had taken the name of Amethyst Wrent, but continued using Amy.

Tanya and Amy had given a knockout performance at the Junior Prom. Amy's identity was not discovered since the dance.

Gloria has decided she is more comfortable being heterosexual, or at the very least bi-sexual, after the death of her grandmother. She felt that she didn't belong with a woman.

These next chapters reveal her development through high school years. The results of the formative years since her creation have posed her on the approach to adulthood.

As we follow her along this path, we find the test of friendship and society's liberality. The social acceptance of the 'Queer Persona' is in question. As the western cultures are giving way to gay marriage, others are outlawing the homosexual practise.

When you look at the zero tolerance for bullying, taken by communities and educational institutions. You find the stance is hard to take, for the victims. Bullying is an ever present threat, that is not just alive, but thriving without the targets' nerve, to stand up and accuse their molesters.

The original purpose, for Amy's existence, has been and is still, to collaborate on the similarities and differences, between male and female suffering.

The twist in the story, took place when Amy had revealed to Mr. and Mrs. Wrent, her homosexual orientation. Consolation came when Amy declared her intent to have children, but without a husband. Artificial insemination will be her chosen method for reproducing. I hope you will enjoy her evolution and how she will approach the stage, where she had lost her past incarnation.

When you have had the loss of a parent, prematurely, you fear the point of their death. It is a great release to pass that point, without incidence. This and others, will be among the trials faced, by some of the characters of the story.

Chapter One

A New Beginning

my is finally a regular person, with an identity, given to her, legally. She had waited two long years for this day. She has chosen the path she would like to take, to her career. The beginning steps have been taken. There is much to learn in all areas of life. We will be challenged on every point. Amy will not be spared that position, or will she? It is a long road to cover with certainty. Even longer with doubt.

Amy and Tanya are fourteen. I have got to get this under control. I have let this go too far. I don't have energy to chase them, or the strength to defend my accusations. The only thing I have, is the power to say no. No without going into details, and reason. I went on trying to protect her emotional state of mind. I have ignored the power I must use, to keep her safe, morally. I can't stand up to a confrontation. I collapse when I get over anxious. I have been sparing myself, and spoiling her. If I let this go on any more, I will lose her, my sanity, and I will not be able to face the good people around me. I cannot hide from God either. He gave me this and I am not handling it well.

Tanya's father has divorced Brenda, and she plans to marry her partner. Tanya doesn't know what to do. On one hand, her parents have split up, because of this other woman. On the other, her mother is in a lesbian union, with her long time best friend, and plans to solidify it with wedding vows. This is Tanya's chosen path. She can't be two-faced with her mom. She has to accept the loss of her father from her life. He has abandoned his family, so she can't feel the change is all her mom's fault. He could have fought for her. He left her because she was gay and her mother was too. He had no sympathy for Tanya. She had chosen to be the same, as her cheating mother. This is Tanya's reasoning. If it helps her cope, it is right for her. The truth is, she can't take on the world's problems, and that stance, is a sure start.

Tanya wanted Amy to attend the wedding of Brenda and Millicent Imovitch. A private ceremony in Millicent's backyard. I have to say no and I am challenged. All this time, I have let this go on. Now, I'm saying no? Did I sit through this, and even aid and abet the relationship? I did. I did nothing to spoil my relationship with my daughter, not even being a father. I have put her, in the commanding position. What can I do to rectify the situation? The only thing I should have done. I have to say no. I have played from my weaknesses. I have one strong point to back up my stand, Marie. She will be the strength behind my stance. I have to have her stand behind this decision, and she will.

Amy asks Marie, if she can go to the wedding. Marie reminds her of what she was told before. The order still stands. She has to come home after. She cannot stay the night and must be home by ten.

The small gathering is centred around a large white floral arch. The brides are dressed in matching gowns that, when together, form a floral heart. After the ceremony, the party is arranged together, in the yard, encircling the happy couple, in a heart shaped ring, as the photographer records the event, from the roof of the house. It is a grand display, for such a small gathering. The emotions boil over, as they often do at weddings. The couple had wished to marry when they were young girls, still in school. Now that it is legal, they enjoyed the occasion right through the weekend, with guests staying as long as they could. As the population dwindled, the entertainment became more intimate, to bring the guests closer. There was nothing illicit to the event, but they included all the revellers, in every point of the party. Once the last guest left, on Sunday afternoon, the family collapsed in there beds, to sleep until Monday morning.

Tanya told Amy about the things she missed. She had been good and came home as ordered, before ten. She wished she could have been there.

I don't like to be the romance cop, but I have to hold it apart, for at least until they're sixteen. At that age, they are within their rights, to leave home. It would not do any good for them, if they did, but Amy could leave us, to go to a less restrictive home. I have to keep her satisfied, with leaving the relationship on the nonphysical side. If they can hold it together, on that standard, we can progress as they show the maturity they need, to face the issues of society.

Amy had been thinking about the weekend with Tanya, that she missed out on. She had hurried to be with her and ran out the door early. Marie hadn't seen her leave and I was still sleeping and it seemed like, just another of our shared fears, were playing again in my head. It was, but more a cry for help, than a dream. I slept on.

Tanya had not noticed the difference, because she had also, been anxious to see Amy. When they got to school, they seemed to be getting a lot of attention. They wondered what could be wrong. Kids were staring and pointing. They had been seen together before, and they had not been holding hands, or anything. What is going on?

Jayme catches sight of them and hurries over to see them. "Wow, what happened to the clothes? They've shrunk!"

They look down at what they are wearing. Tanya is no different, but Amy has forgotten her baggy clothes and is showing her figure. She had been so good, so far. Now the damage has been done. The whole school will know, that she is a well formed beauty. She doesn't want the guys coming after her.

Amy asks Jayme, what she should do. Jayme replied, "Just go with it. You'd have to do it sooner, or later. May as well be now. That cat is out of the bag, and it's prowling."

That brought Amy out of her fearsome funk and set things straight for her. She laughed. Where does Jayme get these things from? She always cracks her up.

Now that that is out, she may as well bring it all out. She reaches up to Tanya and plants a big kiss on her mouth. They all felt the shock of that. Even Tanya, was caught off guard. They did not repeat it, though. 'There is no displaying of affection allowed, in the school building, or on the grounds.' The staff had not seen it, so they carried on, as if it hadn't happened. Although Tanya was grinning like a Cheshire Cat.

How can we get over this? I was awake now. I had opened my eyes just in time for the kiss. I felt the warmth of Tanya's lips and the tension that gripped her entire body. It was reverberating through Amy's fingertips. Wow! Amy grins. 'I'm out now!' she shared with me.

My reply was a vocal, "I'll say!" Once you open the floodgate, you can't get the water back behind the dam. Like pushing a cooked strand of spaghetti, it's out of your control. When it is too big for me, I just let go, and whatever happens, happens. I lie back on the bed and wipe my hand across my face. I've stopped trying to handle things like that. If it is going to be bad, it will. If not, we've survived. That's all there is to it. The dust will settle and we'll sweep it out the door, or under the rug.

Even though she was dreading the day, when something like this would happen, it is feeling more like relief, than panic, that she feels. She is going to be okay. She feels like, the world can go on about its business now. There is nothing to see here. Tanya is still grinning. Life is good.

There is a minor buzz around, as she passes kids in the hall. She doesn't catch any of it, but she feels centred in it. When she sees Jayme, she hears what it's all about. There is speculation that she, is the girl from the prom. They can't settle on it, as her height, is so much different, to the mystery girl. Amy is content. If that's all they are talking about, what was she worrying for? Sheesh!

The days past smoothly. There was not one to try to demean her, or Tanya. It was as if, there was no stigma to attach anymore. They could walk together and even hold hands, off of school grounds, that is. They would get the odd stare from people on the street. Those that don't know them. Even then, there were few to take notice. They weren't flaunting themselves, or their attachment to each other. They kept that, for their alone times.

5

Tanya's house, was the first stop, on their way home every day. They would listen to music, or watch a show. Then, when they finished, Tanya would walk with Amy, up to the stoplights and with a quick kiss goodbye, they each headed home.

The hormone storm had, for the most part, blown over. I was breathing easy, and so were they. The sensations, they had thrown into the world around them, had dissipated. I was able to carry on with my days, tiring only, from my own efforts and not, as a result of the sensual typhoon, that had been with them for so long.

Tanya's home life was better now. Her mom was home earlier and wasn't running off to meetings. She didn't put it together, but Amy did. One night, her mom and stepmother, went out to a show and left the girls with a pizza and a movie. Once the ladies had made their exit, the teens started to discuss the improvement in the living conditions. Amy suggested, that they had been meeting, everyday after work and going out together, to the 'Meetings'. Tanya was caught in an epiphany. Like a flash of lightning, tore through her mind. She just stared, blinking. How could she not get that? "You were too close to it to see." Amy explained to her. "Your dad hadn't caught on either. He was as blind to it, as you were."

"Could they have been doing this, since before Mom and Dad got married?"

"I would lay odds on it."

"Holy COW!" Tanya dropped back against the couch. "It was like Mom was cheating with Dad, on Millicent!"

"She probably only married him to have you. That way, nobody would point fingers at her, being unmarried, with a kid, and living with another unmarried woman." Amy spelled it out for her. "Back then, it was still a shameful thing, that was just not right, to the general public. She wanted a family and they worked it out, to have you with your dad, and stay together."

"How do you come up with these things?"

"I talk with my dad and my mom, and I listen to them. I also have a habit of looking at the world around me, of watching things that go on everyday." she gave Tanya a sideways glance, "I pay attention."

"So my mom did not, necessarily, love my dad? She just used him, to have me and make me legitimate?"

"That is the way it seems to me."

"So Millicent loved my mom enough, to let her go through all that, just to have me, for themselves." Tanya's gears were turning. "I don't know which way to go. Mom used Dad, so she and Millicent could have a baby."

"Not entirely. She did let your dad, have sex with her, for all the years they were together. That is a pretty big gift for a lesbian, to give to a straight guy. Now he, was the one to end it. So, really, the debt is paid, with interest." Amy gave a satisfied smile. "He got off pretty well, seeing as he is still young enough to have another family. PLUS, he can say, he had kinky sex, with a lesbian."

"I love you, and how your mind works."

"Although, most guys, would want to have two lesbians, at the same time, but then, that's what made it kinky."

Tanya pounced on Amy, and I covered my head and thought, 'here we go again.' and the girls were wrestling and giggling on the floor.

'And you're gonna hear me roar!'

Chapter Two

A Homecoming

Tanya and Amy were just getting ready to sit down and listen to some tunes, when there was a knock on the door. Tanya went to answer and found her dad, was on the other side. "Dad, what are you doing here?"

"I came to see you."

"It took you long enough."

"I had to get over things, that your mother had done."

"You mean you just now, thought about someone else, other than yourself?"

"Oh, she's turned you against me. I figured she would say all kinds of things about me, to turn your head."

"She hasn't spoken much about you. She tried, at first, to get in touch with you, to give you her blessing, to come and see me anytime. You wouldn't reply, or call for me at all, for over a year. You ran off and abandoned me."

"So, how is Ms. I'mabitch?"

"She is great to Mom."

"You calling her, Mom too?"

"Grow up Dad. You could have come back, and things would have gone on the way they always have, but you didn't. Did you not notice, that they were together, even before you married Mom?"

"What are you talking about? They were just friends."

"So, you didn't see, that they were in love with each other, all along?"

"Get outa here! How do you know all this. Is that what they told you?"

"Actually, some body else did. They were seeing each other everyday. Since before you were married. They wanted a baby and they let you be the father. To pay you back, Mom let you have sex, anytime, since the day you both said 'I do'. She let you play house with her, so that you could share me, with them. If you don't believe me, then why did she go out to meetings, all the time? What kind of meetings were they?"

Her dad just stood there thinking of all the times they would have sex. She was always up for it, without any foreplay. She would practically jump him when they got in the room. It was great for him. All the guys at work were jealous of him, for coming to work everyday, with a smirk on. He would admit to his wife's eagerness and stamina.

Tanya thought she could smell smoke, as he stood there, mulling it over in his head. "Come in and sit down, Dad. You look a little beat up. Did I hurt you?"

"A little bit. I never even noticed. She was always late coming home."

9

"You were her second job. She had to stop off to see Millicent, between jobs."

"I think, I can see it more clearly. That is why she never wanted to buy a house with me."

"Yes. She didn't want to take anything from you, when you split up. She knew that some day, it would happen."

"Who told you all this, Millicent?"

"No. It wasn't Millicent. I can't tell you whom it was. I can only say that Mom, did not try to hurt you, or take advantage of you. Besides, now you are still young enough to find another wife and have another family. You never blamed Mom, for me being a lesbian, but you made me feel, like you were blaming me, because she was gay."

"I'm sorry, honey. I never wanted to blame anything, on you, or hurt you in any way. Will you forgive me?"

"Only if you will forgive Mom and Millicent."

"I guess I can do that. If, what you told me is the truth about it, I guess it is best I do." he looked over at Amy as if he hadn't seen her. "So, Amy, how are you doing?"

They sat and watched their movie and let Father, process the information. In a short while, the moms arrived home. It was confirmed and explained to him, so that all was clear in his head. He still felt a bit cheated, but realized, that she could have left him, years ago. It is never good to keep someone in the dark, about his whole life, and how it was manipulated. He decided to just let it go, and enjoy the reunion with his little girl. He stayed with them for the night, and went on with his life in the morning. He said to Tanya, before he left, "If there's anything that you want, if there's anything I can do, just call me."

Chapter Three

All In The Family

Amy has now been revealed to the immediate family, for whom she is, a sister and an aunt. The next circle has not got the word yet. I am hesitant about saying anything. It will be very stressful, for Amy and myself, as well as Marie. In fact, Marie would rather not be there. It is hard to imagine a warm reception, from everybody. I can handle the positive, but I don't know how the negative reactions will affect us. I don't envision any and that is the problem. I like to be ready for anything. If I can't formulate an acceptable answer, I choke. Amy can show them evidence to explain it, and that is the only thing, that is clear to me. My part, is where it all goes south. I like to play things out in my head first. I get my arguments down, then have a drink to bolster my courage, and then I forget everything and go forward. The answers will always come, if I know there are any. It is like being on a trip, and leaving the written instructions at home. I get there and realize what I've done. I stop to ask directions, only to find, I am right where I am supposed to be.

One place to start, is with Marie's family. It's not too bad. I could anticipate their objections. I was ready to cover it all. This gives me courage. I think I might be able to go to my family.

There's a much bigger discussion, raised from the liberal members, than I expected. The conservative ones, were more open to see the evidence, to support my account of what was happening. Well, you know that you can't keep them all happy, all the time. I settled for what I got. The others may come around yet. Sometimes you do need to walk away. In fact, when they all understand the first try, there must be something you left out, or did wrong.

Our friends are next. I am confident, with them, I know they won't believe me, whatever I tell them. I shouldn't say that. They may be better prepared to accept it, than I anticipate.

After a whirlwind tour, Amy has been shown off to our family and friends. We each have our sanity, left intact. Well mine was never really there anyway. There are some that feel we are promoting a hoax. We don't know how those people got in. We sold the idea to about eighty five percent. That is better than I expected. I can see one, or two of them trying to get us on the news, to have us exposed, instead of helping us to keep it between the friends and family. I would have to counter by denying it was possible for us to engineer such a hoax. We are hoping it will never come to that. I am surprised that anyone would think me capable of faking this. I didn't realize they thought so highly of my abilities.

Amy shakes her head at the disbelief that some of them clung to, when confronted with the evidence. It doesn't profit us, to purport such an oddity.

We gave them a test to perform on us. I would have them separate us to different rooms, with no means to view each other. One of us was pinched and the other would wince in pain. It would be me that would holler, being the more sensitive to pain. Amy would point to the part of her body that co-responded to where they pinched me, while I would grab and rub the co-responding location on my body to where they pinched her. Eventually they came around, but not before we received a few bruises. I tell you, some people are just too suspect of new things.

Having won them over to reason, I invite their opinions, on the merit of the experiment and their conclusions, formed on the results of the tests they had performed. Some admitted to wanting to be a part of it, having imagined a similar scenario in their own lives. They decided, that it would not have been, as they had imagined. It was one of those times, when they would be glad, that their prayers would not have been answered. If they had gone as far as to pray for it. They all concluded that we were in for a rough time. They could see that there are dangers to having this link between us. Some thought we would go mad, when the real struggle started. There are some among them, that will forget being shown it.

Amy could find the memories, that I hold in the recesses of my cranium. It gave her thoughts, that we should talk this over. How is it that I have felt it, so early in my life, and the others, either felt it later, or not at all? The fibromyalgia is at question. My maternal grandmother was diagnosed at age seventy five. My father's maternal great grandfather had suffered from it, and there were signs that his mother, had inherited it from her grandfather. My father also suffered great pains, of the same sort, from his teenage years. There were other contributing factors in all the cases. When these traits are brought in by both sides of one's parentage, the odds are very close to one hundred per cent, that all the children would have this disease. As one grandparent had been diagnosed late in life, after suffering for several years, and my dad and I, suffered in our teen, or preteens, shows how the disease can differ within a group, as small as we have. It started for me, when I was about seven and I was diagnosed close to thirty five years old. My sister was diagnosed in her fifties, after suffering for many years. My other siblings have other health problems, that may, or may not be connected to it, but the distinguishing signs, aren't there yet. My doctor had told me, when I received his diagnosis, that three percent of the total population may have the disease. Three percent of them, may feel some of the symptoms, during their lifetime. Three percent of them, would be bothered by it. Three percent of those people, would feel it enough to seek help for it. Three percent of that group, could be diagnosed with clear, recognizable, symptoms. Out of those, only three percent, would be disabled at any time because of the strength of the illness. That is a simplification of the effects, but it is more, or less, an accurate portrayal, of how the disease can operate.

It seems to Amy, that she may have difficulty with it in her life. I try to calm her suspicions, with the fact that, each generation of an affected family, would half the probability, by mating with a family that does not carry the genes. Marie's family does not have any known cases in her family's history. With that, Amy is only fifty percent likely to have the malady. This would go for many of the diseases that are passed on by heredity. Because Amy was created, she was touched by the hand of God. As this is so, all disease is erased from the genes in her line. She will not pass any genetic impurities, down to her children.

"What a heritage. I am glad for the little mercies you find in the family trees. So to keep that reduction going, I should screen donors for diseases like fibromyalgia, in their bloodline."

"Good luck with that. Unless you know the donor personally, you won't be able to screen the father's family history for that particular trait."

"So for my child's sake, I should find someone I know, to donate their sperm."

"That is the only way to screen for it, but not all families would be able to have that information. Many people don't even go to the doctor, for any ailment, if they can help it. It's either fear of what they might find, or they don't want to show weakness. There are also people, that have been adopted and have not got access, to any information."

"How did your side of the family, come to have that kind of information?"

"Remarkable people in the history of the family, that took an interest in recording information, about the family history. They wrote about a significant member, and followed the progress of the families marrying into it, and where those people went. We were fortunate, in finding people on all sides, that collected all that data, and published it, within the family, or to the general public. We have a lot of history, connected to our bloodlines."

"Does it scare you to think about other things, problems we may have?"

"You can see that if you look for it, but no. I don't worry about what I don't know, and I try not to worry about what I do. It solves nothing to worry. Fear is going to get you, anytime in your life. You don't need to seek it, and you don't need to welcome it in."

"I wish I could keep it out of my life. I remember the things of the last one, and that scares me, that it might happen again."

"I know. You must remember though, that that was not an illness in your ancestry. It was a disease of society. People all over the world, are working to take that away from the human nature. The problem is, that there are also those, that foster that hate, and try to infect the rest of us. It comes down to our own, individual outlook and insight, to make us make that choice."

"I hope I can inherit your outlook and insight, so that when you're gone, I can pass it on to my children."

"The best way to do that, is to do this. Talking about it. Care enough, to bore them with it. It will get deep inside them, so that they will use it, without thinking." I have watched her thinking about her fears and I know she will face them well. I had concerns about her sexual orientation, when I found out. I have found that, I can not keep from loving her anyway. It stopped bothering me, when I saw her good heart and her similarity to myself. I have found enough wrong with myself, without blaming her for anything.

"We see so much in each others head. It seems strange, that it still feels better, to talk about it out loud."

"Yes. We get it out in the open and let go of it. It floats off, into the wide expanse of the universe, where it is lost. Venting is best done out loud. If all we do, is think about it, it all is trapped within us."

'Up, up and away, in my beautiful, my beautiful balloon.'

Chapter Four

The Bridge

Times are tough all over. I've heard that excuse too much. Still it hurts you when the trouble is close. Tanya's father, Dave, was drinking with some buddies, that weren't too swift. He got talking about his family life, and how his wife had left him for another woman. They told him, if their wives did that, they would kill them. The drinking and discussion got worse and heated. Finally Dave had got enough bad advice, to go to his wife's home, with a gun. He burst in the front door. Luckily, while forcing the door open, the gun discharged. It alerted the house. Fearing the worst, Brenda got Tanya and Millicent out the back door and over to a neighbour's house, where she called 911. Other neighbours had heard the shot and also called in. The Police were there in about five minutes. There was always cars in the area and one happened to be at the mall nearby. Dave was wandering in the house, looking for Brenda and the 'wife-stealer'. He was not used to drinking that much and was soon starting to feel overcome by it. He was staggering across the living room floor, as the Police caught sight of him. He tripped and went headlong into the side of the fireplace. Gnashing his head hard on the stone, put him down and unconscious. The SWAT team had arrived and slipped in through the open front door and the back door at the same time. They found Dave in a lump on the floor. He was bleeding and motionless. The officers got the gun away from his side. It had not been reloaded. They secured his hands and tried to revive him. He was spaced out when he came to. Paramedics had just come in and took over. The first responding officer, had gone to the neighbours and was interviewing the women. A member of the team came in to let them know it was safe and that he was in custody.

They've seen this happen too often. Dave has just thrown the rest of his life, into the pile of stuff he had been advised by. He will face charges and, if convicted, he will likely spend time behind bars. He will lose his job. He may not be able to see his daughter again. The rescued relationship he had, is gone. There will not be a second chance to have a life, where there is trust, and affection from them. They had just got to the point, where he was welcome in the house. The guys that had given him the advice, were not even aware, of what they had done. They talked tough all the time. They drank and remembered little of it.

Dave spent two weeks in hospital. He received no visitors. He went from there to jail.

During that time, Brenda and her family, started thinking about moving. They wanted to distance themselves, from the chance, that he could do this again. Their lives were thrown into disarray. They were startled easy, by the slightest thing. A knock on the door sent fear ripping through their minds. They approached it gingerly. It was a delivery for a neighbour. The neighbour wasn't home, would they take it for them. Nothing helped. They had someone come to counsel them, to try to set their minds at ease.

During this time, Tanya had come to stay with us. The girls slept together, when Tanya was able to sleep. They were not thinking about anything that, would be normal, when they were together. The fear of the upset got revisited. It brought back Amy's fears. This time, it would serve to help Tanya, come to grips with hers. Amy would put soothing music on her stereo. It would play softly, while she would cradle Tanya's head on her lap. She would stroke her hair with one hand, and hold her hand with the other.

The thought that, her father, would try to kill her mother, or Millicent, took away the innocence from her life. If he had not been drunk, he would have been able to get in, with no trouble. Amy tried to reason, that he may never have had the idea to try that, if he was sober. It was a small chance to cling to. The thought that he was that easy, to push to that extreme, took away that small comfort.

Tanya was with us for two weeks, while her mom and stepmother decided what they were going to do. During that time, Amy was completely under control. They went to and from school every day, together and were pretty much inseparable, outside of class. Only once, did someone make a crack about her parents, but the others around him, shut him up quick.

Together they would go to the movies and window shopping at the mall. They were keeping busy. They weren't allowing each other time to dwell on much of anything.

When Brenda came to pick her up, there were many tears. They learned that, the decision was made, and they were staying put. They assured Tanya, that he would not be coming around anymore. When they got back, things were not easy. The wall damaged by the shotgun, had been repaired and painted. The physical damage may have gone, but the memory was still there. Tanya had heard plenty at school, and on the news, about fathers that would kill their exes and their children. How was she to know, whether he would stop at killing the women, and not her?

Because he was so intoxicated, he did not remember, what he had done. So they had to go to trial. He could not plead guilty, since there was no knowledge of the deed. The court would not accept a guilty plea. This means, that all the evidence needed to be set forth during a trial. They will have to give what evidence they had. That evidence was very little. They had not seen him, but heard someone break in, through the front door, and a gun was fired. When they had phoned the emergency number, they had just said, that someone had broken in, and fired a shot. They had not seen him, at all that night. The only evidence that places him, with control of the gun, was the first responding officer, and the SWAT team. He had seen Dave, with the shotgun, saw him trip and fall, headfirst, into the fireplace. The tactical unit had seen him with the gun, while he was laying on the floor. If it was not witnessed by the police officers, he might have been acquitted. The search light had been shining in the window, to help the officer identify the gunman. Dave was subsequently, sentenced to two years, for attempted murder. The judge had given the lenient term, because it was his first dealings with the law. He had not even had a parking ticket. The judge had recommended psychiatric counselling, while in jail.

With Dave in jail, they could relax again. He can hold nothing to them. Their testimony had, nearly, set him free. The police were the ones that had placed him there, with control of the gun, that had just been fired. The family had had no idea, that it was him. With the relationship that had been rebuilt between them, Brenda had no reason to suspect him at all.

Now both Amy and Tanya had violent memories to haunt them. Children that age, should not have to have these kind of things in their lives. The sad thing is, that too many children, much younger children, have them.

When Tanya goes for counselling, she brings Amy with her. Amy says that she is helping Tanya, build a way to get over this.

'Like a bridge over troubled water, I will ease your mind.'

Chapter Five

Silver Linings

The spring is going to be early. That's the word from the groundhogs this year. It's time for our trip to Cuba. More friends are coming along and we are excited about all the mischief we will be into. I have decided to go along on the speedboats this time. I may not have many more chances to do it with friends. This is the biggest contingent from the UK yet. The Canada crew are always fluctuating. There are many of us with health woes and it gives us the wakeup call, every time we get into winter. With new parts, still under warranty, we brave the tropical elements. The sticky white coral sands, the hot humid temperatures, the glaring bright sun, and that seductive salty air, are not going to get us down. Not even the free flowing rum, will spoil our winter season. All those friendly people, we see every year, gathering in this sweltering paradise, are going to help us with our determination, to be set in our ways.

We have started our packing earlier each year. New comfort aids are coming along. Padding for those long days under the palms, in those beach lounges, will ensure that we will not abandon our posts without a fight. All the activities we will be avoiding, don't stand a chance. The food will have to come to us this year. It is possible, to stay on the beach 24 hrs. a day. Working overtime, although they stop bringing the drinks to us for a few hours during the night.

Seriously though, we are counting on better conditions. Not that they were bad in the past.

Amy wants us to take her with us this time. We are almost all retired, and most of us, have still not reached maturity yet. She will know every move and thought I have, so I will not be sparing her anything. I will have to have her okayed, by the committee that okayed me, to go along. The chances are slim for this year. We would have to get a last minute booking and these flights are usually sold out. Especially after the winter two years ago. Finding room at the resort would be easier, as she would be with us, or one of the others, that might be alone.

After much deliberation, the committee has said no. Amy is heartbroken. I promise her a spot next year, if it doesn't interfere with school exams. Amy assured me the exams were over in January. I did not even notice that she had had exams. Boy, how alert can I be, if I know all she sees and does? I must have been concentrating on the trip and didn't take any notice. I apologize to her. She just shook her finger at me. No, not that one.

I suggest to Marie, that Amy might stay at Tanya's, while we are gone. She thinks it's alright, if Brenda is on board with it. I give her a call that night and she agrees. Amy is instantly ecstatic over it. She had not made a move, in thought, or deed, since I picked up the phone to make the call. Suddenly the trip is forgotten. I could not have come up with a better consolation prize.

I did want to take her with us this year, but that was something beyond my control. We have one short for a room, and it would even that out. Instead, they will have three in one room. This year, the Brits will outnumber the Canucks.

Tanya and Amy have apportioned out their two week allotment, and are losing sleep, over the sleep, they will be losing then. There is nothing to compare with excited teenage girls, getting ready for something planned on short notice. I can see how I missed the exams. They think so fast and talk faster.

All the possibilities that occurred to me, prior to this experiment, were so naive. Having two people thinking and feeling each other's thoughts and feelings, was mind blowing. Amy has that and one more person, to add to that. I think of God, with all those people praying to him, all around the world, in every time zone, in every language. The din would never cease. I thank Him, for being Him.

As the departure time approaches, we finish packing and start testing the bags, to see if we can close them, and lift them. I thank God, for the people that put wheels on luggage. Now if those vacuum storage bags would work better, we could use them, to help us pack it all. Each year we bring more things, to give away to the schools, and the villages, that are out of the way, and neglected by the current regime. Like many countries today, they have a struggling economy.

The day soon arrives and we are taking Amy to Tanya's, the evening before we leave. Brenda and Millicent have us in for quick drink, to celebrate another vacation trip, come upon us. We enjoy a glass of Irish Cream, and chat about the good things happening for the girls. They are growing up before their time, with this nonsense of Dave's idiotic move and the reasons to soon forget that. We discuss the chance that we would become in-laws. We are warning, that they have so much to learn about themselves, and they really haven't had a major disagreement, yet. The time goes by and we need to get back home and prepare to leave the next morning.

The alarm goes off, to our surprise, we have actually slept a few hours. We get dressed and ready to head out. The bags are at the door and the phone rings. It's the gang we are to meet. The plane is delayed. There was a problem with one of the engines. We will be picked up a half hour later. Marie and I decide to go over there anyway but stop for breakfast on the way. We don't mind the delay. As long as they fix the problem, we will be fine.

After we eat, we head to our meeting point. We arrive just as the others do. We have a chat, after we have arranged the cars. "Are we ready for the snowstorm to hit tomorrow, after we leave?" Everyone laughs. It will be consistent with the last seven years. They try to guess which luggage will be overweight this time. As we are embroiled in the game, the limousine pulls up to collect us. I was wrong, the Canucks and the Brits are even. There had been an unannounced change.

If we were teenagers, we would think the time dragging by while we wait. As retired adults, some of us senior citizens, the time flies by with a passion. In just a couple of minutes we are clipping along the highway to Toronto. Just as the years past have been, we are chattering away, all along the route. Once at the airport, we check our luggage and get our seat assignment rechecked. We will have no repeat of the trip, two years back. After that, we go through security, and look for a place to snack.

We pick a spot near the gate and then take turns hitting the restrooms.

We hear the call for pre-boarding, and Marie and I get over to the gate. We are on quickly, being at the front of the line. Just a few minutes later, the rest are coming down the aisle. They take their seats across from us. The plane is loaded in no time at all and we are heading down the runway ahead of schedule. That is, the revised schedule. If the air currants are favourable, we could be there by the original ETA. We are excited, and are still jabbering on. We break out the snacks, that were brought from home, another tradition. I dig out my headphones for the movie. I have brought a few to share. I get a little nervous about flying, because we have flown so many times, without incident. I keep wondering about the odds of never having a problem on the flight. Marie calms me, and reminds me that they just fixed a problem and it will not likely happen again on the way down.

~

Amy and Tanya are up early to enjoy breakfast together. They chat away about the things they want to get done that day. They are even out the door early. They're too caught up in the conversation that they are absentmindedly moving through the routine. They notice when they are on the bus that the usual kids aren't there. They look at each other and laugh at themselves. They get to the bus stop and wait. They surprise Jayme when she gets off.

"How did you get here so early?" Jayme asked.

Tanya answered, "We were too busy talking. We left early without noticing."

Jayme asked, "How come you're not staying at our house?"

It was Amy's turn to answer, "I wanted to go to Cuba, so they had me stay at Tanya's to keep me happy. Next year, I'm going though. Dad told me I can."

"Lucky." Jayme looked envious, "I wonder what my mom will say about that."

"I know. They didn't go places like that, when they were my age."

"Yeah and they won't take me." Jayme says.

"Mom said if they had the money, they would take the whole family. But they would have to win the lottery to get it. They don't even buy lottery tickets anymore."

"Yeah, so they won't have to take us with them." Jayme complains.

They get on to classes and the couple are feeling quite like they are living together, outside the parental home. They imagine themselves, in their own apartment. They think of being married and having children of their own. The fantasy goes on and they feel as though it was really happening. They start discussing their future, in terms of college, and careers. Tanya would like to be a veterinarian. While Amy has her sights on being a family counsellor. They start finding out about the courses they would like to take, and those they would have to take. Amy had done that for herself, last year. They started coming to terms, about the sacrifices they would have to make, to have this vision come true. They are planning their life, in earnest, and doing a good job of it. They see their guidance counsellor, to get this all mapped out for them.

~

I tell Marie about what the girls are up to. She is impressed. "All this, because we wanted to make it up to her, for leaving her home again. What will they do next to astound us?"

The heat is not bothering me as much this year. We have the room we wanted. I get to walk up the five stories, to get my exercise and cool off in the room, as well as the ocean. The hotel staff had wanted to upgrade our room for us, but we insisted, that this was the best room for us, because we wanted to walk up. It was not common among their patrons to want to walk up five storeys. Especially someone like me with disabilities. Marie and I were getting up there faster, than the ones taking the elevator. Of course, we were pushing the call button on each floor as we passed it, so the elevator would stop at each one. I will be able to stay on track with keeping in shape and losing weight. We still get to relax on the beach and keep fit. I do have the drinks as our normal Cuba routine. Our good friend, Johnny Cool, keeps us supplied and entertained.

Some of the staff, has changed here and we are missing the ones, that have moved on.

The outings this year cover the spectrum. The newcomers, John and Pat, are getting to see what they have missed, these past years. They don't go on them all, but do go on something from every type. There are enough excursions, to go on something different, every year.

We are still a supplement, to the entertainment, offered at the resort. The annual water ballet is duplicated, by the girls, the next day. It is a farcical performance that many are now gathering to watch. The word has gotten around, about the prowess of the ladies, and their support team. They count on me as usual to catch the star performer and I miss her every time. It's like the clown show at the circus. Dedicated, to bringing the lowest form of flattery, with the highest level of ineptitude. The spectacle should not be missed.

I find I have answered out loud, something Amy asks me. She has also been seen, giggling at somethings we say, or do. These are the hazards of living within the dynamics of our lives. I can get away with it, because I look as crazy as I seem, with my one eye small and fully dilated. People are giving me a wide berth. I just say, "tourette syndrome," Amy just says, she just thought of something funny. She keeps a few memories handy, to tell them, if they insist she share the joke.

~

In the girls' room, they have set up a spread sheet, of a sort, to list all of their goals and necessary qualifications, or pre-requisites. They include a timeline, to set limits, for the required goals to co-inside with the qualities needed, for the next phase. It looks very professional. This is Amy's training from that past life, that gets this so organized. They include recreational goals as well, to keep from becoming too focussed, on the work portions. Who does these things?

Brenda is amazed, at the change, that has come over them. She finds that she is becoming more organized, from keeping pace with the effort, they are putting into this.

Milli, as the girls have started calling her, is also impressed by them. She finds just being with them, is driving her to arrange things in her life, more efficiently. When faced with someone with a purpose, who quietly strives for that purpose, without seeking influence over anyone else, you are inspired to do better in your own life.

The girls, although focussed and driven, also take time for romance, to reward their efforts, and keep the prize in front of them. While stuck in that snowbound environment, Amy draws warmth from me, as we bask in the hot tropical shade. With an average temperature of thirty degrees Celsius in the Cuban days, my body is transmitting to her senses, and she, in turn, is wanting to share that warmth with Tanya.

~

There are some exceptions to that principle, I am one said exception. When faced with someone working diligently toward their desired goals, I am drained of the energy, so desperately clinging to me. I have such a weak grasp on the motivation I try to surround my thoughts with, that I find it sticking to anybody that is working near me. I know this to be connected to the fibrositis. That malady affects so many different parts of your being. The muscles, organs, brain, all are at the mercy of this merciless condition. It is a nuisance disease that will not take your life. It will, however, suck the life essence out of you. It mimics so many things that are much worse, but it robs you of the motivation to work at fighting it, and the only way to keep motivated is to keep working to fight it. Exercise is the key, to overcoming its ravenous thievery. Hence my choice, of staying on the top floor and using the stairs always.

The sound of the gentle surf, against the reef protected shoreline, lulls you to sleep. The slow sway of the hammock, keeps you cradled and safe from harsh activity nearby. Exercise is the key, but comfort is the elixir that rewards the efforts. There are people all around me, swimming, playing volleyball, chatting ceaselessly. It all fades into the sound of the surf, the wind through the palm leaves, and the call of the tropical birds.

The call of one in particular, Johnny Cool, alerts me to a fresh opportunity. 'Rum Punch, por favor. No ice!' It doesn't matter much about the ice if the drink is going to be nursed along, but if I want to drink it, I don't want the ice to remind me of what we are escaping. Besides, it gives me indigestion.

The excursions are slowly emptying our stores of gifts. We are replacing them with rum and other souvenirs. I am going to the market, this time. I want to get something for our cottage. I want one of those Cuban drums and some maracas. I had seen them on a previous trip and was dissuaded from purchasing them. I have a reason now, as I move swiftly from my sixtieth birthday, and stepping firmly on the threshold of my sixty fifth. I am approaching a time when I may not be able to come back. I want to play these instruments, during my alone times at the cottage. I do need to have a prize to keep my eye on.

We have two couples to go on the speedboats. Marie and I, with Tom and Sally, are riding the wild surf. Really, it's only wild, because I'm driving. I'll be following Tom. Marie will be holding on for dear life. She doesn't know why, she let me talk her into it. Tom and Sally have been going on this excursion for years. They've wanted us to go, ever since we met. When we get out there on the water, it's calm and serene, until we start moving. There are eleven boats, all supposedly following our guide. Tom has his own agenda, and I'm following him. You start to see what looks like a demolition derby. Thank God it is not that bad. With only one eye, I have to be careful with my depth perception. I am glad, that I watched all that 'Bass Masters' TV show, to learn how to handle a speedboat. I review those lessons, and go through it step-by-step. Most important is 'How to make a sudden stop, from full speed.' Put the throttle in the off position and crank the wheel 90 degrees. Then put the gear in the neutral position. Okay Tom, take it away. Good thing I wasn't watching those surgical shows.

Well, that was exhilarating, for me. Marie looks kind of white. "Put your head down, Marie. You did your duty. If it wasn't for your colour, I would think you had full faith in me."

No answer from her. I think I should keep my eyes open tonight. Amy lets me know just what Marie is thinking, and I won't be asking her to come on the speedboats again. I don't think I'll be driving anything, with her in it.

I told my sister one time, when she had me take her, in her new truck, to my brother's place. 'You're pretty brave, riding with a blind man.' She hadn't heard my telling her about my sight problem before. No matter how much she protested, I kept going. She does a lot of risky stuff. So, I knew she could take that. What did she do in her seventieth year? She took flying lessons and became a qualified pilot. She has flown before, with hang gliders. Now she can fly a plane, on her own.

~

I always entertain my kids and grandkids with my scary stories, about my driving adventures. They've ridden with me, so they know they're true. Amy gets to experience them, safely outside of the vehicle, on solid ground. She decides to have Marie teach her to drive. After I tell Marie this, Amy thinks she'll take a training course. She is content to wait for her sixteenth birthday, before signing up.

Safe at Tanya's home, she is enjoying a relaxing soak in the tub, with her girl at her side. Saving water with her BFF. I will never be able to get used to these things. Candles surrounding the tub, the stereo playing and nothing to go outside for, in the cold. Brenda and Millicent are watching TV in their bedroom. Romantic scenes throughout the house. No males around to spoil it for them. A place of peace, with the memories of that night, set aside. I can't help but be glad for them. The teens are getting pretty pruny, sitting for so long and warming the water when it cools. They are using up the tea lights while they soak. It is so nice, warm, wet, slippery bodies, laying there, they gaze into each others eyes. Amy thinks, 'It's strange that she can hear Marie's and my thoughts, but the one she wants to hear are denied her.' They lay there while, one by one, the candles go out. As the room darkens, they hold each other closer.

Finally, they are down to the last two tea lights. They climb out and dry each other. They go to the bedroom and climb under the covers. The mood is kept alive as they lie down and just hold one another in sweet, seductive, bliss. They don't go any further. This is the way they find themselves, as they are awakened by the movement of the breathing. A peaceful night of wonder, their energy spent, in the silent stillness of their loving embrace.

Amy wakes first and stares at Tanya's face until she finally opens her eyes. She greets her with a kiss and Tanya rewards her by telling her, "Man, your breath is bad."

I find it hard to believe that that could have happened, with a boy in her bed. I guess I could, have a chance, to get used to this playing in my head.

They have two weeks together. They are playing house, ignoring the presence of the others except to bring them breakfast to delay their trespassing, in the idyllic game they are portraying. They start a fire in the fireplace and settle in each others arms again. They know real life, alone, will be more than this and so much less romantic, but this is why they prolong the wonder. They do everything together, as if attached. The serenity of the scene is soothing to me. As I am moving about at the resort, I can't help moving in their rhythm, their mood. They start to dance to the slow tempo of the song on the stereo. Pressing themselves together. No space to let anything come between them. They feel the wonder in their minds, at the extension of the heightened sensitivity. The sensuous sensations are engrossing them in an aura of rapture. They feel enclosed in a cloud filled with the warmth of their own body heat. They are separated from the world about them. They don't notice the other women come in and share their music in a dance of their own. They are suspended from the reality and are being carried away in the embrace. They are flying about in a vista of their own creation. It is more real than real. More peaceful, than any hope for heaven to hold. They are high on the drug of their own imagination. It is a closer connection than Amy holds with me. It is the creation of their own minds entangled in the firma about us. The atmosphere is as intoxicating as I have ever felt. I am caught in this field of being. I am with them, but ignored. I dare not move, lest I awaken them from their paradise and dash them into the reality, so harsh and acidic. They slowly become aware of themselves. Their features becoming inflamed with the rawness of their nerves. They have gone as far as their physical beings can allow them. They slowly relax their grip on each other. As they let go, I am released from their clutch and remember the feelings I had shared with Marie. This blissful emanation does not come along many times in one's life. You hold these feeling in your memory, more precious than diamonds.

They collapse on the couch and catch the stare, of the others in the room. They look back and smile. They have experienced a non-physical sex, as good, as anyone could hope for, in their whole existence. I feel honoured, to have been witness, to that expression, of gentle care.

~

I find my way to a lounge. I had been suspended where I was standing. Unable to feel the physical pain, from my numbing limbs. I had used up all the energy, I dare expend. Had I lost any more, I would be laying on the walk. The others around me, look at me with indignation. I had sat down among people I did not know. I excused myself and explained that I was about to faint. With no more strength, I asked them to help me over to my friends. As they take me along, Marie and the others rush to help. The questions are flying at me and right on past. It is the helpful strangers that answer for me. They ask if I should see a doctor. I manage to wave them off. I utter, "I am just exhausted from an experience and anxiety." They allow me to rest, and chatter among themselves, about me and my conditions. They talk of fears about heat stroke. I manage to wave that off. They look at me in wonder. What had gotten to me, that would leave me like that? When I have the strength, I explain the anxiety. I tell them about the experiences I had regularly at work. I say, "I am quite accustomed to the feeling." I do not explain the true cause of the collapse. I would tell Marie, later in private. She will remember the occasion we shared, and a similar feeling. It is true, that you can climb in someone else's mind, if you bring yourself close enough, to caring about the feelings they can get from you. An out of body event of sorts. I have been part of that connection with Marie, twice and have longed to repeat it. A singular event shared by two people.

I have felt a similar feeling, while engrossed in the hymns being sung at church. I could feel myself, outside my head, rising into the rafters, and looking down, at the congregation, as if I was being allowed, to stand beside God, in His house. It was explained to me, as astral projection. I felt it was as much as, letting the music into you and you, into the music.

Johnny Cool has come to see how I was. He had seen me standing there, not moving. When he could come over, I had gone. He takes the refill orders and heads off to retrieve them. The gentle breezes help me to recover. I am fortunate, to have friends, and the wherewithal, to be able to come with them, to this earthly paradise. This, our seventh year, is satisfaction to, at least, have led a life worthy of the happening enjoyed by us, this day. You've heard the expression, 'While the cat's away, the mice will play.' Well I tell you, when the cat's away, the cat, will play as well. Amy is quite used to the innuendos, that she takes little notice, to all the references within our conversations. We keep the language clean, but the innuendos, dirty. We are sixty somethings, still living our teenage years.

Once recovered, I warn Amy to be careful. Keep to the cerebral and stay away from the physical.

If you can age, without fully growing up, you can stay young enough, to at least have an idea, of what God means, when He asks us to live like children. You may embarrass your kids, but then they may, be doing the same thing. You can only hope. So far only one child of mine, has grown up. I think his kids will help him back. It's like the movie 'Hook'.

Sitting here on the beach, I think of all those things that should have taken my life. The fall off the bridge, the third story falls in the barn, the car crashes, breaking my back and neck, and the near impossible fitting of my van between a concrete wall and a semi tractor trailer closing the gap at highway speeds. Oh, and driving through a blinding blizzard, at top speed, with faith that God was getting me through, and that no one else, would have the gall, to be driving that night. One hundred kilometres, of driving blind, without incidence. You can't tell me faith doesn't work. And here I am, sitting on this beach, still as much alive as ever.

That is why, I feel, there is something for me to accomplish yet. This experiment, may be that something. This telling, may be that deed that I must do, before I can finally be allowed to pass, from this world. I have said before, that only the good die young, and that is why I, still live.

Chapter Six

Are You Still Here

We have still some time yet, before we head for home. The weather is amazing, and if it wasn't for the families at home, we would stay longer. Plus, being with the same people, day in and day out, soon, you run out of things to say and do. We all feel it, and no one, is offended by it.

We've gone back to see the dolphins, the poor fishing village and school, and the speed boats. We've done the paddleboats, kayaks, and Hobie-Cats. We've visited friends, shopped at markets, and strolled along the beaches. We've seen weddings and were invited to join one. We've planted trees, held wildlife, and helped celebrate anniversaries. We've shared our pictures with our local friends, and taken new ones of them. We don't know how much time we have, so, we wasted none of it. The last few days we have, are needed to recharge, after recharging.

At home, Amy is getting anxious to have us back. Things have been epic between the girls, but she needs to recharge too. I have doubts, that they will ever stray, from each other. It is almost impossible, to find a love like that, from the first one you care for.

I see the things I've done in my life to find what they have. I know, it is all that, that has given me what I need, to relate these experiences to you. We must live life, to know anything about it.

Amy knows enough, from her former life, to know not to waste it, when you find that you have it. Tanya may just be able, to see it through her eyes, enough to recognize it. They are smarter than I am. I went through hell, and took others with me, to get to where I am. Amy did it all alone. I don't know if I could live up to the expectations of others. How could I expect others to live up to mine?

We always celebrate the birthdays here. It doesn't matter whether you count them or miscount them. We celebrate another accomplishment, another year of life led.

We return to the Indian village, for John, Pat and me as well. There are so many things to do here, and this attraction is one to remember. Amy tells Tanya and the others about the painting. It is put on their bucket list, to see and to try. The ceremony is also a big draw.

"The time has come," the walrus said, "to talk of many things." And what we are talking about, is the trip home. We are packed up and shopped out. We head to supper and some time at the bar. It's our last night and we have our carry-on clothes on, so we do not disturb the packed suitcases. In the morning, we don the our travelling clothes and say our last goodbyes. We go to breakfast and a stop at the bar. Then we head out to the doors to wait for our chariot. We are both sad to leave and anxious to go. We will miss the warmth and fear the icy reception, in Toronto.

The bus pulls up and this year, it's on time. We are herded onto the bus and our bags are aboard. We are off, to pick up more passengers, at the other hotels. That done, we cruise to the airport. We have requested seats at the front where I will be able to straighten my legs. When we get to the check-in counter, we are surprised to get what we asked for. Things are looking up. We are preboarded and then the others are loaded. We get away quickly. As we rise up to the clouds, we look back and say goodbye to Cuba. We are half way home when the captain comes on to announce the change in flight plan. Toronto has just closed due to a storm that has just hit bringing the visibility down to ten feet. A blinding blizzard that has several hours of continuous dumping at Pearson. We are being rerouted to Hamilton International, where the storm is not expected to hit for two more hours. That is a window big enough to land and be disembarked. Our limo will be sent to pick us up there. Yes, things are looking up beautifully. For us, this is great news. For the people catching a connecting flight, it is questionable. They will be shuttled to Pearson, unless the connecting flight has been rerouted to Hamilton as well. If we had had the storm hit while we were still in Cuba, we would have been returned to our resort, and kept there free of charge until it is safe to go back. We were torn. We didn't know which we would prefer. We are happy to be landing in Hamilton.

We land in Hamilton with the snow just starting to fall. Once in the airport terminal, we breathe a sigh of relief. Going through customs is quick and easy. There were no long corridors to trudge through. Luggage and customs, over in half the time as of that in Toronto. Stepping out of the terminal, we see our ride pulling up. We toss in our bags and climb inside. The driver said he was called in plenty of time so did not have to turn around. A quick and short ride to our destination. As we get out of the car, we are hit with the heavy and blowing snow. We get right into our car head for home.

We just get in the door and the phone is ringing. It is Grace. She called our number by mistake. She was surprised we got home so fast. When we told her what had happened, she was thrilled for us. As Marie talks to Grace, Amy comes in the door. Millicent brought her home since she was heading out to pick up dinner. They would have had her stay, but she was tired and missed us.

Amy helped us get the luggage sorted out, and then got ready for bed. She came into the living room and sat on the loveseat. We sat down and chatted with her for an hour, before she got up for bed. We went to bed early also.

'I couldn't sleep at all last night, 'cause I got something on my mind....'

Chapter Seven

Floating Upstream

Sometimes you go through things without realizing what it takes to get through it. It's done before you get it. You look back and then it hits you. How the heck did that happen? That's when you become more aware, that someone is looking out for you. You thread the eye of a needle with a four ton vehicle and a semi. You lose control of your car, spinning on black ice through traffic, ending up on the other side, up against the curb. How could you explain it? You get caught in a ridge of snow on the highway. It pulls you sideways. You know you are about to lose it, but by some chance, you make the right moves and get back in control. How did you get out of that one? That is why I have faith. That is also why, I am the only one, that would choose to ride alone with me driving. On purpose!

The sweet times, the ones that make you glad of the struggle won, and the effort spent. The times you can let down your guard. You put yourself in the arms of another and trust them to take care of you. You are not easily led, but you go against your nature and let it happen. Of all the lessons you learn in life, is what brings you to this, when your reluctance has been beaten into you. You feel the eyes on you and that it will be alright.

Imagine the soul of Amy. What she went through at the end of her past life. Being brutally murdered and tossed away like garbage. She is among the ones asked to, not only take on another life, but to be attached to another's painful life and death, to share with him all your inner most thoughts and dreams, and the most private moments of your life. Being able to hear the thoughts of not just one but two people, without relief until death ends each life. She steps up and volunteers to put herself in that situation and has to remember the agony of what she had already been through. Would you sign up for that? As if that is not enough, she gets hitched to my wagon. One that a number of people have offered to 'fix.'

When I first saw her, I thought, 'Oh, man, I'm in trouble now.' She was developed past her age. I saw other young girls in that stage, being chased by men, let alone boys. When she told me she was gay, I was like, 'Ha, those guys don't stand a chance,' and then I think of the ones that won't take no. I think, 'we could have a problem after all.' A father's mind can get such a beating, when his little girls are teenagers, or even tweenagers. I was the one to ask for this. I deserve the punishment I get.

Just watch the waterfowl in the slow moving streams. They look so at ease, so graceful. Like they are floating upstream. Under the water, they are paddling like crazy.

Right now, I'm paddling like crazy. I don't know what I'm in for. Amy is, well, too into Tanya, for our trips up north in the summer. I don't know if I can, take responsibility for the two of them. I have been counting on Amy for help, during the time that Brad is working at his jobs at home. I can't imagine my role as 'Grampa' on 'Heidi'. They are a little too mature for their roles. Amy still wants to go, if I can take Tanya along. Assuming you were in this position. What would you do? Remember that you have already come to terms with their relationship and it is sanctioned by Tanya's parents. The cottage is run down and only used for the working bathroom and rudimentary kitchen. For sleeping arrangements, there is a camper trailer and two tents, with tarps above them for weather protection and cooling. We are by a river's exit from a lake. We are a half hour from the nearest store, on a bike ride, or a boat ride from the nearest marina. Would you be able to take responsibility for two, fourteen year old girls, setting aside their being gay? You're not much help. Some say yes. Some say no. It looks like I will have to try it, and hope for the best.

Our work will include some demolition and some carpentry, some electrical and plumbing, but first we have to set up camp. I take the tents down and pack them away, the trailer is packed down, and the tarps are put away. We have a solar panel electrical back up. Until it is ready to power the camp proper, we haven't got a big battery bank for it, just two car batteries. In the tents are queen-size BYO beds, with foam on top of them. They have side tables and lamps. These have to get set up and it will take two days, with all hands on deck. It is a beautiful camp, but that is only until the cottage is finished. My workers need some comfort, if they are going to be of help to me. It prepares them for some real jobs, when they are of age.

The decision is made and the girls will be coming with me. Marie stays home to work. So the trip is for just me and the girls. Marie may come up for some R-and-R, but not to stay too long until the cottage is done. We bought a large canoe to get some exercise and exploration done. I have my trike and we have bikes for more exercise and shopping. Brad has brought my old fishing equipment up for us to get some fresh food now and then.

Once the school year is done, we get up to the cottage, as quickly as possible. The girls are hyped up about it. Tanya only knows, what Amy has told her. The departure is planned for the midmorning and that will depend on how much 'I' can get hyped up. I am excited, but it's always conditional with me. Coolers are packed and that is just enough to take us four days. When I get up, I am shown pictures of the area we are working in. This is to get me ready to drive three to four hours. My breakfast is made and the girls have packed the supplies in the van. It's a good thing the cottage has room to store almost all the camp equipment. We would be very tightly packed if it didn't. Wait a minute! I haven't told you about the how we got the cottage.

It was after Amy said goodbye to Gloria. We headed east, for some quick shopping in the real estate offices. We found the cottage in between two stops. It was remote and had a sign at the entrance to a gravel road. It took awhile to worm our way through the woods, to where the lake came into view. The road split and the sign directed us to the left. At the end of the lane was a clearing, right up to the shore. It was on a rise, maybe ten feet high. The roof looked okay for my eyes. Amy thought it was just okay. Inside was neglected. We called the number on the sign. The one on the other end told me the price and we decided to go for it. The owner came down to see us and while we waited for him, we walked along the sandy beach. Most lakes here don't have sandy beaches. They are usually rock, or marshy shores. I asked about the beach. He said his grandfather had it trucked in.

There is some rocky areas and marshy, but they were on opposite ends of the sand beach. He said that it was a lot bigger when he was a boy. It was a more solid area that got the sand. The man told us the cottage is an estate sale. His father had inherited it and left it to him, when he passed away. It was too rundown for him to fix and that is why the price is so low. He had just put the signs up the day before. We agreed on a price and thanked him for the opportunity to bring it back to life. So there. Now you know.

We got up to the cottage in mid afternoon. The trailer was still sitting level, so we didn't have to mess with it. Amy and I just cranked it up with a tarp over the roof. While we did that, Tanya brought in the supplies from the van to the cottage. We set up the beds and made them. This will be our shelter for the night. Tomorrow we will set the tents and tie down all the tarps over top of them. The tarps channel the breezes over them and draw out the warm air underneath. Like the airflow over an airplane's wings. I used that form of air-conditioning while we were camping on Long Point. We were well noticed for our big gray roof. We wanted a cottage of our own and quit camping there, to concentrate our vacations at my sister's cottage. I was supposed to get rid of the trailer, but held out to give us somewhere to stay, while fixing up a cottage.

We have brought up a new tarp, to take care of the roof, if we found any leaks. There were none to be seen, so that tarp went into the cottage for emergencies.

The night was cool but we were comfortable in the trailer. I had one end and the girls had the other. The wildlife kept startling Tanya, so Amy held her close to protect her. They were considerate of me and my sensitive role here. They kept it down to just holding each other. They couldn't hide anything, so I know they were good.

In the morning, the girls were up and out the door. They got the preparations ready for the days work and then took the canoe along the lakeshore. They went quite a way up there. They passed the other side of the marshy spots and came upon another cottage. It was in better shape than ours, but there was nobody there. They went a little further, before they turned around. By the time they got back, I was awake, but not yet alert. They got breakfast going and did a fine job of it. When we had eaten, we placed our plates and flatware in a basin of water, to loosen the food, while we set up the tents. The first one, was the nylon, that went up nice and easy. The tents are being set up on temporary decks composed of four by eight tongue and groove three quarter inch plywood. This keeps the moisture from getting into the contents of the shelters. The second tent is a very old cotton tent. To peg them down we are using spiral, or ardox nails. When they are set up on real decks, they will each have their own deck. They will have a lounge in front of the tent, still under the tarps. They call this glamping. It gets pretty luxurious, when it is all finished. The girls are doing very well, helping to get things done. They do have a vested interest in the camp being finished. They will be sleeping under their own shelter. It won't hide anything from me, but Tanya will feel like she has some more privacy. The tents are finished by supper time. That includes all the tarps. Tomorrow, we will furnish the second tent. Tonight, we do the first one, where the girls will sleep. They are thrilled to no end, to have it all dressed up inside. Another thing we need to do, is walk the boundary of the property, according to the survey that had been done for the transaction, last year.

The night had been milder and that was a blessing, for the girls in particular. They were up early again and had taken the canoe the other way, past the river mouth. They are energetic and that's helpful. When they get back today, they find me, still in bed. They get breakfast and bring me some. I could get used to that. After the meal, we go for our walk, looking for the markers along the boundary line. I tie a rope to a tree and wrap it around each tree as we proceed. It will help me keep from getting lost in the woods. The property is nearly ten acres, mostly forest. It will take us tying several ropes along the border, to help me learn the limits. We are starting to get bitten, black flies. One of the big disadvantages, of owning a place, in this part of the country. Another is mosquitoes. I have a method of ridding us of some of these around the cottage, but not out here.

When we get home, to the cottage, we still have some time to decorate the second tent. I want it ready, in case we get company. If Brad comes up, he may bring Bradley, or maybe Jayme. I want them to have a comfortable place to sleep. They will get the trailer and I will take the second tent. We have put metal pots around the place, to burn some sage bundles, for repelling the bugs. We will have to build a fire pit, this year. We need a dock, too. The time the three of us spend together, are so enlightening and rewarding. Tanya has a great propensity for entertainment in intimate gatherings. It is truly a blessing, that I decided to bring the girls along. When faced with a challenge, that would make you step outside your comfort zone, step.

The next day, I am up before the girls. I only beat them by a small margin. They were surprised that I did it. After breakfast, we get into the cottage. We are looking for soft, or rotten spots, in the floors and the walls. Once the exterior walls have been stripped on the inside, we will be looking to find rotting underneath the painted exterior. I ask them to check the floors first, for rotten or sagging spots. Tanya is the first to find a bad spot by having her foot go through it. We go to work, ripping up that section of floor and check the supporting grid, while we can. It was built nicely, with a ground sheet that was probably added later. The flooring has rotted from the top down, and the joists are sound from what we find. The girls catch onto what I've shown them. While I take a break, they go to work, checking out the rest of the rooms. They like the responsibility they've been given, and respond well to any requests from me.

The conditions are tolerable and the appointments, of our shelters, are aesthetically pleasing and comfortable. This makes the work inside more enjoyable. Every now and then, we take a walk in the woods, to get some fresher air and limbering exercise. The work is not fast, by any means, but it is satisfying. I had hoped to be able to get employment, like this, but my health kept me from it. However, being the boss is not so bad. The work I do get done, is therapeutic for me and I bond with the girls all the more, by giving them free reign, to work as fast, or slow, as they want. This is one thing Amy had said she wanted to learn, so that she can blow off steam. Every two, or three days, we go biking, or canoeing. We get to the marina, or general store, twice a week. The store is reached down a path along the river. By car, it would take as long as it did by bike down the path. The road is winding, so much that, if you didn't know it, you would get disoriented, trying to find the way to the store. It is a wonderful summer job for the girls, and they get lots of lessons, on the ins and outs of building homes. They will not need too much training, for a job doing this for the summers, when they can get work that pays. For now, I call them my interns.

Every night, we check my schedule of appointments, and check off the days of the calendar. I take care of the bills, when we go home for appointments. Tanya goes home to her parents, for that time and Marie is happy to see me, and I, her. Amy always lands on her luxurious bed and feels like she is floating on a cloud. Many things have happened this year and the time away at the cottage, breaks the memory line, and helps those things seem so long ago. After those appointments are kept and new ones made, we head back up to work on the cottage.

Our drive is dependent on me being lucid and strong. We make stops as frequently as we need to, to keep me functioning. Small meals keep my blood sugar and energy levels, level. We get out and walk to keep exercising my legs and limbering my back. The girls enjoy the trips that way, too. They don't feel antsy and aren't always asking, if we're there yet. We see things that you don't see from the highways. The wildlife get used to the sounds of the traffic, and go about their usual habits, as the cars go by. We get some good pictures, when they aren't being spooked. We climb a hill on our walks, if there is one. That helps stretch those leg muscles. I love being with the girls. They love exploring. We get back on the road and do well because of the stop. Each trip is different. We stop in different places, as my needs demand.

Tanya's moms are thrilled with the stories she tells them. She is happy and energetic. It seems I 'am' suited for the role as 'Grampa', on 'Heidi'. I will invite them up when the cottage is finished. They are pleased, but wish they could come up and help. I say that I will consider it. I know what they are hearing and the reaction of Tanya is great, but adults, in those same conditions, would not be as easily pleased. I may be wrong about that, but it is the romanticized image, they like.

Once back, we take a walk through the woods, to plan our work itinerary. We have used up much of the plywood for the floors. A few joists had to be replaced. It seems that damp carpeting was left on the floors, for quite some time and that, is what rotted out the floors. We will have to look at sealing all the cracks, before we leave and make sure the place is dry, when we leave it for the winter. That will make the costs go up for this year, if we need to replace windows. The flooring will be left as plywood, until the exterior is finished. I probably should have attended that first, but I needed to see if the foundation, of the cottage, was sound. We were glad to see there were no ants, or termites, in it. That was a surprise. I get the girls checking for rot and spaces, in the exterior walls. They just have to look for light coming through and tap the wood walls as they go, to listen for dull thuds. The dry wood has a clear knock, when hit, but the rotten wood will either sound dull, or give way to the hammer altogether. Thus, this work will go fairly fast. We are gluing the wood, as well as nailing, to help prevent squeaky floors and give strength, to the walls. We are leaving the bathroom for last. We may have to rip up the floor there, too. The kitchen is being done along with the rest, because we have an outdoor kitchen at the trailer. We leave that wall for now though, to have our supplies piled along it.

We are moving along, more like pros now. The work is good, and the walls are not as damaged as we thought they would be. The lower walls were mouldy and were replaced with new clapboard. The cracks are being sealed with caulking. Amy and Tanya, have sound sleeps every night. They are thoroughly exhausted, from pushing themselves all day. It is a pleasure to see them work and play, more as friends, than lovers. In fact, they have had little in the romantic direction, while they were here. It was shear enjoyment, that has kept them going. When I think of it, they could be seeing this experience as romantic. Up here in the woods, with the one you love. Glorious night skies, filled with a billion stars. Fresh clean water to swim in. All the fresh healthy air, that makes your chest heave, when you're playing and falling in each others arms. It seems I can miss a lot, even connected as I am. This is romantic, even without the making out. I have such a good time with them. They fill up my time here with excitement. The play and fast paced work, they are doing is, as much for themselves, as for me.

Looking at this summer, I start to feel like we, have been floating upstream. The girls have made so much progress, for inexperienced working under the leadership of, until now, a theorist. I expect that, we will have made some mistakes, but we will be living with them. Having built it, we should be better equipped, to fix it. There is little sign of wildlife infestation. That makes me wonder. How can a building, in a clearing, between water and woods, get ignored by the wildlife? Maybe I should wonder, what other wildlife may be living near here. We start to look around for signs of predators. While the girls look around the outside, I take a look up in the rafters. I find some droppings up here. The wet carpet may have been recently removed. That would take out the evidence I had not found down there. I can see we will have more cracks to fill, in the attic. No light coming in through the roof. We will continue this, when we get back, from our vacation. We are going to my sister's cottage on Lake Huron. It needs work as well, but we won't be doing it, because we, are on vacation. We close up the house, put lavender by the doors and windows, close up the tents and trailer, and head back to civilization.

'When the weather's fine, we've got women, we've got women on our minds.'

Chapter Eight

Lounging By The Lake

We get home, and we have dropped Tanya off, on the way. We get our luggage unpacked and repacked, ready to head out to the lake. Marie is still at work. I grab the shopping list and go out to do that. Meanwhile, Amy gets in the tub and has a long soak, in the hot bubble bath. I hear her thinking, of the dirt and grime, from all the work, getting rinsed off. She is still in the tub, an hour later, when I get back. She hears the door and sits up, to scrub herself down. I feel better, feeling the dirt come off of her. I get feeling the dirt all over myself. Now I, have to get in there. Oh, what a feeling, to be really clean, after working in that filth. It didn't feel filthy, while we were there. Amy steps out of the bathroom and I step in. I get in the shower, step under the rain shower head, and get wet. I wash my hair and then turn on the body sprayers. I get scrubbed off and feel ten pounds lighter. My skin feels like it can breathe. The things you miss when you can't have them. I know what will be going in that bath at the cottage.

I look down at the tub. Oh-oh, I get the cleaner and scrub down the tub. Marie would have a fit, if I left that for her. All clean and out of the dog house.

I get the groceries packed for the cottage. Amy's on the phone to Tanya, talking about being clean. I hear Tanya, telling how her mom reacted, when she walked in. She said after her bath she felt so much lighter, so she stepped on the scales to see, she had lost ten pounds. She looked in the mirror. Shock hit her. She looked skinny. She also looked like she had grown! The things fresh air and exercise can do to you. The girls feel justified to pig out. After she hangs up, Amy checks the mirror. She does look thinner, but not taller. "That's not fair! Tanya grew an inch and I didn't!"

"What can I tell ya? Sometimes it just isn't fair."

"Oooh. That's deep." she gives me a dirty look, and she thought she was clean.

"You don't have to give me that look. I know how you're feeling. I probably shrunk that inch Tanya got. Besides, good things come in small packages."

To me, Amy is no different than any other girl. She wasn't out to convert girls to lesbianism. She was just like any teenage girl, with her best friend. She shares things like any BFF would. The only difference is, how far she is willing to go, with the best friend affection. In some cases, there is very little difference.

Amy is remembering Gloria and comparing her with Tanya. Two girls sharing an attraction for her. One wants to stay, the other doesn't. Who does she love? The one who will be there for her. Good choice.

I look at my choices and where I am. What brought me to this point? The girls I dated, were all nice and for many different reasons. So, what made me move on instead of staying? According to some, I went from a prize, to a booby-prize, to a prize. I was in so many places that would accept me, and some that threw me back. Why did I move on from the ones that wanted me to stay? Was I being steered toward where I am now? For what reason? I look at my kids and they are all remarkable people, who have done very well, being dedicated in their chosen fields. I anticipate that Amy will be too.

Marie is getting in from work. She is happy to see us and that we are all cleaned up. I tell her that we are ready to go for tomorrow. That is well received. We have supper ready. I see a smile for that, as well. I am batting a thousand so far. I take a quick look around. Marie asks, what I am looking for. I reply, a post. She looks sideways at me. "I was doing so well, I was trying not to hit the post." I tell you, complete strangers, have a better chance, at making her laugh.

In the morning, we are all up on time. We get the van loaded. Tanya will not be with us this week. Her moms are going on vacation and want her to come. She and Amy are talking about it. She says her goodbyes. You know, the ones that go on and on. When she's done, we get in the van and go. We stop on the way, for lunch. This is calculated into the travel time and we will get there on time. There is one more stop to make, Anna Mae's. We will pick up some baked treats. Marie's sister, Alice, is riding with us. With four going, there would not be enough room in the car. Marie is leery about the old van, it is twenty two years old. Nothing I can say to make a difference, but I still try.

"Steve and Rick's Garage, gave it a thorough going over, and did not find a thing wrong."

"If you say so, I still don't like going so far in it."

She gets to drive, because she isn't comfortable, with me behind the wheel. It is a two and a half hour drive to the cottage and she knows the route, better than anyone. As we get close, we see the landmarks that we all like to see, and we yell "It's Teletubby Land." We refer to a show, our grandkids watched, a long time ago. It is the wind turbines in the fields. We are approaching the turn. As we arrive at the cottage, we see my sister is about to leave. This is my other sister. She is the one that shares my disease. We back in and she comes to help us bring in our stuff. She's been waiting to visit, before she heads back to the states. We drop our stuff inside and sit down on the deck to visit. An hour later, we say our goodbyes, and she is off. We live four hours apart, so we don't see each other often. This was the second time she has seen Amy. They had a good chat and got along famously.

We unpack our bag and coolers. Then we go down to the beach, to test the waters. It is cool to the toes, but not cold. We climb back up the stairs to the cottage and wait for the rest to come. It is quite the climb, which is alright by me. It gives me a great workout. It is not long before they arrive. We go up right away, to lend a hand. It goes quite quickly. We get the celebration started, with a cocktail for all, but Amy's is without booze in it. Pina Coladas really make it feel like summer. Amy gets many questions about her school and amnesia. They are alarmed to hear her say that she never had amnesia. She told them about what had gone on. She related her time in limbo, that was nearly to drive her off the edge. We had explained it to them, last winter. They look at us. We tell them that, we had talked to them before, about it. My brother-in-law remembers us talking about it, four years ago, before it came true, when I had told him about the experiment. He remembered that, we were in the water, having one of our talks, about our religion. We do that every year, to sharpen our belief, and recharge our faith.

The girls go down to the beach and take a walk to see how the beach has changed since last year. While they are gone, my brother-in-law and I start making the beds. When we got done that, we stepped outside with another drink. He asked about the connection and I tell him how it has turned out. He asked me, how I knew, that she was what I thought she was. I tell him to check out the traits that I had asked for to prove that she was real. When they got back, I had told her to walk right up to him and show him her belly and ears. I had told her by thoughts only. When she did this he nearly fell off his chair. He turned to me and asked, how she knew to show him these things. I explained, that I had told her to do that, through my thoughts. He asked me how I knew it was God and not the devil. I told him that the devil can't create. He can only distort and destroy things. He agreed and showed his acceptance of Amy's story, by giving her a big hug.

When Amy told them about what we were doing, so far this summer. They were amazed. They had a ton of questions for her, about the work and Tanya. She almost felt like, she was being interrogated. We showed the pictures we had taken with my phone. We told about the walks in the woods and just, how much property came with the cottage. We showed the pictures of the tents and the trailer, all set up. We got some ideas and instructions, for implementing those ideas. We do a lot of this, at this cottage. We let our imagination go and come up with different ways, of tackling a problem. When they hear the knowledge of carpentry, coming from Amy, they are very impressed. We decide that we will set up a surprise, for Marie's youngest sister. She works for a building supply store. She had surprised us, when she became so well versed in her building products. Now we will surprise her, with Amy's expertise. Until then, she would talk about things to do, with this cottage. She invites her uncle, to come up to see our cottage, and see what we can do up there. The biggest deal of it all, was how much room we have, in the driveway and the garage. All the camping equipment went up there. The extra furniture was, either up there, or going up there. Much of our tools are there. With the place gutted, it's easy to learn both, how not to do it, and how to do it right, or as right, as we know how. I watched all the reno shows and she collects what we need to do, from my memory.

We spent some of our time there, talking shop. We got out on the water for exercise. We went on walks down the beach. Most of our time was loafing on the beach, with a book, or loafing on the deck, with a book. At night, we would gather on the beach, to watch the sunset and sit by a fire, roasting marshmallows and having something to drink, tea, coffee, liqueur, or anything else, that struck the right cord at the time. Uncle Jim asked her to yell up to her father and have him bring him down a beer. She said okay and didn't move. He asked her again, and she said that I was already on my way. Amy and I would enjoy dazzling the others, with our mind games. We would tell a story, with each of us alternating, word-by-word. She would go on walks with the girls, who walk faster than I could, and I would tell where they are, at any given moment. I would see things, Amy sees and tell her, if she should bring it back, for crafting into something useful. Marie would talk to me, through Amy and I would talk back with her. Amy would also, let me know, what Marie, is really thinking. She would give me a heads-up, on signals that I may not be picking up. We did have some great advantages, with this setup.

The water is warm and the sand, is covering most of the rocks, this year. Of course it could all change overnight. If a storm comes through, the sandbars could move and the water could get frigid. So we enjoy it day-by-day and hope for the best. There is a tradition, anytime we are camping, or at the cottage, Jim dives out of the water with his suit in hand, or around his neck. It has been going on for forty years, or more. Amy is out with us and after the jump, she says "You're not going to switch me back to guys, with that move." That cracks him up.

Nan, my sister-in-law, is a gourmet cook. We eat very well on these vacations. Jim runs the bar-b-q, according to instruction from Nan. I get to be the gofer. I'm not good with the bar-b-q, and I don't follow instructions well enough. Besides, it is easier for her, to get after her husband. I'm just too cute.

Alice is Marie's other sister. She's the one that rode up with us. She is re-singled, and loving it. We always have good conversations, and they help to get us through tough times and enjoy good times.

This cottage has four bedrooms, an indoor bathroom with a shower, kitchen, and a large living room, with dinette. It spoils you for others. Our cottage had two bedrooms, an indoor bathroom with a shower, and a kitchen and dinette. This one is on an escarpment slope, about forty to fifty feet above the wide sand and stone beach. Ours is on a ten foot high knoll, in the middle of a field of high grass and shrubs, with the woods behind and the water in front. There are stands of trees by the water. Marshy area at one end, beach in the middle, and rock and earthy shore on the other end. This beach goes for miles in either direction.

This is Lake Huron, one of the largest of the great lakes. Ours is a small lake, with a name of doubt. Some call it one thing and some, another. Opposite ends of the spectrum. They both are wood frame buildings. Both are in need of attention. In my case, there is lots of room to improve and the freedom to do it. There is no cottage owners association to appease. The municipality is small and fairly liberal with requirements. As long as the building is up to code, and doesn't need environmental assessment, it is usually given permission to go ahead. I have to draw up plans for an addition, to present to them and Jim and I, can come up with a good, detailed plan, while putting our feet up, sitting on the deck.

Amy wants to have a part in the design stage, too. She stays close, so she can put ideas in her Uncle Jim's head, as well as mine. "We need at least three bedrooms and a sleeping loft, or bunk room. A great room, would cover a multitude of common uses. A storage barn, for a garage, would be near the top, of the list of extras. We want to be able to handle the group that is here now and an extra capacity, for special occasions. I would like to have it insulated, enough to be safe, if we are ever stranded there, for any reason. Right now, it draws water from the river, that drains the lake. That is one of the borders, of the property. The road into the property is solid, as it sits. It has its ups and downs."

"He means it's hilly." Amy puts in.

"That and there are places, where it could become impassable, in storms, or spring runoff. The cottage is on a knoll, of about ten feet in height. I would like to have the barn, up above the flood plane, that surrounds the knoll. There is a place near the woods. I would also like to put an elevated perch in the trees, for a wilderness experience."

"You mean a tree fort." Jim says.

"Yes. It will be more than that eventually. I would like to put in, an elevated walkway, to other platforms and a zip-line." Amy looks at me as she's thinking, 'What's left to ask for? A waterslide?'

"I'm wondering, if I own my own, timber rights. Some places have the mineral and timber rights owned by companies. The land owner has no control over them. They can't even cut trees for firewood."

"You'll have to look into that. This will take a bunch of cash." Jim says it plainly.

"Yes, but, it will have to be put in, as we can, and I intend to salvage some of the supplies we need, from recycling areas. If it is found on the side of the road even. I will scrounge as much as I can. The more stuff I find, the richer the design. It will look like, some of those west coast island cottages. I've got an article on them, in this magazine. I have to be resourceful." I hand the magazine from the pile of others. "A rudimentary barn would do, at first. Once the building is there, we can upgrade it, without further applications, to the community planning department. We can use unconventional materials, too. Like used tires."

"We need to put in a dock, once we get some boats." is another point for Amy. "Our canoe is okay on the beach, for now."

"If you have any scraps of material, that we could use, or find any in your travels. That would give us another pair of eyes, looking for them. We will stop around the dumps and construction sites, to pick up discards. They will only be for smaller projects, but we will be doing the work ourselves."

Amy offers, "Tanya and I will be doing as much as we can. We want to build our own house, when we get married."

That sets Uncle Jim back a bit. It wasn't real for him, that she was gay. Even what she said in the lake, didn't bring it home to him. He sat kind of shocked, for several minutes. He didn't give it away, that he was shocked, but he sat very still. He would speak his mind, and he usually does, make his thoughts known. He was concerned that he may hurt her, and he didn't want to do that.

I was starting to get uneasy. I felt his tension. It was almost imperceptible, but I felt it.

Since I felt it, Amy did too. She went over and sat on his knee. "It's okay, Uncle Jim, I know it's hard, within your faith, to accept. But, I couldn't live my life, for someone else's feelings of right, or wrong. I have to live it, with my own feelings. I will love you, for who you are. Just love me, for who I am."

Uncle Jim nodded, "I don't understand it, and I have a hard time, accepting it. You're right. It is the way you are, and I just have to love you, for who you are."

She can't change anybody and wouldn't want to. She can let them be, if they can do the same, for her.

He sees her as she is, but she seems more than that. I will be talking with him, about her, next time we are in the water, away from other ears. I must remind him, that whatever I hear and see, she hears and sees. The strength of our relationship, will carry us through. I just remind anyone, Jesus told us that, of all the qualities we should hold, love is the most important. God knew, what He was doing, when He accepted her, as the volunteer He would send us.

There are many things, we must try to change. The only one, we can do for sure, is to change our own attitude.

If we are intolerant, we can not ask for tolerance.

We do talk anyway, Jim and I. He says it's easier, when she isn't there. She is ready for the harshness that others have given. It comes down to the golden rule. Love others, as you would want to be loved. Marie went through the shock, and Amy heard every word she thought. I can no further, change his mind, than I can walk to the moon.

The walking up and down the stairs, to the beach is keeping me, up to my workout level. Canoeing and walking on the beach, are helping out too. I have to stay in the shade. I am getting my rest, even with the routine.

I know it's vain of me, to want a cottage. I just have so many memories, of my Gram's cottage. Amy brings many others to my attention. When Gramp died, the family sold his place and when Gram died, they sold her place, and the cottage was sold before that. Even if we just break even, when we sell, if we have to sell, I would be happy. One thing I will not do, is put carpeting, on my cottage floors. Many times the guys that build things like this, become over extended and have to sell. If they don't, the family does, after they pass it down.

Have you ever noticed that cats, will cuddle up to people, that don't like cats. Amy knows that Jim doesn't care for her sexual orientation, so she sticks by him most of the time. She talks to him about building practises and cars. She likes trucks and hotrods. Almost everything he likes, she likes. Finally, she lays it on the table. She tells him the they have so much in common, all those things, and women too.

He warms to her. He can't dislike someone, with that kind of personality. She is loving and not going to let people change her. Now I tell him about her previous life, and how it ended. He feels bad about saying those things. She went through that and still has this amazing outlook. I tell him, that it's because she went through that, that she has that bright and hopeful outlook.

We put some ideas down on paper, with notes and drawings. We decide what kind of things, we might be able to scrounge. We make a list of priorities. Finishing the existing cottage, is the first priority, that includes insulation. He reminds me about the government assistance program for upgrading efficiency. That helps put some cash into our budget. Second, is preparing a basic pole barn foundation. Getting a roof on the barn, is incorporated with that. A raised platform in the trees, would help entertain the kids that come up. Then comes the zip-line. After that we can work on filling in the walls of the barn. Using straw for this, will insulate and soundproof the building, to quiet the build noises from the shop section. A foundation of tires, filled with earth, can recycle tires and give a solid and insulated base, for the additions. This would really stand up, to the spring thaw waters, flooding the lower spots near the cottage. Amy and I are getting so wound up, about our plans and the work we have to do there, we are wanting to head over and get started right away. I call a contracting company to have an audit done on the building. That is set up for when we return.

We are so eager to go, that it takes all we can muster, to stay out the week. Marie feels our tension and energy, and corners us for an explanation. We tell her of the plans, and what we are wanting to get started on.

She asks us, "Where are you going to get the money for all this stuff?"

We reply, "We have to scrounge around recycling centres, dump sites, transfer stations, and wrecking yards. We also need to finish the existing cottage and prepare a spot for the barn. We are going to check with government for any grants that we may qualify for."

"Well you can't go yet. So just calm down."

"We're going to go for a walk, to use up some of this energy."

"That's a good idea. Don't go too far. We'll be having supper soon."

We get ready and start out, for a scavenging walk. We can start gathering right now. Driftwood and fallen branches are gathered and set in a pile, near where the road comes down, close to the beach. We go back and get the van, to take it all back to the cottage. We pile it next to the sheds, by the driveway. We pick the best pieces, and put a layer in the van. We leave the rest, until we have loaded up the luggage, on Saturday. That's all we can do until we get back home. Once there, we can scrounge up the rest of the load to go to our cottage.

For now, we just take it easy, and enjoy the rest we need, before we head out. We talk Jim into loading up his truck, and going to see our cottage. Anything he can scrounge, is all extra for us. It can give him a vested interest in the project. If my sister decides to sell her cottage, they will need another place to take their vacation. We can either sell, our place and buy hers, or just use ours. She's been using time at her cottage, to barter for work on it. We can do the same with ours.

Amy and I take the canoe out, the next day, and take advantage of the calm lake. By going up and down the shoreline, we can look for ideas, in the neighbouring cottages. We've got a bunch from the internet. We found one place, that sells unusual furniture and statuary. I saw some animal figures that look so real, that they may fool people, that come nosing around while we aren't there. They may even fool the animals, and keep them out of the cottage. There is a pair of panthers, one in a submissive pose and the other in a dominant pose. Put them in a spot visible from the outside, and have a recording, on a variable timer, give out various big cat sounds. It would be fun to watch from a concealed spot. We love coming up with these ideas, to amuse ourselves. In this family, we try not to mature. It's highly overrated, and it isn't much fun.

We have an amazing amount of people taking themselves seriously, while being surrounded by those that would never share their assessment. What they are achieving is a mystery. So much of what we do today, is undone and rarely remembered. This account of our lives will be read by some and discarded. Some would keep it to pass on, or reread it. Will the results be remembered? I very much doubt it. It's biggest achievement, will be to make someone smile, or even laugh. That is my goal. They may shed a tear, but not too many, I hope. It is helping me improve my short term memory. Amy tests me on it. I have to remember where I went that day, in the order of occurrence, while Amy is busying herself, to hide the answers from me. I write them down, and when I'm finished, she checks the answers. If she finds there isn't anything to busy herself with, she will do disgusting things, to distract me. Thank goodness, she doesn't have to resort to that, very often.

I have times when I zone out and am lost, and don't fully know, where I am, or what I am saying, and I grab for things, out of the blue. Most of the time, what I have grabbed for, does not make any sense at all, to anyone, including me. It's gibberish. Amy has tried to help me with that, but there is no common threads available to me. The best thing to do is stop trying, and go on with something else. If there was any basis in fact, it will work its way around in the conversation. Then you have people looking at you, as if you are nuts. That's okay though, because nuts are good. You just look at them, as if, 'you can't follow that?!'

I am often reminded of songs. I can hear a rhythm from a machine, someone's walking, or breathing. A bird's song, or a bug's chirps, will bring to mind a melody. I start singing it and launch into other songs. These thoughts are....often...lost...

Chapter Nine

Back To Work

We are at the end of our time out. The rest of the group, are dreading, having to go back to their jobs. Amy and I, are looking eagerly, to get back to our project in the woods. We are looking forward, to picking Tanya up, for the trip back. We have things to show her, that we have in mind for the cottage.

I suggest getting some driftwood and fallen branches from here.

"You're not allowed to take wood from this area to another. You would have to process it here, before you can take it anywhere."

"I forgot about that. I'll keep the driftwood. The time it spent in the water should have got rid of those bugs. We can seal them up when we get home. They can use the other stuff for firewood on the beach."

"Are we going to have room with all the driftwood?"

"I'll make room." I start separating the driftwood. After loading the driftwood, I pack the baggage in on top of it. That is one thing I am good for, packing stuff into vehicles, or any space for that matter. The others carry it and I pack it. While they clean the cottage, before we leave, I finish stuffing every space I can find. If I was driving, I could fill it to the ceiling. However, it's Marie that is driving, so I have to leave space for her to look out the back. I would just use the outside mirrors. While I am packing and the sisters are cleaning, Amy carts the rest of the wood over behind the shed, so it will be seen as firewood, and used down on the beach. There is a nice big spot where we have fires there. It's far enough from the trees, and the lake, to be out of the storm surge, and still have a safe distance for sparks.

When the work is done, we gather on the deck and say our goodbyes. Hugs and kisses all around. A few tears, there is always one that gets teary. I wipe my eyes and they just pat my back. Really, you saw that coming? I might need some hormone replacement therapy.

I get in the van to turn it around, for Marie. She has trouble backing up, so I take care of that. At our cottage, there is plenty of room to turn around. Here, we are on a narrow drive, on the side of a steep slope.

We are all ready to leave and the cottage has been given the once over, looking for anything we might have left behind. Our garbage is loaded, to take home. We can't leave it for the people following us. We have locked it in an empty cooler, to keep the smell down. Anything that is recyclable, is separate. Plant waste, is put in a compost bin and turned in, so it can be used in the planters and gardens at the cottage. Anything burnable was burned. There is only a small amount we need to carry home. The recycling has been washed, so that doesn't stink up the van.

We pull out, up the hill and away homeward. It is a long drive and Marie is always the one to drive. She comes up several times each year. She brings her girlfriends up twice, and this trip, as well as any other time that we can get, that the cottage is open. It doesn't go through Toronto, so she doesn't mind the drive.

Our cottage is past Toronto. I can feel the tension she will be having, to get there. We will be able to fit in a stop, at Nicholas' place, to see them. It will be either on the way home, or on the way to the cottage. That would help Marie cope. There is the toll route we can take, to reduce the traffic volume. We keep that as an option, but we're cheap, and we already pay taxes for the other highway. If we move during the less travelled times, it is bearable.

I've invited Jim and Nan to come, and bring Marie with them, for a few days. I've given them a map of the area we are in, so they can find the driveway. It's one of those ones you can only find, if you know where it is. I'm sure Marie will like the camp we have made of the cottage. It is protected from the rains, comfortable, and spacious. The bathroom is indoors, private, clean, and close. We have our little fridge in the cottage, away from the wildlife. Jim is to bring some lumber pieces that he can scrounge. If we are all to share the cottage, we all need to pitch in, with the little things you can find.

For now, we still have to get home and finish the driftwood. I hope Marie will find our place is worth the drive. While the girls find things to chat about, I have a nap. Getting up early, will do that to me. Early for me, is late, for most people. I have been making the usual time, earlier lately. Alice talks to Amy about school, the cottage, and even, about Tanya. Alice is very open, to accepting people for what they are. That had been a downfall, at one time, but she has turned that to the positive. She has been careful, to discern the differences, and is quite within her faith. She is one of the most Christian people I know. She will love without judgement, and keep to herself, as much as she can, any negative thoughts about others. The conversation goes smoothly and Amy feels very close to her aunt. They get into personality quirks, and have a good laugh, about some of the stories the family has seen, within their ranks. Alice is surprised, that Amy knows so much about them. Amy tells her about the unique relationship, that she has with her mom and dad. Alice is amazed that this is possible. Amy shows the detail signs, she bears, to identify her, as what she is supposed to be. She tells about the challenge that was proposed by God in heaven, to the spirits that had gathered to consider it. It was not to proceed, unless there was a volunteer. She told her of her prior life, and how she was told, that she will retain that knowledge. She told her of her volunteering for the return existence. She related the events that took place, before anyone in the family could know. She told of the reason that this is still, only for those close to her, and the family to know. This took quite a bit of a stretch for Alice's imagination to follow. Alice questioned Amy, about several points, and they discussed it for some time. She said, she will have to go over this again, to really have a chance for it to sink in. I start to come to, as we are approaching home. Thankfully, I had not snored too loud, the whole way. They had poked me a few times, and I felt the bruised feelings, where they had.

When we pull up to the house, Alice gets her car out of the driveway. We pull in. She backs in, to load her stuff into her car. We get everything out of our van, and set aside the driftwood for treating. We get our things inside, while Alice loads hers. When she's done, we pause to say goodbye. I fake some tears and give them a laugh. She wishes us luck, for the cottage, and pulls away. When we are done unpacking, Amy and Marie get working on the laundry.

I go to the store to get some things to treat wood with, for finishing. I get something that is an insect repellent. It will allow anything inside the wood, to stay inside and die, and keep others out, or so it says. I have another piece that I was going to do for the Lake Huron cottage, but decided to use it on ours. I bring the wood out and get right to work, with a rest now and then. Amy comes out and takes over, some of the jobs. I don't have to tell her what I'm doing, she knows. We work without vocal chatter and give each other a hand. It is done so seamlessly, that it gets the attention of the neighbours. They work together and are always yelling at each other, to do this, or to do that. They ask us how we know, what the other is doing? I say, "We're" and Amy says, "psychic." That really freaks them. It's just like our story time, at the cottage. We get back to work, and leave them, to marvel at this. The wood gets three coats, of varnish and looks amazing. We cut it level, to use it as an end table and a coffee table. Once the varnish dried, we show our wares to Marie, for her stamp of approval, and we earned it.

Amy asks her, "Is it as good as the pieces you made, when you were a teenager?"

Marie reflects on those times and agrees. "It is very nice. Where are you going to put them?"

Amy replies, "In one of the tents, for now, and in the great room, when it's built."

"You'll have to come up, with Jim and Nan, when they come. I've already talked to him and you can come for a weekend. We have room for everyone. It's clean and comfortable. Just bring some food and drinks, and it will be better than camping, and more private. We think you'll agree, when you see it."

"I'll talk to Nan." she goes back inside and we put the pieces into the van.

I go to the building supply to get some deck blocks, lumber, nuts and bolts, and some more adhesive and caulking. When I get back, Amy agrees, that it will make a big difference.

We stay until Marie goes to work on Monday at noon. We are all packed and head out as she goes. We grab some food and get on the highway. We nearly talk, the whole way. Going over the different ideas we had on paper, and some new ones we think of as we go. The traffic is light as we go toward Toronto. It gets heavier as we pass the 400. It is getting close to the homebound rush hour, and we are just getting through before it starts. We stop for some groceries, and some odds and ends, before going on to the cottage.

I know, I had not mentioned Tanya. Amy got a message from her. They were held up, and her moms, would be bringing her to the cottage. They are coming from that direction anyway.

We got up there and sat back to enjoy a pizza. A treat to reward us for staying with the job. After dinner we got the supplies out of the van, and put the tables by Amy's bed. They had more room in their tent. After that was done we got ready for bed. Amy asked, if she could sleep with me that night, because Tanya wasn't there. It was different here. There is wildlife around, and she's a little frightened, being by herself in the tent. I agree and we get to bed. She giggles, about me sleeping with a lesbian. I let her know, that I wasn't easy.

Amy is still in bed when I wake up. She is lying there looking into my eyes. "I wanted to know how it felt, to wake up with a guy in my bed." she said with a big grin.

I give her a big kiss and get out of bed. She says, "So that's it wham, bam, thank you ma'am?"

"If you don't count the lack of wham and bam."

We got left over pizza for breakfast, or brunch after we see the time. We go for a ride in the canoe. It is now, the middle of the summer, and the water is warm. We get in for a swim and lie on the rocks, to dry in the sun. We hear the car pulling in by the cottage.

"Tanya!" Amy screams. She runs off to greet the visitors and her girlfriend.

I come strolling around the cottage after they have greeted each other appropriately. Amy had nearly tackled Tanya. Tanya is five foot eight now, and thin from this growth spurt. Amy had landed on her feet, as she swung past, and swung Tanya around like a stuffed toy. The moms had a big smile, when they saw me. We sat down and visited by the trailer. A short time later, I gave them a tour of the cottage and camp, while Amy showed Tanya the tables we made. They asked if they could spend the night. I agreed and gave them the choice of accommodations. They opted for the trailer, so I got the bedding changed for them. They went for a tour of the woods, with Amy and Tanya as guides. They were impressed with the hominess the place showed. The cottage magazines were out on the table, when they returned. I was busy drawing up some plans. Amy didn't tell them, before they came upon the scene. She thought it better left among our side of the family. She takes them along the shoreline, pointing out the different types, marsh, sand, rock, and earth embankments. They come back to the trailer, where I'm still at the drawings. I set them aside, and offer the ladies a drink. They accept and I go to retrieve the bottle of wine. I had brought it up to help me get to sleep. I pour the adults, some wine and the girls, have juice. I have the fire place all set up to burn, so I light it up. We sit around the fire and they comment on the absence of bugs. I let them in on the secret. The flames are enveloping the wood with a rainbow of colours. I offer the explanation for that, passing on the secrets of magical fires.

"We set the fire going, to chase off the bugs, before we go in for bed. It's much more comfortable sleeping, without scratching. Before the fire is gone we get ready for bed. I'm the last one to go in, and I spread the wood apart, to let the fire die down quicker. Whenever you are ready, we can go inside."

They sit warming, in the heat of the flames. At last they all stand and go into the cottage. They use the bathroom and come back out for a short stand by the flames and then head for their chosen shelters. Once they are inside, I go to the cottage myself. I come back, spread the wood apart, and go into my tent. I sit inside the tent and see the faces, looking out at the coals glowing. It was overcast, as the sun went down, so we missed the star display. Now that we are inside, dry, and warm, it starts to rain. I watch the embers slowly dying, with each drop that attacks them mercilessly. The smoke rising out of the ashes and then nothing. It is too dark now, to see the faces, and I suspect, they are looking for each other, for comfort, in the drumming beat of the rain. I am snug in bed, when the rain pours down, in earnest. I think of Marie. Two hundred kilometres away, cozy warm in our waterbed. I hope she's missing me, as I am missing her. Amy lets me know, how much Marie is thinking about me, and missing me, glad of the quiet.

In the morning, it is still raining. They stay put until it stops, about an hour later. They start filing out to get some brunch. Amy and Tanya are quick to get the cooking started. They are cooking in the trailer's add-a-room. Brenda and Millicent, sit in the add-a-room, where we have dry chairs. Each night, all the chairs are put under the tarps, to keep the weather from getting to them. Each tent and the trailer, have oversized tarps, that keep a wide area around them dry. It doesn't take long, before the girls come out with trays of food. They are quite resourceful. Now that Amy has had some lessons from her Aunt Nan, she has some crepes to offer. The moms are thoroughly impressed. They had enjoyed their talents before, but their game has been, definitely upped.

After eating, Brenda and Millicent load up the car for the trip home. We gather round the car to see them away and wave, as they disappear past the edge of the forest. They have a map with the route marked out, to the nearest familiar landmark route.

I turn to get back at the job and the girls are making out, right in front of me. So, I stick my face, right in the middle of them, and they start kissing me, on both sides of my face. I slap their butts, and push them toward the cottage. They break apart and go off, to get their tool belts.

We have some work we can do inside, until the place dries up outside. The interior walls, that had not been stripped, are taken apart and the debris is cleaned up. When the mess inside is cleaned up, we go outside to take a canoe ride along the shore. If we find anything that looks interesting, it is loaded into the boat. Our canoe can hold 1200 lbs., and we tax that capacity, frequently. When we feel the treasures are drier, as we find them, we head back to camp.

Back at the cottage, we unload our booty, then we get setting out the deck blocks. Once they're properly placed, we set the upright posts in them. We have nine posts for each tent platform. We fasten the beams to the posts. The level is checked and the beams are adjusted. Then the joists are spaced out across to tie the beams to a grid. They are nailed to temporarily hold them. The level is checked and the joists are adjusted. The beams are then bolted to the posts and the posts are cut flush with the joists. After the deck is solid with spacers between the joists. The facia is attached with deck hangers, across the ends of the joists. We take the furniture off the platforms and they are lifted, and slid onto the grid. They are loaded up, with furniture again. The tarps are attached with heavier ropes for year round protection.

I tell the girls about the metal deck posts, I had heard about. I think we will have these temporary decks for quite a while. When we are ready for a permanent placement, we can use the new metal posts.

When we were still at home, I had ordered, the two panther statues. I just got a text, saying that they were ready to be delivered, to the cottage address. I make the arrangements and we go down to the main road to meet the truck. It is not long before we see the truck coming. We step out to signal the driver. He pulls up to the pathway. We put the packages into the van, and wave to the truck driver, as he gets back on the road. We take these packages back to the cottage and unpack them. Aww, beautiful. They will be real attention getters. I imagine what that might look like to people, just passing by. Yeah, like there is anybody just passing by, out here in the wilderness.

Imagine, walking up the path, in the daylight, and seeing a black panther standing there, looking back at you. You may not even notice the soiled underclothes, for the first two hundred feet.

Now imagine, looking in the window of a cottage, late at night. You knock, but no one answers. You go to the door and try it. It's not locked. You open the door and turn on the light switch, and there, in the middle of the room, two black panthers, staring back at you. I would think you lucky, if you hit the doorway, in the first two attempts to flee.

I almost, don't want to warn our guests, before they come in looking for us. Just for entertainment purposes. Marie would give me such a beating. Ohh, it's very tempting. The girls want them to be outside their tent. I wonder if a black bear would be put off by them? They aren't adult size cats. They don't have a scent. They are still impressive. The sight of them would startle anyone. No matter how big they are.

Well, enough loafing. Let's get back to work. We have old knob and tube wiring to remove. I'm surprised that they left that in, the last time they fixed the place up. With the walls stripped, it will be a cinch to replace the electrical, and put in the new circuits you need in today's world. The plumbing will be changed, just before we go home for the season. Then when we come up, in the spring, it will be ready for us to hook it up to the pump, and get on with the other work. Amy will be graduating then, and will be thinking about getting a job. I will not be ready for that, no matter when it happens. If she gives the place one more season, it should be close, to being finished, in the main section.

Once Amy is gone on to working and university, Tanya won't be there to help. Hopefully I can get other family interested in helping. Tanya objects to my surmising that she would abandon the project. She says that her moms would pay to come up here to help out.

I have the power to the house turned off. There is still power outside that was hooked up for the trailer. We can run the fridge in the trailer until we have the wiring done. We can also, run the tools we need from the trailer feed.

We have staked out the area for the great room addition. The wiring will be run into a spot on that wall. The insulation we will need, is not going to fit well, in the studs we have. We need to extend them, at least two inches, better going four. Just insulating, will help with comfort, for most people, but also pain relief for me. Temperatures are bad for any chronic pain sufferer. Either extreme is very taxing. A well insulated place means, less money for heat and pain relievers. The girls are amazing help for me. Amy knows whatever plans I have, and the choices I am considering. To make the choice she forms her own opinion and confers with Tanya. She never asks me, because she already has that. Tanya feels like it is their decisions, that are moving this forward. When I need my rest breaks, they do the job they want to do. Or so it seems to Tanya.

"Don't you think you should talk to your dad about these things?"

"I have already talked to him about it. He trusts me to do what we've talked about, but allows us to add the feminine aspect to it, so that my mom will like it too."

"It feels like we are making the decisions without him, as if it is our own place."

"It might be someday. If my brother and sisters don't want to use it, we could buy them out. I'm sure the sisters will want it. They love the country cottage by the lake. It's not like the great long beaches of Lake Huron, or Lake Erie, but it is nice just the same. I think, we will need more sand, for the beach. We need to get more 2X4s for the outside walls. Then we make the same walls that we have already and set them in front of the others and nail them together. That will give us room for putting the insulation in."

"How do you know about all these things we're doing? You hardly ever speak to your dad about anything. You just go on and do it all."

"We talk before and after the work day."

"I've never heard you talk about this stuff."

"Okay Tanya, I have to let you in on the secret we have. You've seen that I don't have a bellybutton. Why do you think that is?"

"I don't know. I thought you said, that you were created, and not born. I never knew, what you meant by that."

"You've heard the Bible story about Adam and Eve. Haven't you?"

"Yes. And the snake and the apple."

"So, how were they made?"

"Adam was made of dust. Right?"

"Yes. And God breathed life into him. Now, what about Eve?"

"Eve was made from Adam's rib."

"Right. God made Adam sleep, so that He could take the rib from his chest. Then He made Eve the same way He made Adam."

"Okay, so what does this have to do with you?"

"Well, my dad wanted to feel the same pain and feelings, that women have. So that he could compare them to those that he has. So he prayed to God, to make this comparison possible by creating me, to be psychokinetically connected to him."

"So what does Psychokinetic mean?"

"It means that whatever I feel, he feels. Whatever I think, he knows. And vice versa. Our thoughts transfer the pressure from one to the other."

"How is that possible?"

"With God, all things are possible."

"So, if you hurt yourself, he feels the pain too?"

"Exactly!"

Tanya looks ponderous. "So, what does that have to do with your bellybutton?"

"God created me from parts of my dad and mom. So, I was not born. I was made."

"You mean God took a rib from each of your parents?"

"No. My dad said that Eve was created from Adams rib and she was bad, to listen to a snake, so I was made from soft tissue that wasn't needed, like fat and cellulite."

"So you are made of fat?"

"Yes, to make me more humble. Humble enough, to listen to God, and my parents."

"So, God is real?"

"Very real. I have all the memory, from my past life and I have the memories, of meeting and talking, to God."

"You've talked to God."

"Yes, I have. When my dad prayed, he had only one other person that agreed with him and God asks for three people, to agree on the prayer. He had decided the third person should be the soul that was going to be given to the created body. So God asked for a volunteer. I was the third person to agree to that prayer. I was the soul to volunteer to come back. Because I was created to come into these advanced and complicated times, I needed to retain my memory of the life I had led before this one. I was given six years of my parent's lives. So I was twelve and they were each six years younger, to give them a chance to live long enough to feel the experiences I have."

"Wow! I don't know what to believe about all this. So, what about your amnesia?"

"I did not get an identity that would be acceptable in this society. So, I had to act like I had lost my memory of my life, up to the day I started life. That way they would give me the identity, when nobody could be found to claim me. That is why I have no bellybutton and pointed ears. If someone was to claim me, they would have to know about, those two things. Since nobody could, they couldn't claim me. My real mom and dad asked to be my foster parents. Just like Moses' mother asked to be a nursemaid to Moses, when the Queen had him. So that I could be with them and they could adopt me, legally, as soon as I was made a crown ward. When that happened, they let me choose my name, and that gave me my identity."

"So. Your mom and dad can feel what you feel?"

"No, only my dad and I share that. My mom doesn't get that. I can only know what she thinks and knows. My dad and I are the only ones connected to feel each others pain, and other feelings."

"What do you mean 'other feelings'?"

"When I am happy, sad, sick, or anything else."

"What else?"

"When I make love to you. He feels all of that. I feel it all, when he has sex with my mom."

"Ewww. He feels me, when you feel me?"

"Every little bit. Even what you taste like. I used to punish him with that when we first started. He gets something else to keep him busy when we do that. He eats something spicy that burn his senses and does things like listening to very loud music with his headphones on. He feels like you do about that. He said 'Ewww' when we first started."

"Can you ever, like, turn it off?"

"Not until we die. Him or me. Until death do us part. We can't get a divorce, or an annulment."

"Wow, I'm almost sorry that you told me. So, you would taste your mom?"

"I do the same as he does. He warns me."

"I never, ever, thought that that would be, even, possible."

"Like I said. With God all things are possible. He made the 'Big Bang' happen. He brings things together and takes them apart. He creates things all the time. He enjoys His work. Would you stop doing things you loved to do after only seven days?"

"NO WAY!"

"So, neither did He. They scientists say the universe is expanding. That is why. Because He loves to create new and different things. Sometimes His creations go bad and ruin things. Like us. Man is ruining his own planet. God makes other ones and when the time comes, He will take the souls that He wants to put on another planet and let ours have time to fix itself, or burn up, when the sun dies and swells up, to consume its planets, as it goes. God has a plan and it doesn't matter, whether we believe, or not. It is only better for us to believe."

"So, He is alright with you and I being lesbians?"

"It may not have been His choice for us. He is alright with love. Our choice of whom we love is up to us. He did punish Sodom and Gomorra, by destroying them. That was the Old Testament and in the New Testament, He forgave us our sins, through Jesus Christ. So, if I am not forgiven, I have to die with that. After I died in my past life, He forgave me the sin of being a lesbian, as well as all the other things I did wrong. He loves us. He wants to forgive and all you have to do is ask to be forgiven, through Jesus Christ, and you will be. If He can forgive Saint Paul, for aiding in the murder of Christians, He will forgive me, for loving you. I know that for a fact. Jesus did not, and still, does not lie."

"So, you know what your dad has planned for the cottage. Can you tell me?"

"Of Corsican. We want to build a great room, right over there."

"Why not on the lake side?"

"I will decide that when he wakes up. He fell asleep in the hammock."

"You can't help him decide while he's asleep?"

"He started thinking about it when you asked the question, but it isn't right to make a decision in your dreams. You need to be able to face facts. In your sleep, you are at the mercy of you heart and not your head. Which is all wrong. Your artistic side rules your dreams and your mechanical side works on facts and figures. You can dream of the facts and figures, but the mechanical portion will not accept the ruling."

"How do you think he will choose?"

"He will probably want to agree with you. There may be another piece of information that he hasn't thought about. I can't find one. I may have got turned around by his dreams. They don't go in a logical order."

"What if we took a nap?"

"You're not thinking of a nap. You want to fool around."

"How can you see what is in my head?"

"I don't have to. I know what you think with." Amy wants to be the responsible one and keep working, but she can't fight her desire to do just what Tanya wants. She grabs her hand and they run off to their tent.

"Isn't this going to affect his dreams?"

"Yes it is. He might just remember when he and mom were younger."

"You mean he did that with your mom?"

"I can not tell a lie about that. He did. And he liked it."

'Look through any window, yeah. What do you see?'

Chapter Ten

Let The Little Girl Through

The supplies of lumber were dwindling. We had to go to town and pick up some more 2X4s, 2X8s and 2X12s. We had used up the wood for the decks and now we had to get started on the inside so we can get ready for the insulation. I have just driven up to the lumberyard and had an anxiety attack. While I sit in the van, the girls go in and start gathering a cart full, of the pieces we need. They are sighting down the length to check for nice straight pieces. Some guys, down the aisle, see them and think they should get to know these new girls in town. The girls have the cart well on the way to being full. They see the guys watching them and they see them start toward them. They want to finish filling the cart, but they don't want to deal with guys like these. They decide to take what they've got, and head to the cash register. They start to go, but seeing this, the guys quickly surround them. They become a nuisance, making lewd suggestions, to them and grabbing at their arms and clothes. I can see it happening and try to get to the store, but I have another attack and collapse in the parking lot. People are running to help me, and I am trying to have them get the girls. The attack worsens the more I try. No one can understand me. My speech is slurred and they start to think, I've been drinking. They are checking my breath, but don't smell anything. They ask if I am sick. They are wasting the time the girls are running out of. I hear a familiar voice and look for it. It's not by me. It's by the girls.

"Excuse me fellas. Can I help you?"

"Nah, we got this."

"I think you need to step aside guys."

"We're just talking to our girlfriends here."

"I know that's not true. Now step aside and let the little girls through."

"I don't think you understand. This is none of your business." said the one holding Amy's left arm.

Amy knows that I am in trouble but the boys have a hold of her.

"Do what you want to these guys, Amy." She recognizes the voice now. She kicks her heal back up into the groin of the guy behind her. Brent grabbed the two guys closest to him, while Tanya rips free from them and goes after the guys holding Amy. She sees the one guy go down and both girls push the other one back into the stack of lumber they had just depleted. He is sprawled over the back of the pile and can't get free. The girls grab hold of the one Amy kicked and pushed him down flat on his face. Tanya sat on him and Amy went to give Brent a free hand. She kneed the first guy in the groin, as she shot her hand up under his chin, which at the time was coming down, to meet the hand coming up. His nose got the worst of it.

"My dad is having trouble in the parking lot. I gotta go. I'll be right back."

"Go, I got this." He called security and the boys were held in the store until the police came.

Tanya had stayed with Brent to help hold the guys and make a report on the incident.

Amy found me outside the door and stepped in to claim me. She explained about my health problems. When the police arrived they thought I was one of the guys they were called about. Amy directed them to where the assault happened. One officer stopped to check me out. I was exhausted but the anxiety had let up. Seeing that I was okay, he went inside to catch up with his partner.

Inside, the boys were questioned about their conduct, and what they were supposed to be doing, in the store. They gave some question about the girls, that attacked them. They blamed Amy, for beating them up. It was at that moment that Amy and I came back to where it happened. The policemen asked the boys, to pick out the girl that had beat them up so bad. They all pointed at Amy. Five foot nothing and ninety pounds. The cops laughed got the other statements. Security helped the officers, take the boys to the cruisers outside. They were loaded into the cars and taken to the station.

Amy gave Brent a big hug. "What are you doing here?"

Brent replied, "I am working here. We have a cottage up here, so I applied for a summer job and I got it."

"You remember my girlfriend Tanya and you know my dad. We were just getting some lumber for our cottage. Tanya, Dad and I are renovating a cottage out here."

Brent looked at me and asked if I was okay. I said I was. "Is this the girlfriend, you had introduced to me, when I was stalking you?"

"Yes she is. This is our third year together." Amy gave Tanya a one armed hug.

"Where is your cottage?"

She gave him the description of the road through the woods.

"Oh my goodness. You're my next door neighbour. When that road splits, our place is on the right side of the fork."

"What do you know about that? We were wondering if we were going to meet any of you."

"Now that I know it's you there, I'll bring my folks over to meet you. Are you the ones with the maroon canoe?"

"Yes, that's us."

"Well, stop in next time. C'mon, lets get your order together." And we all worked through the pile and came up with a good load. Brent helped us through the check out and out to the van. We loaded it all into the van and made arrangements for Brent to bring his folks over for a barbeque.

We climbed in the van and drove over to a butcher shop. I went in and got a bunch of steaks. We got back to camp after dark. We put the meat in the fridge and got ready for bed. We didn't light a fire that night. We went straight to bed.

The early morning sun, found the girls ready to rise, but not until they wrestled a bit. When they stepped out of bed they literally bounced back inside. The temperature had dropped down to eight degrees Celsius. "Holy mackerel! Someone turned off the furnace. It's freezing out there." They lay back down and huddled together to warm themselves.

I was still sleeping in my bed until around eleven. When I stepped out it was back up to about fifteen degrees. That was chilly enough for me. I got some warm clothes on and went to check on the girls. As I passed their tent, I saw a mound of bedding piled on their bed. I looked in to find they were still there.

"I thought you were in a dark, soft place. What has happened to my undeterable workers?"

Amy's muffled voice said, "We were tossed back, by the reaction of hot feet, on icy cold floors."

I went into the tent to see them all cuddled up. "It is not too cold now. It's fifteen. What would you girls want for brunch?"

"Warmth!" they said in unison. "Bacon and eggs with home fries. Please!"

"Right you are. It will be done in six jiffies."

I guess the connection we have is dulled by cold. I should have been aware of exactly where they were. I get cooking on the stove in the add-a-room, it's out of the wind. We still have a couple of days before company comes. It's not important, to work every hour we're up here. I finish making brunch, that is more lunch, than brunch. I load it on the tray and carry it out to the girls' tent. "Sit yourselves up to sup!" I holler as I come in. As the girls sit tentatively up, checking the temperature. "You'll have to start wearing warmer clothes to bed. Sorry. You'll have to start wearing clothes to bed. Those little things aren't exactly clothes. It will be cooler, for the most part, now and downright cold, once in a while."

They eat up the meal quickly, to get it while it's warm. I'm finishing soon after them.

"So, Brent is our neighbour. I hope they don't mind the condition of our cottage. I would like to see theirs."

"What are we to do about the great room? Which side are we going to put it on?" Tanya is asking.

"I had originally thought of the forest side. I have considered putting it on the lake side but am undecided."

"What would be the negative side of each?"

"Well Tanya. On the lakeside, in the spring runoff, it could be eroded faster on the lake side. On the wooded side, it would be, looking at the woods."

"And on the plus side?" Tanya is pushing.

"On the lake side, you would be looking out over the lake. On the forest side, the erosion factor is much less."

"Which do you want."

"I do think the view better, on the lakeside. The wood side has some merit. The problem lies, in the strength of the foundation. The knoll is untouched and may be less erodible for that reason. Using a tire packed with earth foundation, could be a better base for the addition. I will have to talk with Uncle Jim. They are coming this weekend, weather permitting. Well ladies, lets get something done today. I would like to have the inner walls done for their arrival."

"Is it decided yet?"

"I do think the decision has yet to be made. If the great room was on the lake side, the water flow, could get trapped against the foundation and the knoll, which would provide the water, a reason to dig into the softer hillside. That would threaten the main cottage. I might want to put it on stilts, or as a second level."

"Your dad is talking to us, isn't he?"

"Yes, but himself too. He's thinking out loud, and coming up with new thoughts, to convince himself."

"Lets start on these walls now. We put one of the long 2X4s on it's side. Then we start fastening the short ones to it. Nail through the long, into the end, of the short, every 16"on centre. That is the centre of the 2X4 being attached. I have put marks, where each board is to go. Angle the nails in an alternating pattern. Show her what I mean, Amy. I'm getting anxious again." I sit down against the adjacent wall. Five, or ten minutes, might be enough.

"He'll be like this for a few hours. Off and on then, for the next few days. If you nail on the top side, angle it slightly, toward the bottom. On the bottom, angle to the top."

"How will we match this to the height of the existing wall?" Tanya wondered, looking at the thickness of the wall base.

"We'll nail a strip to the floor along this long board. This will match the height and keep the nails from working their way out as the wall flexes in the humidity. We will stand the wall up in place and then put a few screws down through the whole lot." she looks over at me with a hint of worry. She knows more about me than I do. If she looks worried, why should I?

We hear a shout from outside for Amy. It's Brent. Amy and Tanya come over and help me up to take me outside. They wave to Brent to come on in. He stands there pointing at their sleeping deck. We look over and see the cats. We have a chuckle and wave him in again. They help me to my chair and, while Amy goes to escort Brent and his folks in, Tanya goes to hold the cats for them. When they are close enough, she knocks on the cats heads, to let them hear that they are fake. Then they get to laugh.

"They're doing the job well." I tell them. "And they're cheap to feed."

Brent introduces his parents, and Amy introduces Tanya and I. We talk about the cats and then switch to the renovations. His dad asks if the girls are helping me much.

"Actually, they are doing the most work and I am helping them."

Amy takes over the conversation as she hears me slurring my speech. "Dad and I do the planning and then Tanya and I do the work, while he recovers, or does something else. Dad has a few health problems, and we can learn from him, and then do it right. Tanya was just learning to use an air-nailer." she reaches and holds Tanya's hand up, like a champion. "We're doubling the inside exterior walls, now." She is still holding Tanya's hand, gently swinging it.

Brent speaks up, "Tanya and Amy, were picking up the wood yesterday, when those guys, I was telling you about, started harassing them. I grabbed two, Tanya and Amy took out the other three before Amy took the leader from me, and took him out. When the cops came, the guys tried to pin it on the girls. The cops might have thought about that, until Amy got back with her dad, from the parking lot. When the tough guy pointed to her, the cops just laughed and our security helped to get the guys to the squad cars. It was hilarious. We had it all on video."

His dad looks at the girls and laughs, "I can see what was so funny. How tall are you?"

"Five feet."

He shakes his head. "Mighty Mite."

"Would you like a tour?"

"Yes please. I've never been here before. What are your plans for it?"

The five go off to the tour and leave me to rest. Like Amy said. I could be like this, for a few minutes, to a few days.

Amy tells about all the plans, and the concerns for spring floods, on the proposed additions. He tells of the flooding, around the lake, and near his place. He was impressed, at the scale of demolition, and how clean it was inside. "Brent, you should marry this girl. She really can do the job."

"Amy is the girl that I told you about. She was the one with amnesia. We are just good friends."

Amy closes the gap between her and Tanya. Then she leans her head on Tanya's shoulder. Tanya turns her head to face Amy, and kisses the top of her head. The parents get the message and look uncomfortable. It got awful quiet.

Brent breaks the stillness, "Are you updating the wiring and plumbing too, while the walls are open?"

"Yes, we are. We're putting in solar panels and a battery bank. And inside we will go to a two level wiring plan, where we can switch off the grid, or back onto it, if we need to. The plumbing will filter gray water, and recycle it, before it gets to the tile bed. There will be some settling tanks, for solids, and a treatment to liquefy them."

"Who's going to do the plumbing and electrical for you? And the solar?" Brent's dad pushes.

"Dad and I will, with Tanya's help. We also have other tradesmen in the family that we can call on. We will do most of it. We'll be getting it done with inspections all along the way. We have our permits posted, and have it all insured. That, being tied to the inspections."

He looks at her with reluctant admiration, just for taking on the project, being so young and small. "I can't get over this. Some girls your age don't even want to think about work, and you're taking all this on, with an ailing father, and another girl your own age. Plus you are still too young to be employed in this type of work."

"Well, I have to learn sometime, and the younger you are, the faster you absorb things, barring any disabilities, or illnesses. We aren't being paid for this because we are the employers."

"I am a fan. You are remarkable kids. What are you going to do after the cottage is done?"

"Build a barn-workshop over by the woods on that slope there."

"No, I meant school wise."

"Oh, I want to go into counselling, in the health, education, marriage, or career fields. Either that, or this line, as a developer."

"Very impressive. VERY impressive! It's a good range of fields there. I could see you going for all of them, and doing well in them, to boot. Very impressive. If you ever rethink your situation, keep Brent in mind. He could use your influence."

"Dad! She's not switching teams in midfield."

The girls look at each other and smile. "No, I'm not going to do that. But we will keep Brent in mind anyway. We might need a hand with the local gentry."

"You know where we live. You can call on us for that, too."

Brent starts singing, "You just call out my name, and you know, wherever I am, I'll come running..."

Chapter Eleven

Help Is On The Way

The Youngs left feeling good about Tanya and Amy, and about our work over here. Brent stayed around, after his parents left, and helped the girls catch up, on the work they were doing, when they were interrupted. It was to make up for his Dad's remarks. He did say that his father was sincere, about his admiration, and his offer to help. I went for a walk in the woods, along the rope we had tied to the trees. It would get dark in there, faster and sooner, than in the clearing. I would follow the rope, until it ended, and then turn around, and follow it back. I had anticipated this scenario and planned the solution. As long as the rope was where it should be, I could trust where it took me. There was no problem, with that not being so. If my sight were to worsen, I could still enjoy walking in the woods and find my way back. They had the fire going, and the tricks for the bugs, and entertaining colours, were in use. We also had the herbs, in use elsewhere too. Lavender at the doors, sage in the fire, and others to keep the place pleasant.

Brent and the girls were quite involved in their conversation. They barely noticed me come in. I sat down and leaned back to look at the stars. I missed a whole summer of star watching, three years ago. The eye surgery, made me keep my face down, for nearly three months. It feels so nice, to watch them now, and the northern lights, are visible here, as well. I watched the sky until Amy gave me a kiss and told me they were walking with Brent to the end of our lane.

"Okay dear, take a light with you." I paid more attention to Amy's thoughts, until they came back giggling, about the faces of those guys, when they were being beat up, by some girls. They turned off the light before getting close to the camp. They sat down by the fire again and warmed up. It gave the bugs a chance to leave. When they were warm enough, they got up, to get ready, to go to bed. A quick repeat of the previous stop, to warm themselves, and then off to bed. It was my turn to get ready. The bathroom being free, and I, being at the end of the line, took my time and had a shave, shower, the whole bit. When I got back, the fire, was nearly dead. I spread it apart and stirred it up. I could watch the embers die from my bed and so, to there I went.

The frame extending moved along fine the last of the week. We were finished it along the walls that had been stripped. We finished stripping the walls that had been neglected. I took out the fuse old box. There was a big mess from that to clean up. There had been signs of overheated wires. Scorch marks behind the box as if the whole box had been overheated at one time. We felt like we had just dodged a bullet there. We cut away the charred wood and other debris. We had to do some shoring up back there. I built a box to fit inside, fastened to the uprights, on either side, with a piece to go where the stud had been cut out.

Then we put up the stud extender grid. If we were going to err, we tried to err, on the overbuilt side. We put in the new box and attached the wiring to the extension and kitchen and bathroom. We called to have the box installation inspected and the other stages of the construction. We had the camp on a circuit from the pole outside.

We put in our two stage power selector switchbox, our electrical wiring throughout the cottage and had it all ready for the inspection. Then we could hook them up when we got the okay. The cottage was now ready to have large appliances and a furnace installed.

Next we got up in the attic and cleaned out. This is where the natural elements had had their way. We cleaned it thoroughly and then opened it up over the common area, while putting in a floor to make a sleeping loft. This resembled an A-frame cottage loft. We reinforced the roof collar ties and thinned them to every third rafter. We laminated some joists to form beams, over the common area and removed the rest. We put up a ladder to access the loft. Now we were ready for a break. Help was on the way. We could relax and be proud of our efforts. Along with inspector, we had a tradesman coming to critique our work and offer direction beyond the inspector's scope. We will need to do the same on the roof, that we did with the walls. Then we can insulate and enclose the walls and ceiling. The time left before company came was spent extending the rafters with a 2X4 on every third one. This beefed up the roof structure and left a cavity to be filled with Styrofoam board insulation and air flow under the roof. We have then to put in 2X2s over the insulation board. These will be screwed to attach to the 2X4s through the insulation boards. I have to check with our advisor on this. This is something that I had not seen in the shows, yet. How do I beef up rafters and insulate, for loft rooms? The girls are having fun. They're learning aspects of different trades, and they are learning where to let the expert step in, to get the critical connections made. You save money on labour and costly mistakes. We are ready for an electrician to come in and do the things they do best.

Now that we are done, we invite the Youngs to come for dinner. They are delighted to come and see the progress, and visit over a meal. After cooking the food and eating, we give the grand tour. We ask Mr. Young, if he could recommend an electrician, to do next step with the panels, and appliance lines. He said he could have one here in no time. He goes to look at the things we have done. He then turns to me and asks, when would I like him to start.

"You're kidding me. You are an electrician?"

"I was before I retired. I went into another line of work that was easier on my body. But I don't mind getting into it, for a day, or two. You have all the grunt work done. Running the lines, are the things that get you on your knees, and straining what hasn't moved for a while. I hardly need to bend over, and if you had a table, for the tools, I wouldn't even have to do that."

"I do have tables." I chirp, "What do we need inspected before we go any farther?"

"Everything is open and he's able to see everything. I could hook up most of the completed lines, if you want to install the switch, and outlet boxes, I could do it all. You don't want to have lines, with power to them, that are hanging loose. You have some of them done. Just do the rest. Have you got any up to the loft yet?"

"No, not yet. I'll run one up there now."

I got the girls to hook up the switches and receptacles, while got the line up into the loft. We had each line going to one room, so we could see what is being put on that line. That will reduce the chance of fires, from overloaded circuits. It would minimize tripped breakers, and that is the first sign that you're overloaded. The girls slender fingers, helps them get the wiring done fast. Amy pops up at the ladder, to see the space I'm in, from a distance away. She felt me feeling claustrophobic and came up to see, if I would let her take over. I had some room around me, but trying to get my fat fingers into receptacle boxes makes me feel more claustrophobic. I am getting too old a body, for these jobs. I come to doubt my abilities, and worth. Once I do that, I spiral into a depression. So with that offer, I give up my position, and get down to an upright space. If I know what is about to happen, why would I not take appropriate action? At least having conditions for long terms, you can anticipate things, and make corrections.

Now that I am put out of a position, I check all the wires from start to finish. If I find any loose, I flag it, with a coloured clothespin, at the end of it, and check for more. The rooms now, have a second line come in, where there may be a need for them.

Mrs. Young looks in, to see what we are up to. It has turned dark and she's ready to go home. Her husband holds up two spread hands, to either say ten more minutes, or hold your horses. Sure enough, in ten minutes, we were finished. But where is Brent? We call out for him and get a knock on the floor. He has run lighting wires, through the crawlspace. Two more minutes and he's at the door as filthy as can be. A good time to end the day, when everyone is spent. We give a heartfelt thanks and our working guests start down the road for home. Having asked for his bill, I was turned down. He had said that, he did not want to give the impression, that it was his job. If I paid him, it would stir up bad memories. I understood completely.

I hadn't realized, that Brent had gone home and brought over work lamps, so that we all could do the work. He had done it so well, that nobody mentioned it being too dark. After seeing them off down the dark road, it dawned on me.

We then, turn ourselves in for the reward, of a well earned sleep.

When asked, in the fall, at school, what they had done for the summer. These girls can now say, 'I nearly tore a house down, and rebuilt it.' What other 14, or 15 yr. old can say as much. Plus they did it for free.

The morning comes too soon. The work is done, for now. We enjoy the warmth of the sun, by staying wrapped up in our beds. We are encouraged, each of us by the others' determination.

Hence, on the stroke of twelve, we roll out of our cocoons, proud to have outlasted, the morning. We skip brunch, and break right into the thick of lunch, vowing to work harder, to make it to dinner. One must set goals. Even if it is, to be a sluggard. Although, having already accomplished so much. We could hardly, with all humility, claim such a title.

Odd, that lunch, looks suspiciously, like brunch. We may be breaking the eleventh commandment. Thou shalt not, kid thyself!

After we have eaten our breakfast, at lunch, we get the canoe out. We tack a note for the inspector, that we shall be on the lake, and will come, when called. We get out for a quick spin, around our end of the lake. We have a good workout, for our arms, and are back long, before the inspector comes by.

When he does show up, he is in a foul mood. I escort him through the cottage, making notes of anything we wants changed. At the end of the tour, he finishes his report, signs our copy, and tells me when I need to have him back. We have passed our first hurdle.

We now can do the insulation. Here is a big job. Putting in batts of fibreglass, that will make you itch to no end. Cutting boards of Styrofoam, with the shavings floating everywhere. We decide to get the white suits, and cocoon ourselves up, for the torture it will save. Before we start on that, our company has arrived.

Jim, Nan, and Marie, have braved the hornet's nest of traffic through Toronto. They were able to find the sign I posted at the road. It is a hard road too see. It is a private access road for the two cottage properties on this portion of the lake. Because of this, it is not on the maps, or marked by municipal signage.

They get out and comment on my usual camping style. They do notice that there isn't the huge amount of ropes and bungee cords. The decks are a stray, from the old camping on the ground. An improvement in their opinion. They look out at the lake and love the view. We take them on the grand tour to stretch their legs. The first point is to the marshy section of the shore. Then along the sandy beach, past the stand of trees that hide a small section of our view of the lake. We come to the rock outcropping before the earthy embankment. When we got to the stream, by the rocks, Amy lets me know, they will be wanting to get into the cottage, and the bathroom. I swing them down toward the woods and stop. I make a point about the woods and suggest we leave that until later. I offer to get them in, to use the facilities, and see the cottage interior work. I get reaffirmation to that plan, and we quicken the pace to the cottage. The ladies get inside and the rest check out the sleeping quarters closer. Then Jim notices the pets. It almost startled him, but he isn't easily surprised. At least to get a reaction from him. He laughs and suggests a plan to get the girls. I tell him that Marie knows about them, so he plots to get his wife. We quietly stick them down behind the decks between the two tents. We go in and see the cabin interior and get the girls reaction to our labours. They are pleasantly surprised on how much work has been done. Marie even stood on the ladder to see the loft.

"I couldn't see my friends climbing up there on our girls' weekend. It looks nice though." she climbed down to let the others up, to check it out.

"Wow, there's a lot of space up there. It would be good for the grandkids. The older ones. You need to put up a railing."

As Nan lets Jim up to see, I tell them that last week it was all closed in and filled with animal nests and feces. "The girls cleaned it all out and opened up the ceiling over the common room. They put in the floor and I did all the beams while they did the rafters. Last night we all did the wiring, with the help of a friendly neighbour, and retired electrician. We did all the lines and he did the connections at the boxes. We've got a panel for the lights and receptacles with a separate box for the appliances and lines to go out to the outbuildings to come. We have a switchbox for connecting the solar and wind powered battery bank. We will be able to switch over to it and be off the grid and back in case of trouble."

Jim says it looks very nice. I know he's got some suggestions for me. I can tell by the tone drop of his voice. I tell him to let me have his ideas, since that is what I've asked him here for.

"Well I don't want to step on anyone's toes."

"Go ahead. I've got my metatarsals on."

"Well I can see right away that you're gonna need a pile of money and frankly, I can't see how you could do all this on your income. I think you're getting into a money pit. No offense but, this is gonna take a pile, and I mean a big pile of money." He said most of this looking at the floor. He didn't want to see the hurt in my eyes.

It was time for my surprise news. "I am selling my first book. The royalties have started coming in. I am nearly ready for the second and the third will be done within the next year. I found a publisher that likes the premise and my style of writing. He thinks, if I can do the series of books, that people may want to see it on film, too. I have the book series and a great response on the sales of the first one."

This is a surprise for Marie too. She got excited. Finally I have something finished and a future plan that has a direction. She even likes the cottage better. "How much do we owe on this cottage so far?"

"At this point, I would say, not a damn thing. I even have an account to see the project through, as long as I have my workers. Which is why, I need to get it done to a level that, we can then do the rest with hired help. And I would want to hire family first."

My wife gave me a big hug. "So when can I retire?"

"I would say, as soon as you want. I should have this second book done before long. Probably in October. Barring any more health surprises. I think I have learned enough in my life, to get this down on paper. Amy is helping me recall all of those experiences, that tie it all together. So, now, if you want."

"Oh good. I'll have to give my notice, so she can hire someone to replace me."

"I figured that."

"How long have you known about this?" Marie looks sternly at me.

"I got a letter at home, the last time I was there and I called them from up here and we talked a few times and struck a deal. They wanted to be sure, that I could come up with the second book, at the very least. We met before Amy and Tanya, had that trouble, at the building centre."

"What trouble?"

"Ooops. I guess we forgot to tell you about it. Amy and Tanya went into the store to get a load of 2X4s to do the extensions on the exterior walls. I stayed in the van because I had just had an anxiety attack. It was because of this deal I was doing. The girls were sighting down the lumber and some guys in the same aisle, came down and started harassing them. The girls saw them coming and had started toward the cashiers, but the guys trapped them and really started being jerks. I started in to help them, but had more attacks on the way and it knocked me down. People were coming to my rescue and I was trying to send them to their rescue, but I was slurring badly. Then I heard a familiar voice. I looked around but it wasn't around me it was in the store around the girls. Amy didn't recognize it until later because she was being molested by these guys. Well, the voice asked the girls if they needed help, and the guys told him, plainly, to get lost. So he grabbed two of the guys and told Amy that she can do anything she wanted to these guys. That's when Amy recognized the voice. It was her friend Brent. The girls started taking the guys down and doing a number on them. When they had kicked their butts enough, Amy ran out to help me and Tanya, sat on a couple of them to keep them down. Then security got there and then the Police showed up. They first thought that I was causing the disturbance, but Amy got there and sent them inside. One of them checked on me, before leaving and then went in to help his partner. The guys started to blame the girls for starting it and while the cops were considering this, Amy and I came down the aisle and the tough guy, pointed at Amy as the instigator, and the cops roared laughing, at these five toughs, getting beat up by these two fourteen year old girls, weighing about ninety pounds each. After that Brent caught up with Amy, and it turns out, he is at the family cottage for the summer, and is working at the building centre."

"Where is their cottage?" Marie asks.

"Right next door to ours. And, his dad was the electrician, that helped us get all this wiring done last night."

Jim says, "How did you see in here?"

"Brent went home to get some flood lights, and set them up, while we were too busy to notice. Then he ran a line of lights, through the crawlspace, for us. We had had them over for a barbeque, and when I asked if they could recommend an electrician, he said 'when do you want me to start?' When I said 'anytime', he started."

"Sounds like he's a real nice guy." Jim said.

"He said he didn't want money, because he wasn't going to do that anymore, for money. He was retired from that."

"You're doing alright then. Are you sure that you want to do this, here? You have to go through Toronto all the time, to get here."

"I like this place, but I could let it go if I had to. But it is a real nice big place. Almost everything we would want. I like having it my way, and my way is a better way than having to have it, someone else's way."

Amy and Tanya have left and gone to their tent. They're thinking about their summer and the work that they have put into this place. They would like to be more involved in the say, about what goes and what stays. I tell Amy, she will have more say. They've put the work in it and the book is based on her life. If she wants to stay, the place is hers. I will still work at developing it, and would do the same on another place. If I was to get one. She can't own it yet, but when she reaches the age of majority, it will be hers and Tanya's. They lie on their bed and Amy whispers in Tanya's ear, the words I have told her. They give a squeal of delight. Wrestling around the bed. They celebrate the promise I've made them.

Jim and I sit down, and draw up some plans. Me, with the artistic flair, and him, with the eye of the tradesman. We plan the great room and the barn. The tree-houses and the zip-line. We compare them with what we drew up in the other cottage, and combine the best ideas. He gives me some things to think about, for the next few weeks work. We get out on the lake to see the area and the other cottages. We hear a yell, look at each other and I hear Amy tell me, Aunt Nan saw the cats. I tell Jim and he has a great laugh. We go back and they have the fire started. Jim can't hide his expression and gets scolded. That just makes him laugh more. We sort out the sleeping arrangements. Nan and Jim, have the trailer. Marie shares my tent with me, and the girls stay in their tent.

During the night, Marie admits it is a nice place. "There's no bugs at night, at the fire. There are no spiders in the cottage, or tent, and the bed in our tent, is very comfortable."

I am having to struggle with my 'gift', as the girls are celebrating the news of the day, in a most intimate way.

I celebrate with Marie and do a fine job. We have no connection to spy on our guests, but past information could lay odds on a similar situation.

Hearing Jim's laugh, won my bet.

The girls are up early to make breakfast. Apparently last night gave them an appetite. I must remember, to give them a stern look. The smell of the bacon and the coffee aroma entwine in a long lure reaching into the trailer and drawing the quarry out by the nostrils. It's almost like the cartoons we saw as kids. Those afflicted with the desire, for one, or all of the components, meandered witlessly toward the origin of the cacophony of scents, in other words, everyone. On my arrival, I shoot my sweet, innocent, daughter a stern expression. She beholds me, with raised, questioning, eyebrows. I simply form a wrestling hold to make them dissolve into a hidden spot, where they tittered with delight, and embarrassment. I couldn't manage to do anything about it now. I tell Marie about it and let her dish out the punishment. I am weak and mouldable, by a ninety pound, five foot version of me. This tiny piece of my psyche, is undoubtedly wanting to call the shots. I believe, she has taken my spine, and stowed it away, for me to gaze on, to remember when it was mine. I have the not-so-secret weapon, her mother.

They are taunting me. Not purposely, I am sure of this, but out of their powerful thirst for each others company. If I stood up to them, I would be trampled by their blind stampede. I could be thousands of miles away, or inches, from grasping them, to attempt to ply the only strength I can find within myself. Just to have them wisp, through the very flesh and bone, of my former physical being.

If there was any hope, of my posing in the dominant role, that I personally cast for myself. It was quite possibly, that I was the only being, that believed in its existence. I had a noble purpose and order, that was posed and in which, most wilfully, I was bound for its success, or unavoidable failure. I was intent on being the clinical judge, of an argument that, at least a few, have indulged. I no longer view my judgement as clinical, but farcical. I am lost in the mists of Avalon, and my reality, is drifting from this world, to the infinite.

I am lost in thought and I realize there is something wrong. I can't move my legs. I fell asleep and when I opened my eyes, I could not move. Only my eyes would respond. I have been here before. An out of body dream, followed by a waking to this. I try to go to sleep to get a release. It doesn't work. I don't work. I can't think back to that point I was at. I had flown without difficulty and when I awoke, I felt that I had not been able to get back inside properly, and I was unable to move. My body had felt as it does now. Very heavy and awkwardly inept, at a simple basic movement. Doctors then were dismissive and I have no desire to have their opinions on the phenomenon. All I want, is to get to that breakfast before it is gone, or cold. Amy knows. She's looking and now getting up to come to me. The others are busy talking and eating. They don't see her coming to help me. She holds out a piece of bacon, to tempt me into forcing myself. I see it, but I can't move. She brings it closer, and nothing. She touches my lips and then tries to push it into my mouth. I cannot even move my mouth. She remembers the other times. She plays it over in her head. She pulls my legs off the place that was supporting them. They fall. Is the spell broken? I start to slide down, but am caught on a fold in the chair. We wait and the others take notice. "What's wrong?" her mom asks. "He's stuck. It's happened before, when he was working. Some kind of astral projection dream, gone wrong. This time he just drifted off and when he woke up, he couldn't move. He can only move his eyes. I put bacon to his lips and he can't even salivate. It's like he couldn't fit back in his body properly. That is something that came to his mind. He might slip in, now that he is moved from his original spot. He wants to get his breakfast, and he doesn't want it to be cold."

They look at her, and it's as if they didn't really believe that this was real.

Marie puts together a meal for me with the warmest of what is there and puts it between two plates and wraps it in some towel. She puts it inside something by the table that I can't see. Amy says its a jacket. Marie gets a cloth and wets it. She comes back and puts it on my head, just like she did when I was like this from a sunstroke. Amy moves my arms and fingers, to stimulate my senses and muscles. They work at it until my mouth starts to move. At first it was just my lips pursing like a nerve response, or maybe it was voluntary. Amy says it's hard to tell. My jaw moved slightly and my mouth started to salivate. I felt like I had been frozen in a pose, like being paused. Amy could feel the muscles starting to get signals again. A spasm moved my right hand sideways. Amy smiles. "That has happened before many times." she tells them. "He is coming around." She lifts my legs and puts my feet under them. She and Marie put their hands under my arms and start to lift me from my chair. I move as much as is being allowed. I try to take my weight. I feel functional now, but it is still tentative. I open my mouth and stick my tongue out, as much as I can.

"Oh, he's been joking. He just stuck out his tongue." Nan said.

Amy said loudly, "No. He's checking to see if it could have been a stroke. If his tongue is straight, it wasn't a stroke."

"Oh, yeah. I remember him telling us that, at the cottage. A stroke would make the tongue go toward the side, that was weakened, by the stroke. He said, he has so many of the symptoms already, that that would tell, quickly, when the other symptoms were questionable."

"He says he's not wanting to chase doctors about it. They feed him mumbo-jumbo when they don't want to try. He said he just wants to finish the books and all the other things he's working on before he goes."

"What does he mean 'goes'?" they ask her.

"Dies." she says plainly, "He says he's not in a hurry."

Marie looks at him and smiles, almost to keep from crying. She's like Nicholas. She wants things in a fair order. She doesn't like some of the things I say. I won't let anyone really control that side of me, because I want to be heard and understood. We often butt heads, because we are opposing players, and we each have our own rules, of logic and of reason. Hers is orderly and mine is abstract.

Amy decides she is ready, to tell her own version, of this familial triangle. In her head, she is more an extension of her past life, but this time, she has a family that loves her. She also sees Tanya as an adult. Like she feels she is. Fourteen is just a number for her. She thinks, this is what you get when you go changing the rules, and messing with peoples lives.

I did get my breakfast and after what Marie did with it, I didn't care if it was ice cold, because she cared and believed.

I do come around and fully recover my faculties. I tell them that I am glad that I have an interpreter now. Tourette syndrome symptoms have been happening more often. Not the cursing, but the spasms and arm flying up in the air after I have an unpleasant memory. I don't know if this is a function of the mimicking fibromyalgia, or if this has been caused by one of my many injuries. Doctor are not sure about a lot of the conditions and are happy, it seems, to just be able to diagnose it. Many diagnoses are in error anyway. Like they say, 'They are just practicing doctors.' I would hate to see if they got serious.

'I'm still standing. Yeah, yeah, yeah....'

Chapter Twelve

Pulling Out The Stops

I walk over to the Youngs' to introduce Jim. Mr. Young was glad for the company. Brent had to work and Mrs. Young was doing some shopping in Peterborough. He had work to finish up and didn't really feel like doing it.

He and Jim talked about things and instantly they found they had a mutual friend. That happens to Jim wherever he goes. In Mexico, Indianapolis, or Timbuktu. There was always a two degrees of separation with Jim. Jim worked with the guy that Joe Young had apprenticed with. Back when Jim was an apprentice carpenter. Jim had many trades now.

Everybody just can't get over how it happens, wherever he goes. I tell him that Joe lived in Hamilton and sure enough, Jim knew his next door neighbour. I ask them to pardon me while I walk a while. Joe puts his shoes on and walks along with me, still talking to Jim. He tells Joe about the problem I had had at breakfast. Joe tells me to have the girls call on him if they need help. He tells Jim about him telling his son to marry Amy and then finding out that she was a lesbian. "They are some remarkable girls though. The work they're doing in that house is amazing. I've never seen two people that work as hard as they do. Never."

"They are good. Amy is helping to design some of the details with her Dad here."

"Remarkable."

These two guys could sure talk. I knew Jim would get along with him.

Meanwhile Amy and her mother were talking about how I was doing here. She was feeling very lonely and was wanting them to come home. She didn't care if I didn't finish here. She wanted me home. That scare this morning made it very real. She lost her dad when he was younger than I was. She did not want me to die up here and leave her without the last of my days to share. Amy tells her to retire. She would send me home to be there with her while she works through the two weeks notice and then they can come up to see the end of the work up here. She and Tanya can keep working and the Youngs could watch out for them. Brent would come by every day. They agree. Amy will be able to get my attention and help from anywhere we are.

Marie decides to ask Jim to stay, while I get all the supplies for the house in, and then come back in the van. Nan and she would go back, and she could hand in her two weeks notice. I could concentrate on finishing the book and then go on to the next. Amy has the cats to protect them. We've proved that. Amy tells me the plans. I turn to Jim and Joe and put forward the proposal. Jim has no trouble with that, and Joe says it would be an honour, to look in on them. He would have Brent check everyday. I excuse myself again and head back to start the shopping list. I look back and Jim is right behind me. I stop to let him catch up, although he would have anyway. I talk out the list as I walk and Jim adds things to fill it in. Amy is writing it down as we say it. She adds ten percent to the totals for shrinkage.

Tanya and the women are expecting to tell us when we walk in. We measure up the place and we were close with our estimate. Amy is getting hyper. Tanya is planning. This is a big step for her and Amy. They feel that they will be essentially married for a two week trial. No chaperone. They will be free to do all the things that adults do. She feels a little anxious. I can't hear Tanya's plans but I know Amy's. Right now there are only fleeting glimpses, of her honeymoon plans. Her anxiety is interfering with her thoughts.

'I would like you two, to behave like young teenagers should, as far as your romance goes. Don't do anything, that you might have done as an adult, in your past life. It makes a difference, when you are still physically developing. Some things could make basic functions become uncontrollable. I don't have much knowledge about these things, but there are ways you can harm yourself, if you are too young. You can't do things that an adult can, at your age. That is why carnal knowledge, is taken from us, before we take on another life. Be content to be young and careful.' Lecture done, I go over the instruction with Amy in our heads.

Not thinking of our talents Jim goes to give Amy some instructions. She surprises him by saying them as he does. "You know these things?"

"Tell me about the vapour barrier." she lets him give some of the finer points of insulating, having a general knowledge from me.

He feels better that he can be of service to her. He gives her a bunch of things to do and some things to be careful not to do.

They will be fifteen this year and if it wasn't for the Youngs next door, I would not leave them alone. I will be able to be there mentally, but I have to rely on the phone to contact anybody else up here. Way out here in the bush, the lines are fairly primitive. A strong wind could knock them out easily and with all the branches along the length of the line, it makes that an imminent threat whenever a storm appears. Brent will be seeing them everyday. Those guys from the store, may be able to find them, if they were wanting to make them suffer, for having them arrested. It is a stretch, but parents imagine the stretches, when they are in a compromising situation. They do have the threat the cats might look capable of, to protect them. It will be nice to have the cottage moving along. It will also be nice to have Marie retire early. She won't get much from her pension, but working until she is sixty five, won't give much more. We will be able to come here more often and travel more, as well. Her schedule will not be as full, but her life will be fuller. I tell Tanya, that I will stop in and see her mom and let her know, she is doing well.

So now the plan has been set, and the tension, is both easing and tightening. Marie is anxious about retiring and leaving her boss with the task of replacing her. I am feeling anxious about the retirement, because we will be together more than ever. What if we don't like being together that much? What if I can't handle her scheduling our lives. She knows, that I have been up here working on the cottage, and she sees, how much is being accomplished. She may not know, that it is the girls that have been doing ninety per cent of the work, and that I am still, unable do be as productive as she would want. I have always kept an easy attitude about my shortcomings. I keep a sense of humour, to put my problems in a comic light. I can't do much about them, that I am not already doing everyday. I had plenty of supporters in my final years at work. They knew me. After forty four years, I am not sure if Marie wants to know me, or support me in the same manner. I try not to complain but, it is talking about the things that happen to me, that shows them why, I can't get up in the morning, and run off to do an errand, or fix something. I need to give myself time, every bloody day, to let the energy build up slowly. I can occasionally, get things done right away. That is only a short window, before I have nothing left, for the rest of the day. I never let myself worry much. It doesn't help. When Marie is with me all the time, that may change beyond my control.

People say they would like a crystal ball, so that they could get all the answers. I have one, and they don't work that way. They help you see inside your thought processes. It helps you see, what you are too busy to, normally. You stop and concentrate, meditate, looking at a focal point. You can look at a spot on the wall and get the same effect. You just don't get a picture of the future. You get your vision of your possibilities.

My fears about my life, when she retires, must be met and faced, the same way you conquer all your fears. You face them and don't back down. I just don't want to hurt her, or lose her. When you haven't any choice, have fun. This is how I face everything. If people want too much from me, I disappoint them on purpose. If I can help, I do. Marie wants more, than I am able enough to deliver.

The ladies are leaving early today. They want to be able to beat the traffic. Nan will take Marie in the pickup. Jim and I will go to get the supplies for the girls. We've put in the basic plumbing, that we will need to get by. When Marie and I come back up, we will put in more of the water recycler-system. If the girls can get the insulating done before we get back, we've left some dry-wall board and they can start putting them up in the loft. I will probably find them enjoying the lake and canoe. They do have the option, of cutting out the window space, on the end of the loft. They can seal it with the vapour barrier plastic sheet. At least that will bring in more light. The girls have had a wild, few weeks up here. It has been more work, than I thought we could manage.

It will be Tanya's birthday, the week after we should be back, and I intend to invite the moms up, to celebrate it with her, up here.

Marie and Nan, got home alright. Jim and I, will pick up the rest of the batts and boards tomorrow. We cleaned out, what was left, at the builders' supply store, and Brent said, there will be a shipment in tomorrow. It's amazing, how certain people, are destined to be part of your life, and in the most surprising ways.

"Hey Jim, I was looking through some genealogy information, and I found your last name on a castle in Belgium. Then I heard, that it's not uncommon, to have nobles in your family tree. But a long, sharp stick, should get them out. Have you gone in the lake yet?"

"Not yet. How is it?"

"Nice! The water moves well, off the beach and toward the stream. Away from the marsh. There are leaches in by the marsh, where the water is barely moving. We've swam and the water is clear, enough to see sunken tree trunks and huge boulders, in deeper areas. We've seen them, while we canoe around the lake, at this end. It would be nice, if we could haul those logs up, out of there. Then I wouldn't have to cut any down. I have an idea, to make some furniture for the cottage, from wood grown on the property."

"Those are rotting down there. They will fall apart when you try to move them."

"Too bad. I don't like cutting trees down, if I don't have to."

"Just thin out the forest. Take them from where you need some space. First around the barn area, and then, wherever they are too thick."

The girls are starting supper. The sun is disappearing earlier. It's a shame, the time passes so fast. I won't be able to enjoy the summer much more. When we get back, it will be nearly time to get the girls back for school. Life just goes spinning off out of control, it seems. So much seems to happen all over the world, but at home, I can't seem too get much done at all. Here, things move fast wherever the girls are. It's like, I am in the vortex of a tornado, just standing there. Is it like this for everyone? The girls will feel the summer went by so fast, because they are doing so much. My summer is going so fast, and I don't do much at all. I will just get started on something and it's time to quit. I move so fast, there are cobwebs hanging from me. It doesn't make sense, I feel like I am busy, but don't get much accomplished. This place will be Amy's. She and Tanya have done almost all of it.

After supper, we all get in the canoe and follow the shoreline to explore. We skip over the bays we have seen and head for the ones we need to go in to see what we can't see from beyond the mouth. There are a few more cottages. Some look like they are older than ours. Some look 'brand new' in the eighties. Most are kept well. A couple are worse than ours was. I feel like I could enjoy doing this for many years. Then, they will be gone, so fast, that I could not feel it.

I told my Uncle John, that the years were going by faster all the time, and he said "wait 'til you're my age."

Back at camp, we start the evening fire, throwing in our special ingredients. We get something to sip on. Sit back and enjoy some quiet. The girls get ready for bed early and then stay by the fire longer. Jim and I start the star attraction. It is tradition to talk about the happenings in the sky around the fire. First up, Venus. Next is, Jupiter. Just before the satellites are seen, the Northern Lights steal the show. Jim is pointing out things for the girls. "Right between those two stars." Tradition,.. tradition,.... Tradition!

It doesn't matter, whether we are camping, at the cottage, or wherever we go. Sitting down in the evening, and enjoying some conversation, is the payback, for being apart for so much of the time. Sure, once in a while, you get on each other's nerves, but the together times, are the best times.

Jim has noticed that there are no bugs biting. "I wonder why there aren't any bugs around?"

Amy says, "Ask the sage."

"Who is the sage? Your dad?"

"The sage is in the fire."

"The sage is in the fire? What does that mean?"

"We put sage in the fire pit to drive away the bugs." she explains.

"Is that right? I never heard of that."

"Yeah, it sits on the edge of the fire there and burns slowly to drive away the bugs. And we put lavender at the openings in the tents and buildings to keep the spiders out."

"Where did you hear of that?"

I tell him about the one thing he did not like when I announced it before. "Remember me telling you, that I was going to study witchcraft?"

"Yeah."

"Well these are some of the things I learned about. I don't have to practice witchcraft, to use the wisdom it can hold. I was looking for natural ways of healing, that I have not tried. I came upon this sage advice, and used it."

"What else did you learn?" he is a little more interested.

"To get new things into your life, you need to get rid of the old, broken things. Things like chipped glasses and stuff. And if it's going to be thrown out, try to fix it first and if you can fix it you can give it to someone to whom it is useful."

"Well that makes sense. Are you getting rid of the broken things in your life?"

"Nope. If I do that, I'll get new things and I am used to the things I've got."

With that twisted logic, we get ready for bed.

The mornings come so soon, when they're getting cold. A chilly night and a heavy dew. Something to stay in the blankets for. The sun is bright, but it needs to do a job on the thermometer. The girls are cuddling close and not jumping up to make breakfast. Very smart girls. Jim gets restless and gets up first. Dang, now I feel like I should get up. I lie perfectly still. Maybe that feeling will go bother someone else. Oh good, it's gone. Jim makes coffee and waits to see what it draws out of the sheets. Hmm, nobody? I call out, "Try bacon!" I hear laughs all around.

It's not that he wants to get us up, but that was an idea whose time was always coming, around here and his favourite smell, anytime. The stove is on, and the smells are working their magic. We are still in bed, but we are getting hungry.

I can no longer stand it. Apparently neither can the girls. We throw on some extra clothes, and stumble out, for a reluctant start, to an unappealing feeling.

I set the table and Jim finishes the cooking. The girls sit, like most teenagers do, and for them, it is unusual to see. They do know how to take advantage of a good thing. They sit on the bench and leave the chairs for us. They keep huddled together and I want to huddle with them. I get a heater out of the trailer to hang up in their tent. It will hang down about half way between the roof and the bed. The nylon tent is not good to have heaters too close to, but that ought to be safe at that height. It is a type that isn't supposed to get hot on the outer parts.

They can move into the trailer, if it is not enough. I will need to get a woodstove for the cottage. We have lots of firewood from fallen trees in the woods and scrounged wood along the lake. We sort it into three groups, suitable for building structure, good enough for building accents, and good dry firewood. Anything not good enough, stays in the forest to feed the trees and wildlife.

Once in a while we get animals poking around the camp. Explorers, seeing if we are a food source. They see the kitties and give a wide berth. I saw a bear statue fishing by the lake, in a store website. Thoughts about putting it up here, have been flitting about in my brain. Reactions from guests, are worth the price.

Breakfast done and we're all cleaned up. Jim and I head to the building supply store and check out their woodstoves. Brent tells us of a place in town, that has a wide selection. It's a small town, but there are some good shops that draw the customers, from miles away. They have one that we want to get. It will be great for the cottage, until we get the great room with the fireplace. After that it can go for the barn-workshop. We get that loaded up and then head back to see young Brent Young. He's got our order forming up on a trolley. We give him a hand putting it together and then we can get back to the camp.

When we get close to the cottage, I see trouble. The boys that harassed the girls are walking along the road. I tell Jim to keep on going, past the driveway and down the road a ways.

"What's wrong?" he asks.

I tell him about those boys and we think about how we should handle it. If we turned in the drive and they knew the van, it would bring them around looking for the girls. I don't know if they know the van. They might be looking for Brent. They would recognize him, and could be looking to get revenge, for his interference. We decide to go to camp. They hadn't seen the van at the store. They saw me for a short time. We go back. We pass them on the way. They have passed our road and could not see me in the van. They were looking a different direction. I feel better, but not easy. I set one of the cats on the path to the camp and the other one is visible from the lakeshore.

I tell the girls, to talk with Brent about the boys and to keep an eye out for them. Amy did know, as soon as I was aware of them, that there was a problem.

We load all the supplies into the cottage and go over to see the neighbours. Joe is out fishing with a friend, but Evelyn is there, and we arrange for the girls to get some groceries with her, when she is going into town. We tell her about the boys, and she'll pass that on to Joe. We thank her in advance and head back to the girls.

We say goodbye to the girls and head for home. An uneventful trip, Jim drives all the way to his place, and I drive an hour back home.

Chapter Thirteen

Retirement Postponed

Marie was intent on retiring until she found out the cost of not waiting six weeks until her birthday. As appealing as retirement looked, the bottom line is looking a whole lot more so.

I came down to keep her company. This extension, will leave the girls alone too long. I decide to stay the week, and drive back with more stuff, from our house. I have stacks of wood pieces, that can fill some needs, and old furniture, as well. I can bring up more food and I can be back down in a week. Do one on, one off. The girls have to come back in three weeks, to prepare for school, and then I can stay with Marie. I will shut the cottage up and the camp down, for the season. Once we have it finished, next year, we can use it year round.

I call on the moms, and invite them to the cottage, for their daughter's birthday. They are thrilled at the chance to go there again. I tell them to pack warm clothes, to layer up, for the nights and mornings are getting cold.

I load up the van and take care of business here. I go to find things to take up with me. I get in on some end of season sales. Floatation jackets, for members of the family that wouldn't have their own. I bring the utility trailer and load it up. One more thing out of the driveway and lots more out of the garage. My buddy, George, has some stuff to get rid of, and I take it off his hands. These things, are destined to make special features, for the property up there. The names of the donors, will be engraved on the features they have contributed to. I load the old propane tanks in the trailer. That takes the last eyesore from the driveway.

I knew that I was going to need these things that I had been holding onto. I have had this dream for decades and now, it is defined in our cottage getaway.

I pick up some space heaters, that will be stable enough and safe for use in the tents. I get another trike, so I can have one here and one at the cottage. I can stick to my exercise in both places. I won't have to cart the trike back and forth. Canoeing is good for upper body strength, but not so much for the legs. I get this one set up for me, so that I won't have the gearing problems, I had with the first one.

This is a new dimension in our lives that will last, being both a struggle and a respite. We will not enjoy going through Toronto traffic, but the prize awaiting us, is worth the effort.

Amy is thriving in the freedom of space between us. Having the illusion of a married life with Tanya, is giving them renewed energy in their work, to get to their domestic activities at night. They are in their utopia. The appearance of Brent at night, and his mom in the daytime, bracket their routine.

Brent has been keeping an eye on the foot traffic around the property, with some surveillance equipment he and Joe picked up. They had had it on order and when it was finally delivered, it seemed a good idea to put it down at the road, to check on the migratory path of certain individuals.

The court date is going to be in September and we will all have to be there, to give our evidence. It is going to be good to check on the camp and set things right. To enjoy the fall climate here also. The September warmth of sunny days and cool of frosty previews at night. Sleeping in the cottage might be possible then. Three sleeping areas inside and three sleeping areas outside, give us a great place for the family to gather en masse. We will be able to close down the trailer and tents for the winter. An October visit with Marie, after her retirement, will be so amazing. The woodstove installed and the furniture moved in for the weather safe environs of the newly refurbished interior space. It is enticing a dream that will keep me working on it.

The results of the cameras scans show the boys go by there and they don't even give the place a second glance. They are likely from the area, or are visiting someone in the area. The girls and the Youngs relax. Marie and I take the time easier, as well. It consumes you, to fear for someone outside your reach. The cats are a good visual deterrent and now there are the cameras. We feel much better.

I want to look into the foundation for the barn-workshop when I go up there. Amy looks over the area for me and measures it up. We want a pole barn with straw bales for the exterior and insulation. A place to create, relax and escape to. Amy is thinking the greatroom should be part of the barn. I think I like that idea. I will have to draw up some plans to include that.

The insulation is done on the main floor. The loft is next. Amy is excited about bringing in the furniture and is working longer hours. Tanya quits about a half hour before Amy, to fix dinner. The vapour barrier goes up after dinner is over. When Brent checks in on them, he gives a hand to finish the room they're in. They stop for the evening once that is done and visit. They have the space heater in the cottage, while they are in it. Welcoming friends into their house, is a real turn-on for them. When they need to put the heater back in the tent for the night, they start the fire in the fire pit. They continue the visit with Brent for a bit, by the fire. They get ready for bed and Brent goes home.

They hop into bed and wrestle each other to get some heat built up in the bed. That's a good excuse for it. They get set to watch the moon on the lake, on one side and the dying embers, on the other. If it was a warmer evening, they would watch the stars. Instead they cuddle each other to sleep.

The next morning, they are out fishing on the lake. They enjoy catching their own meals. When they catch anything. Some days, it's a fish and some days, just a chill. They cook up the catch and get right to work. The Styrofoam is much nicer for them to work with. They score and snap and score and snap all morning. The afternoon has them screwing in the panels and putting up the barrier. I feel tired from seeing all this work and get outside to get something of my own to do. They keep on moving. They put some planks across the beams over the common room for a scaffold. They feel empowered with each day they put in. By Friday they are finishing the insulation and the vapour barrier. Next week we will go to work on the wall panels. I need to get the roof done.

Marie sees me off, before work and I start my trek up to help the girls celebrate Tanya's fifteenth birthday. I hop along, stopping every hour, or two, to rest and walk around. It is about a three hour drive for some people, but more like five, or six for me, on my own.

Marie and Tanya's moms, are coming up together after work. Millicent is one that drives everywhere. They get along with Marie and wanted her to come up. They are bringing up the party, they say. Amy doesn't want to let me know, what Marie is thinking, but as she hears it, I catch a bit of it. I remind Amy that Marie is nervous, and is like this for everybody. I know there will be tension in that car. It is a strain on Marie to meet new people. Once she's got to know them, she warms to them.

'What are you giving to Tanya, for her birthday?' I ask as I take a stroll to stretch my legs.

Amy replies, matter-of-factly. 'I've been giving it to her all summer.'

'Amy!'

'Relax, Dad. I've been giving her a place to come to, to get away. Get your mind out of the gutter!'

'You've been putting it there all summer.'

'Okay, I'm sorry. I've been working on this, to give us a place to come on school breaks. We love the place and if we could live here, we would.'

'You're right. You two have been pushing yourselves all summer, to get things done. You have paid for a big part of the place, with your labour. I will be putting your name on the deed with ours. I have some stuff to use for projects up there.'

'Yes, I saw. You don't have a clue what for.'

'Nope. It is wood and will be needed someplace.'

'True. I'll help you think of it. Don't push yourself. I don't want to have to tell Mom that you've had an accident.'

'I've been taking it easy.'

'Where is that place you're at now?'

'I don't know the area well, but it's got a wide enough shoulder, to pull over on.'

'Don't get lost. Have you got your GPS app on?'

'Yes, it's on. I'm just going to have a nap now.'

'Okay, Dad.'

The three moms made it to the cottage before I did. Right away Marie was worried. "Where's your father?"

"He's nearly here. He had a nap and got a little disoriented. He couldn't find his phone right away and he panicked. I helped him calm down. We found the phone and he sat for a while before getting on the road, so he could relax."

"Oh, thank goodness! I thought he might have got lost, or had an accident, or something." Marie was getting hyper from the scare. It's been seven hours since I left home. "I'm not going to have him come down on his own anymore. He can stay up here, until you come home for school."

"I think that is a good idea. It's too hard on you, to worry about him on the road. He's safe and has been careful, while he's been on his own. I got busy and didn't recognize the road when he pulled off."

Brenda came inside to see if there were any space heaters, for the trailer. "Whoo, it's cool out there, with that sun so low. It's going to be cold tonight!"

"Dad is bringing some new space heaters, for out in the trailer and tents. He'll be here any minute now."

"Oh. Did he call you?"

"Yes, he did." Amy winked at her mother. "He called to say he was taking a nap and then, to say he was on his way again."

"Oh, good. Your mom was worried when we didn't see his van."

"I think those are his lights coming down the lane."

Marie went out to check. She saw another set of lights behind the van. "Who could that be?" she said to Millicent.

"Isn't that your husband's truck?"

"Yes, but there is someone following him in."

I pulled up to the trailer and got out. The car behind me was Joe Young. He wanted to welcome me back, and give me an update, on what was happening here. He told me about the boys, just walking by without noticing the driveway. He said the girls are pretty good fishermen. Recounting the fish he saw them pull in a couple times. "They don't practice catch and release. I think they're enjoying them for meals. Real outdoorsmen there."

"I think they can give a pretty good imitation of one. They are both remarkable young ladies." I puffed out my chest.

"They could give a contractor's crew a good run for their money."

"Yes, they could. I am very proud of them and the job they have done here. Get Evelyn and come over tomorrow. We are celebrating Tanya's fifteenth birthday."

"That would be great. I'll tell her as soon as I get in there."

"Great, we'll see you tomorrow then." Marie has been standing back waiting to talk to me. As Joe walks off, she steps out of the shadows. "Hi, I'm sorry I'm late. I didn't want to take any chances. I had to have a nap."

"Yes, Amy told me. I'd rather have you do that, than have an accident. Do you have those space heaters handy? I think we'll be needing them tonight. Brenda was asking for one for the trailer."

"Yes, I've got them just between the seats. Did you bring any food up for dinner tonight? I'm starved."

"Yes we brought a cooler with chicken and pizza. I'm going to get it now, from the car."

"Pizza at the cottage. What better could I ask."

Marie gets the cooler from the car, while I get the heaters from the van. As we take them out, another set of lights pull in. It's Brent on his rounds. "Hi, Brent. Come on in for some food and meet the folks."

"What, are you having a party?"

"Tomorrow. Tonight is the warm-up with chicken and pizza. I just saw your dad. That was before I found out there was food. Give the folks a call and have them come over."

"No, I can't stay. I was just going to see how they are, but now that your here, I'll go home to bed. I'm beat. I'll stop in tomorrow though. I'll talk to Dad and give him your message. G'night."

"G'night Brent, and thanks for watching out for them, all these years."

"It's my pleasure."

I get the heaters started and then get inside for food. I get inside the door and Millicent hands me a drink. As I take it from her, she says, "Some antifreeze for the coming chill." I step up to the counter and grab some pizza. I greet the company and inform them, "the heaters are heating, as we are eating."

"Here, here!" the throng replied. We got the warm-up party going and toasted the diligent work crew. The girls blushed and hugged each other. I commented on the scaffold. They were all ready to start putting up the wallboards. We had a good visit and then got ready for bed. Marie and I went last. As we got into bed in our tent she noticed there was no heater, just as she felt the electric blanket.

"Oh, nice. Does it still work?"

"We will find out soon enough." I was hopeful but not confident. We slid down between the sheets and the icy crispness made us recoil. Forcing ourselves on, we felt the warmth in small pieces of the bed. The warmth built on the pressure points of our contact with the coverings. If we lay in one spot, that spot would warm us. If we dared move, we were jabbed by frosted shards of pain, stabbing at the raw nerves. So still we stayed, and until morning broke, stiff and rigid we looked, as if frozen to the bedding. Warmth against us, but nowhere else. We opened our eyes to the light. The chill of the air gripping the orbs beneath, and the lids snapping shut. "It's time we get a new electric blanket." I clouded the air above me.

"Here, here." came the reply. I didn't dare move to nudge her. A moan from this side and then that. Showed that there was life yet around. No movement noticeable, but low muffled sounds indicated that there was truly, intelligent life. Too smart to peal back toasty blankets. We remained inert. Thinking of search parties finding the lifeless bodies stuck tight within the shelters.

Chapter Fourteen

Happy Birthday

P atience is the word for the day. We lay in the confines of our sheets. Blankets and comforters are piled deep atop our inanimate figures. Marie and I dare not move a millimetre. I don't think the heaters were effective, since the others have not made a move either. We hang in the balance of the teetering thermometer. The sun has risen high but the air is still chilled. Amy and Tanya are clinging tight to each other, but still behaving. I imagine we all are clinging to our partners. We are getting restless and Marie challenges me to brave the cold and put the kettle on. As the resident male, I am at odds with the sexist role pressed upon me. I would be happy to give the leadership to anyone else, should they desire the role. Amy says "suck it up, Dad." I get respect only when I would rather not.

In a grand display of testosterone, I jump to my feet. Actually, I slide rather slowly, but am on my feet, in less than five minutes. I get bundled quicker. Stepping out from under the tarp, I find it quite comfortable, in the rays of the late summer sun. I put the kettle on, and the teens step out, to keep me company. I call to the rest, to enlighten them on the cosiness we are enjoying. One by one, they emerge from their dens. They are gratified that I had been truthful in my description.

The young ones get warm clothes on, to go into the trailer and start cooking. Amy makes Tanya, stand and watch. It is her birthday, and she is not to lift a finger to do any work. Our guests walk down to the riverside and lay on the rocks, to sun themselves. Marie joins them. They shed their extra clothes and pull up sleeves and pant legs. They talk about how beautiful the scenery is around us.

Amy is moving quickly in the add-a-room, trying to convince the meal to cook faster.

The tarps offer protection from the rain and heat, but not for very much of the cold. The heaters should have been more efficient. I walk over to check them and none are working. I check the pole panel to see if the breaker had been tripped. It had. The two heaters, and the electric blanket, on the heavy extension cords, were too much. I switch the girls heater, to a cottage feed, and set up another for our tent. The trailer will be able to work better now, with only one heater on it. I had done a foolish thing. I am embarrassed at what I had done. It was our body heat, that was keeping us warm and not, the electric blanket.

I own up to my mistake, and get a razzing from the women, all the women. Breakfast is ready, in time to draw off the heat, for the lack of it. We sit in the sun and enjoy Amy's labours. The warmth of the food and the sun are soothing our ravished nerves, from the chilling we had last night.

I had made sure not to overload circuits inside the house. Why I didn't think of the trailers circuits, is beyond me. I must be sure the heaters are all working tonight, before the women start to get ready for bed.

We are getting ready to go for a paddle around the lake, when we hear a siren coming very close. It stops and we hear the engines coming down the lane. They go over to the Youngs' cottage. Amy and Tanya start running over by the path to the driveway. The rest of us start a quick walk. I am falling behind but wave the women on. Amy tells me it's a fire truck and an ambulance.

She gets to the trucks and sees Brent at the door, looking in. One hand is holding the door and the other gripping his forehead. She runs up to him and he turns and grabs her in his arms. He cries into her hair. His head is buried in her shoulder. "It's my Dad! He collapsed, and I couldn't feel his heartbeat. I tried to do CPR, but it wasn't helping. I think....he's dead!"

Amy held onto him. He was so tall, and she felt awkward, hanging from him. She would not let him go. Tanya arrived and joined the embrace, holding Amy and Brent as Amy's legs started to dangle. As comical as that could have looked, not one of us paid much notice of it.

We started to congregate near the door, but afraid to block the doorway. The firemen were coming out of the house. They came to the kids in the doorway and talked to Brent.

They assured him that there was nothing he could have done. They said he had died instantly. They used the defibrillator, without success. They said that if they had been there when it happened, it would not have made a difference.

The paramedics were consoling Evelyn. Brent goes to his mother and they embrace, as the tears flowed. The firemen and paramedics stayed by them to offer any assistance. The family was too contained to look to anybody. One fireman came to us, to see if we were going to stay with the family. We said, we would, and they started to gather their things. As they loaded their equipment in the truck, another vehicle pulled in.

It was the coroner. He talked to the men and then proceeded into the house. We stepped inside to help Brent and Evelyn. The coroner talked to the paramedics after he examined the body and then went to speak to Evelyn. The paramedics placed the body on the stretcher that the firemen brought in from the coroner's wagon. They had put him into a black bag and rolled the stretcher out to the wagon. The paramedics came back for their equipment and left after offering their condolences to the family. The coroner left shortly after and the house was quiet, except for the sobs from the group left assembled there.

The coroner was called in as he was driving in to his office and was still close to the scene. It was surreal, how fast it had taken place. It left Evelyn and Brent, feeling the emptiness of the house and their hearts. He had suffered an aneurism. There was absolutely nothing, that could have saved him.

Brent came to us and thanked us for being there for them, but asked us, if we would mind leaving them. They did not want to keep us from the birthday celebration, and would like to be left alone for a while, to rest. The doctor had given them some sedatives, to help them rest and recover, somewhat, from their ordeal.

We left the house, and walked slowly and silently, back to our cottage. We did not feel much like celebrating. When we got back to camp, we looked around at each other, to see the feelings in our faces. We all wondered what we could do to move on from this. A friend, a short time known, was taken. It was as if your house had been robbed. Something very tangible was missing from us. A hole left in the heart, of each one of us. We decided to go on with the canoe trip, we were about to embark on, before this loss was revealed.

We loaded into the craft and pushed off. Paddling slow but steady, it was as if a dirge was playing, and we were keeping time. If the mood was lighter, this would break us into laughing fits. This was not one of those times, and it won't be for most of the day. A pall hung over us. An empty, inky, gloom, blocking out the bright, cheerfulness of the sunny day. We took in the length of the lake, without seeing anything we passed.

When we returned, it was still difficult to make any move, to accomplish any part of a plan, or consciously travel the courses left before us. Time was moving absurdly slow. What is usually a swift blur of events, seems to be a series of stop-action scenes of a contrived script. Nothing close to the realism we found about, on any other day. The day had been tranquilized, and was floundering in its tracks.

I started to cook the dinner, more to do something, then to satisfy any hunger. The table was being set absentmindedly. All the movements were robotic. Tanya and Amy disappeared into their tent. No one noticed, not even me. Our connection numbed, by the events so alarming. The man was a dozen years my junior. Even that realization, did nothing to break open the vault, in which our emotions were locked.

The food cooked now and the diners approached, as if drawn through some hypnotic haze. We came to the table, and sat down to pray, for the survivors, and the soul. Half of us, had no religious affiliation, but prayed, as if it was their daily routine. As the meal was consumed, not a word was uttered. At the end, we brought out the cake, with the autonomic movements, and sang a disappointing tune, hardly enough to be noted, but performed all the same. The candles extinguished, the wishes expressed, all with an emptiness, that threatened to implode within the gathering, and swallow all in attendance.

Tanya received her gifts without emotion and no insult was felt by it. We all went early to bed, to the comfort of our mates. Sadness, was a joyous romp, compared to the mood, by which we were all consumed. The days end was a blessing to us all.

Chapter Fifteen

Revival

Sunday morning came peacefully. Our funk, had sunken into the mist. There were no brass bands. No fanfare announced our arrival, back into the light. We simply stepped out of our abodes and pleasantly greeted each other and went about our day.

We revisited the lake and did a more perused tour. Comments were made on differing points, and even a laugh, presented itself, to the welcoming ears present. We had returned. The afternoon was well spent, in the touring of the estate within the forest. The ropes explained and understood. Pleasantries were fitting of the day.

When Marie and the moms left, the sadness was a little deeper than at other times, because the buoyancy was lost, with their departure.

We still stepped up to the tasks left for us, and performed them ably. Within the next few days, we put up wall boards, and finished the jobs that will enable us to go home, fulfilled and confident, that all is well. We have yet to clean up the mess, around the dumpster, behind the cottage. We had thrown all the debris out the back door, and it did not always land, where it was bound for. We sorted out all the reusable pieces and then arranged for the container's pickup. That date is after we head back home. The window for the loft is installed and sealed.

We attend the funeral for Joe Young. Evelyn is very distraught. Sudden passing always leave the survivors in a bad way. Long illnesses afford you the luxury, of grieving over time, while the person is still alive. You know the end is coming. You are prepared. Sudden deaths rip us apart and leave us flayed, for all the elements to ravage us. Brent will care well for his mother. His mother will care well for him. It will be a teeter-totter effect. Day-by-day, they will find their way.

Brent said to Amy, that he was glad he had the chance to work with his father, on her cottage. It helped bring them together more, and just in the last few days of his life.

He would be there for her and Tanya, if ever they need him.

The summer of the cottage build, was a thrilling, and rewarding event in their lives. It will always stand, as their favourite summer.

We have yet to do the plumbing, and now is the time, we must rip out the bathroom. We shut off the water and drain the pipes. From this point on, we are on pioneering style bathing. Out comes the fixtures and up comes the floor. The plumbing contractor of the family, will be up with us to set this stage, in the next month.

Amy may be at school, but if she can be there, she will be there. Brad and I have done this work before, but Amy wants to have her chance to learn this type of work. I believe, I am living my life through her. She is all the able I wanted to be.

I am starting to believe, that it is fortunate, that she is gay. I would find it hard, to let some guy, have her. Brad had said, at one time, that his girls, would have to be gay, for the very same reason.

The girls and I go in to town, to the builders supply store, to get a composting toilet, to use while our plumbing is out. It will be left with the trailer, to act as a half bath, to add to the amenities of our place. Brent is still working there and is glad to get that taken care of for us. He shows the girls what it needs in upkeep. He also shows us a solar powered shower, to help give us some better hygiene for the coming period, as the need may arise. He tells us where we can get an enclosure for it, for privacy. I ask him about gray water filtration and recycling systems. He knows someone, who handles those things, and gives me the address.

We head back to camp with our treasures, and get them set up in their places. Then we go shopping for the water system. When we get to the place, we find that Brent had announced our coming, and all the information, was put together in an information packet. He showed us the display system, and we could study it thoroughly. We take the information with us. I will show my sister that packet, for use in her cottage. It will lengthen the life of her system, and allow her to keep her cottage longer.

Now that that is done. We put the kitties inside and close everything up. We will be back. I don't know when. But we will be back soon.

After we pack our things and load the van, we get in and go over to say goodbye to Evelyn. She is much better today. Some tears fell, but it was not mine this time.

We are back on the road and headed home. Amy asks, "How much did we raise the value of the property?"

"Until we finish the reno, it will not be any better than when we bought it."

"How can that be?"

"We had a bathroom and a kitchen, before. We don't have either now. When they are replaced, it will likely be, about three times, what we paid for it."

"Wow, I feel better about that."

"If something happens to me now, it will be up to you two, Faith, Grace and Brad to finish it."

"What about Nicholas?"

"That is for him to decide. I know the others would help out. Nicholas is very handy at some of those needed tasks."

"Well, lets not have anything happen to you."

"I'll try to oblige you with that. Although I was ready to go, long ago. Each new day, gives me something to stay for and I wish, it would cut that out."

We have a few stops coming home. Some are just to shop for more cottage supplies. Some are to eat and exercise.

We go straight home this time. Tanya has rarely been to our house and wanted to help unload. After the unloading, we reload for the next trip up.

Amy takes Tanya in to see her bedroom and give her a tour of the house, including 'the dungeon.' When Tanya tried Amy's bed, she wanted to stay.

Amy walked Tanya up to the stoplights, where they usually parted. As they walked home alone, they replayed the scenes of the summer, and lingered on their tent scene, with its most glamorous tables.

Chapter Sixteen

The Fall Guys

Amy and Tanya, are to appear in court, to give evidence against their harassers. Brad and I are going with them, to work on the plumbing. The courthouse is in Peterborough and we will count on being there the whole day. We head up two days before, to get the plans down with Brad and to pick up our special order parts. We also make the camp comfortable for our stay.

Brad is impressed upon entering the house. "Great job, Father."

"The great job was done by the girls. I gave minor input and paid the bills."

"Great job, girls!"

Brad works three jobs. The third is his own business and he is on the go whenever you call him.

We talked about the plan, and where we need to place it all. We will be putting in a bathtub-shower combination, to keep all involved, happy. The wash water will filter through the bio-filter bed and into a holding tank. The water for the toilet will come from the holding tank and exit to the septic tanks. The overflow from the holding tank will go to the septic tanks. From there it all goes through the septic bed. This system is to save the cottage from too much traffic. Plant watering, also comes from the holding tank. The big thing is, that when we are closing the cottage down for the winter, we need to drain the holding tank, and put some antifreeze, in the tank, to keep it from cracking. In the spring we must pump out the antifreeze to keep the pets from ingesting water from the tank that contained the antifreeze.

With all the plans straight, we begin the job in the morning. It is all hands on deck, after breakfast. I am soon weeded out and return to my tent. When I wake up, I find them doing great things, and decide to let them be. I walk over to the Youngs' cottage, to see if they are there, and how they are doing. Evelyn answers the door and we greet each other like long, lost, friends. Brent is doing some errands and will be back in a few hours. We sit and chat about the usual topics. She mentions, that she is concerned that the cottage is going to be too much for her. I tell her to wait on any judgement for one year. If there is any problems, they will show themselves, and we will help if any is needed. I warn against quick decisions. Brent should be in on any of her thoughts. The ones that push you to quick decisions, are after something, or listening to the wrong sources.

She thanks me for the advice and we go out to see the property. I tell her about my mother being told to sell the farm and everything, to get the best price. She had three sons that could step up and handle things for the first year, if she had asked. She sold quick and regretted doing it, almost immediately. She sees the wisdom my mother had learned from that. Nobody can tell you, what your life will be like in one year. The hardest part, is coming to grips with the fallout from snap decisions.

I enjoy the casual talk and walk. The countryside is showing its full array of beauty. The wildlife are busy around us storing food and winterizing their homes. The hints of Joe's life were strewn carefully throughout the property. The memories overflowed from his widow. She recalled each item she saw, and the story behind it. I listened to every one of them. It was wealth beyond measure. Irreplaceable evidence, that Joe Young was here, and cared for his home.

The time went by quickly, as we covered the entire circumference, of Joe's summer retreat. We see Brent's car, pulling in the lane. I walk her over to greet her son, and after offering him a ride in to the Courthouse, I sauntered back to my retreat. I knew they were still busy, and the job was passed the point, where an old man could help. So I offered my assistance.

What? You think I'm old?!

They did need me and I knew they did. The girls are very adept at doing things and moving fast around the jobsite. However they needed brute strength and body mass to wrestle big tanks around. They have wasted away, while working so hard. I was wasting away to a ton, as my uncle would say. Brad needed me. We had to put these tanks, one close enough to support the other and keep the weather from causing them to shift. We need to build around them and winterize them. With each of us on a tank, we manhandled them into place. They were set for their installation in the spring. The site was secured and the parts are protected and will be out of the weather.

I love to feel needed. Even if it's to be a paperweight. Brad gets it. Amy knows too. We need a purpose and a slight piece of self-worth saves lives.

If you know someone that has lived a great deal. Someone whose experience, is something that could help you understand. Talk to them, while you still have them. Once they're gone, so is their wisdom.

Brad has the girls strap the tanks to the wall and build a casing around them with the lumber from the teardown pile. He and I go over the plans to see what finishes we would like to use. Right away, we are interrupted by the girls. They want to have a say. They did all the work, and want to be in on the choosing. I agree and we prepare the pamphlets for them to see, after they finish the job they are doing.

Tanya's tastes are wild and garish. Amy reigns her in some. She shows how the combinations can keep us up at night. "Trust me. We don't want them up at night." she points out. She shows how a little flair can go a long way in keeping the place bright and exciting. It can also be soothing to the old folk and help them unwind.

"Hey! I take exception to that old word being loosely tossed around!" Marie has been coaching Amy and it's not funny.

"Don't listen to them, Father. They're just trying to get a rise out of you." Brad speaks up.

"That is not possible with this one. She is in my head 24 hours, seven days a week. But I am also in hers."

Amy blows me a kiss with a toothy grin.

"We need to get up here in the spring, before the runoff, has run off. We need to see, where we can work out the additions. This is a floodplain, and it doesn't show itself clearly. We need to take down the camp, and move it into the woods. The decks break down easily and the furniture can come in here. I will get the trailer, up onto the top of the broad hill, behind where the barn will go. The day after tomorrow, we can get all this done. The girls can move the furniture into the house, and set it up for us to use that night, and again in the spring. Brad, you put a floor in loosely in the bathroom for the toilet, and then take down the tents. The girls can help. Do the tarps last. I will put down the trailer and move it. We can all work on the tarps and see if we need to put any on the roof of the cottage."

"I won't be going to court." Brad reminds me.

"Brad, You can work on getting anything that needs doing, done. Before we do all the moving. If you want to start on the move, while we're at court, go ahead. Start with the toilet, then the canvas tent and then the tarp from that tent. The decks we can do the following day and they come apart easy." I look at him and add, "If you want to lay about and relax, do it. You need it."

"Thanks, Father. I might just do that. I like that big bed in the trailer. I can enjoy that for a bit longer."

"There is also the hammocks, to try." I thought to point that out. Nobody but these girls, work as hard as Brad.

"Thank you, Father."

Amy has to ask, "Why do you call him Father?"

"You don't want to know the other choices." he laughs.

We are done for the day. We have a clear sky tonight and it will be ablaze with the aurora borealis and the milky way will entertain us. An immense array of colour and light. We are far from the town and farther from the glow of any city. There are no street lights, and the moon has just begun its rise. We have the heaters on in the tents and trailer. We light a sage bundle and place it upwind. We position the chairs and fill our glasses. Settling down in the position of our choice and relaxing as much as we dare. My impaired sight is supplemented by Amy's keen eye. The wonders of the near universe are on display. The steady glow of the planets. The quick clip of the satellites. The waving Northern Lights. A few meteorites and some planes to interrupt the twinkling stars of our own galaxy. The Milky Way stretches before us, and with the naked eye, it hides the wondrous emanations of our neighbouring galaxies. I tell the girls to be careful or they will get freckles. They need to laugh. Exercise for the lungs.

We are trapped in the theatre. I try to sit up and the cool dampness around us has caused a spasm in my neck. Amy gets up to help me and nearly has one of her own. I tell her she's getting old, but laughing doesn't help a neck spasm. But laughing with a neck spasm helps to extend the laughing. The more I laugh, the more it hurts. The more it hurts, the more I laugh. The more this goes on the more people are laughing and so on, and so on, and so on. We stop trying long enough to stop the laughter. Once we are under control, both girls and Brad lift me to my feet and send me off to bed. I hate to do it but, I must forgo my usual preparations, and get straight into bed.

Now that I have broken the spell, the remaining gazers give up their watch and prepare for bed. No fire to watch die. They crawl into their cocoons and wrap up the edges. The girls have the warmest stateroom as they huddle together. They are behaving, but enjoying the simple pleasures of sharing innocent body heat. I am happy with the way they have accepted the restrictions, and embraced the allowable freedoms. I feel the heat from their bodies and imagine Marie here with me. I know the pitfalls now. The stimulation of their senses, will do the same to mine, and I am alert to the feeling. I can now react, to the slightest infractions, with both girls aware, that this is the danger of overplaying their hand. How I both hate and love the responsibilities of our dynamics. The girls behave. The sleep comes to them, and to Brad, and eventually, even to me.

The morning comes early. I have set my alarm to wake us so that we are fed and ready to go to court. I warn the girls to leave all fluids, creams, sharp objects, and anything that may be construed as a threat, at home. We need to just go there, and give our accounts, and leave. We don't want to lose our favourite pen, or our nail file. They elect to put all necessary items, in one purse, and have me check the items, before we leave. We are finishing our meal and see Brent, walking up the path. Brad can do the cleanup, while we get off to our appointment. The girls fix their needs and report for inspection. I find nothing offensive, and we go to the van, and climb in. Brent is riding shotgun and is my navigator. I have been to Peterborough several times in my life, so I know absolutely nothing about it. My family has a branch here and there are several cousins. My great aunt and uncle lived here. So long ago with so little tie-in memories. They are all disjointed to me. Amy tells me that is, in truth, all wrong. She can follow my memories, and link them to all the places I have visited. I am thrilled to know this. Next year, we can go to visit the relatives, and I can astound them, by going straight to their homes. That is, providing they still abide, in the same places.

We spend the morning in the court, without being called. The case will be up, after the recess. We go to lunch nearby and enjoy some pleasant conversations. Getting back to the court room, we are approached by the crown prosecutor. She asks if

we are prepared to testify. We all agree. She shows us where we
should sit. We hear the case called and I get anxious. It is time for
an Atavan. I can relax, because I will not likely be called, but tell
that to my subconscious. I can just try to meditate, or concentrate
on something else. That really should have been started before. I
am just leaning back, to pose as I did, the night before. A court
official comes over to see what is the trouble. Amy explains to
him, that I have problems, and will be okay, if I can just be left
here beside her. He agrees and steps back. The magistrate signals
him over and the request is relayed to her. She allows it and turns
to the docket before her.

The case is called. The defence asks for an adjournment and
the court deals with the request. It is quite common for this to
happen. It is both good and bad for me. It might ease the anxiety,
but at the same time it would mean we have all been wasting a
day here. The judge, however, upon hearing that the complainant,
and witnesses, are all here and ready to proceed, sees the ploy as a
stall to a time when there is not so many waiting to witness. She
denies the request and orders to proceed. These boys have been
in front of this court before. The court heard the plea and the
statements of all the principals involved, and heard the witnesses
testimonies also. The accusation against Amy was presented, and
the judge needed to have clarification on why, Amy ran from the
scene. She explained that I am oversensitive to tension around
me. She told how I had suffered an anxiety attack, before they
entered the store. She said that I was left to calm myself, while
they chose the lumber. She explained, that I was having more,
strengthened, attacks after the boys started the harassment. She
knew that I could sense that, and had to get to me, to stop me
from hurting myself, more seriously. The judge looked at me,

and saw how I was propped in the pew. Amy added, that the police, had found me in the parking lot, on the ground, and that Amy was attending me, before returning to the scene, with me in tow. The judge asked for the policeman's statement and he substantiated her statement. The judge found the boy guilty and subsequently, found one of the others guilty. The afternoon was spent, but satisfaction was attained. Like I said before, it is usual for requests for an adjournment to be granted. The ruling of the judge may be challenged in an appeal. This story may be visited again. Today is over and we can go back to the cottage. We stop and pick up some pizzas and head back to camp.

I have found on many occasions that the exceptions to the rule, just present a new rule. The deceptions are real and the proof is not in the pudding. The proof of the pudding is in the eating.

Our little cottage camp is moving on. Today we pack it away for the season is dying. Brad enjoyed his day off for the most part, but got restless and put my tent down. I slept on the other bed in the trailer, and woke up late but stiff. The others had gone on with the plans I laid out. The furniture was placed in the cottage rooms. It was basic decor, but functional. We will be spending the night in the cottage and leaving the following day. It was a productive trip full of mixed emotions.

After I have my meal, I don't know which one, but at least it's food, I start on my chore of packing the trailer down. The bedding from it is going in the loft. The girls are putting the tarps away while Brad takes down their nylon tent.

Brad comes to help me finish the trailer, and we hook it up to my van. I drive it out and take it on up into the woods and up to high ground. It is firm ground now, but in the spring, it will be too soft, to pull it down. I do have room to bring it around, so I keep going and get it back to the lane.

The others are finished cleaning up the tarps and turn their attention to me. Amy sees my position and my plan. She sees the flaw and the answer. She outlines the steps for me to take as I look around the woods for it. Brad and Tanya are walking up the path to the lane to see if they can help. Amy has taken that whole trek by seeing through my eye. I get moving up the lane to turn around at the split. Now I have the angle right and can follow my path in reverse to get back to that promontory spot. Tanya and Brad have stopped and are watching the vehicle with trailer bouncing through the bush, down one hill and up the other. They don't believe I can get through it. Amy knows me and has faith, that I am likely, the only one for miles, that would try this with a 22 year old van and a 25 year old, twelve foot, popup trailer. I am dredging and grading, as I go. It is clear, where I have been. The other direction did not make me dig in so much. The angles of this way are sharper and I am getting through by pushing on with speed. I am shaken and both the van and the trailer are showing their collection of flora and earth. It was a rough exhibition of determination and gall, but I stood triumphant, beside my van, in a garish pose. Applause rewarded me and one shaking head, mine......

The trailer is in position and ready for winter. In the spring, when the low ground is dry, I will be able to winch it down from its lofty perch. I will think more on whether it should stay there and become an outpost for one wanting seclusion. Amy thinks, that would be the preferred answer. To build a deck out and around the trailer, and make it a permanent fixture. I have a feeling she is onto something.

I decide to set the trailer up, on its jack stands and make it level, while the ground is firm. I call to the others, to bring up some of the lumber and deck blocks. When I look up to see if they heard me, they are half way up the hill, with the pieces I had thought of first. They start piling it near me and head back for more. It looks to me, that the sleeping decks just might, be in the woods next year. I fit the timbers under the trailer, through to the other side. I feel someone handling the other end. I peek under and see Amy grinning back. I know I won't need to say a word. I am surprised that I didn't feel her there, or know, that she was there. I can feel things she's touching. Was I too into my own thoughts, to see hers? Is my allergies a factor? How did I not know? Amy tells me to shut up and get to work. Okay, I was too preoccupied. We slide the deck blocks under the timbers. We level them up and fill the space and shim it. We do this in a few spots. The trailer is now set for the winter. The wind will keep it from getting too damp underneath. The trees will keep the snow to a minimum on it.

The decks have been dismantled with the lumber and blocks up the hill by the trailer. The furniture is in its place inside the cottage. The lamps and heaters are on to make our project look amazing. It is still in its basic finishes. It will be dressed next season. We took it from fire practice chic, to cozy comfort in two and a half months. Two fourteen year old girls and a decrepit sixty five year old disabled man. Well, aint that a kick in the head. I look around to see the others and we seem to have grown. Evelyn and Brent have joined the party. "Welcome. How long have you been with us?"

"A couple hours." Evelyn said.

"Well, thank you very much. I seem to be out of touch with my senses, today. I didn't notice a lot of things."

Amy tells me orally to lay down. Apparently, I'm not feeling well. She puts me to bed and they celebrate as I drift off. I can feel the room swaying and the band playing, but there is no band. I am lost in the night sky. I don't feel Amy and I don't know what she is doing. Have I lost the connection? I am drifting on my hammock on the beach in Cuba. It is so hot there. I can't hear the waves. I see the beach is covered with snow. I can't feel my legs and I can't move. I'm stuck again.

The place is dark when I open my eyes. I don't know what time it is. The cabin is dark. I feel Amy move. She is right beside me, keeping watch. I look up at her but I can't see her. I feel the cloth on my forehead turn cold. No, she put a new one on. I can see her more now. It isn't very dark anymore. She tells me that I have been sick for two days and they are going to take me home when I can sit up without being sick to my stomach. What is going on? I am drifting again.

They decide to take me home, laying on the floor. Brad will drive and Tanya will navigate, while Amy takes care of me on the floor.

I feel the room rocking and Amy tells me that we are in the van on the way home. I had been unconscious for three days. I had been put to bed after the trailer was level on its stands. The rest of what I remember, was done by them, while I was in bed. Amy had done the blocking of the trailer, as the other four carried up the leftover supplies. I had hit my head on the van, while I was getting the trailer up the hill. I had passed out by the van. They called Evelyn and Brent as soon as I collapsed. I don't know what is real. They got me in bed right away and Evelyn had watched me. I still don't know what is going on. The things Amy said are strange.

I open my eyes. Am I in the hospital? I am. Amy is beside me. What is real?

"Welcome back." Amy says to me as she leans toward me. "Are you going to stay for awhile?"

"Where am I, Amy?"

"You're in the hospital in Peterborough. When you collapsed, we dialled 911 and the ambulance brought you and I here. Tanya and Brad are taking care of the place. They are going back, as soon as Mom gets here. She's coming straight here, and I will text Brad, so that they can go home. You might have hit your head on the van when you fell, or in the van as you bounced around taking the hill."

"Have you told me this before?" I am puzzled.

"Not out loud. I tried several times to reach you, but you were out of your mind, literally. You were saying that you can see me, from the loft. You were not even in the cottage. They think it's just a concussion. We have been trying to wake you. I could not get a clear thought from you."

"We didn't have a party?"

"Tanya said that she and Brad celebrated with Brent and Evelyn. You seemed to roll over, when she was telling me this, on your phone."

"I think I was there."

"You could have been. Because you were not here. Mom's here. She just pulled in. Brad was wondering if he should have been here, because he has Power of Attorney. I told him to stay there. You weren't going to need it." Amy explains it all. She texts Brad to let them get on home.

"How am I? Did they tell you anything?"

"You've just hit your head and put yourself in a coma for three days. You've got a concussion. I think you're fine. Some touch-ups and a coat of paint and you'll be fine."

Marie enters the room and Amy jumps up to give her a hug. Marie looks me over and asks Amy how I am.

"He just woke up a few minutes ago. I'll go tell the nurse that he's awake. You sit and chat with him."

"Oh, he's awake? I saw his eyes closed and I thought he was still out."

"I am awake. My eyes were open. They just look closed."

"How are you feeling?"

"Great! How are you?"

"Seriously, how are you?"

"I have a haddock and my stomach is queasy."

"You're joking. So you must be alright."

"I have been better."

"Amy was afraid, when she couldn't reach you, or get through to your senses."

"I thought I was losing it, when I couldn't reach her."

"What was the last thing you remember?"

"I thought we were having a party, after we set up the trailer and were going to sleep, in the cottage."

"Did that happen?"

"Apparently not."

"Are you going to have the problems that your sister did?"

"I can still smell. In fact I stink."

"You kind of do."

"I should ask for a bath."

A doctor walks in and introduces himself. "You aren't the one I spoke with before."

"No, I am his wife." Marie introduces herself.

The doctor comes to check me out. He does the awareness tests and checks my head thoroughly. I ask if I can have a shower. He says, he will order a bath for me. I am not to get up, for the rest of the day, and then, only with a nurse.

Amy comes in just ahead of the nurse. She and Marie step outside the room, for her to do what she needs to do. Someone else comes in, and helps me take a bath in bed. They let me do some of it and help me get the rest.

Once they are finished I tell Amy to come back in with Marie. They come in as the others are preparing to leave.

"Oh, we've just finished." they said.

"Yes, he told us you were done." said Amy.

"I'm sorry, who told you?"

"My dad."

They look at me and I nod. They look at each other and leave.

"That was fun." Amy laughed.

"You know what they say about simple things?" I warned her.

"I would hardly call that simple. It took a miracle from God, for us to be able to do that."

"You're right. I'm sorry."

Marie asked, "So when do you think they will let you go home?"

"I have no idea. I just found out I was here, not too long ago."

"So where are we going to stay?" she looks at Amy.

"I've been here since they brought him in. We can go to the cottage to sleep."

"I'm not sleeping in a tent now!" Marie protested.

"You won't have to, Mom. We've moved the furniture inside for the winter and the tents are packed away. The trailer is in the woods, up on the hill, overlooking the cottage."

"Wow, I'll have to go see it. Is there any heat?"

"There are heaters there now, and they're on."

"Is there water and a toilet?"

"Yes, Mom, there is some jugs of water and a composting toilet."

"Food?"

"No we can get some on the way."

"How far is it to the cottage from here?"

"About an hour or less. It took 45 minutes by ambulance."

"Well, I'm hungry. Should we go get some lunch?"

"Sure, I'll keep in touch with Dad while we're gone. He won't be able to eat today, at the least."

"Okay, we will see you later, Hon. Let Amy know if you need us."

"She'll know, as soon as I know. She might even know, before, I know."

They give me kisses, and they're off to do their thing. I should have said, 'they're out to lunch,' but that would have got me in trouble, again. Oh, Amy just confirmed that.

Those boys got probation for public nuisance. I just found the note left for me. I think, being bested by little girls is good punishment.

Chapter Seventeen

Sitting It Out

Marie and Amy, got home to the cottage, just as it was getting dark. They couldn't get a good view of the layout. They stepped into the door and Marie was pleased at the room there was with the furniture.

"The toilet is in there and just be careful because the floor isn't fastened down yet. It's just tacked there."

It always amazes her when Amy does that. She knows just what she wants, or needs. She rarely gets to ask for anything.

"On the floor, on your left, in the back corner."

"Thanks." It always gets her.

"Brad was in your room on the left and Tanya and I were in the other room. Dad would have had our bed, if he hadn't got hurt. It was really hard. It hit the pillar beside him when the van got knocked side ways and back. It nearly made me cry. I had a hard time with it, but I had to get to Dad."

"Okay, Honey, let me say my line before you answer me. It is a little spooky when you do that. Efficient, but spooky."

"Sorry Mom. I keep forgetting."

"So, is the place all done for the winter?"

"Yes. I might get some things done for the spring setup, that can be done now. It is all set though."

"When are they going to put in the wood stove?"

"In the spring, after the ground is firm. They'll need to wait until they can back the van up to the stairs, to unload the stone."

"Yes, I guess that would be better. I was wondering if we could use it in the winter."

"Yes, if you don't mind the cold until the heaters warm it up."

"It would be pretty in here, in the winter. Even more, when the chimney is puffing out smoke. It would be like a Christmas card."

"I would love to see that. Ouch!"

"What?!"

"Dad just put his head down on the bruised side."

"That's incredible that you have that all the time."

"I know. The only consolation is that, when he hurts me with that, it hurts him, too. It's all his sisters' fault. They gave him the idea."

"They did?"

"They were saying that the pain he felt wasn't as bad as what women feel. That is what got this started. They thought he was going on about it. Every time someone asked him what was causing his problems. He would start to answer the questions and they would say that to keep him quiet. Meanwhile the others still didn't understand. So, it's their fault. I think he already had the answer. Men would feel the pain and never want to go through it again. Women would feel it after having a baby, without an epidural, and turn around and want another baby. Bingo, there is your answer. Men win because they would not want it again, so it must be worse. After feeling what he felt with them digging through his foot, when the freezing wasn't working, or shoving those needles through his eye, when the freezing wasn't working. At least women have a canal to pass the child through."

"Why didn't he say that?"

"He had said it and it wasn't enough for them."

"Well, at least I've got you. Without passing you through that canal!"

"Thanks, Mom."

"So, how's your dad doing?"

"Same as always, lying awake. It hurts and the stuff they can give him doesn't help at all. It never helps. That's why he doesn't take pain medication for the pain. He only takes it so he can move his neck and hands. Just so he can move around."

"He is always talking about it. I just ignore it."

"He tells you so that you will know, and when you ignore him. He feels that you don't care about him. Then when you get sick, he dotes on you. Because he cares. You tell him and he listens, because he knows. If he told you every time it hurt him, he could never stop to take a breath."

"But, everyday?"

"But, every second?" Amy mocks for emphasis. "In my past life, I never felt pain like he does until I was being beaten to death. I didn't have a baby. If I did? I would want another. I wouldn't want to die like that again."

"So, after we die, we come back?"

"Only those that want it, come back. If you don't want it you can try to help those that do. The ones that come back, want to feel again. They want to live again. You don't give birth in heaven. If you want to have children you have to take on a physical body. They take away your memory so that you won't be afraid to go through it and it will be new for you to discover and to strive to learn and do things. Now that I have come back with all that memory. I would love to not have it. I like communicating with Dad through thoughts, but enough is enough. It gets old fast because you don't have any privacy at all. When you were young, you could hide things from your parents. I can't even hold someone's hand, fifty miles away, and he knows it, and can get after me, for anything that doesn't seem right to him. He says it is his responsibility. It wouldn't be, if I had the same privacy, that anyone else, in this world has. Even those locked in glass cages, with cameras and microphones around them, have more privacy than I do. They can think private thoughts. Dad agrees with me. He says it is his obligation to keep me from doing things that others think is wrong. He says it would be evil and vile, for him to allow me to have sex with Tanya because of our ages. If we had any privacy, nobody would know. I agree, that he has an obligation, to teach me right from wrong. I just would like to have some privacy, in my thoughts. The worst thing about this accident is that I felt good that my thoughts were private, while he was in a coma. That short time was, at the same time, horrible, and wonderful. It would have been evil, and vile, if I had taken advantage of that coma, to have sex with my girlfriend, in privacy. I knew I needed to be with him. I may yet, in my lifetime, want to kill him, for that, precious, privacy, in my own head!"

"Amy, I am so sorry for you. I had no idea that it was really like that."

"For him and me, both!" she bursts into tears and lands in her mother's arms. And I am inconsolable, too. Laying in my bed.

Blubbering in my private room, where the only one that knows, is my fellow prisoner of thought, my Amy. God is punishing me with the answer I wanted. To settle a question, that had no business being asked.

"What can we do to help?"

"We can't escape this. People have been trying to invade the thoughts of others, so much, in the last century. They have machines, drugs, hypnosis, all to get into someone else's head. They want to read your thoughts and control your thoughts. They want to control you. Dad and I know everything about each other, down to the smallest detail. I know that he and his brother parachuted toy figures out of the landing window of Gramp's house on the hill. They were half my age then. I know that the fireplace in that house was fake, and the house had a humungous amount of chimneys. Dad knows the names of my brothers in my past life. He can see that. We, he and I, are like you and him. We're together until death parts us. One difference. You can get a divorce! I can't! Until death parts us!"

"Why would God allow this? He knows everything."

"Mom, He has faith in Dad, and Dad has faith in Him. Dad has survived some amazing things. He has a purpose and he is trying to find out what it is. So he can finally go home! He is tired of this body that is torturing him, day and night. He wants out! But he will not take his own life. He wants to do the job he came for. Maybe, maybe this is it. Writing about this, stupid, experiment!"

"I wish he wouldn't talk like that. He says that a lot. He even jokes about dying. Why does he have to say those things?"

"He is tired. He is exhausted. People don't understand. He jokes to make it smaller in his mind. He has to live with it. So, he jokes about the pain. He laughs about his mortality. So many people want immortality. If they got it they would soon be like him. In constant pain, with new problems coming at him all the time and nobody wants to hear about it. If he doesn't talk it out, it will make him go insane. The only things that are soothing to him, are being stolen by medications, and other people who are so damned impatient with him! He just wants to go home now. He wants your love. He wants intimacy. And he wants to do his job and go home. If he has to stay? He wants to play. He wants to make miniatures. He wants to build things that will look like he wants them to. He wants you. He helps you with what you want and you won't even try to help him with what he wants you to. Simple. That is all he wants."

"I don't want to do that stuff. I don't know anything about it and I would just like it gone."

"He will tell you what you need to know for the moment and once it is done, you can forget it. If he can't have this little part of his father. He won't want much of what you want. He would be miserable. And you would too."

"I don't have to listen to this."

"No Mom, you don't. I know all your secrets, too. I know about the boys you liked and I know about, the thoughts you had about all of them. I hear all your thoughts. I hear you build him up and knock him down. You don't have any privacy from me, either."

"What do you want me to do?"

"Be happy and help him to be happy. He is trying to keep you happy. When he has his strength and you want him to do something for you? Remember that, it will take him farther away, from what you say you want him to do with his things.

His energy goes too fast. He's been hit by cars, trucks, farm machinery. He's fallen off third storey places and been bent like a pretzel. He can't keep going with all that scarring. Physical and emotional. If he doesn't do the things he wants to do? Why do you ask him to do more for you? Especially if you want him to do what he wants to, too."

"I don't know. He sits at that computer for hours and won't even go down there. He's up all night, on that computer."

"He would be up all night anyway. The pills rarely make him sleep. He's had insomnia, since he was a teenager. He would stay up all night building models, or reading a book. Now he's up all night writing a book. It doesn't matter what he is up doing. All the things people tell him is keeping him up, is crap. They don't know what he has given and they don't know what he can take. They may have studied millions of people, but they haven't studied him yet. The only guy who made an effort to study him, took his own life. They should let him alone. Give him what he needs and leave him alone."

"It's getting late. I'm going to bed. Good night."

"Good night, Mom. I love you. I have to tell you, because you are a part of it. You are a big part of him, too."

The night is quiet and a little crisp. The wildlife around the cottage can be heard clearly. They are calm and subdued. An owl hoots here. A raccoon chatters there. The scene was serene, but not the thoughts. The words were many and the tone was harsh. Emotions flew high and bore down on the sleepless figures. Opinions shared without reserve. Cutting and sewing, remaking the tapestry of the family, so differently viewed. A different light on a difficult subject. Tears came and anger flared. Remorse and indignation. This ride was as terrifying, as any amusement park rollercoaster. The comfort of the beds gave little solace. The darkening night in the moonset. The northern lights offer a distraction, for moments on the run. The knowledge shared in emotions. The heart thump echoing the loneliness, of one's position. What secrets kept so close, now aired on communal post. Not one shared, but souls left bare. The night wore, on a frazzled ego, cast on the rocks and pummelled into a shelter-less corner. Pushed against an ugly marquis, flashing insults and blame, in neon-bled names. Non of this lost on uncaring plebs. Only those close, know the feeling and reflection, going on within this lodge.

Amy crawled into bed with her mother. She turned away in pain. Amy wrapped her in her arms and whispered apologies and love. They lay there, allowing the feelings to meld and soften.

Sleep comes to Marie and lets Amy give in to it. The morning comes in the eastern window, and allows for lengthened slumber. When they wake, with stinging eyes, they hold each other, to loose the hurt and let it slide away.

Marie doesn't have to say anything to show her feelings, and in an attempt to hide them is betrayed by the nature, of her nature. Amy feels all and knows all, and she tells her mother that she loves her too.

"He is awake, but the same as he is at home. They are pestering him to wake up. Why does everybody think, you must not sleep, in the daytime?"

"You need to get up and see the daylight."

"You need to get a longer sleep than three hours. For us it is once in a while. For him it is everyday."

"For me it's every other day."

"Yes, I know. Yet you get up and go do things, without much trouble. You've seen how he is. You know, it's not the same for him. They don't even care."

"Amy, calm down. Let him fight his own battles. He has a mouth and he can use it. He will show them how he gets and they can learn from him."

"Okay, I'm sorry. I just get so caught up in his struggle."

"You've got lots of passion. You have to spread your battles out. He picks which battle he can handle. He only fights when he needs to."

"He only fights when he has the energy and strength."

"Still, it's his fight."

Tension in a relationship is like a poison. You have to relieve it, or it will spill into other areas of your life. The least you can do is to accept their premise and let it go. Ask yourself, 'is this worth fighting for?' Amy and Marie are holding on to this, like it has value. It only takes value from your relationship.

'You don't need to bother with this. I can do what I have to when I can. She is putting herself through it as much as she does me.' I try to stop the one that will listen. I am in the hospital and they are at the cottage.

'I'm doing this for me, as much as you. She gets after you and I feel her tension, at the same time as I feel your pain and frustration. I'm caught in the middle and I want out.'

'How can you get free? We're both trapped in this.'

'We can pray! Ask Him to set us free!'

'What if He wants us to see it through?'

'Then we will see it through. We don't know unless we ask.'

'Talk to your mother, and see if she will join us in asking for an end to it. Amy, be careful what you ask for. His solution may be to remove the connecting entity. That would be you. He may take you back. I don't want to lose you. I would let you do whatever you want, and just let it happen, rather than lose you. We have to think this through.'

'I do want to live. I want what was stolen from me. I want my life with Tanya, you, Mom, Nicholas, Faith and Grace and their families. I don't want to lose any of it.'

'Then we have to live it through. I don't want to take the chance of losing you. I will let you enjoy your life and just accept it and assess the reason's findings. I will treat the whole thing clinically. I don't want to take that chance.'

'Are you sure? It means putting up with our sex life and not interfering.'

'It will have to be. I would not wish even a remote chance of losing my daughter. No matter which way it would end. If I die, you will still be listening to Mom's thoughts. I can't take the chance, of putting anyone's life at risk. If He decided to answer that prayer. No. I could not take that chance.'

'I agree. It is too big a chance, that one of us, will have to die.'

'I promise, Amy. I promise to let your life continue on your own recognisance. If you choose to do something. I will just observe as a lab technician, and not your father.'

'I promise, Dad. I promise to not do anything harmful to myself, or anyone else, I will behave as much as I can, in having relations with Tanya, or anybody else. I will try to keep it under control.'

'That is the most I can ask for, in view of our circumstances. I will have to act like a doctor, detached from involvement. God have mercy on my soul.'

Chapter Eighteen

Up And Around

After another week in hospital, I was given the green light to get back out there and enjoy life. I have to stay away from actions, that might be too rough, for my old man's body. This was my twelfth concussion, judging by scars on my skull. It looked like, it was put together like, a jig-saw puzzle. Marie and Amy, are bringing me home, but first we must have the weekend, at the cottage. We will enjoy the work that we have had done there. If anything happened to it during the winter months, we will, at least, have enjoyed it together.

Amy has regained some of the weight she lost on the work crew. It softened the lines of her face a little. Marie has had a break from work, and that has taken some of the lines of her face away. I have lost nothing. I have a peaceful feeling, in knowing that I will no longer, have to berate my daughter, for having a life. All three of us have had some benefit from this sabbatical.

The cottage life agrees with us. I have hopes of enjoying it for years to come. I will stay on in this life, as long as I am supposed to. It may be a pain, but it's my job. I expect Amy will be testing my resolve, when we return home. I don't care to think of not having her. No matter what I must endure.

We go out in the canoe to show Marie the lake in all its fall glory. The reflection of the leaves, at their peak colours, captures our gaze and hooks us, to this countryside. We will brave the traffic through Toronto, as long as we can have this place to ourselves.

On Sunday morning, we clean up our things and get into the car. The major part of the equipment, went home with Brad, in my van. We have just enough room in the little station wagon. At least we're not crowded. With Marie in the driver's seat, there are no stops and it is strictly business. Amy and I can enjoy the scenery. Marie will see it and enjoy the colourful trees, but only while it is not a distraction. If I was driving, we would stop to enjoy a walk and maybe a meal.

We arrive home in mid-afternoon. Tanya is there waiting on the porch. She springs from the chair, as soon as we are in sight. She nearly falls coming down the stairs. We let Amy out before we back in the driveway. They are all over each other. Marie hollers "get a room!" which gets some control. They help get things in from the car. I see there is still evidence of my foray through the forest. Mud and needles jammed under the bumper. Marie sees it and gets after me. "What were you thinking?"

The neighbours are out to welcome us back. George is much healthier now. His battle with leukemia was scary, but he won and is doing great. He is careful and I guess we all should be.

I can see me having to wear a helmet, when I drive. Like that will ever happen.

With the car unpacked, Amy and Tanya have started to test me. They've gone into the hideout, in the back of the garage, to make out. I just go inside and have a soak in the tub. I take a deep breath and let it go. If anyone has any objections toward them, they can take it up with them. I am re-tired as well as retired. The warm bath soothes and eases my wounds.

"Where did the girls go?" Marie is amazed at the speed with which everyone disappeared.

"Tanya is still welcoming Amy home."

"Yes, but where are they?"

"In the garage. Why?"

"I wanted to see if Tanya is going to stay for dinner."

"Yes, she is." This will be my purpose, from here on I am the liaison, for those two. My, soon to be, fifteen year old daughter, is to be treated as an adult, by me. Marie will have to be the one to exact punishment. I have bargained away my responsibilities and it doesn't feel so bad. She is like my grandkids. I bond and Marie adjudicates. I have no choice. I gave my word. I'm not going to be stuck in the middle, just as Amy will not, either.

I will just enjoy the expression of young love. Young, passionate, love. I wanted to be young and virile. Now I will live that, vicariously through my daughter, Amy. I will just have to avoid direct eye contact with Tanya. I have a long way to go to be clinical.

Amy is in her last year of high school. I have forgotten the plans she had about university. Short term is still a struggle. Oh, She has chosen Queen's University. I was just reminded. They need to get involved in the community, as volunteers. That will give them some distraction from each other and attraction of the sources of the scholarships.

I was never a program student. I tried, but never really was fully accepted and felt like a visitor, even to the groups closest to me. I saw a program once, on serial killers. I fit the mould, slow developer, genius, loner. By the way, genius refers to potential and the ability to reason, not how smart you are, in terms of knowledge absorbed. I guess I had just the right amount of social success, to keep me on the light side. Instead, I use my power for good. What a geek. How did I turn out this way? Many people blame Marie. There were others that helped. I have to hand it to Marie, though. She stuck with me, well after things had gone south and she helped to steer me back. My father-in-law played a big part. He asked me to help Marie to stay with church. As I tried to help her, I found myself becoming drawn back. I found an interpreter, that could speak my language. Since then, I could talk to God and later, with Him. I knew where to find Him. He was right beside me. No matter how bad things got, I had a friend in Him. It did not need to be in church, or with any one denomination. I had a home church, where I had welcoming friends. I found I was close to Him, wherever I was. I guess that is what led me to this situation. Was it inspired by God? Was He the one that planted the seed in my mind, to pray for this? The more I think about it, the more I wonder. What has this brought to my life? A champion in Amy, she promotes my case to everyone. An understanding of her, I had not thought about having a lesbian daughter, in answer to my request. I have become even more understanding of people with differences of opinion to me. I have learned that, I didn't have a clue about some things, and their value in life. She opened my eyes to things and made me the better for it. Is there a long way to go yet? I don't know. Judging from how far we've come, I would tend to think, yes.

The summer is at an end. The girls are back in school. I have time to try different things. I can work on my hobbies more, without having to keep Amy and Tanya under control. Oh happy days! I have nothing to clean up in the garage. It is nearly empty. I have the model railroad working, thanks to Amy. I can work on my favourite parts now. This my form of art. Like my landscaping, but in miniature. I can sculpt the scene and populate it, to present a story for the viewer to enjoy. There is a story in every scene. I realized the reason for my life to develop as it did. I had to experience life from all directions, to be able to express it in my art. I don't know if anybody, will see it all, or even enjoy it. I do know, I can now express it. The stories I build, I can write about. Feeling the pain of others, can help me relate it to people, that will help prevent it from affecting others.

A fellow approached me in hospital once, and described what he felt after his treatment. He seemed to know me. He talked to me as if I was his best friend. He told me that they took his blood out and treated it and put it back. He said the blood, going in, felt like razorblades in his veins. I know that feeling from a different cause. I could see in his eyes, that it helped him to tell me this. I was like his best friend, and yet, I could not remember, ever seeing him before in my life. I do know, that God sends us to those who may need us, for whom we are. I could very well, have been host to an angel. One that would use me, for him, to recognize a friend. Is there a better explanation? Not better. I have not seen him since.

Having an experience like Amy, is enlightening, refreshing, and livening. Her lack of pain, is soothing to me. Her outlook, is empowering to me. Her energy, is invigorating to me. Her femininity, is comforting to me. She can wear absolutely anything and look good in it. It fills me with warmth, for her to enjoy something, as simple as that. Since I am no longer a censor, I enjoy her expression of life. To feel the embraces with Tanya, and the happiness it brings to her. I wish I could feel this all the time. I wish everybody has that feeling in their life.

Amy's fifteenth birthday, was a celebration of the work she and Tanya shared on the cottage that summer. The friends came by to see her, and Brent brought Evelyn with him. She wanted to come, to express the influence Amy had had, on Joe, before his death. The moms were there. Valerie came by with her new boyfriend. It made Amy happy, that she had someone now. The nieces and Christian were there, along with her sisters. Nicholas was away on business and Brad had Bradley with him. There was a full house. In a bungalow, it was full with half the people. We usually go to Grace's, or Faith's, but Amy insisted that we stayed here. She is a wealthy woman, at fifteen. A wealth of caring, loving, friends.

We were almost going to go to the cottage for Christmas this year. We knew though, that we needed to get it to a more finished state, and better equipped. As the sales of the book are doing well, we are more optimistic, about our ability to proceed, with the development of the property. It fills us with hope, for the type of summers, we always wanted. We will be able to spend entire summers there.

After New Years Eve, the eye is on the Caribbean again. Amy and Tanya are coming this year. The friends were reluctant to have them along, until we reminded them, that through Marie and I, they were already with us. They will have a room next to us and we have been assured, that we are in one of our preferred rooms. The moms have also booked a spot with us. The Canucks are taking the lead in the numbers race. There are six from the UK, and ten of us. It is our largest group ever. We have had to get a bigger limo, to ferry us to the airport.

The exams are finished before we go. We will not be with the huge March break volumes, and the teenagers, will help us elderly folk, pull our walkers through the sand. Thank God we aren't at that stage yet. We are returning to Brisas Guardalavaca, in Cuba, again. It has been our home away from home, for so long, that instead of going elsewhere, we have booked another place to go, at another time. Besides the girls, the moms are the youngest of the group, this year. That was a title that we had enjoyed, up until now. The plans are the main topic of conversation, for weeks before the event, as it is our habit.

The feelings are on high alert, with emotions riding atop them.

Chapter Nineteen

Globe Trotting

As I have said before, each year goes faster than the last. We are packed and ready to leave for the airport. This year, we are taking my old van, to leave at our pickup point. We are stopping at the Imovitch home, to get Tanya and her moms. Then we are off to the meeting place. With this many, we have had to get a stretch SUV. If this growth keeps up we will need a bus. To handle the luggage, they are pulling a trailer. The introductions are made. The group have never met Tanya and her moms. The driveway is crowded with people and luggage. The neighbours are probably wondering about this crew out here at 4:00 AM. The limo is spotted just in time. We were expecting to see a police cruiser, from the other direction.

There is climbing and clamouring, as we are packed into this year's mega-ride. For that many people, it's surprisingly quick. Our driver is a familiar one. She took us out the second year of the limo. Having all this taken in one ride is great. There is nothing lost. We all arrive at once, so we only get lost in the airport. There are more groups going every year. It makes a lot of sense, to travel in groups. Security is a big reason, with the unrest all over the world. Not being forgotten, is a big one also, and one of my favourites.

The airport is always changing. It's no wonder we lose someone there. Finding a place to wait for the flight, is the order of the day. We had a beautiful bar to sit at, one year. The next, it was gone. I need to keep calm and with this many, there is a fine line between calm and comatose. Although, either is good, as long as they get me there. Amy and Tanya are raising the roof, with the exuberance they are emitting. I am in need of a drink, to stop the vibration of the canyons in this terminal. I had one before leaving home. It has been burnt off. The girls are becoming shrill. I have no influence in this matter. I have been drowned out.

Marie has found seating by a coffee shop. I turn to one of our regulars that is thinking in the right direction. I get the message to him and we are off. If we can find the duty-free it will have something we can share. I found a restaurant that might serve liquor. The duty free opens at 4:00 a.m.. There is hope. I really don't want to take an Atavan. We are on our way and have collected some of a similar ilk. The moms are with us and the other regulars, stay put at the coffee shop. Getting to the duty-free first, is good enough for us. We can get a bottle to share, and get the mix back at the coffee shop. "Two birds" I say and we are agreed. It is as if we share the gift that Amy and I have. No, we just understand the basics.

We settle on a Capt'n Morgan spiced rum. Since we will be drinking rum at all hours, in Cuba. We may as well acclimatize ourselves. We grab a 26er and head back to the girls. Amy has got some mix for us and Marie has the seats. The party has begun to warm up. We know better than to overdo it. We want to make it down there. Now that we have the essentials, there seems to be more hands out for the bottle, than were in on the hunt. The hunters get two and the rest get only one. We lay the poor soldier to rest. Life is good. I did see some teenage hands come out for the rum, but they got slapped, and they can't blame me. As we catch the last drop from our glasses, we hear the call for pre-boarding, so Marie and I are on our feet. The rest will soon be loaded onto the plane, but we get to avoid the crush.

I have arranged for the wheelchair at Holguin Airport. That will get me through with more reserved energy. Keeping with tradition, we have ducked another winter storm, back home. They are well prepared there. The regularity is uncanny.

I enjoy the in flight movie, and have spare headphones, for those that want them. The regulars are in one row and the newbies are in the row ahead. I offer the headphones to the group. Amy asks for the headphones from the other side of the plane. As she does it in our usual fashion, no one hears her and we gather some odd looks, as I pass them across. I like getting the outsiders interest up, just teasing them. It is just a little thing. There are others that can communicate this way, but they are few. I wonder if we could be heard by the other telepaths. Since ours is of unique design, I start to think not, but check myself. How could I expect, this is different from that? Amy asks me to cut out the mind-chatter and watch the movie.

The flight is smooth and turbulence-free. We land in the warmth of a bright morning sun. It is just approaching noon.

I have to wait for the rest to disembark, before I get up. I have Marie go ahead with Amy and they wait at the bottom of the stairs. My chariot awaits. I don't like having to ride, but it means, they won't have to wait for the slowpoke. In the customs booth, I am nervous about the chair and Amy. I don't have anything to worry about, but it doesn't stop me. I guess, if I worried more, I might be better at it. Amy tells me to cool it. She is through with no problem. I am through with no problem, and all is well with the world. Security is another hurdle for me. It was bad enough with the canes. Standing up and getting through the sensor screen is quite difficult. The back and legs don't want to co-operate. They hold my hand to help me through. I am glad that I left the belt and boots, I like to wear, in the carry-on. Fewer dirty looks from Marie. Getting to the bus is easier. Finally, we are off to the resort. Another hour of sitting.

The resort is coming into view. The familiar terrain and rows of classic cars for taxis. As we pull up, we hear the music playing for our arrival. Familiar faces are there to greet us. Hugs and kisses with the introductions, and cocktails in hand. I love the greetings. Even security is smiling their welcome. They try to look stony-faced. Here is the big test. Getting the rooms we asked for. No, don't upgrade us. Yes, we have what we asked for and the newbies are next to us. Problem averted. The long procession to the rooms. We see that the girls are in and they're next door to our room. The teens are sandwiched between us and the moms. Perfect.

Quick changes and down to the beach. The girls in their bikinis and - wait, bikinis?! Amy is not hiding her missing navel? 'It's okay now Dad. Relax. No one is going to take me away now. I don't think they will even notice, that part of my anatomy.' I look again at the whole picture and I have to admit. They might not even look close to her stomach.

Into the ocean and this is what we came here for. Warm saltwater and coral sands. We are home again. No connection, this year, to the frozen north. Amy's here, and we are totally immersed, in the warmth of the sun. I hear the Beach Boys' song in my head. 'Aruba, Jamaica...'. I love the Caribbean. We haven't got our towels. The mature ones, are taking care of that. The guys and the teens, hold the beach chairs for them. Amy and Tanya, grab an empty hammock. They are SO here! It doesn't take much training, in enjoying this. I could live here, I think to myself, and Amy says, 'Amen.'

I think we can handle our situation, now. Now that I have foregone the role of moral censor, I feel free, to be a part of something big and yet private. I no longer have the guilt feeling. The arrangement was for me to observe and compare. Now that we are sticking to that, I feel right, that I can let Amy do, whatever she could have done, without my knowledge, had she been in a normal existence.

Amy feels like her life is hers now. She tests that frequently, by touching Tanya inappropriately. With no response from me, she sighs for relief.

Marie has never felt a part of the ordeal. It included her without feedback, other than Amy's telling her, she would not have known.

Amy no longer feels the need to champion me.

I feel that, because of our concern for each others' survival and love, God has approved of our decision. Life is indeed, good.

Our compatriots from the UK, are arriving tomorrow morning and we will gather the clan, to greet them. It is this way, or that. One year, they are first. The next, we are first to arrive. Because of the time their plane left, they will be leaving, the same day we do. They should have arrived the same day, that we did. It's an oddity in the business of travel.

As planned, we are all at the doors to greet them, as they arrive. It is an early day for all of us, but too much for me. I go up to the room to take a nap. There is plenty of representation down there, to go around. As I get back to bed, Amy tells me of the disappointment the others felt, that I wasn't there. I ask her to assure them, that I will be down before noon, and they will have more than they want of me, then.

John and I get along well. We have very similar tastes in humour. It is so good for us, that the others will distance themselves, from us. We like to carry-on, each adding to the joke, to bring it to the ultimate in objectionable humour. The theatre of the absurd, in dry humour.

We meet some people from past trips, to which I introduce Amy and Tanya. They say, "Is Grampa treating you to this trip?"

Amy replies, "No, this is my brother."

I play along with, "Yes, she's 49 this year. It's the last year I can call her Kid."

Spoil sport Marie says, "She's our daughter. She's 15 and will be going to university next year. She'll have to pay her own way, then."

That got more of a rise out of them than 'our' comments. Truth is stranger than fiction.

Amy found some Tolkien fans and put her hair up in a ponytail, to expose her pointed ears. She then proceeded to argue about the height of true elves. She said to me, 'They will never see me again.'

'I'm not too sure about that.' I replied. 'You feel freer in foreign countries. You should always be careful, in those places that you are not familiar with. My cousin was not allowed to be named Lynda, by Juan Peron. It means pretty, in Spanish, and that was not allowed. Simple things may mean something different to other cultures. This is your first time in another country. You must play your cards closer to your chest.'

'Sorry, Dad. I never thought.'

'That is what puts people in foreign jails. Not thinking.'

'I'll be more careful.'

We stick close together, after that incident. It could entice an inebriated fool to do almost anything. She will think twice about doing that again. I just hope they don't think twice, about her.

I find a show about crimes and have her watch it. On the show, a girl is having fun with some friends and is approached by a ne'er-do-well. He is attracted to her, because she looks like fun to him, and fun to him, is not fun for any girl. The following scene finds her dead in a dumpster. With Amy's past life, it hits home to her. Then, she remembers.

"I'm sorry, Amy. You have to know. What happened then, can happen now. That was just a show for morbid entertainment. You've lived it. It's real. I want my kids to bury me. I don't want to bury my kids, or my grandkids." I held her close. I didn't want her to fall back into that dream again. I had Tanya come, to help me hold her, to surround her.

She told us she would be okay and I passed her to Tanya's arms. She had one breakdown. I did not want to risk another.

I talked to Marie and the moms. I asked them to keep the girls in sight. I will know where Amy is, but I will not always know, where I am, in relation to her. If they are always within sight of us, we may be able to get to them in time.

They ask me what the danger is. I can only say, "complacency." I tell them about her argument, and the ease at which boys can be aroused. "It will only take minutes to lose, either of them, to someone here."

Marie feels I am being an alarmist. Thankfully, Tanya's moms do not.

Now, back to our originally scheduled mayhem. We gather the girls into our circle, and include them, in all that we do. They can enjoy freedom, on their own time.

Adult humour is expressed, in gentlemen's terms, in this group. We don't use fowl language, but we do mean fowl terms. There are continuous entendres of the multiple kind. You must watch what you say, because we will, too. Nothing is too personal. Nothing that we say, is sacred. For that reason, I say nothing sacred.

We take the tours and enjoy the reactions of the newbies. We show them the scenes, you may almost miss, while being ushered around by some guides. The poverty in the small coastal villages. The school in the shack. The forgotten people. They are hidden by the patriotic guide, that wants to show, how great their country is, and ignore these blotches on the flag. We tell of the championing guides, that bring you to see, those that are passed by. They tell of the fishing village, that shares an income, too small for one family. They love their country, but know it needs help, for these forgotten. We bring our supplies for the school, and buy the wares of these people, that can't afford to go to the markets, so far away.

We understand, that even our country has some forgotten souls.

We pass the torch.

We enjoy the fruits of the labourers, in our hotels. The free rum, that we get for taking a tour, or returning to a resort another year. It isn't free. We pay for it in our packages. We are given them to promote the country. The best food goes to the resorts. The country is broke, like many countries today.

We return to the resort, to enjoy the amenities. We need to do this, to convince ourselves, to return next year. You must reward yourself, to make things better for them.

People have left, in the staff of the resort, that we felt very close to. You only find them, through other staff, that were also friends of theirs. The management will not tell you.

We hear a familiar voice coming down the beach. It's Johnny Cool! The bartender that delivers. More introductions. He is surprised at the teenagers with us.

"I know, we are too old!" I say. He is embarrassed. "Don't feel bad, Johnny. We 'are' pretty old to have a teenager, but we aren't dead yet!"

He enjoys the joke, but still feels bad. "I didn't think of your children, being young, because you talked about your grandchildren."

"Yes, we have grandchildren older than Amy. We have four grandchildren, older than her."

"Ayayay, how many do you have?"

"Four children and six grandchildren, so far." Marie says, proudly.

"Amy will have a Pina Colada, without the rum. She has that at the cottage." I hand her mug to Johnny. "Rum punch for me."

"Pina Colada, no rum, and rum punch, no ice."

"You remembered. It doesn't surprise me anymore. You're the best, Johnny."

"You can order what you want, next time, but this time, I'm buying." I say to Amy.

Amy looks puzzled at me, "How much are they? I thought it was all included in the price of the trip."

"It is. Johnny works on tips, though. He doesn't get paid by the resort, unless he is behind the bar. He is better paid in tips, on the beach. He doesn't pay taxes on tips. It is an incentive, to provide better service and customer relations."

"I guess I should get some money."

"We didn't know it either, at first. Our first two resorts discouraged giving tips."

She would have understood, if she had not got conflicting memories. She saw us looking for money, in our thoughts. She doesn't search our heads all the time. Just when she needs answers.

Some guys have assembled near us, and are checking out our girls. Amy notices them through me. She sends a dirty look their way and snuggles up to Tanya. She puts her arm around her and nuzzles her neck. She can't be much more plain about her message. Especially on a beach, in front of children. I keep my eye on them, and seeing enough, they get up and leave. I can see the coming storm. As I roll it around in my head, Amy becomes aware of it. She wonders if I am not just imagining it. I let her see herself from my view. She sees how alluring she looks.

"You don't have to hide. Just stay with the group. Keep Tanya close and stay with one, or two adults. More, if your away from the main building here. I will come with you, if nobody else is available. You can recognize Mike and Marketa, from our thoughts. You know Johnny. If we get separated and you can't recognize the area you see us in. Go to one of them, or just head for the main building and I will go there, too. I will intercept you on the way, if I can. If anyone tries to molest, or bother you, in any way. Scream and put up the biggest fight you can. To avoid all that, just stay close to the group."

"I promise."

I get carried away when I am trying to protect them. I know that I run off with the mouth. I would rather do that, than find them being hurt.

The girls have a darker complexion, like Marie and Brenda. They spend a bit too much time in the sun, for my liking. I ask them to be careful, but Amy knows Marie. When she was their age she fell asleep in the sun and when she woke up, she looked like she was from Trinidad. Her skin was nearly purplish black. She had gone way beyond brown. With that memory, Amy figures that she would do the same. I remind her of my fairer skin. That doesn't phase her. I must remember my promise. So I sic Marie on them. Marie reins them in. She relates how it changes with puberty, child bearing, and menopause. Even the darkest skin can burn. She convinces them to put on better sun block, and limit exposure to twenty, or thirty minutes.

I remember having health issues, I can't remember what it was. I had to stay in the shade and wear long sleeves and wrap up in towels and blankets. It was the strangest summer ever. Everyone else was enjoying the sun and sand. I was frail that year. Amy said it was at Outlet Beach. I would shiver in the heat. She tells me about the medicine I had to take and that it wasn't good to have sun exposure, while on it. Steroids.

I still have to sit in the shade. I don't have to wrap myself, unless I am in the sun.

The girls in their bikinis, are making me want to lay in the sun, with its warmth on my skin. I burn enough in the shade. In heaven, I would enjoy the light and the warmth of it. In my heaven.

A vendor comes by wanting to sell cigars. We have been warned about buying from them. Those cigars are contraband and would be confiscated by security at the airport. No one is buying here.

People come by to offer coral, but that too would be confiscated.

There are so many things to be aware of in other countries. Some simple thing may land you in hot water, with the local government. Saying things, that are within your rights at home, could put you behind bars. We must check with fellow travellers and locals, on what is legal in that area. Viewing comments online, will help, before you go there. Adults, for the most part, think of these dangers. Teens may not. With the innocence of youth, they do and speak freely. Not having a thought on the delicate outlooks of some cultures.

Seeing Amy and Tanya, laying beside each other, reminds me of the laws being passed in some countries, against gays. While they are laying there, they don't present a problem. If one of them should kiss, or touch the other inappropriately, it could even be life threatening. I am glad that we don't have that threat, here in Cuba, yet.

It rarely occurred to me, that any of my kids would be gay. Now that one is, I find myself wanting to champion their cause. I am not even able to speak out, most of the time, but it is almost enough, to get me strength from some obscure source. In the past, I would only think of it, when someone I knew had a child that was gay. I wish that such things would not be an issue, anywhere, and people would live and let live. I wonder, will that ever be attainable? Will there ever be a time, where threats of all kind, do not exist? I guess not. There will always be someone, who wants what you have and will try to take it from you. One, who doesn't agree with the way you look, or think. One, who puts their thoughts, above the rights of others.

Amy and I, are getting a headache from these thoughts. "Johnny, Johnny Cool, another rum punch! Por favor!"

Amy enjoys seeing herself with Tanya through my eyes, and will make me look at them by giving me a thought of them. I don't mind being used that way. Pleasantly, harmoniously, being, existing, in paradise. I would not mind being used like that for anybody. Me, with my one good eye, would love to see beauty for others. It is so appropriate, that the bad eye, has a view for beauty, in this brilliant light.

I love being alive for moments like this, when even my constantly painful entrapment, finds joy, from the lives of others. It makes it worthwhile, to be me.

The group around me, grabs my gaze, in this moment of reflection. I look at each couple individually, to see their enjoyment show through the idle expressions. I go from one to another, until finally coming to rest, on my Marie. Now having been married for forty two years, and being together for forty six. I remember what brought me to ask her, to be my wife. I reflect on what made me stay with her up to that point, when I had gone from one to the next, so quickly. All it comes down to, is the knowing, that whomever you choose to be with, you will need to make a conscious decision, to be happy together, and work at making a life, that will be rewarding to the other. You don't need to find something that rewards you. That will come from anywhere. You can get that on your own. It is hollow reward, without one to share it with.

I fell in love easily. I found that the next girl I saw, was just right for me. And the next, and the next. I had to learn to make something out of it. If any of the others, had decided to show me, that they wanted to be with me, I would have stuck with them. I even proposed to some of them, and it was accepted, but that means nothing, until you are mature enough, to back it up with action.

Now, here we are, with a legacy passed down, with children and grandchildren, that we are proud of. Here we are, stealing time from our lives, to relax in paradise.

Time here means nothing, until it is almost over. It is well wasted on friends. You never know how long you have with friends. So many have left your circle, through one way, or another. You would love to have them back. There is always room for friends. 'Some are yours for an hour. Some are there for a day. Some are with you for a lifetime, constantly going your way. Some come to you through heartbreak. Some show themselves with great joy. Some make you always feel pleasant. With some, you are often annoyed. Whatever the way they come to us. Whichever direction they leave. Emotions run high when they're thought of, and you're wearing your heart on your sleeve.'

It feels great to walk into the ocean. The waves within the reef, gently lapping the shore as you enter. I went for a walk through the sea grass. Walking straight through. Tom stopped me. He was snorkelling, and saw that I was passing straight through a mass of sea urchins. He guided me back to the other side. We don't know how I got through that far without getting stung while stepping on one. When I looked close enough to see them, they were everywhere, and were thickly packed. I live a charmed life. What will it take to end it? I suppose it will finally end, but the suspense is killing me.

Amy finds that funny. Ironic, she says. Sometimes I want to just kiss her. She helps me see my outside, when I am stuck here, inside.

Without being judgemental anymore, as much as I was, I love the feelings I get from her. Almost everything is enjoyable to her. Touching something that would make me cry out in pains, feels intricate and enticing to her senses. She, like me, finds beauty everywhere, but she can enjoy it so completely, whereas I can only look.

She is another dimension to me. She is me. I exist through her. Sometimes I envision my soul joining hers, when I pass on. We could make it work.

"Oh no we can't!" Amy breaks in. "When you are gone, you are gone. No pets in this house."

Everyone stops and stares at her. She did not think she was saying that out loud. Tanya starts to laugh at her and the rest still stare.

"I was being a pest. She did not want me thinking like that. Remember, she knows my every thought." I forgot, that our UK friends and family, did not know that. "She can listen to my thoughts. Not yours. Just mine and Marie's." That did not seem to help much. There are still shocked faces.

"How is that possible? I mean I've heard of it happening, but I never knew it to be true." Sue speaks up.

"Okay, this is for our UK folk and Tanya's moms. You can see that Amy does not have a navel. There is a reason for that. She was not born in the usual fashion. She was created like Eve was in the Bible. It is the result of a misguided prayer, that was granted for a specific reason. God created her from the flesh of Marie and I. You remember three years back, that Marie and I were much slimmer. That was the reason. We regained that weight, because we hadn't changed, any of our habits, enough to prevent it. Amy was twelve years old, when she came to be. It is a miracle of God. Amy and I feel each others senses, all of them. Amy knows what Marie and I are thinking and what we have stored within our minds. She can access that knowledge at any time. This is the life we lead, and have led, for the last three plus years. I had just thought, of something so intrusive to her, which is why, she blurted that out. Amy is a miracle. Tanya and our closest friends and family were told that, about a year ago. We had not told you folk, because of the proximity to us, and the danger it could hold for her, in communicating it through the internet. Brenda and Millicent, you were not within our confidence at the time, and we left that to Amy, to decide when she should tell you. Now that you all know, we hope you can keep this information, within our circle."

Amy looked on as I explained her whole identity. She felt naked, strangely enough, something the string bikini, had not done. She was exposed yet again. I went to her and held her, to give her a break from the stares, as they decided what this information means. She brought her arms in close, within mine, to let me wrap around her. She felt that I had splayed her on a rack, for all to see. She felt defiled. She made me feel it too. I had made her speak out, like that. It was my fault that she was exposed.

I had betrayed her again. I tried to make her feel protected. I tried to rebuild the safe zone she had had. I apologized for my stupidity, for my crass handling of her most private being. She stayed within my embrace, but still felt exposed. 'They would have to know.' I told her. 'They are our close friends and Tanya's trusted family. They will be able to help protect you.' She did not reply. She was just reacting and letting it take her. She was not willing to show her thoughts, until she remembered that girl, in her past life, yelling, LEZBO! This she showed to me and it made me feel the extent of my trespasses. I did not intend this to hurt her, but I caused it. She thought she saw me, walking to the microphone on stage, and announce it to the world. I had never thought of my words hurting her like that. It was as if I had stripped her and shamed her, inviting the world to stone her. I felt as though, I should be the one that is stoned. I felt that I could, at this moment, take my own life. I felt the guilt of the world, heaped upon me. I felt the sins of the world laid on my shoulders. I realized then, what Jesus might have felt, as he walked toward his fate. He did not deserve that feeling, but accepted the mantle. I fully deserve, knowing what I have just done, to my daughter. She now hugs me back and says, 'I forgive you. Forgive yourself.' She then reached up and kissed me.

All was quiet in our world apart from the outside. We lay down and let ourselves heal from the emotional stripping we had been through. The others seemed to understand what we were doing, and let the quiet surround us on the outside, as well.

They stepped into their books and magazines. There was even an emptiness, in the air apart from us, as if, not one person on the beach was speaking.

We emerged from our social coma, to look at the group. We needed them now, to give normalcy to the day, to bring our stars back into their place.

Amy said, "Hey! Who died?" That healed the mood and put the world right. Laughter erupted again. We were still alive.

"I need a drink." Bernie offered, "You up for one?"

"Yeah, I could use a drink!" I answered.

"Anyone else?" the mugs are all passed his way.

"I'll come along. Give you a hand." I grab my canes and get to my feet. The teens come along to help.

"Aw, there he is, our Johnny." Bernie spots him on his way. He waves to us.

As we give Johnny the order, I hand him the girls' mugs and say, "Two Pina Coladas, por favor. Light on the rum, just a splash."

As we turn to walk back, Amy says, "Contributing to our delinquency."

"Expressing mine." I justify.

They looked at each other, Amy thinking to her about my guilt.

'I'm the one who can get that, not her.'

"She knows. She doesn't need to hear." she says aloud.

If that was true, I could be in more trouble.

Chapter Twenty

Wild Eyes

There has been some running away with, an almost, Walter Mitty twist. For some time, the attractions of the resort get an involvement within the group. The promoters are always mixing with guests. They make friends and promote involvement in the entertainment. Our girls have joined in on some of the programs. The guys have done some things to mix it up, also. The hosts and hostesses, become involved with all the big groups, socially. They come to greet us, have meals with us, celebrate our special occasions, sit and have drinks with us. It makes, our trip fun and their jobs easier, for the most part. Then there is the 'student crush syndrome,' when someone goes overboard. They take the attentions personally. They will follow their voice, like the child and the pied piper. You want to find them, you listen for the voice, and in the audience, with a great view, there they are.

You also have the one that plays the groupie role. They go for the entertainer. They follow the cutest, or the most dramatic. They gush over the idol and hurry to watch each performance.

It's easy to fall prey to the allure of their talent, or personality. They have the larger than life, quality. Easy to set on a pedestal. It has happened often, within our friends and acquaintances, people you've met here, that are back year after year.

We've been around to their homes. It gives you an attachment to the resort, and the region in general. They bring us gifts, made by their children. We bring them gifts for their children. You become more than attached, if you feel too much the centre of their attention. It can happen to anyone, especially if they are not one, that gets the attention they want elsewhere. One who works, or is a homebody. One who may be overly busy with family stresses. They don't admit that it is a personal involvement, because it isn't for both parties. For the one there has been a spell cast. They are under it deeply. Too deeply to see for themselves, or admit to themselves.

Like all crushes, they run their course and there is little harm done. There is a point, when you see it happening, and you don't know if it is going to clear in time. It is like watching someone, trying to avoid a car crash. You see it on their face. There is the look that says, 'Can I make it?'. I know, I've been in the car.

The closer the call, the more the heartache. It was only because, they did their job too well. We all get excited at a great performance. We all feel a closeness when somebody is flirtatious. Most of us see, that it is their duty to the management. They are prostituting themselves in a way. They have to be nice to the customers and the bigger the group, the more attention they get. Everyone is happy, when it is all on a casual bent. Once in a while, you see the expression. The look of the fish after the lure. They are intent on finding this same feeling, every time they are in range. Then the fish becomes the angler. Offering candy, to get them in the dirty old van. Trust me, it is a dirty old van.

After the spell is broken, you don't know what they will do. Have a rebound crush, to disguise the first? Sit moping in a dark corner. You are on the lookout for this collateral damage. Those close enough to feel the fallout.

They say, 'What happens in Vegas, stays in Vegas.' That doesn't work in this town.

Over it now? We'll see. You watch them slowly picking up pieces, to hide their disappointment. Their gaze is averted. Tension in the throat area. Clenched jaw. What can you do? Nothing will help. They still think nobody knows. They will feel better, a thousand miles away.

I remember a kid in my class at school. He was head over heels for the teacher, and she was beautiful. But it all came crashing down, when she married the gym teacher. He was six foot four. The kid had his first lesson, that he actually learned, in that school.

It is a little dicier, when the kid is an adult. One that should know better. One that may not have the right, to go looking. There have been a few. There wasn't just one. It doesn't seem helpful to watch it happen, but that is the only thing you can do. So let it run its course.

Until next time, you watch for those wild eyes.

We are still on the beach. Another day, another rum punch. The sun is looking for its worshippers. Nothing to see here, move along. Don't take the heat, just don't fry my skin, thank you.

Amy and Tanya, are in a competition with their mothers. To see who can get the darkest. Tanya has the edge. She is tall and thin, the lean skin seems to darken faster. It is a close race, even with that edge. Marie, I always say, gets dark, just thinking about the sun. A warm weekend in January, saw her go from paper white, to milk chocolate brown, in two days. The game goes on until we board the bus for the airport.

I saw the teens laying out under the stars. I said, well, you heard it before. It wasn't funny then, and it wasn't funny now.

It is tempting to go out into the countryside, to get away from the resort lights. We could lie under the stars and see the amazing show of God's creation.

They told us there are no dangerous animals in Cuba.

There is a poison, in every paradise. I don't want to be the guy to prove them wrong. Just to treat this place as your own back yard. If only I could. Just imagining the freedom you feel, to walk in your own neighbourhood, and have it be here. No winter.

Amy isn't agreeing with me on that. She would like something different. She wants to travel, to find a better place. I would like that for myself. With Marie retired now, we have the time, but not the ability. We can do one more trip a year, but that will not give us much time to cover many countries.

"Enjoy this trip, it may be the last, for some time. University will keep you busy." I advised her. "Oh, what a sad face." She gives me the pouty face.

This trip has been great. Getting together with friends and family, from so far afield, is great in itself. To enjoy it here is wonderful. Now it is time to prepare to leave. So much, we wait for, to come here. It goes so quickly. It was worth the drive. Marie's mother would always ask us if we had driven to Cuba. She had dementia giving her unique outlooks.

I feel like I have actually lost weight, this time. The walking, and taking the stairs to the fifth floor, really helped. I did behave in the meal selection. Marie and I both feel the better for it. Amy, Tanya and her moms all walked the stairs with us. Amy doesn't think there was any loss for her, but she feels more fit. That seems to be in line with the other three. They had enjoyed spending time on our extra large terrace. I was alone, with all that estrogen. How could that be bad?

The last full day, I took a stroll down to the market, to do some shopping, for our cottage. I picked up some company, after Amy heard where I was going. She and her shadow, came walking down the avenue, right behind me. I picked up some bongos and a couple other things that would pass the time up there. I had looked for them last year but I was able to find them this time. The teens got something for each other. I was to hide them, but I could not look at them, or I would give the surprise away. I will have to pass these to someone else, to make sure they will not cause any trouble at the customs. We stop in at the pizza place, and find another of the group to join us. We get the pizza I was supposed to get last year, and it was worth the wait.

Marie had done her market trip, days ago. She did not know about the things I had planned on getting. She would not have approved. Maracas and bongos, the last things she would want me to get. Christian will be able to entertain us, at the cottage. Brent could join him with his guitar. I will play the maracas, and we can jam, around the fire, at night.

We get back in time to pack our stuff away, and get to the beach, before the rest are done for the day. Our last swim in the ocean and then to dry.

We did well this trip. We had lots of fun with the boats and tours. Nary a bored comment within our ranks. We go back to our lives of leisure. The ice and snow and grumbling multitudes, us included. We don't want to trash the planet, but we don't mind this global warming. With our deep chills, we have hardly seen any of it.

Up from the beach to grab our last mugfuls of drinks to toast the island refuge. Saying goodbye, to the place where we are becoming a fixture. That done, we are bound for packing the last of our treasures and our wardrobe. A quick shower and a lay down, to get ready for dressing up for dinner. I have to put my feet up to get rid of the edema, so I can put on my shoes. I put on some shorts, just in case the neighbours drop in on us. It was a good call because, no sooner done than said, through the door we hear the call. It is the moms. They are getting quite used to me calling them that. They are ready to go, and had to come to show their appreciation, for us having them share so much of our friends and time with them. We have a rest on the deck, one last time. We finish the contents of our mugs. They are rinsed, dried and packed away. The time growing short, sees the moms out the door, to prepare for the last supper. We dress and in come the teens, to collect us for some photo-ops.

They want the evening shots, with the lights on the front of the building. We start to get anxious about leaving tomorrow. Usually the two weeks is long enough, but with so many new members of the troupe, it was being cut too short.

I feel relief, from the escape from incidents involving Amy. I have little enough, confidence in our own city's acceptance, of the unusual. Foreign countries are going for acceptance, or condemnation, alternately. Not only is she an attractive woman, she is still underage, gay, and she has shown that she is anatomically different. I wonder what really possessed me to propose this explosive organization, that will be called a hoax and a sham. There will be no results that can be expected to be agreed to. Like everything else in this world, it never happened. Nothing has ever happened here on earth, or in this galaxy. No matter what proof is offered, it will be rejected by some 'qualified expert' and deemed a hoax. We are going through this, for our own inane, curiosity. God will show us, whether it is possible, to live this kind of life, and that will be the extent of it.

I still love having her as my partner in this. We are teaching each other, how to accept those that have differing ideals. I have someone to talk to at all times. We are never alone. I have an alternate reality. I can live a life through her and she through me. I can be reminded, what it is like to be young, single and free. She can see, what it will be like to be old, married and broken down. There are benefits to both. At her age, people don't expect you to be competent. At my age, they feel the same. As a fifteen year old, you are provided for, either by your parents, or a state subsidized charity. As a disabled senior, you are provided for by your pension from an employer, or the state. Come to think of it....nah, it's all good.

The date of departure is upon us. Up early for breakfast and assembling for farewells. Hugs and kisses for everybody, from everybody. So many groups are leaving today. It is like a zoo here. The busses are beginning to arrive. I am glad to be on the first one. I would love to get to the airport first. We are herded into the bus and waved off, by the Brits, leaving later in the day.

The driver is in a hurry today. I appreciate his haste. We are pulling into the parking lot of the airport, to find, we have a head start. I am at the front of the bus and I know that means the luggage is buried. I take the carry-ons and head in to stand at the check in desk, the girls arrive with the luggage at, nearly, the same time. After all these years, we have got this down. Marie has the tickets and we are processed quickly. Over to pay our exit fees and then to customs. I am through and am going through the security, when Amy tells me that Marie is looking for me. I tell her where I am and she passes that on to her mom. Marie hadn't seen me go into the customs. She gets through and catches up with me. She was talking to the others in the group. She was upset with me when she found me. I couldn't tell her anything to save myself, so I just accepted the blame. It worries her, if we are not together, when we go through the gates.

Amy, Tanya and the moms, are filling in behind us. The group had been distracted by one of the sniffer dogs, just as I was going in. The dog had stopped at a suitcase and it was being searched. It turned out to be something the owner, had bought off of a beach vendor. He was allowed to go on, but the box of contraband cigars, were confiscated. Excitement and intrigue, short-lived. What was in those cigars?

I am more comfortable on this trip. I was preboarded, this time. They are being more accommodating, of late. Each year they have improved. I am sitting between Marie and Amy. Tanya is across the aisle next to Brenda and Millicent. The rest are in the row behind us. We are in the front third of the plane. That will help in Toronto. I should get through with no ill effects. The seats on this carrier's flights are some of the closest in the industry, but they are always full. Not much incentive, to have them spaced out better.

As I am so close to Amy, we talk aloud. She is complaining about my back, neck, and leg pain. It is constant for me, because I have had it for so long. To her it is flaring up, and giving her some teary eyes. She asks, "How can you stand it, when it is so severe? It is really painful!"

"I might have missed my anti-inflammatory capsule. It does feel raw. I am used to dealing with it."

"It is like fire singeing my skin. Your joints are really bad too." she wipes away the tears. "Can't you check and see, if you have the pills, and take them for me?"

I look in my pocket for my case, and find this mornings pills are still there. "I have them, but you will have to wait until I get some food, to take them with."

"Thanks, Dad. I am a little tired and it is getting to me."

"I'm sorry. I forget them the odd time. Let me know when it feels strong to you, and I'll check, but don't let it go on so long."

"I am having trouble sleeping because of it. I think you should bring those vitamin and mineral pills you have. I noticed that you leave those home, and you need them."

"I'll bring them for you, next time." That is the first time she has told me about it. I think that her constantly feeling my pain, is wearing on her, as if she is the one that has the damages. I feel empathic pain from others, overtop of my own, because they only come when it is bad for them. If their pain and weaknesses ease up for them, I don't feel them. I think she is getting a stronger dose of my pain, than I do from empathy. I have to keep in mind, what it is doing to her. She is showing it in her eyes. The stress and strain of dealing with it. She will not have the disease herself, but she will suffer as if she does. People with long term pain can build up a callous of sorts, to dull the effect it has on the brain. It is much like morphine does. It is better for the sufferer to build up this resistance, to lessen the pills they take. Some can't bring themselves to do this. Even when it is done, you can read the pain on their face.

Chapter Twenty-One

March Breakers

Getting home this year was a surprise. We are coming from summer weather to spring like weather. A midwinter thaw is taking place. A nice bit of buffering, from the harshness of home. We are home in the middle of the week, and the girls have to get up for school, in the morning.

Amy is in the last term of high school. She is probably going to Queen's University, in Kingston. That is her first choice. It is close enough to home, to get back for the holidays, and far enough away, that she will feel some separation from us, if it is possible. Tanya will be heartbroken, when Amy tells her. She had hoped for her, to stay close by.

It is also close to the cottage, and she would go there, once she gets her licence. The course at Queen's, is only one part of what she wants, and she is debating, what she will do with that.

We have relations in many places, around the country, and would like to have her stay with one of them, but that doesn't seem to be working out. Amy feels that she would like to stay in the dorms, the first year anyway.

I think we'll have to wait and see how that works, once she has actually graduated.

I got a call from Evelyn Young. She wanted to talk about the cottage. I make arrangements to meet her and see what she has in mind. She has a hard time thinking of the time she has there. I tell her it is still too soon, to make a quick decision. She is wondering if she should put Brent's name on the deed. I say that would be the best way of coming to terms with it. It will take the two of them, to decide its fate then, and that is a great safety point to have. She won't be easily swayed, by treasure seekers and conmen. Brent will have less cost, if something should happen to her, further on down the road. She could also have a clause put in the will, and power of attorney, to demand an advisor, to help mediate any discussion, to bring in any change to the ownership, after that. She agrees and asks me to be that advisor. I agree, as long as I am not eligible, to be advisor and purchaser, at the same time. She agrees to those terms.

I think she was overwhelmed, with the variables, in the keeping of the property.

She calls me the next week to say it has all been drawn up and it is final. The fate of the cottage is safe in both their names.

Amy asks me, if I had put her name, on the deed for the cottage, yet. I tell her that, she needs to be an adult, and that it will happen, once she has reached the age of majority. She is disappointed in that news.

The March break is coming up, and we are going up, to check on the condition of the cottage property. Amy wants to come and bring Tanya. We agree as long as she doesn't pick that time to tell her about Queen's. That is agreed, so the invitation is extended.

Marie is much happier, now that she has retired. She is free to go anywhere, or nowhere. It is her choice. She wants to help with the rest of the reno, of the cottage proper. I send her to ask Amy. She thinks it is ridiculous, that she needs to ask her. I tell her that Amy, has directed the build so far, and is the foreman in charge of the project.

Amy agrees to have her come on the team, as long as she lets her stay in charge of all aspects of it.

That is hard for Marie to go for. After thinking about it for a couple days, she agrees. The timing was right, for us to straighten that out, before going up.

We pack up the necessities and get the van fuelled up. We get off early and grab breakfast on the run. I am sitting in the back with Tanya, and Amy is riding shotgun. Marie will not pull over, until we are past Toronto. It is still winter and there is a big weather front coming in while we are there. We will see how much it takes, to get in and out of that lane, in winter.

We won't have the news updates there. We don't have wifi in the cottage. The radio in the van will be out of range for our stations, and we really don't care that much anyway.

I have longed for a chance like this. To get away to our own cottage by the lakeshore, with a treed lot. It isn't what I had pictured in my dreams, but then, when is it ever, as you dream. It is just as I dream now. Marie had never wanted a cottage, until we had camped, for more than thirty years. It isn't like my sister's, but it is ours. We have our own place, and she will love it, once we have finished setting it up, as I have planned.

The roads are clear of the signs of winter. Give it a moment though, it will change. The storm coming in, is one of those reminder storms. It reminds us where we live, and what season it is. It buries your car. If it misses that, it will leave a drift all around it, that will need tunnelling, to get through.

How about that? The driveway is clear. We'll have to turn the van around, once we get in. That will give us a chance for me to barrel through. I'll have the girls down at the road to give me the all clear. That is just if we are dumped on, as it can be here, with an attitude.

They carry the supplies down to the cottage. The midwinter thaw, gives the area a chance to lose the snow, without the frost coming up. The ground stays firm and we can walk on it. While they are doing that, I get the van in position. I walk up along the ridge to the trailer. There are quite a few tracks around it. Rabbit, raccoon, and bear tracks. It looks like the animals like my ideas of camping too. I strain to see under the trailer. I don't see anything hanging down. I give a sigh of relief, and also of hope, that they haven't got in, to set up their own home.

Amy tells me, that the cottage was more appealing for them. There is a hole in the roof. I head down to see the damage first hand, but I can already see, what she does. Old habits die hard. I pick up some wood to patch it, on my way. Once I get in, I have a better idea. Amy is already acting on it. One of the kitties is placed so that it can be seen inside as the flap of roof is lifted. Its mug is pointing right at the hole. I tack it down to keep the coming storm out. When the raccoons come back, they will not want to trust their noses, with that face bearing down on them. We are hoping that will be the end of that. The heaters are on and it will be nice tonight. It isn't that nice yet, though. Marie has the beds made up and is preparing the kitchen.

We will have order. Having the basics, bathroom and kitchen. The rest is all personal comfort, and we have that covered, in spades. I have to feel no pressure points, no rough textures, and to get that in my cottage, I have air and foam, galore. I tried water, but it just doesn't cut it. You feel like you are floating on a cloud, in any bed I put together. I got a bed for our spare room. That is now Amy's room. It has pocket coils and seven inches of memory foam. It is firm and ultra-soft at the same time.

My tents have air beds with your choice of foam thickness. They are at a comfortable height, to give you the feeling that you are in your room at home. I was known for building the most comfortable chairs, to deal with the pain, while at work.

Tonight we have the two bedrooms. The choicest materials are on these beds. If I find they aren't, they soon will be. I have two things I like done right, comfort and efficiency. Amy feels that if it is good enough for me? It is good enough for anyone. She says I have the 'Princess and the Pea' syndrome.

We are comfortable with the fortunes of the cottage, this spring. Now that the run off has been split, and will not over tax the river's capacity here. We will be able to plan out our construction and get right into it, as soon as the time is available. We can start before the frost is out, for the laying out of the site plan, as well as the plumbing layout. Once the frost is up, we can sink the supports for the decking, and do the digging, before the soil dries. It gives us a good stretch of small projects. Our time is tied to the girls' school schedule. Marie and I can get up here to do some things. The most work will be done by the teenagers.

Around the trees the ground stays soft longer. In the cottage area, the ground dries earlier.

I have brought a trick with me that is sure to keep the visitors to the cottage at bay. It's a sound track, with a motion sensor. When the sensor is tripped, the track will give the low growls of a cougar. It will just be the warning growl. If the door is opened, a more emphatic growl will send them away. The door will shut as the pressure against it is eased. The only problem is, if the visitor is stuck inside, by the door closing.

I think we need a bear to sit by the trailer. A visual deterrent to prowlers.

I wonder what an alligator figure would do to an uninvited visitor?

I look to Amy and she is shaking her head. She refrained from thinking of it, until I looked at her. I won't run it by Marie, then.

I need to stake out the base pad for the barn. I also, need to mark trees that will need to be cut and the ones that must stay for the tree house and platforms. I need to choose where I would put a zip-line. I'm having fun just thinking of it.

Amy is unusually silent. She is sleeping. I check her, to see what is going on. Was I too busy to notice something wrong? I go in to check her, and she has just dozed off on the bed spread. Tanya is helping to get the kitchen set up for cooking space. She is helping Marie to see the options. Weird. I try to see Amy's thoughts before she lay down. I find myself doubting my ability, to actually find the answers. I can't recall my own recent thoughts. If I don't pay attention to everything I am doing, it's lost to me, until it filters through. How much can I recover from her, when neither of us, pays the attention I need, to find it.

"Is there anything wrong with Amy?" I have to ask and I feel guilty for it.

"If you don't know, how would we?" Marie looks at me, puzzled. She is catching onto the dynamics of our situation. She has been in denial of the possibility.

Tanya looked between us, wondering what we are saying. She is still questioning the mechanics of it. She goes in to see what's wrong. She sits beside Amy, brushes her hair from her face, and feels her forehead.

Amy awakes to her touch. She looks up at her. "What's wrong?"

Tanya replies, "That's what we are wondering. Your dad didn't know and that made us concerned."

"I was just lying here, relaxing and fell asleep."

"I suppose, that's why I didn't know. It wasn't a conscious decision." I spoke out.

"Then everything's alright?" Tanya is relieved to ask.

"Yes, I'm alright." she laid her hand on Tanya's.

I walked back out of the doorway, to try to remember what I had been going to do, before this worry interrupted me.

Amy reminds me. She had been following it, as she lay there. She drifted off to my description, of the idyllic pictures we shared. We have imagined, many times, the configuration of our family park. Our thoughts are built one on the other. We share the elements of each idea, putting it together, like building blocks. I want to get moving on it, without waiting for the building season to begin. We both get excited about it. We are like kids on the eve of a holiday. We want to start, without waiting for the dawn of the event. We don't betray our ideas to anyone else. Our thoughts are our treasures, to amass in secret and refine them, apart from the pollution of another's input. We play quietly. We are like the children, that silently get up to no good. Our empire is growing in the deepest protective vaults of our war room. We are sending the troops out, to attack the job of assembling our fortress.

We look at each other, with a great grin, of evil contemplation. Our plotting is gaining the element of intrigue. What can we accomplish, without being impaired by rational interference.

Marie breaks our concentration, "Would you two schemers like to come and have supper?"

There it is, rational interference.

The evening meal, in our own retreat, is so rewarding. We see the coming together, of all our efforts. This is the preview, of what this Eden will be like, to our lives together. The gathering of the families, to our private amusement park. We can't resist the impulse to vocalize our feelings, just thought out. Amy and I look at each other, rub our hands and emit a "Bwahaha!"

The other two look startled, which makes us laugh out loud. We are then forced to reveal the thought and why we had to act on it.

Marie and Tanya, look at each other and just shake their heads. They agree, that we must have an evil genius, we share.

We must take the rest of the evening to read. It is to have us take a step back, and let some rationale, have a chance to form in our thoughts over night. It will, help us to get to sleep. If we kept on our train of thought, we would be up all night. Still might.

In bed, we are enwrapped with the peaceful domesticity, each couple in our separate room. The girls envision their world of future plans becoming reality.

I am feeling the years of long ago. I am drawing energy from the mood in which we find ourselves. The feeling is infecting

Marie and it doubles the velocity of the action. The movements are diverse but entwined with the thrills we are feeling. The deepest of emotion, combines in the absence of awareness, of external elements. The height of our hunger feeds the abilities. My blood rushes faster and harder. My strength is multiplied by the fluid in my veins, pulsating and erupting through the recesses of the brain pushing out the physical inabilities and pulling me into an inescapable climax. The power felt urging through me, keeps me suspended and carries me on to further depths of rapture. I can't feel the physical confinement of our surroundings. I am rushed through the portal, into an immensity of sensual explosivity. We are no longer individuals, but an entity gathering the energy of the cosmos. It becomes an out of body compulsion to entangle the egos in an expression of evolvement of multiplicity into a crescendo beyond any capabilities. We finally crash through the bewitchment and collapse into the now, spent bodies, gasping for the air, to feed the physical demands of our hearts.

We slowly become aware of our surroundings. We attempt to reason out, what has happened to us, individually. We start to remember the other couple sharing the chamber next to us. My mind is unable to see the course of Amy's thoughts past the initial emotions.

I start to regain the senses shared with my daughter. I purposely remind myself of my promise. I cannot feel the controlling impulse and react with a clinical response in my thoughts. I look to Marie. How can I contain my thoughts. I see Amy and I know that she is aware. We see our loves lying beside us and they are returning our gaze. We attempt to calm the thoughts we have, we feel that we have succeeded. We are putting up scenes to put forth a diversion. How can we, who share the most encompassing view of the other's world, hope to deceive ourselves into believing it possible.

I thought an experience like that was long past the expiry date. Being a senior citizen, with the blood pressure medicine, stealing my last vestiges of virility. It seems I was piggy-backing on the intensity of Amy's desire. At my age, I will take what I can get. I tell Amy, she is contributing to the delinquency of a senior, and I thank her. She is at once embarrassed and glad to be of service. From now on, I have a new tactic for dealing with my teenage daughter.

It feels good to get up in the morning, after getting up, the night before. I feel more like a normal man again. I do avoid looking Amy in the eye, when they crawl out of bed. I have to let go. It seems the thing to do, when it manifests itself, into a symbiotic relationship. I, the old Croc, and Amy, the little Plover bird. It works for me! I have enacted her desire but I do not look for any other information.

The bacon and eggs, with home fries, are such an appropriate reward, for a good nights work. All smiles today. After we eat and clean up the debris, we step outside to check on the weather.

The promised storm is late. You just can't go by the hourly forecast. It was supposed to be here between nine and ten, and it is already a quarter to eleven.

We walk up to the trailer, so Amy and I can explain our plans, for the trailer decking, and tent decks. They are interested. Tanya more so than Marie. I show Marie a picture I sketched of it. It is rough, but she sees more clearly, what I was trying to describe. It shows the screen room of the trailer facing the lake. There is a deck surrounding the screen area with a Plexiglas railing. At the back, I have added, an add-a-room from our previous trailer.

In that, will be more sleeping space. It will have a curtain across the trailer side, to give it privacy. The tent decks will continue along the forest edge. There will be tarps, to cover all the camping rooms. This will protect the material, from the trees, and weather elements. It will also help draw air through the structures. There will be an overhang that will be adjusted according to the weather conditions.

We are putting in a new septic bed, and raising the ground level, between the cottage knoll and the ramp, from the driveway entrance. This will make it easier, to get to the cottage, in the spring.

Now Marie is feeling better about the house, hosting all these people, that will be sleeping, in the sleeping rooms. There will be at least eighteen in the available quarters. I tell her, the trailer will not have to be fussed with, each year. The tents and trailer will go up at the May long weekend. We will be able to welcome in family, and friends, until the Canadian Thanksgiving holiday. If we want to get a licence, we could open it up to Glamping rentals. Short of that happening, we would, at least, be able to vary our own, sleeping arrangements.

It seems a great undertaking to Marie. It is overwhelming. I ease her mind, by saying, the family is all that it is for, for now, and the foreseeable future. "Okay." she says. The stamp of approval that we were waiting for.

Amy and Tanya, are laying out their work schedule, for the project. I don't need to bother asking. Such a self-driven organization, we have here. I start looking for protection of the trailer, from nosey bears and such.

We are still looking over the area of construction, when the front blows in. Boy, does it blow in! The wind picks up solidly, and a few flakes, turn into whiteout conditions quickly. We are hard-pressed to make it to the cottage. We get inside and toss off the coats. They are hung up near the door, and we collapse in our chairs. "It's he-ere." I joke.

Now we will find out, if this can be used year-round. The heat is on, and when the woodstove is installed, it will be more comfy here. The thing we need to rely on, is the hydro withstanding the storm. That flimsy line from the road, should be buried. I make a note, to discuss this, with Brent and Evelyn Young. I feel my reserve beginning to drop, so I go and lie down. The others sit and read. That should do us for a while. We have games from the trailer. We had brought all of that stuff in, before we closed up last fall. The wind is howling outside and shaking up the women. Yes, it unnerves me a bit, too. I can fall asleep, in any kind of atmosphere, and I do just that. The girls are put off their books, by the noise of the storm. They hear scratching on the side of the house near the breach in the roof. Amy grabs a flashlight and climbing into the loft, she shines it on the cracks of the damaged area. The scratching stops and then, reverses its direction. That is one hurdle taken.

They pull out some cards, to occupy themselves. This game changes constantly and will keep them involved and distracted. Amy is catching my dreams, while I snooze, in the next room. She is seeing the dream vividly. It is reminiscent of the previous nights activity. It starts to get to her. She tries to ignore it. She plays her hand in the game all wrong. Marie tells her that, she isn't on that level. That brings her back. She is still readily distracted, and soon asks, if they could finish the game later. They decide to do that, and let her get over her occupation. She goes to her room and Tanya joins her. Amy starts to initiate intimacy. Tanya is shocked by the timing of it. Her eyes dart to the doorway several times, while Amy's persistence triumphs. She is totally gone, to the outside stimuli. Tanya soon succumbs and they continue on Amy's path. Marie could walk in on them, and they could not even respond, to her objections. As it is Marie is busying herself with getting a lunch prepared for when we arise from our 'naps.' I am engrossed in the dream, and now it is being refuelled. It is familiar to me but not in this state, or this emotion. My essence moves to Marie, and engages her, with the fever we felt before. She is pulled into the unconsciousness. She falls to the floor, with no notice given, by any of the fellow occupants. We are engaged on an ethereal plain. We are there again, in the fall of our psyche beyond our mortal being. It is a labyrinth of the minds inner workings. The populace of the physical is controlled remotely. The souls are spinning the web of their own congress. They are taking the depths to new levels. Never have I been this far before. I have never thought this existed. We are beyond our memory and are drawing on the universal forces to find our way home. Even Amy, with full knowledge of the heavenly spaces does not recognize these vistas. We are now beyond our beginnings and into an intergalactic cruise. We are taken through the scenes, of the ancient creation of the stars, and other entities, that I have seen fleeting glimpses of. We are lost and give ourselves to be brought back. As we descend to our natural shells, we see the insignificance of our beings.

We awake, with a sorry state of retained thoughts, of what had happened to us. Marie thought she had fainted. Tanya and Amy, wondered what they had done, and where they had been. They don't believe the scene before them. They had been beyond this. I retain parts of the ethereal heights. I could not get the whole thing, but Amy will be able to draw this out.

The storm sounds remind us of where we are. The howling winds beyond our walls, tell the story we will see outside our windows. She turns around and goes to our room. The windows are pasted by the fine snows. I think of the direction of the wind and where the van is aimed. I had planned it well. Marie shares the experience she had. I help her to understand.

The girls have recovered themselves, with clothes they had gathered. They are chilled, with the sudden loss of the heat. Marie and I are also feeling the freshness in the rooms. I get up and check the loft. The wind has lifted the flap, made by the raccoon boarders, we had chased off. The snow is coming in the gaping hole. Amy and I get the compressor charged up, and grab the framing nailer and a tarp, we had kept for this very occasion. we go outside to get up on the roof to fasten down the misplaced roof patch. We have to dig up the ladder, that Brad had brought up for us. We get the missing piece and climb up to the roof. We wrap the tarp around the corner, and after nailing down the patch, we nail down the tarp over it. That will have to do until spring. We replaced the ladder in its spot, and get our frozen butts inside, to thaw.

"It looks like we need a new roof." I tell Marie.

"See if Brent can get us some metal roofing." is Amy's answer.

"We can call Evelyn, when we get back, and have him call us."

"Do you think Brad could get some for us?" Marie says.

"He could, but I'll call Brent first."

We sit down to have that lunch Marie was making, before I so rudely interrupted her.

She looks at me to ask, "What happened here?"

"What do you mean?" I stall.

"These two went into their room and I started making lunch. Next thing I know, I am on the floor. I had this really weird dream, in between. The place was freezing, and you ran up the ladder to the loft and then out the door. What happened?"

"The wind blew the broken section of roof off. Amy and I went out to fix it. You may have dreamt the rest. Are you feeling okay?"

"I feel okay now, except for this weird dream."

"I don't know. I was asleep on the bed. Amy do you know what happened to Mom?"

"When I went to the bedroom, Tanya followed me. Then we felt the cold air and I followed you outside. Mom had had some really weird thoughts, about last night, and then, they were showing us in outer space. She could have fainted. It all happened so fast. We had just gotten into the bedroom when the air got so cold."

I think silently to Amy, 'Are you really going to do this to your mother?'

Her reply was a simple, 'Yes.'

'I guess it would do less harm to her, for her to believe, it was a dream.'

"Marie, you should take it easy. You may have been stressed out over something. Relax!"

"I guess it could have been that. I might have been stressed out about them, running into the bedroom so fast."

"But we just walked in. I wasn't feeling well."

"It can't be....I...Maybe that's...but what about the lunch? It was done. After they ran into the bedroom."

"Maybe you weren't feeling well then, either and it was speeding up your thoughts, or perception." I suggest.

"What is making us feel ill?"

"I think, we need to vent the stove better. The fumes from cooking, might have been affecting us. That cold air might have saved our lives!"

'You are wicked, Dad!'

'No more than you, my dear. No more than you.'

To make it safer, just in case there was more truth to that than we know, I put a vent in the plans. Until then, we will crack open the window, and stick one of the heater fans by it, to blow out the fumes. We can do this every time we use that cook-top. I think now, that may have been what had happened. That old vent may be plugged. She may not have turned it on. Why didn't I replace it before?

'Maybe I wasn't being that awfully wicked, after all.'

The storm is raging, still. I try to envision the van, making it out of the lane. Us getting to the van will be a struggle.

"Amy.."

"I'm doing that now. It is puddled up on the floor. It hasn't soaked in yet."

"What is she talking about?" Marie is lost on a lot of our conversations.

"She is cleaning up the snow that had come in, when the patch blew open in the loft."

"I'll get it down and we can do that before we leave."

Marie looks at me with raised eyebrows.

"She's talking about the tarp, we brought up, for the roof."

"Not that one, Mom, a bigger one, that will cover the whole roof."

"That is annoying." she complains.

"A lot goes on, behind the scenes, in here." I point to my head and to Amy.

"Tanya, does this get to you, too?"

"Yes. When we are working on something, and she has to ask her dad, and then just goes ahead and does it. When I ask, she says that he said 'yes.' And when she gets up and leaves, and she says, her dad needs her. And then out of the blue she yells to him, 'No not that one.' It creeps me out sometimes."

"I thought you liked that."

"Not all the freaking time."

"Oh, okay, I'm sorry. I'll try not to do that, all the freaking time."

"You don't need to get upset over it."

Marie shouts, "Alright, just drop it!"

'Amy, I think they are a little ticked with us. If it wasn't in the middle of a blizzard, I would suggest we take a walk.'

'Women. Sheesh. They get a little crazy sometimes.'

'Wait, are you the pot, or the kettle, here?'

'I'm the Brillo pad.'

'Do they still make those?'

'Whatever.'

"The wind is dying down. Check outside to see what it's like." Marie suggests, strangely like an order.

I try to open the door, to find the snow has blocked it. "I was just out there! What happened?"

"It might have come off the roof, when you came in and slammed the door." says Marie.

Tanya suggests, "Check out the back door."

Amy does that after dropping the tarp, beside it. "It's all drifted around this side. We can get out here, but the drift is humungous. We might have to tunnel through it. We may have an out, around the corner, on the end to the left. I can't remember how far down this drops. Get the stepladder to put it down here. It is still blowing snow. We need to plant a windbreak along that end." Tanya hands her the ladder and she slides it down beside the doorway. "I can get out here okay, now."

"I'll go."

"No, Dad, you can't go with your problems. You may collapse out there, and then we will all have to go, to get you back up into the house."

"Amy's right, honey. You could get worse than you are now."

"I'm taller, I should go." Tanya breaks in.

"Come with me then." is Amy's answer. So they both dressed for the occasion and climbed down the ladder. They trudged through some smaller drifts, and around the corner, they found the drift circling around, the other end. They continued along to find that way was blocked by a pile on the stairs. "Mom was right. The snow fell off the roof and is blocking this way and the door."

Tanya asked to get up on Amy's shoulders to see over the drift. She climbed up and leaned against the wall to steady herself. "There is one huge amount of snow out there. It's hard to tell where it gets shallow enough for us. Lets go back and look over the other side."

"Can you see the van?" Amy asks.

"Yes, I can see the roof and the front window, but just the top of it."

"Okay, climb down."

They went back around through their pathway. It was almost as hard as the first time they went through it. They got to a spot that was lower than the rest and Tanya climbed back up on Amy's shoulders. "I can see the trailer is covered. There is a very low spot about twenty feet from the drift here."

"Climb down and we will look at the other end."

Tanya climbs down again and off they go to the other corner. "You get on my shoulders this time."

Amy has more trouble getting up, but manages to make it. "I made it to the top of Mount Tanya." she shouted.

"Funny!" Tanya huffs at her.

"There is a big break on this side. The drift goes out toward the river on both ends of this wall. It is not very far to go through this way. I think we can make it out. We will need a shovel, or something to break this down with. I'm coming down."

"No!" Tanya shouts. "Jump against the drift to knock it down some. If we can get out that way, we can get to the tools, that are by that tank we boarded up there. Jump hard against it and see if you can make it to the other side. I will try to follow you."

"Okay, here goes!" she jumped as hard as she could toward the bank. She landed on top of it and crawled toward the river, pushing against the wall. She found the other side of the drifts slope and rolled down it. Getting to her feet, she was in a very shallow spot. It was the edge of the knoll. She got to the covered tank and found the shovels. There were no snow shovels, but there was a broad scoop shovel for loose stuff. 'Perfect' she thought.

Tanya was not having as easy a time getting over the drift mound.

Amy told her to wait there while she checks out this end of the cottage. She found that just getting to the stairs to get the other door open would be a monumental task. She was just about to tell Tanya to come on out, when she remembered Brent getting in the crawlspace on this end. She digs down and finds the trap door. I go to the bathroom and move the compost toilet out into the common room.

Marie asks me, "What are you doing?"

"Amy is coming in through the crawl space. Turn that switch on by the door."

She flips the switch and Amy sees the light from behind the door. She digs it away and pulls open the door.

Tanya calls to her. "Where are you? What should I do?"

I stick my head out the door and tell her, "Come back inside this way. She is coming in through the crawl space."

"Great! I'm coming up." She clamoured noisily up the ladder. The aluminum ladder banging against the wall.

"Enthusiasm, that's what we need." I describe her action. "At least it will scare off any animals out there."

She shoots me a big grin.

Amy's head pokes up through the loose floor of the bathroom. "I'm glad we only tacked that. We can get out here. We should get rested up first and then plan on going home once we dig out the van. If we go wide around. First to the river and then the lake. Then we can find a route to the van. Tanya and I will go first. You two get the things to the door of the crawl space. We will come back once we have found the way. You wait until then and rest up. It will be hard moving in this snow. We may not get a storm like this every winter, but it is not a good idea to come during the winter until we have an alternative plan."

"Yes sir, Major Minor!" I tease.

"Help me up, Dad."

I pull her out of the hole. We sit down to recover from that excitement. Marie gets the girls some hot chocolate and then hands one to me. The window is open this time.

"The vent has a nest in it. It looks new." Amy informs me.

"Why didn't I catch that when you saw it."

"You were busy. I was busy. I was trying to get in out of the snow."

"Okay, so no staying here during a winter storm." I decide for them. I feel comfortable in assuming their agreement with that.

"If that was the kind of storms they get here, in the winter, I have no problem with that." is Amy's call.

"So, how deep is the snow by the crawl space door?" Marie wants to know.

"Only about two and a half feet." says Amy.

"Lets plan on staying the night." is my suggestion. "It will take a long time and a ton of shovelling, to get the van cleared. While you go to find the path, we will see if we can get this door cleared."

"Dad, there is a huge pile of snow in front of that door. The path in front of it is huge too. We will be better off, letting the snow melt, while we are at home."

"She's right, Tom. We don't need to get hurt, digging snow here."

"I guess you're right."

"Hey, I hear a machine coming, you guys!" Tanya nearly shouts.

Amy climbs up to look out the loft window. "She's right! It's a snowplough! It turned to go toward Evelyn's cottage. It looks like it is turning around. Nope. It's backing up the lane. It's coming our way. It stopped again and is backing up. Hey!

It's ploughing in front of the van! I'm going out there to meet them."

Tanya says, "Me too!"

I put the ladder through the opening in the bathroom floor. As soon as the girls were dressed for it they climbed down and shimmied through the space and out the door. As they stand up, they come to face a black bear, near the bottom of the slope. They slowly slip back in the doorway, and close the door behind them. They scoot back to the ladder. I see them pop up from the floor.

"Good choice girls. He ran off toward the river a ways, when you ducked back in." I watched, when Amy saw it, through the kitchen window.

Marie is in the loft watching the plough operator.

"At least they are coming to the cottage." Amy says.

Tanya gives her the look again.

Marie calls down. "They are coming in on snowshoes."

They make their way around the mound of snow, that is surrounding the cottage. They wave to Marie when they see her in the window. It is about ten more minutes before we hear a gunshot.

"What was that?" Amy shouts.

"They shot into the air to scare off the bear."

She runs to the bathroom, and slides down the ladder. She opened the door, to let them see the opening. They see her, and aim their gun toward her, until they see it's a girl.

"Are you alright?" they call in.

"Except for being stuck, other than this way. We have just this opening to get in and out."

"We'll go around to the side near the lake. Is there a doorway there?"

"Yes, but it's blocked with snow."

"We'll dig you out."

"Thanks!" she calls and closes the door, then slides along to the ladder. Up through the floor, she pops again. "They're going around and dig us out at the front door."

"Great!" we all shout in unison.

After a half hour, they knock on the door. I open the door and ask them in. We give them some hot chocolate and sandwiches.

"How did you know we were here?" I ask them.

"We saw the tip of the roof, of your vehicle. We checked toward the other cottage, and then yours. We saw the light in the window, and after we cleared in front of your van, came to see, if you were okay."

"Do you always plough these lanes?"

"No, it was just lucky we saw the van roof. We were looking down the lanes for any sign of life. What are you folk here for?"

"It was the March break, and we wanted to see what the property was like, in the winter."

"This is the worst storm since 1977-78 winter. We've been finding cars buried on the side of the road."

"Wow! We knew it was bad, but not that bad."

"Yup! It was a southern storm, meeting an Alberta Clipper. Same as back then. Will you folk need help getting out to your van?"

"Since you cleared in front of it, and got the door here free, we should be good."

"We'll knock the snow away from those side doors for you. If you can stay the night here, we would recommend it. Some routes haven't been opened yet, due to abandoned cars. If you're going to stay, we'll leave you and get back on the road. Thanks for the food."

"Thanks for coming along and digging us out. Do you think that bear will be back?"

"Not for a long time, but there are others, and they will look for shelter. Don't know why that one was out and around here. Just close it up tight, when you leave."

"We will and thanks again. How much do I owe you?"

"Nothing. You gave us a meal and that was well appreciated." they went to the door, "Well goodbye folks and good luck."

"Bye!" we all shout as they descend the stairs.

We close the door, get the ladder out of the floor, close up the hole and put the toilet back in the bathroom. Turning out the lights in the crawl space, was the end of that adventure.

"You know, that was exciting!" Amy says, "I don't need to go through that again, but it was exciting."

"The last time those fronts met there was the flooding and ice storm." I inform them.

Tanya chimed in with, "I could stay home for the winters, unless it is somewhere warm like Cuba was."

"What a week this has been and it's not over yet."

Amy calls down from the loft, to the other women, "They really know how to use that plough. They scooped the snow from both sides of the van, so all we need to do is brush off the rest."

"I think we need hoists for the food near the trailer and tents, to get them hanging from the trees, in case of bears."

"Shall we finish our game?" Marie requests.

"Yes please." from Amy and Tanya.

I say, "Sure!"

"You weren't playing."

"I'll just sit and read then."

We settled down to waste the day away, happy to be cleared out. I won't have to barrel through the lane drifts.

That night was an early one. We fell asleep fast and woke up late. It was a satisfying night. It was a beautiful day to be up for. The sun was out and blinding, against the bright, white, snow. This is what we usually miss, when we are in Cuba. It starts the day after we leave. It was an adventure though. We will be happy to get home. Marie is gathering the bedding to bring home and wash. Amy is cooking brunch. Tanya is out walking to the van. She wants to see where best path is, so she can show us where to go. She wants to do her part. I am crashing on the bed, after it has been stripped. I am resting to avoid the backlash.

When Tanya comes back in the door, she looks rattled. "I saw a lot of animal tracks on the lake side of the house, and up the shoreline. It was after the plough had been here. They were around the van and they went off to the Youngs' house. Like dog tracks, or wolves."

"Did you see the animals at all?"

"No. Just the tracks."

"They could be long gone by now then. They could have gone through during the night." I get up and set the sound affects and their triggers. Then we sit down to eat.

After the dishes are cleaned up and washed, we pack up and go out to the van along Tanya's path. At the van, she had already brushed off the snow from the windows and grill area. I pack the stuff in and then pull ahead to get the back of the van cleaned off. Marie has it clean and she is knocking the snow off the roof. I get in the passenger side and she climbs in to the driver's seat.

We get down to the road and see that it is still only one lane. Marie is nervous about that. We switch places and I drive until the roads are wider. The sides are towering above the roof of the van. After only a kilometre, she spots some blue flashing lights ahead. I slow down, to find out if they are coming this way. When I get to a spot to pull off, I stop and wait, until Marie sees where they are going. They are going away from us, she deems, so we go on. When we get to where the lights were, we are able to switch back, because the road is two lanes wide, now.

"Mom, remember the summer Gramma died and you had to drive home from Picton. You had to get by those tractor-trailers. There were three in a row on either side of you. You floored it and went screaming past them. These high walls here remind me of that."

"That was twenty five years ago, Amy. How could you remember that?"

"I saw your fears of that snow canyon and that memory popped into my head from your mind."

We move along at a good clip, for a snow covered road. The main roads and the highways should be much better. There are more flashing lights ahead. We get to these quickly, they are police cars blocking the road. We stop for one cop who asks where we are headed. When we tell him that we're going down through Peterborough, he says we'll have to wait here. There is no detour open and there's a major area blocked by cars stranded in the drifts. They had been using snowmobiles, to help get the ploughs through, and missed one car, that was pushed into another. That shut down the road, until they could investigate it. There were other spots, where the abandoned cars and trucks, had nearly piled into each other, and narrowly missed being damaged. I asked the cop if there were any connections with other areas. I was told that there were but because of the difficulty in moving the road crews, they were still closed. I asked if it would be better for us to go back to our cottage. He said it would help greatly to get recovery vehicles in to pick up the abandoned cars.

So, back we go to the cottage and more roughing it. We imagine the kids flocking to the southern beaches, with white powdered sand. Here we have the wrong kind, of white powdered beaches.

We cart the laundry bags, of bedding, in and remake the beds. We are starting to smell musky. There is no shower, no hot water, and only one sink, and that's in the kitchen. The water is not hooked up. We had not brought anymore water than we needed, for dish washing, cooking and drinking. We had planned on staying this long, but we weren't very realistic on the conditions, and that there was no other source of water, not frozen. We start to gather pots of snow and while they are on the stove, we bring storage containers full to add.

It takes less time to boil water from cold temperatures, than mild. Once we have some hot water, we can get some semblance of clean. At least we will smell less disgusting. All of that climbing, and crawling around the cottage, helped to make this bathing in the common room, necessary.

After cleaning ourselves up, we could think of getting some food. We brought more than we needed, and that will be just enough. Tomorrow, we will go as far as we can, and get to a town, that might have a place to stay.

When we were coming up here, we had been blinded by the emotion of cottage ownership, and we had not planned on this magnitude of storm. Being in love with the idea, of owning a cottage, has fooled us into thinking of the benefits of seclusion and restful pursuits. Thinking of the warm hearth and snowy vistas, was hardly realistic, for this cottage, and in this stage of completion. We have survived our foolishness, so far. The near asphyxiation in the venting disaster, being trapped in a very remote location, with only the electric heat and propane stove, stranded with a buried vehicle, were all against us. The fact that that flimsy power line from the road, all the way in here, stayed up and had not had its feed knocked out was almost miraculous.

We thank God, for our survival and the sharp eyes of the plough operators. Their cab height was particularly advantageous, with the height of those hills and the depth of those snow banks. The trees had kept the lane free, with the wind being funnelled through it. The deep snow was in the lower areas and up against structures. The wind coming down the lake, was wicked and would have been horrendous, to attempt to get through it.

The night was a welcome excuse, to huddle up in our beds, and cuddle close to our mates. The dynamics of our household, was strained until we took to heart the necessary attitude adjustment the situation required. Once made, that adjustment brought peaceful harmony and openness. If the power should fail now, we would have a chance for an exodus, tomorrow.

In the morning, the room was still warm. The house was filled with the bright sunlight of a crystal clear winter's day. We cooked the food we had left, and sat down to eat. The fresh air from the open window, serving as our vent, was very chilled. The cottage was cooling faster than we could take. So, we closed the window and turned the heaters on high, but they were not working. We tried the lights and found the hydro was out. I checked the breakers and they were good.

"Well ladies, we are out of options from this place. We have to leave, while we still have the body comfort we have. Bundle up to keep it, then pack up the rest, and we will start for home." We dressed first until we could just move around awkwardly. Dishes were wiped clean and left, to be washed when we returned. Bedding was tossed back into the bags and the trekking to the van was begun. The path was easier, after being trampled down by the previous trips. We saw no further signs of animal activity. There were more places in the region to get their attention. They might drop by later, to see if we had gone. That gunshot had stirred them to get away from here.

On the road again was easier. It had been ploughed wider. We could move a little quicker, but we needed to watch for things pulling out of the tributary lanes. We followed our preferred route. Swinging down toward Peterborough, then heading southwest toward highway 401. Progress was good today. There had been a concerted effort to open the travel ways. High banks were still a problem, but that will take time. We keep going as far as we can before looking to get a meal. Power outages are evident all along the roadway. All-way stop signs were put up where lights had been out. Signs asking travellers to go slower than usual, were placed along the way. Many temporary signposts dotted the landscape, as narrow as it was. Visibility was good straight ahead, but in many places, you were in a snowy canyon. In Peterborough, we found that some restaurants were closed and most other businesses were, too. We found a place that was open and pulled in. It was a 'mom and pop' business and once inside, we were told that they had no power, but were serving cold food to those that needed some and they had some hot coffee from their propane stove out back. They couldn't use the kitchen, as the vents weren't working, and the gas was turned off, because of a leak, in the area. They said the storm was bad all over southern Ontario, Quebec and the north-eastern states. The Maritimes are being pounded by it now.

We had coffee and took some sandwiches with us. They did not want to charge us, because they were likely, going to have to throw out the food, before things got back to normal. They were just wanting to help people that were in need of it. We paid them the price on their menus, just to have them keep that charitable effort going. They were going to need to replace that food anyway, and that would help cover the deductible on their claim.

It was like that in many places, in this type of situation, people were out to help the ones that needed it. We had to watch our cash, in case we were stuck somewhere else along the line. Our gas was conserved as much as we could. Gas pumps don't work without power and we don't know, how far we have to go, before we will need it. We are driving slow, in case we need to stop quickly, and to conserve fuel. All roads are snow covered.

When we get to the highway, it is just as bad, but without the canyon effect. Traffic is light and slow moving. People are driving responsibly. The wind is light and that keeps the visibility good. It's not often that you get a pleasant, leisurely drive, on a 400 series highway. I should amend that, because you are tense, from hanging onto that steering wheel and watching for brake lights.

Marie does not like driving in snow. With the traffic being light, she is having me drive, while I can, so that she can have a rest. I have always liked driving in snow, because I have had so much practise in it, that it is second-nature to me. I tell people, I took the crash course and nobody ever laughs. I wonder why.

While the driving is slow, Marie trusts me, to continue being careful. Silly woman!

We are getting to Toronto and decide to call Nicholas, to see if we can stop for a visit. We are getting low on fuel, and have to get off the highway, to get it. He says it is okay. We ask him, if he has power, and he does!

We set our course for his place, and find a gas station, on the way. They had not lost power here for very long. When we get inside his house we get a warm greeting from the family. We enjoy a nice visit and then, we have to get back on the road.

Getting on the highway is so much better than other times. The construction in the area is done. The traffic is moving better because of it, and the volume is light. We don't have to conserve fuel now, so we can go a little faster, but we still want to maintain the general caution, that is being shown. The radio is still asking people, to stay off the roads, if they don't need to travel.

We make it home in one piece. Tanya is invited to stay, if she wanted. Of course, that is a silly question. She would do anything, to stay with Amy. She calls home to let them know she is back and is well. She asks if she can accept the invitation. She gets permission and squeals with delight.

Chapter Twenty Two

Hard Facts

Tanya's father Dave, has been sent to a halfway house. He was doing well, and was being given a conditional parole. He is in Toronto, and the family is encouraged by the reports. Many people are put through this placement, before being allowed, to resume a normal life. Dave has been a model prisoner.

Tanya is staying with us, so she doesn't know her dad's situation. The family had not visited him. The 'moms' weren't comfortable, with the idea of being so close to someone, that would do that toward them. Tanya had had mixed feelings about him. She had written and sent pictures of Amy and herself. They were of the working days at the cottage, the days canoeing and some with her moms. She told him how happy she was, and the plans that she was making. It was a picture of a happy family life.

To Dave, it was a picture of a family life, that was excluding him. They had not brought her to see him. They had not written him. They had not seen him, or talked to him, since before, the night of the shooting. He was a model prisoner. Like most models, he was posing. Posing with detachment. He smiled for the viewers. He walked the way he had to walk, to get where he wanted to go. Now he was there. He could go out into society, and do all the tricks, they wanted him to do. He played the game, and played it well. His old firm was considering, having him back, on a probationary period, if he maintained his progress. He can do that. He can do anything, they give him a chance to do. He was hoping for a chance to do something. Something in particular. He had changed. He was calculating. He had a mask he would wear for the viewers. It was nearly invisible. It was very lifelike. Of course, it was his old face. The one he had lots of practise with. It was still familiar to him. His new face wasn't ready to be shown, yet.

When Tanya did find out, when Brenda got the call. She thought her daughter would like to know about him. So she called her right away. Tanya was startled by the news. His letters hadn't hinted at this. She was very glad, but startled. She asked if they were going to visit with him, but was told, no. They did not feel safe. They had an inkling of something, not right. Just a feeling. They didn't tell her. They just said, "no," to the question. Tanya felt down about that, but she bounced back and stayed with her Amy, and just loved her Amy.

The break will be over soon. The women go out shopping. I stay home and write up our experiences, on our travesty of a vacation. What was I thinking? Amy says, that that was the problem. I was thinking. That was always my line. The grandchildren said, 'it's a Papa line.' While Marie taxis the girls around, I try to figure out the best project to handle. We've uncovered some big things. I should have done this before we left.

I lose my place in thought, and I am always scrambling to find it, in a panic. That is connected to my personal power failures. My energy drops and I lose where I am in the world. If my mind was in Europe, I would be scrambling all over Asia. I panic in slow motion. My mind slows down to about five words a minute, or less. My speech slows, I clumsily search an empty space, for the hints, of where I could have been. They would send me for tests and find nothing. They would send me to a different doctor, every time, and I would have to start, at the same place, and go nowhere.

Amy can help me. Amy knows where I was. She can get me to Europe, instead of me going to Asia. She can find the needle in my haystack. She can't find the root, of the cause, and no body thinks the problem is there.

I love having her in my head when I am lost. I don't want to enslave her, to being my guide, to the Tom Wrent universe. Like my dad wanted us to have a childhood. I want Amy to have a life. I don't really believe in the reason for our manacles anymore. I want her to be able to have her life of freedom, to think with only one brain. I don't want her to have the three of us inside her brain. But, I still love to have her in mine. She gives me a day, where there were only hours. She gives me a story, where there were only paragraphs. I have a quality of life, far more full, than I, could ever have filled it.

The girls are already back. It was hours, they say. I hear them talk. There is something in the voice of a woman, that soothes me. I guess it isn't every woman, but the ones in my life do. If I had a choice to live anywhere, it would be somewhere with women. In that case, I have it made to order.

Tanya is going home now. The mood in my head dims from Amy's loss. I have had depression, after years of taking antidepressants. I can handle it, by turning on the light, in my imagination. I do it before the spiral starts. When Amy gets feeling down, it sends me to the spiral, faster. I turn on the imaginary light, and I could hear wheels squealing, as if it was a car. It's like the pilot, fighting the wheel, in his nose diving plane. The scenes you see in movies. I can do it but, I would like to avoid her lows. We get deeper into our synchronism. We feel the vibration of each others rhythm. Sure, we some times are numb to it when we are busy. That is not the case, if we are on our cruising course. No bumps, or turbulence to avoid. I have likely felt different about it, at times and I could get confused about it, but this is how I can see it, now.

Marie gets Amy going with a project, to take her mind off, the empty space at her side. They have a new baby coming in the family, and there are gifts to make. A new baby always perks them up. A new baby, a wedding, a new home for someone, are all good mood makers.

Tanya is missing Amy, just as much, and the ladies are working on her stimuli. They have a trip to take, to see a relative, in London, Ontario. They have some health problems to make adjustments for. They have asked the girls down to take care of it for them.

Dave is being the model resident of the halfway house. The better he seems to be, the more of a chance, he will be able to carry out his plan. His outlook took a dive in prison. He seems to have suffered a personality, failure. It is completely adverse to his old self. He doesn't let it show though. It is as if he was possessed. Possessed by a calculating, manipulative, demon. Sure, it could be. Not many people believe in demons. The TV shows suggest differently though. He has switched his internal side. Whether it is possession, regression, or any other -sions, he is not going to play nicely.

How do I know all this? I am relating the information from the aftermath. Things have happened, as they have in many places, to many people, just like Dave and his family. This time it involves us, and it never gets to you, quite as hard, until you know the people, and are entwined in a part of their life. There was another guy I had known. Someone who could have acted the same way. He chose not to. He had the chance and similar reason, but chose to go a different way. Why couldn't Dave have done that? Why did Dave do this? You get a look into things, that lead to this, and try as you may, you can't see, the purpose, or the reason. Domestic crime is the most dangerous part of a policeman's job. There is no predicting the passion. They can't trust anything in an incident of this type. They have to clean it up many times, because it happens without warning. Either that, or the warning was never passed on.

Dave didn't get drunk this time. Dave had a plan this time. The method and the results were clear to Dave, this time. Maybe it was that bash on the head, that he took, the first time. Maybe it broke something in his brain. That was the cause, of the thousands of others, that have done this. This time, Dave was going in sober and with intent. He walked up to the door of the house. He took out the window, of the door, and walked through the door, he unlocked. He walked quietly, into the bedroom of his ex-wife and her accomplice, he saw the forms in the bed and detonated the bomb he had made. The house was obliterated. They thought it was a gas build-up from a leak. After the investigation got started, and they received a call from Toronto, that reported Dave's absence, and they realized what they were dealing with. The news report was devastating to us. This great part of our lives was torn away. We had lost the beating heart of my Amy. She was with us, but she was not. She was in shock. The news was very descriptive of the scene. The real story had not come over, the first time. The next report, was when we found the worst part. We had called Amy's therapist, from her amnesia case, the one who helped her when she had had her breakdown. We were ready to take her there, to help get her out of the pit, she was in. I had never been there, in that pit before, and it was all I could do, to keep from being there with her.

Marie was helping her dress. I was getting myself ready. Then, the phone rang. I don't usually answer the phone, unless I recognized it, by name, or by number. I don't know why I answered it this time. It was a shock, that nearly blew me through the wall. I heard a very familiar voice, that could not possibly, be real. I heard the sweet voice of Tanya. I said, "I'm sorry, I couldn't hear you."

Tanya said, "We're okay! We weren't home! Is Amy there?"

"Yes! Yes, I'll give her the phone!" I ran to Amy, who was still only half dressed. I shoved the phone in her face, then put it to her ear. I yelled to have Tanya speak, "Okay!"

Tanya cried into the phone, "Amy, I'm okay! I wasn't home! None of us were!"

Amy nearly passed out. Recovering, she grabbed for the phone, "Tanya?!"

"Amy! I'm okay! I'm with Mom and Milli, in London!"

"You're okay?!"

"Yes, we had to go right away last night! I was going to call you today and let you know! We just saw the news!"

Amy cried and laughed at the same time. "Why are you there?!"

"My Aunt Belinda is sick, and she has to have things arranged for her, and Mom is the only one she has, that can help."

"Oh, thank you God!" Amy yells up to Him.

I get my cell phone and call, to cancel her appointment, and explain why. There are screams and shouting through the office. They say okay and let me call the police. Amy can't let Tanya go, but when we insisted, so they can call the police, she relents.

I had told them to expect the call and that the women were alive.

Brenda's call sent a reaction in the police station, similar to the doctor's office. They had London Police go to the home where the family were to check on them and get their status confirmed. They were also there to offer counselling.

We felt that the world, just became weightless. When we woke up and heard the story, four people were dead, that held significant roles in our life. Hours later, three of them were reborn, returned from the dead. My beliefs were strong before and I was thinking that they solidified. I realize that many people do not share my beliefs. I also know that I can't be one to stand and preach. I can believe and so I do. He gives us freedom of choice. For this reason, I let everyone make their own claims and choices. I've made mine. They won't change it.

Amy wanted to climb through the phone to be with Tanya. I wanted to help her. We had to wait. They have no home to come home to. They have a reason to be there, and they need to take care of their obligations. They have a place to stay there. They won't have one here, until the insurance takes care of that, for them.

What were the forms on that bed? That was Tanya's laundry and shopping. They had just thrown them there, and left.

Knowing Tanya was alive and well, energized Amy. Marie and I were feeling very good too. We called our friends, to tell them the news and they wanted to throw them a party, to celebrate their fortune.

Their fortune. With the survival of the victims, we forget that one still died. It was his choice, but he was Tanya's father. There is still an emotional toll taken. She will have a hole in her heart.

Amy goes back to school without Tanya. She is still, right there in her heart. She could not feel down today. She was busy answering questions, about the ordeal, all day. Students, teachers and even the principal. Everybody had to get the story and congratulate her on Tanya's survival. The news media were flashing the story and had sent a crew to do a spot at the school. They got Amy on camera and had interviewed her. They had interviews from London, and the world around them rejoiced. One murder-suicide had turned out right. The victims live.

Chapter Twenty Three

Back Among The Living

The moms had been given an extended leave from their jobs, following the horror averted. They finished the arrangements for Brenda's sister. The insurance has found them temporary accommodations, while their house was rebuilt. They were tempted to say 'forget it', but decided that they had to rebuild to get anything out of the home. They have a rental place near Tanya's school.

When she gets back to school, it is a strain on Tanya. The eyes of the world are, still, upon her and she needs that to stop. She needs to finish grieving for her late father. She has the counselling but needs time away. She has to get it out of her mind, and the only way to do that, successfully, is to be allowed to grieve. She takes a leave from her classes. Amy struggles to see her going through it all. Tanya is grieving the loss of the dad that she knew long ago. The one who was there after working late. The one that helped raise her. He is not the one that blew himself up. He was the one who she played with. The one who taught her to ride a bicycle. The one she lost a few years back after he left. The one she nearly got back. That was her Dad.

Amy saw Tanya after school. She stayed a couple hours a day with her, but let her have the time alone. The time she needed to reflect and cry it out.

When Tanya returned to school the second time, there was still the people staring and asking questions. She could take it a bit more. She had shed her tears and done her grieving. She was not back to her old self. She may not ever be her old self again, but she was moving forward. An empty corner of her heart and mind. A significant blot on her memory. They will not likely ever be gone. They will slip back into the background and become part of the things that shaped her life and her outlook on life.

The school year is drawing to a close. Tanya was able to get through most of what she missed. She did average on her exams. I remember how I had not done well after losing my dad. She did better than I had. Amy had helped her absorb what she could.

Amy had done extremely well in her exams and will be the valedictorian, of her graduating class. She has received awards for several achievements. The future is here for her. The one that was in plain sight. Now she really has to make up her mind. She has to choose her school and set her course.

After the scene at the cottage, Amy realized that she could not choose her college, by its proximity to her dream. She needs to opt for one, that will provide the best course of action, to reach her goals. She scours the lists of courses, offered by the best colleges, within her field of study. She has been awarded scholarships and that helps to home in on the proper choice for her.

She has relatives she could stay with for some schools. Her brother in Toronto, along with a cousin there too. An uncle in Windsor area, and us here at home. Her top three choices. She decides to go with Waterloo University for her BSc. It was listed as a top university for psychology, in Ontario.

I am surprised at this. It is close, but not enough to stay home. We are all disappointed, but it is her career choice. Tanya is likely to go to Guelph. That is still years away. Amy hints at doing some of her studies through an online college. She will be able to work with a contractor, or her brother-in-law, while taking the courses. She wants to be away for the first year, so she can evaluate the field and be sure that it is the one she wants.

I never went to college. All my family went to various universities and colleges. I could not retain much in the school room setting. I realize that my teachers hoped I could achieve more, but I had no idea why. The amount of learning I did since leaving school, would have satisfied some of them. It was just not a good place for me to learn, in a classroom. I did retain some of the work from school. I remembered it twenty or thirty years later. They kept telling me I wasn't applying myself. I felt the same about my teachers. I felt they could do better than that. I got honours math, sleeping through class. The teacher would pick on people that were not paying attention, but left me to sleep. I had no problem with that class. My kids have put themselves through the schooling they wanted. We tried to help with logistics, but that was all we could do. I am proud of what they have accomplished. It was their money, their choice, and their effort that got them through. It got them where they want to be. Happy.

Amy is on the same path. She has set her sights. She is putting in the effort. She will be paying for the tuition. All I can do for her is logistics. I'll take her there. I will get her a vehicle to use. It won't be hers, but it will go where she goes. I think, if she can get through the Bachelor of Science phase. She will be able to go all the way, to get her doctorate. She has some help with the scholarship. She will be able to keep the momentum, with her drive. She will even pull off a trade while she's at it.

I tire thinking about all that dynamic energy, coming from that little package. She is ready to resume the work on our cottage. Tanya is with her on that. I have the plans drawn up for approval on the barn-workshop-greatroom. It will slightly dwarf the cottage. It just makes more sense, putting it all away from the main cottage, for the stability of the foundation. We will be filling in the flood plain behind the cottage. While we do that we are putting in a new septic bed and the water system. All of this will be to prevent erosion and keep our structures safe. We will still have the low lying area between the cottage and the lake and river. Leaving that untouched will help keep the rest safe. It allows the runoff to take place as usual. Undisturbed ground is so much stronger, than freshly shored up fill that hasn't had time to settle. We need to let it settle for the tile bed is underneath it.

So with plans, gathered materials and a good supply of food, we are off to the cottage. I have Tanya riding shotgun for me. Marie has Amy riding with her. This gives us free communication between vehicles and a safety net. It also allows for more cargo room. Marie is comfortable driving her car and not having to ride with me. I am comfortable with Tanya's good eyesight. Amy is comfortable riding with her mother. That leaves poor Tanya. If she could sit on the edge of her seat safely, she would. She has a strong handle on the door post in front of her, and the seatbelts are good. I also have airbags in this old van. Tanya is tall so they are okay for her. Amy however is glad to ride with Marie for that reason as well.

I am scheduling the stops to my conditions. Everyone is fine with that. If we come in at night, it won't be a problem, so time is not of the essence, this trip. We are heading out on a Tuesday morning in the area of noon. This will bring us into the city traffic well away from rush-hours. We will be able to get through before it has started. It will still be a busy road. I will take an off ramp, whenever I start to feel the need and we will get into position to get back on, for when I have rested. We will either buy food if it is available there, or eat what we have brought with us. This is low energy travel. We save fuel for the vehicles and we don't wear ourselves down either.

If I see a nice shoreline to visit, or a ravine of exposed rock and fallen trees, I will pull off there, to explore and salvage raw materials. I have been doing this, since Amy and I started our camping trips. I feel it is the most enjoyable way to get where you are going. Marie gets uneasy about stopping so much, but Amy reminds her of the frailty of my energy supply and that it only takes a second, to die on the road. She also points out that "The people we love are in the other car, and we want to be with them in an emergency." A sobering thought, for her to consider.

Once we are out of the city, I am comfortable taking any road if the highway gets too busy. I have GPS on my phone, and we can get the directions to the other car, by me just hearing them. We are far enough north, that we can go up and then across, instead of heading to Peterborough. I went that way, the time I had to take the nap and got disoriented. It is a beautiful ride in any direction.

I tell Amy the change in my plans for the floodplain. I want to put down a load of sand on our beach, while we can get a truck down that far, this summer. This lake is a detached part of another lake which has a more typical terrain. Our section has been filled with sediment that has provided the floodplain shoreline. A marshy bog surrounds some of the cottage properties here. Most lakes in this region are rocky shored and timber lined. The clear lakes and Canadian Shield terrain are the romantic dreams of people looking for cottages. Thousands upon thousands of postcard beautiful lakes dot the province and this region is one of the most comfortable to live on. As if there weren't enough, there has been man made lakes built in this region. I remember my aunt and uncle's cottage on a man made lake near Peterborough. It was a playground as well as a water source for the city and the locks. I have only been there one time. Beautiful memories.

Amy knows the lake I was talking about. She says it is Rice Lake. I got to steer my cousin's boat across it. There was a hive of bees terrorizing the cottage, that weekend.

Well we have arrived at the drive to the cottage with only three stops and scored some nice pieces of wood and stone for the features we will incorporate into the design. I have been studying engineering and architecture since I left school. All of it was casual instruction from friends, family, libraries, and some on the job training with heavy equipment. A hobby rich with diversity and some sources for technical assistance. The people you meet in the day to day social excursions. Just like our neighbour at the cottage. Joe Young was an electrician, turned engineer. I met him through Amy's connection to his son. An example of the rich sources you nearly trip over that will come to be an advantage unplanned for. Blacksmiths, welders, carpenters, glazers, plumbers. Many, many people in your everyday life, that you can provide with work, or learn an aspect for your personal use.

I have looked through magazines and books to absorb as much diverse information on equally diverse topics. I said one time, 'I could write a book.' and was told to do just that. Someday I will write that book. But until then I have a cottage to finish and a barn to raise. Oh, you caught that did you. You are quick.

We get to the house with plenty of light to spare. I love daylight savings time. I unpack the car, while the girls cart it up to the house. This will be our food and clothing, our deco items and utensils, appliances of the smaller variety and some of the niceties of civilized life. In the truck will be the equipment and the materials. That can all be unloaded tomorrow.

While they put things in order, I go across the way to see if Evelyn and Brent are to home. I don't see a vehicle, but Brent could be working, so I continue on my path. I knock on the door and with a short wait Evelyn answers. We greet like old friends that we have become. The mood is bright around my neighbour and it feels good to see her thus. She is getting things opened up for some friends to visit. They will be coming anon, so I give her my best hug and take my leave.

I walk back the way I came and take it slow and easy. There is nothing that I can add to the commotion in our place. Amy is busy and I take the opportunity to review the position of our outbuildings, such as they are. The trailer looks to be steady and stable. The position of the barn is unaffected by the course nature had taken. There does not seem to be any sign of erosion this year. I suspect there may have been, if that blizzard had not followed the thaw. There is ample room to get the decks spread out along the tree line. The view from the tents will be amazing, as amazing as it can get, on our land. I walk down and across the area to be filled. I have marked it all on the plans to present at the township office. I want Brent to give me a hand with that.

Amy will be busy setting up the decks for the tents. She and Tanya will be getting the accommodations ready for the warm nights. It will be cooler out here and with a smudge pot of sage, we can be more comfortable in the tents. Marie will have to be convinced of that. At least the views will help her decide in our favour.

I forgot to ask Evelyn about Brent. I suppose, I will find out soon enough. I see her guests arriving. I head in to survey the condition of the loft. When the girls had gone into the cottage, they heard the sound track and it startled them. They scolded me when they came back for the next load.

I get inside the door to be right where they wanted me at the time. My dinner is ready and they did not have to call for me. Amy's thoughts were busy up until I entered the door. I could not have timed it better. They had taken care of the main floor arrangements and had not looked upstairs. I wonder if we have any new pets up there.

We sit down to eat and enjoy a leisurely pace. They can have some time to breathe some. The events of the drive are reviewed and Tanya gave my driving a shaky score above average. I'll take it. I was scaring myself at times, as Amy had told Marie. Marie didn't ace the review either. I thought Amy would have avoided that rating. She asked, so she was told. The meal made up for the bad driving experience. We all were in agreement there. After the meal was done, I peaked up in the loft. It was messy but hard to define from the ladder. I climbed up to see there had been some probing in the damaged area. I checked the sound track there and it was still operable. It startled the two unconnected girls. Amy got a laugh out of that and took the scolding, I would have received. The ruse had worked with the raccoons, just as it did with the girls. I was a little disappointed that there wasn't a furry pet, stuck up in the loft. Amy was too, but reminded me of the damage they can do.

We play a card game and then read for a time. After that the girls are off to bed and I read on. I need to get a laptop. I have done all my writing on my desktop and it is suffering the test of time.

The night is alive up here. Owls, raccoons, bears and wolves. I know they are here. When they see someone is here, they make themselves scarce. The cats will have to stay around the tents.

One thing I have brought up with me is a bunch of solar panels and some batteries. This is the start of our solar bank. Once we get the placement ready I will build a rack for them near the trailer. This will be the main power source for the trailer and tents.

The sleepers are adding to the night sounds. I need to join them and bring the orchestra to its full compliment. Tanya seems to be at ease here. I think her grieving as nearly run its course. She will always have times, but don't we all. All that have lost a parent, or a friend. It never completely ends.

Chapter Twenty Four

Finish What You Have Started

I am sleeping in, when the morning comes around, trying to make it 'til noon. That is always a plus for me. The girls get up to get things done. Amy has to stop Marie from waking me again.

"How are you going to know what he wants done?"

"Mom, you and I have talked about this before. I know what he is thinking, as he thinks it, asleep or awake. I work better if he is sleeping, because then, his thoughts are all mine."

"He needs to do something too." she complains.

"He does better on his own time. I do better on my own time. We work well together, if he is well rested and thinking straight. Give him a chance to get his rest. He fell asleep at two. I want him to be able to work. Let him sleep."

"What should I do then?"

"Come out and help Tanya and I get the decks started. We will need that done first."

Marie did as Amy directed and saw how well everything fit together. "How do you know how to build the decks?"

"From Dad's head. I play it like a DVD player. I see it being set up and reinforced. Where I need to put this and that. I get it all from his memory."

"He has a bad memory."

"He has bad recall. He has a good memory. He is like an encyclopaedia set. Anything I want to know is in there and I can access it easier, than he can."

"He can't remember much when I talk with him."

"You have bad recall, too. I can get clear thoughts from your memory, but not from your mouth, Mom. I hear you arguing about something and both of you are getting it wrong. You both are bad at remembering anything."

"How do you know?'

"I can get inside your head and find what I need with out you even trying to remember any of it. I have private access to anything you think."

"What would you like me to do?"

"Get on the other end of this board and set it in the slot on the other side."

Once they started working and not talking, they accomplished much of the deck quickly and were ready for a ride in the canoe. I had been up a little while and Amy asked if I would like to go for a ride. I was all for that and headed for the beach. I brought the flotation vests, which surprised Marie.

"Whose idea was this ride?"

"Mine."

"How did he know about it?"

"I told him a few minutes ago. Mom, you really have to get with the program."

Canoeing everyday is the reward for getting things done. Getting an early start and accomplishing the days project, will give you a break to enjoy a gentle paddle along the lake. After that, we get at the next job and go for another ride. Until I have lost the weight I need to lose, I cycle and canoe and then work on a project as my reward. This system gets things done and keeps us healthy.

When we get back they go to finish the trailer deck and I get cycling. Half an hour is my goal, but in good cycling weather I stay as long as I can. I head for the store, when there are any groceries on the list for a 'need today' meal. Otherwise, I go to find something new. I would like to get Marie cycling with me. She has a bike, but would rather walk. Up here, the scenery may help her to get cycling again. Cycling has less wear on your body, and gets you out to see more than a walk would. We will still hike through the woods. We all like to do that and it gives you some movement in places the other modes don't.

I have some issues when walking. I have the vertigo and holding the canes aggravates my arthritic hands. That is the basic problem. I have the scar tissue from having the broken needle removed, because it was sewn up so that the flesh was drawn into a lump. It doesn't stop me. It just doesn't let me enjoy it. Hence, the use of an adult tricycle. I can also haul treasures found, in the trailer I've rigged on it. I have picked up things along the roads that I can burn, or use as fill in the building foundation and walls. Things like plastics that aren't recyclable in some areas. I either put the in whole bottles with caps on, or melt them into balls and thrown in that way. I have some tires, I have picked up off the roadside, to use around the dock, when we build it. They will keep the ice from crushing the dock in winter, and keep the boats from being scraped along it, in the other seasons.

I had wanted to use old tires for foundation walls, but that has been shelved to use the 'easier to work with' straw bales, on a slab foundation. The trailer deck is done. Now I go to work in setting it up. The second add-a-room will need the channel installed along the roof. The awning will attach to it and the room, to the awning. The deck in back of the trailer is lower to fit this addition in it. It folds up in winter, to make a storage shed for the camping gear. Out in front, the deck is supported by the weight of the trailer, and some temporary posts in concrete deck blocks. I hope to have a more stable configuration, for next season.

It is a peaceful, but impressive sight, with the shelters done and that is our goal for the end of the week. Having installed the channel, I leave it to let the caulking set and cure over night. This will keep moisture from getting in through the screw holes.

It is important to minimize the power tool use, when neighbours are entertaining guests. Evelyn's guests are with her still and I wouldn't want compressors and saws, annoying my guests either. It is a good excuse to go and enjoy the lake.

We get the canoe out for another paddle, around the lake. We have four of us paddling, in one canoe. That moves us along at a pretty fair clip. When we come upon an idyllic scene, we stop paddling and coast along. We see a moose getting out of the lake in an inlet. We watch until it gains cover of the wood. A beaver is repairing its mound. A heron glides across the water, a few feet above it. He's just moving to another spot and takes no notice of us.

Time is getting short for our cruise. We turn around and head for home, to get our supper. We wave to Evelyn and her guests, as we pass. Pulling up on the beach reminds me to get hold of Brent. The girls hang up the life jackets, while Marie and I, tip over the canoe and set it off the beach. Heading in to the cottage, we catch sight of Brent arriving home. He waves and then turns in and pulls up alongside the van. We greet him and I get to my point, before I forget. We set a time to go into town, and we leave him to visit with the girls. I help Marie, by setting up the dinner table, as she prepares the food. We eat more cooked food, with her here. We cooked before, but it is a requirement with Marie.

Marie heads to the door, to call them in for supper. I ask her, where she is going? She tells me, as if it is a strange thing to ask. I tell her to just send the thought to Amy, and they will come. She never thinks of that, and she says, "I prefer to do things the regular way." I can't argue with that. Amy tells me to have her call. Brent is talking and she will need a reason to interrupt him. Marie opens the door and calls them in. Brent says he'll talk later and lets them go. Walking back across the room, Marie sticks out her tongue at me and I have to laugh. Seriously, if I don't, I will pay. Amy shows me another good reason for the regular way of communication. The fact that she does this silently, does not make her point clearly.

Brent and I meet to take the proposal to the town offices. They give me the forms for submitting it and the request for dumping and filling near a water front. I let Brent go, and I sit down to make sure I have all the information, and then to fill in the forms. Besides showing me where to go, he got the initial talking done, that I would not have been able to handle. I stayed there, filling in the forms until they were complete. I handed them to the receptionist and paid the fee, then left.

On the way home I found a pile of rocks that had been cleared from a farmer's field. Gold! These rocks are coming up through the soil in fields, where they have been since the last Ice Age. They pile them there to clear the fields for ploughing and keep obstacle free for the livestock feeding. I have to unload the van before I can load them up, so I head back to camp. I pull in and get close to the decks to dump the load off. The three girls help get that done and we go to load the rocks. With my helpers, the pile is gone in two loads. "What are you going to use these for?" Marie asks.

"These are for the fireplace and gardens." I point out that, "The great room will demand a proper fireplace, and one to match the region."

"Where is the greatroom going to be?"

"It will be on the end of the barn. It will be better there, because there is room there to have the reinforced foundation, all in one pour. Amy and Tanya decided that. We can have gatherings in there, without disturbing the sleeping areas."

"Attached to a barn?"

"Barn is a loose fitting word for this. It will have a garage in the lower level, a workshop in the upper level, and a two storey greatroom on the end. If the cottage doesn't hold up well, we can convert the barn to living space."

"Boy you think of everything. Don't you?"

"We think of everything. I'm including you."

"What have I contributed?"

"Besides labour? A reason to do this. A family that you provided. Let's finish these shelters. It looks like rain coming. They have to be covered with the tarps." The crew got busy covering up the tents and tightening the ties to hold the tarps solid. There needs to be railings put up but that is another day. Another tarp shelters the load, we took from the van, to get the rocks. We get the tarps tied down and then get the lifejackets inside.

The rain hits hard. It's coming from the east, so it could be a big soaking, we're in for. The inmates get comfortable. The games come out and we are ready for a long stay indoors. I need to get a dish put up here, a phone line would be good. I like to see the progress of the storms. With this one and that blizzard, I feel the need to be connected here. I don't need to let everyone that comes up, know that though. I just got an image of the canoe floating down river. I get up to go tie it to something and I see the door close. Amy is on it and back at the door dripping wet in three minutes.

"Thanks." I hand her a towel.

"It's not very cold. We could shower out there. No one will see us. Visibility is nil. Step out, lather up and rinse off." She takes her clothes off and grabs the soap. Steps outside and gets cleaned up. She is back in to dry off. I have left the room to let them have some privacy. Marie comes and lets me know, when it's my turn. I was afraid of that. I get outside and it is torrential. It takes no time at all to get cleaned up, under that rain shower head. I take my time, though. I don't need to topple down these stairs. We need a bigger porch.

I just thought of how to get things placed here. The bathroom is just the other side of the wall. I will put the biological filter trough along this side, and the holding tank under a nice big porch. An outdoor shower is already planned for the tent area. We don't need two of those, yet. The porch will protect the door, so it won't be blocked by snow again. "Thank you, Lord!"

I step back in to get dried off and dressed. Amy is drawing my vision on paper. "If we could insulate the tank well enough, we wouldn't have to drain it." Amy suggests.

"It's worth looking into. The barn would have to have the floor poured next year. We do need the water system done first. I'll go to town to get the insulation. You give me a total square footage, that I'll need to get. Write out a list. If we do that, we should insulate all the plumbing, and the crawl space."

"Don't get going crazy, Dad."

"It will give us water for flushing in the winter. The woodstove will be installed And we could come here anytime. We will need an off-road vehicle to get in and out during the winter."

"Yep, he's gone." Amy says, her lips pulled to one side and her eyes roll.

"Honey, we need to take it slower. The money can only go so far." Marie points out.

"You two just watch what we can do, on a shoestring budget. Tomorrow, after the storm has moved out, I'll get to the store and see what I can get." The storm, however had other plans. It was raining for three more days. The centre was stalled over Lake Ontario. It just spun around in one spot, and poured down, the whole time it was there. "I hope the canoe doesn't take that bush, it's tied to, for a ride down the river."

When the rain did stop, it was a real mess. The flood plain was covered and we were just lucky that it stopped when it did. Our equipment was fine. It was up high enough. The car and the van, were surrounded by the new lake level. The canoe got tangled in some other bushes, so it was still there. The depth by the cars was about five inches. We might not get out of here for another couple days.

The teens went out to mess around outside. There is a current through the floodplain. They untie the canoe, flip it over and pull it up to the stairs. They tie it to the bottom step. They play around in the water. 'If you have no choice, have fun', is one of my favourite things to advise. They walk over to check on the neighbours. They find, all is well, except for some cabin fever. They play in the water, sloshing about. They slip on the muddy roadway and boom they go up to their necks. Nearly flat on their backs. Straightening up, they grabbed hold of each other to get on their feet again. You have to laugh. Seeing it, or being in it, will be fond memories. Nothing like a hopeless mess, such as this, to help you let go of your pride, and enjoy.

When they make it back, I meet them at the stairs with some robes. They start to peel off the sloppy mess, slip on the robes and take off the rest. They dump the clump of mud-soaked rags in a hamper. I give them some hot water to rinse themselves. They have stepped back in time, to those years when getting filthy was half the fun. Being free to enjoy adversities. With a semblance of order restored, they come inside to some hot food and soft seating. I envy their adventure.

The following day, the water has receded to its normal levels. New treasures deposited on the space around us. Debris from water swept forests, are dotting the landscape. I am anxious to get the insulation, but that will wait. The slope of the laneway will still be slippery. I could make it out, but at the cost of a chewed up drive and deep ruts to fill. There is no need to go slogging in the muck outside. The clothes, so thoroughly soiled, are strewn along the railings of the porch and stair rails. We had an example of what tropical storms are like down south. It had pushed inland and sat over us until it found its natural course. Swirling above us and the great lakes, it picked up from the lakes and dumped it on us. Two extreme weather events within a few months of each other. We are blessed to endure and survive. How many have not had the good fortune we have, out of this storm? I shudder to think of the possibilities. I wonder how things are at home.

Another day in and our patience is rewarded. The slopes of the lane are dry. I can now, get in and out, with little effect on the landscape. There are many new things in the ditches along the road. I ignore the urge to pick them up. I need to get what I have set out to get. I can scrounge around later.

The women are going over the lodges at the tree line, looking for any damage, and fixing things. There are no furnishings in them so far. We didn't get the wind strength here. We were sheltered by the thick woods to the east of our enclosure. They found some branches had come down, without detriment. They gather these for processing, at a later date. Water inside the shelters concerned them, so they search for tears in the tarps.

I am met with a jammed parking lot, full of people buying materials to repair their buildings. I get through to the insulation section and rest, hoping for someone wanting to help. I am anxious in a different way now. Like the day of the harassing boys, I am drained. I lean over my cart to support myself. I hear a familiar voice call me by name.

"Brent, am I glad to see you? I needed to get insulation for my plumbing and water tanks. I should have waited another day."

"You are better to be here today. The building materials section will be picked clean by tomorrow. The suppliers will be taxed by the storm damage. We got more than usual and we didn't get the full force of it. Have you got a list?"

"Yes, Amy filled it out with the dimensions."

"She's a good person to have for your project. Give me your list, and you go get a scooter, or a wheelchair, and I will get this ready for you."

I did as I was told. It will help him to have me sitting in one of these things. I normally do get one right away. They can help me without as much interruption, while I'm in a chair. He can take the order out for me, and it will go so much faster. He is quickly filling the trolley and then another. He grabs one of his buddies, to get the order filled and to the checkout desk. I will be pushing the limits of my van. I am glad the seats were left at home. I bring the van to the loading bay and then rejoin them. They have rung the order through, as I arrive back. I pay the tab and we sort out the load positioning. It fits! It is to the roof and as tight, as you would want it. I thank them well and get out of their way. There are trucks lining up for space in the loading bay.

The drive home was excruciatingly loud. Styrofoam rubbing, even with it jammed in tight. Brad will be coming up next weekend, to help install the water system. I want to get the parts ready to set in place, fast. Wow, that noise is bad. The radio can't drown it out. Its high pitch cuts through all other sound. Marie would go insane riding in this cacophony. I am so glad to bring this truck to a stop. I get out and just drink in all the sounds of nature. So soft and soothing to my tortured brain. It's like crawling in a toasty warm bed, on a cold winter's day. We have a lot of adhesive for this stuff, but I'm thinking, it is not enough to stop the squeaking.

Amy draws my attention to the shelters. I head up to see if I can figure it out. I check the tarps for wear. We conclude it had to be wind blown moisture. The spray from the force of the water, hitting the surfaces. It was bouncing back up. Virtually raining upwards. We remember seeing it at different times. Hilarious, the phenomenons we are witnessing this year. Wild weather affecting all the corners of the globe. The greenhouse effect is taking all order out of weather systems. It can put snowstorms in the Sahara, heat waves on the mountain tops, and drought in the rainforests. We will worry wickedly with wacky weather. Global warming isn't an orderly occurrence. These storms though, are not the unusual type. They are the heritage of the weather scene, from natural patterns. We are to expect this and have had examples of it, sixty or so years back. Hurricane Hazel was even more devastating in the area this far north.

We set up stairs at the back door. We need to take down the front stairs to place the tanks and filtering trough. The trough has a drain tube running through it, with layers of sand and rock covered by soil and finally plants. Bog plants and vegetables can do well in this filter bed. The wash water passes down on the bed and soaks into the trough. It then filters down through the layers and out through the tube and into the holding tanks. The plants remove phosphates out of the water and they thrive on them. Food solids and dead skin cells will also feed the plants. Things like hair that are washed through are easily scooped out of the beds. In floating homes on Vancouver Island, they use these filter beds to purify water for drinking. Their beds are larger and they don't have the freezing temperatures we have here. I will be placing a greenhouse structure over the filter bed. I will also have a sensor in the soil, to switch on a pump to water the bed during under used times, to keep the plants healthy. The trough can be put in place now, and filled with its components. It hugs the wall on the southwest corner, wrapping around and up to the placement point for the tanks. Underneath it are shelves to house supplies and specific tools to care for it. Insulation will enshroud this area as well. The trough goes into place well enough. The two troughs are joined and sealed. The pipes run through and out on the end near the steps. We fill in the insulation and build the enclosure. The greenhouse kit fits to the troughs upper edges and over the cupboard beneath them. We cover the troughs to keep the rain water from flooding the holding tank. We will put in a water catchment tank later, but that's another story. That is the second tank and will provide water for washing and drinking.

The four of us are putting things right. We dig down along the cottage wall to have the tanks partially in ground. We wrap it with the foam board. We have more around the tank than is called for. The chance of it freezing and cracking is too much of a risk. After placing the oversized container in the depression we made, finishes our preparations. It is quite a job, outfitting a rundown cottage. I love it for the lessons I learn, the peace and serenity of the surroundings. Amy and Tanya, love the freedom it will give them. They enjoy the work they do together. The lessons they learn. Marie loves that we have a place to get away from the city, and look out over the lake. The lake is mostly calm and is great to canoe in. The river is enticing us to canoe down it, to explore beyond what we know.

We need to get more furnishings for the tents and the loft. The mattresses in the loft have to go back in the trailer. The trailer, that is my next job. I need to set up the new addition. It is time for our 'canoe around the lake' ride. We did our project. We must reap our reward. Never forego rewarding yourself. It is why you get at the job. It is why you work hard. Don't overdo it, but do it. Reach for your goals and reap the reward. It is the complete package. The results of your work, may not show soon enough, to satisfy you. Enjoying a reward, for doing the necessary steps, will keep you at it, until you see the finished package. It may even push you to redo, if it isn't perfect. This cottage was built in an age of utility, by an utilitarian. We are artistic personalities, in an age of self expressionism. Anything goes in this day and age. Some of this place, had to go. It is coming into its own now.

There are very few windows in this house. There is one window per room. No windows face the forest and there is only a small bathroom window, facing the lake. That is nearly sacrilegious. How could you not feature, a window facing the lake. We are going to have to make changes. I don't know why, I didn't think of this sooner. Amy agrees that we were too wrapped up in the utility, we forgot the luxury. When we ask for input, Marie wants the plumbing done first and then the porch. "Finish one thing, before you take off on another tangent." is her demand and we must concede.

Back from our rewarding trip, we have a look at what we need done, on the plans. These plans spell out every component of the recycling water system, and it is very well explained. Exploded diagrams show the different steps and what we need to avoid. We have set the wash water holding tank in a depression of the knoll. We did not leave a route, for water that may gather there, to drain. We set to work, digging a small trough out and away, from the building. It is lower than the depth of the pit is. We fill this trough with sand and stone to keep the earth from filling in. We get the catchment tank in next to it. It also is well wrapped in insulation.

Brent has just driven in and is coming over, to see what we are working on. I show him the information. We talk about the system and he gives me some mail he saw in our mailbox, while he was getting theirs. I look over the items and they are from the township. Permission to add sand to an existing sand beach, has been allowed. The barn proposal needs some additional information. He goes to visit with the girls. That sends Marie over to me, to check the mail. The sand approval is what excites her. A nice deep sand beach for her to lie on. That is romantic to her. She loves to lie in the sun, and it just isn't the same, without a sandy beach.

I look up the local quarry, and order a load of sand that will last us, for the rest of our lives. Marie goes in to get our supper arranged. She is full of energy, suddenly. The thought of new sand on the beach, is really having an effect on her. She has a new song stuck in her head. She is humming the tune and that in itself, is very strange. I think I did something right. Amy takes a moment from her visitor, to confirm my victory. The load of sand will be here in the morning. Brad will be here tomorrow night. He will be bringing the whole family, this time. I relay that message to Marie and she freaks. "What will I feed them?"

They are bringing supper for all of us. That sets well with Marie. Grace is always considerate, in these things. "What is she bringing?"

Again I have to say to her, "I don't ask those questions." Knowing that that was a wrong answer I text Grace and ask. I get the menu and relay it to Marie. She will have to go shopping now. She has to overdo her part and I let her. No use in arguing about anything like that.

I will have to get those furnishings for the tents now.

Marie is out to the grocery store, with Tanya in tow. Amy stays, to direct the sand delivery. When it arrives, Amy's appearance will get the driver to do just about anything. He practically drools all over himself. He drives down as close as he can to the shoreline and dumps the load as he drives right around the cottage and back to the driveway. Because he kept it moving at pace, He didn't bog down as he turned. The sand is very close to the beach, and we just have to spread it out. Amy thanks him and when he asks her out, she tells him her age. He was so disappointed at that, he nearly left with out getting paid. I came outside, at Amy's bidding, and paid him. He drove down the lane and out of her life. Such a shame.

She asks how we should spread it, to the beach. I think about buying an ATV, with a plough attachment. She shakes her head and lets me know Marie's view on that. "Fine, I'll rent a small Bobcat."

Marie returns and she carts supplies to the cottage with help from the teens.

Moments later, Grace and Brad come in with all the kids. "We were finished early and I had things ready all day."

"I have to get the furniture for your rooms. Tanya, can you come shopping with me to get some beds, please?" and off we go to town to find some BYO beds. Amy has to stay, to be my hands free, communication device. We end up going to Peterborough, to get the beds. We get back before supper, only because they waited for us.

"They brought PIZZA!" I get all worked up for it.

It was a feast. I heard from my grandkids, that our place was 'awesome!' Grace agreed. She thought it was more rundown. We told her, it was. I outlined my projects that are yet to come. They were all excited about those things. Grace told us, that Faith was coming too. We have our air mattresses for the loft. and the trailer will help. We go out to finish the trailer and furnish the tents.

With seven working in teams, it is done before dark. They choose their accommodations. Faith drives in and there is a rush to greet her. Christian is with her. I tell the kids to gather some firewood and that gets them going, even more energized. It almost shuts me down. Amy is there for me. Seeing Amy rush to help me, sends Grace my way too. Together they get me sitting near the fire pit. Amy gets the special ingredients for the fire. She gets a bundle of sage for smouldering in a pot. The kids come back with wood, and leave to scrounge for more. They are working in two teams. With an element of competition going, Bradley is going crazy from the tension. He is very excitable.

The nights are mild and the days are warm lately. I won't need the heaters out. There is room for the whole lot here. We have space to spare. If Nicholas would bring the family up, we would be near the limit of beds available. We would still have room. Grace and Faith have their own tents. That would add six more beds. Two dozen beds. Wow, we would be spreading out into the woods.

Faith brought her Kayak. We can go out five at a time now. I need to get another boat and canoe. "Or just take more trips." Amy scolds me. "You need to hold back. They can get things, just as well as you can."

"Okay, Mother." I've wanted a cottage ever since they sold Gram's cottage. I've wanted a boat since I first rode in Pogo. I don't like holding back. I know I can get in too much debt real fast that way. It really is hard to pace myself. It's a lot easier to tell someone else, to pace themselves. 'Do what I say, not as I do.' Have you ever heard that before? I hauled myself out of debt before. It took some unexpected income and some millionaire's advice. But, I did it. I really have to pace myself. I don't want to do that again. I did stretch the bounds already, with this water system. It was a real value for the longevity of our septic bed. The next big thing should have gone first. That is the solar power system. A big enough investment there, could bring money in. Amy's right. I just have to make more trips.

Grace got Brad to set up the solar panels in front of the trailer deck. They hook up the batteries and connect it to the trailer through the tongue wiring. They will run it on battery power all night and the sun will recharge it during the day tomorrow. We have only lights on it and no large drain. We should have a good system there. That would only be for lights for the trailer and tents. One less job to do tomorrow.

We have a great celebration. We nearly have to hogtie Bradley. He is wild. He's eleven this year. I hope he gets a little of that slowmo attitude soon. You know the teenage boys that just sort of hang there, inert. That would be a big break for Grace. It is not likely going to happen with him.

Brad is up early, to start on the plumbing. Amy is there and Tanya is not far behind. Grace has been up for quite a while. I am glad that the plumbing is done with hand tools and very little power tools. Although I know how to do it now, Amy wants me to stay away and preferably in bed. No problem, I'm all over that. I have got it covered. My body, that is. The others take no coaxing, to get them down to the lake. The canoe and kayak are out with a full crew of five and two extras. With six in the canoe, they are still under the 1200 lb. limit. It's an eighteen foot canoe, so space is not an issue either. Even the dogs are in for the ride. This is what I got the place for.

The hook ups are done and tested. It is working just the way it is supposed to. The power is on for the pump, to draw water from the river. The compost toilet gets set outside, and will go to an enclosure by the trailer. We will rig an outdoor shower there, as well. The floor is fitted into the bathroom. Thinking of the blizzard, we add a trap door in the bedroom, next to the bathroom. Now the fixtures can go in. We have a tub with a shower. A low flow toilet and a sink are rounding out the basic equipment. The shower head fixture steps these amenities up, one very nice notch. It has the rain shower head, a hand held wand, plus three body jets. This will invigorate your senses and tempt the tub soakers, to try doing the shower thing, they say they can't do. They have to put in the floor tiles, before the fixtures can be installed. Brad gets the girls started on it, and leaves them to finish it. They will do the rest of the floors, so they need to get the room that has the most issues, done first. I am up and gathering strength now. I watch Amy through her eyes. I haven't done this job before, and want to know, how to do it.

Brad takes a break and puts his feet up. He is lying on the bed, next to the bathroom, to be able to help, if required.

The paddlers are coming back from their ride around the lake. Faith is in her kayak. Grace has the canoe, with her kids, dogs, and Christian. Marie is sitting on the beach, watching them. None of them had ever been on this lake before. Nobody in the crafts, was connected to Amy, to give us a rundown on what they had done and seen. I went down to join Marie and listen to the report of the excursion. Christian jumped out on the beach, as they ploughed up on it, and pulled the bow up further, to help the rest disembark. He then grabbed the bow handle of his mom's kayak, and did the same for her. We hear the glowing reports, of the beautiful scenery, and the wildlife along the route. They had seen enough to hook them on this retreat. The teens and Faith are ready for another trip, and ask Marie and I to come with them. We take the place of Bradley, Grace and the toddler. The dogs want to come again also. They are small and don't affect the balance at all with their running back and forth. They have to see the water, from every spot in the canoe. My brother and I, used to take his beagles camping on Tim Lake, in Algonquin Park, years ago. They would do the same, but they were beefy little dogs. Our canoe was loaded so full, there was very little room to rock, without taking on water. That year I nearly froze, after I fell into the water. The next year we towed all of our equipment in my inflatable boat. That gave us much more room to rock with the dogs exuberance. That inflatable became my bed that night, and I was very warm in it. Even when we woke up in a snowstorm.

We were so wound up with the kids enjoyment, I feel that I'll put up the hammock to rest in, when we get back. I think we will see them up here again, this summer.

Amy and Tanya have finished the floor in the bathroom. Brad gets to work with the tub installation. It is a heavy piece. Amy tells me they need my weight again to fit the tub into its spot. Because Faith is as strong as I am, I ask her to go back, and help push it into place. She scoots along in her kayak, much faster, than our big canoe could do. We head out to the far end, to show them the other half of the lake. We slip through the reedy straight, joining the two halves. It was like the African Queen movie. Mosquitoes were all over us. Once we got through, we were afraid to make the return trip through there. There was nothing for it. We had to do it. We worked together, and stroked in time, in a rhythm that had us shooting though those reeds so fast, they were stinging our arms, as they slapped against us. We still got some bites, but not nearly as many. The next time we do that, we need to try the sage in a pot, burning, in the front of the boat. We just get back in time, to see Jim and Nan, arrive on the beach. This is a surprise. We had no clue that they would be coming up.

Nan said, "We thought you might like the surprise. I didn't know everyone would be up here."

Marie stayed their concern, "We have lots of room. There are only fourteen of us now that your here. We can hold eighteen, at least."

I add, "I think I'll have to build some more decks, for additional tents."

Jim says, "We can go if it's too much."

"Not too much at all. We have eight or nine in the trailer, the same in the cottage, two to four in the nylon tent, and two more in the canvas tent." I break it down for them.

I relate the storm and the ideas that that brought. I show the power system for the campers. I show how the trailer is configured. They were amazed at that. They loved the tent decks. There is a big improvement, in having them up here, overlooking the lake. I tell them the installations going in today. Jim wants to see that, so we all go, to check out the progress. After seeing the state of the room, we look out the door to view the tanks and filter beds. I talk about the porch to go over top of the tanks. I also mention the greenhouse kits that top the filter beds, and how that works. I take them back out the other door, to show them our escape route, from the blizzard. I explain the obstacles Amy endured.

Jim asks, if Joe is up at his cottage this year, yet. I had to tell him how Joe had died last year. "Evelyn, his widow, and their son Brent, are here. Brent is helping out at times, getting orders filled for me, and showing where things are up here. I visit with Evelyn and advise her on things."

"She's still keeping the cottage?"

"On my advice, she is waiting a year to see how it is affecting her life before she makes any decision on that. She also added Brent's name to the deed, to make him a signatory to anything cottage related. She did the same for her house in the city. She has named me as an advisor on any deal, except where I was the purchaser. She won't be easily swayed that way."

"Are you sure she can handle that?"

"That is what the year is for. To find out if it is manageable for her and Brent. The minute they sell the place, it becomes too expensive for them to get it back. My mom regretted selling everything so soon after my dad died. I don't want to see someone else in the same boat."

"I can see your point. One year won't make that big a difference in the value. It would likely go up, before it would fall."

"Exactly." I finalized it. "Lets get some drinks ready. I didn't bring all my stuff up here. I did bring the essentials."

"Lead the way, McDuff. We should check on the bathroom progress."

"They are nearly finished. They are putting the toilet down on the seal, right now."

"How do you know that?"

"Amy."

"I keep forgetting that. That's a handy thing to have."

"Everybody forgets about it. It is handy sometimes. It is hell at others." I told him the horror stories and how his casual view, is one reason, we need to let people know, about the downside of it. I related the talk Amy had with Marie, while I was in hospital.

He had no idea how bad it could get, but that opened his eyes. "Lets get those drinks."

We got the barbeque set up and lit. We let it burn off the things that settle in it. We enjoyed sitting and having a relaxing conversation with the girls. The teens and Bradley are off in the woods, exploring. Tanya and Amy were still working with Brad at finishing the bathroom. It will not look very cottagy, when they have the tile-work done. We will have to do that with rustic accents. That is Marie's venue. She will see the need as soon as she walks into the room.

The BBQ is ready to be scrubbed. Instead I spray the, still burning, grill with water. Short blasts dislodge debris and grease build-up and keep the fire going. A few of these blasts leaves it pristine. I spray the area down to rinse the fallout away. Voila, it is ready to begin cooking. I hand it over to the chef to begin the meal. It just has to get the heat back up for slapping meat on. We have steaks and tube-steaks. Jim and Brad are better grillers than I am. I am not adroit with those contraptions. I can do myself irreparable harm, using them. I offer the honours to Jim, as our guest, he should have first choice. I don't need to extend the offer to anyone else. Jim is glad to show his skills. I keep his glass full and that, will oil any squeaks of dissention from him.

We get the announcement that the bath is finished. The tiles are still to go in. But it is ready to be used. I am asked, as the heavyweight champion, to be the first to sit on the throne. Okay, they didn't exactly say 'champion'. I am the resident paperweight. I do the honours and the fixture is tightened. I vacate the room to allow the anointment ceremonies to continue. Some did not want to use the compost toilet, out in the trailer bathroom. They held their piece and now must put asunder.

275

The tiling will begin tomorrow. The diligent workers are off to reap their rewards.

I get back to the sous chef. I refill his lubricant vessel. I get myself another drink as well. The outdoor kitchen will have to be improved upon, for this level of gourmet talent. A camp barbeque and a spray bottle, is not quite enough. Nan, as head chef, okays the steaks. "Does anyone want their buns toasted for the hot dogs?"

"No thanks. We're warm enough already." I say for the rest.

Nan says, "It's just you that likes that."

The call to dinner goes out to all in earshot. I go to check for the kids. I see them gathering things among the trees and call them in. The chairs are being gathered around the fire pit area. We have log seats that have been set out. Log seats and decking joists are made into a makeshift buffet. The sage is burning. The feast is set to begin. Jim says grace and we get under way. It is a lively bunch. We have a raucous conversation going. This we could not have at the other cottage. Too many people for the facilities.

"Finally, you have finished what you started. Now we can do the decorating." Marie says to me. Even though, it was not me to do the actual work. "We now need the kitchen done."

Chapter Twenty Five

Visions

The first major gathering, was a booming success. We had a great meal and time with much of the family. Everyone was having fun with a capital F. The struggles we had up to now, have been revealing and instructive. We have seen the great image we were aiming for, materialize before we have even had time to be ready for it. We will not be disappointed in the outcome. It can only get better from here on out. Disasters may come, but we are set, with gritted determination, to see our life here at our cottage camp blossom into full bloom.

Our guests stay through the next day, and we invite the Youngs and their guests, to come and join us. We salute Joe and others, that could not be with us. It was a very good thing, that we are so remote. We were louder than we ever thought this band of introverts, could possibly be.

Brad did the tiling, with Amy, while Tanya stood watching, intently, over their shoulders. It was an amazing room, when they were finished. They took out the copper stink pipes and replaced them with PVC. We can sell them at the recyclers, for the money to see us into the next project. The drains from the sinks and bathtub-shower, go into the troughs. They get water from the catchment tank. We will install eaves troughs to fill the catchment tank, and in dry times, a buoyancy switch in the tank, will start to pump from the river. Eaves troughs, a new roof and porch, are high on the list for building.

Our guests go home and leave a big empty space. We have no illusions of being stuck here alone. They left with such reluctance, we nearly cried to see it in their eyes. We are left to continue the renovations alone. Just the four of us. It will diminish to two, when I have to go back for my appointments. I have to have cataract surgery on my left eye. I hope it will make a difference. Marie and I, will leave the girls, under the watchful eyes of Brent and Evelyn.

The cupboards are coming in, from our friend and neighbour, George. He had built these for family and friends before, and was happy to build some for us. He is enjoying his life, healthy and strong after his fight with leukemia. He has finished restoring his truck, that he started before it all happened. He is keeping busy at a relaxed pace. He and his wife are enjoying the time that God has given them. Our prayers were working steadily, throughout his ordeal. He had many people pulling for him.

We make sure the girls, have enough supplies and food, before we go. They are glad that I am getting this done and hope it will give me back the vision in that eye. The doctor has said, not to expect too much, because the retina is lifting. There is not much they can do for me after that. It is more than I have hoped for. I was resigned to remain with impaired vision, after finding I was immune, to the topical freezing they used.

We go home and I take care of the banking for the month. We make note of anything coming up, that we had not remembered. Marie stocks up on things we need to take back with us. I am going to take down our swimming pool. We will be at the cottage almost all summer and as much of the fall we can manage. The pool is less than useless now. It will not be useable for us. It will be in terrible condition whenever we come home. I try to salvage it if I can but my hopes are not high. I start draining it out the front of the driveway. I am cleaning it as it empties. What doesn't get done today will have to wait for my eye to recover.

I am excited to get up to the cottage with George. I've talked with him about the place so many times. I think he will be astounded at the job the girls are doing there. The cabinets are getting their finishing touches and will be ready when we are, to go up to the cottage. We will be loading them in our van and George's truck, and the four of us will take them up.

The pool is just about empty. Marie is home now and helping me clean as it drains. The vacuum will be getting the last little bit.

Now that it's empty, we need to get it apart. We hang it up to dry on the clothes line. I hand dry the pump and other parts. I get them inside as soon as they're dry. They are arranged for me to catalogue the parts. It has all gone smoothly and I can donate or sell the pool.

We just need to get help in drying and flipping the liner. I have run out of time. I go for the procedure in the morning. It is supposed to be done with topical freezing. Since I'm immune to it, I must have a general anaesthetic. I know I am going to have a fight in the morning, with the anaesthetist. They don't want to do it, so they would rather make me suffer the agony. They want the job, but would rather not do it. I went through it last time. This one may not mind doing it. I shouldn't prejudge. I prepare for the worst and expect the best. But I just had to vent. I am sure this will actually give me back my sight. Going by what I see, it should be good for a time anyway. I am nervous over it.

I have to be at the clinic for five. It won't even be open for five.

Marie is expecting to get blasted for my snoring. Sleep apnoea. If I was to die, I would like to die in my sleep. So, is it a problem? I don't think so. I hear no arguments from Amy, on that point. She feels the same way. Marie would like to go in her sleep. Most people I know would rather die in their sleep.

No food after midnight. I used to do that every night, until I saw a dietician for my diabetes. She told me that I needed to eat something before I go to bed. That was the hardest habit to break so that I could lose weight. Then I have to eat before bed? Now I am trying to break that habit again.

Tanya and Amy have a project they are working on. They are building furniture out of the fallen branches and driftwood they are finding. I have seen some really nice pieces and they want to duplicate them. They are stripping branches of bark and entwining them, one to the others. They are combing the forest and roadsides, for promising items to use. They have found more table logs. Some good ones for seating too. Once they find the pieces best suited for it, they will use the same methods we used before. They have the nailers there, to tack them together, to help the glues to set. I hope they find some nice ones. I forgot to go back for the ones I saw coming from town. They are using my trike to gather and drag them back. The canoe is handy for that as well.

We had gathered a large and growing pile of wood. Gleaned from the forest. Recovered from ditches. Brought in by friends and relatives. They were sorted in the different classifications. The girls are now cutting and fitting pieces for a railing for the loft. Strength is the key and aesthetics is the goal. They are trying to match shots picked up online. The best wood to build with is that which comes from a living tree. Pruned or cut soon after the tree was damaged. This wood has more natural moisture in it, bonding the fibres of the wood closer, than if it has had time to dry out. They have wound pieces from both ends of the branches. This gives it an overall thickness that is easy to grip. Wider bases are at the bottom of the railing, closest to the floor.

They have replaced the ladder we had been using. Installing one they made with thin logs. They used a mortise and tenon joint to build the ladder. They used pegs to secure the tenon point, on the outside of the ladder. This will keep it solid, with the movement of energetic kids, going up and down it. The ladder is sealed and coated, to give it a smooth surface and protecting hands from wood splintering. Their work is giving the room, a big touch of class and frontier charm. The ladder juts out more into the room. This will give a safer stance and allow the railing to be more useful.

They have an eye out for a larger log to cut a slab for use as a table. I think I need to get more supplies for them to keep moving. We may even have a cottage industry in the making, here. When handling raw woods, they have to wear gloves, to keep the skin from drying out. Moisturizing the hands after each work session, is important to keep them healthy. Fungal infections are picked up easy with dried skin.

They have put up a makeshift barn, near the house. They built a frame and put one of the heavy tarps over it. These two are very inventive, or I have more information stuck back in there than I ever imagined. They asked Brent to find some animals that could graze around here, to clear most of the high grasses and brush out. They would have to enclose the property, or tether the animals. Tethering is the way they would have to use. Are they getting in over my head?

I may not be back up there for weeks. Faith and Grace, offer to take turns going up to take them some supplies and visit. What is it with me and losing my summers to eye doctors?

I have had the operation. They did not argue this time. I had a general. I just saw the doctor and my sight is noticeably improved. I still have issues, but they are liveable. I have appointments that will keep me here for the foreseeable future. Marie has vowed that we will go up, between the doctor visits. I suggest, inviting the doctor up to the cottage. I actually got a laugh out of her.

A goat, a horse and a deer. These are the animals that Brent has found, to forage on the field around the cottage. He stopped at a vet's office and asked if they had need of any foraging space. They just happened to be wanting room for some new patients in their corral. The deer is nearly ready to be released after surgery recovery has done well. Foraging on the brush here will be good for her. The horse is one of theirs. The goat is looking for a new home. Marie says, "No! No more pets!" They take the three animals and tether lines are put up. They are strung like clothes lines between the forest and the stand of trees by the lake. The girls have instructions to follow. They have to move the animals to a short tether at night to keep from having problems with entanglement. It is a short term stay. One week for the horse.

Two weeks for the deer. The goat however, is optional. The vet comes by to check them often, and it is a good arrangement for everybody.

Amy is going to tackle the new porch. Brent sourced out the new metal piles. They are wound down into the ground. There is no need to dig or use concrete. They are installed for us. Amy just needs to mark out the insert locations. She is a little nervous about doing the porch. She needs back up. She goes ahead and marks out the placement of the piles, and they are installed two days later. She waits for more bodies to be around before going on with the build. She sees the shows in my memory, but one key point is unclear. We don't have a TV, computer, or even wifi, to get the knowledge she is unsure of. She has yet to cut the piles to height. She needs to get across the top of the tank to attach the ledger.

'Take your extension ladder apart, and put each half at opposite ends of the tanks. Put your ledger board on top of the tanks. Each of you climb a ladder half, and place the ledger against the wall. Level the board and mark the top and bottom sides of where the board is on the wall. Using your framing nailer, nail the board to the wall. Once you have check the level of the board, drill through the board and wall. Knock the bolts in with only one washer on the bolt. Go inside and fasten the bolts with a flat washer, a lock washer, and a nut. Be sure the nut is tight.'

'Thanks, Dad. How about the posts.'

'Get the ledger done and you can see my thoughts on that once that is done.'

'Where were you?'

'In surgery. They did a general.'

'Glad to have you back. I couldn't find these things in your thoughts. I wondered why?'

'The general was a good one.'

'Great! Glad to have you back in my head.'

They put up the ledger. Then they set up the laser level and marked the spots on the piles. They then, cut off the piles at those spots. They set the post saddles in the end of the piles, plus a post in each saddle. They drilled through the holes in the saddles and through the posts. They knock in the bolts and fastened them with nuts. Making sure the posts were plumb, they nailed a board across the posts, just above the saddle sides. That held the posts steady. They can now, use the ladders and long joists, for a scaffold. Using the laser level again, they marked the height of the ledger onto the posts. Marking a spot seven inches below the previous spot, they found where to put the girder support beam. The joists will lie on top of this. Two 2X6s are nailed together to form this piece and are fastened on the outside of the posts with a third piece on the inside. These are bolted through the posts and girders.

The girls are confident, that they can build the rest of the deck. They work hard at it, but give in for the day, so they can get a ride in. Rewards to help them come back tomorrow. Brent stops in just as they are leaving. They invite him along and grab a lifejacket for him. They're off to the far end of lake. They engage in shoptalk all the way down the lake. Just as they are turning around, Brent tells them that he has met a girl. She lives in the area, and is a senior in high school. The girls stop paddling, to hear all about her. She was helping out at her father's shop, and he went in to get something, for his mom. She is as short as Amy, and is quite petite. Her name is Lidia. He has gone out with her, for a couple dates. She is kind of different. She looks a little gothic, but doesn't have any piercings or tattoos. She has short shaggy hair, and wears a little too much makeup. He wants to bring her around to meet them and his mom.

"Wow, when are you wanting to bring her?" Amy plied.

"Tomorrow. I want to know what you think of her. She just turned sixteen. I am a bit nervous about doing this, but I value your opinion."

"Bring her over. Bring her and your mom to dinner here. We have to eat up some steaks so that they're not in the freezer too long."

"I'll talk to Mom about it tonight. Thanks." He was nervous. He fiddled with the paddle whole time he talked. They started paddling back to the house. They talked more along the way. Amy thinks he needs her approval. She is glad he has that kind of respect for her.

When they got to shore, he jumped out to pull the bow up on the beach. He gave them each a hug and a kiss, then left for home. They looked at each other. "Our little boy is growing up." they kidded.

They put the animals away for the night. It is nice to have them around. It gives them something alive, with beating hearts, for them to care for. Night in this wilderness, is both scary and comforting. A release of the muscle tension and a heightening of a tension of the senses. Your imagination comes alive again. You shut down your mechanical side, and wake up your visions, waiting to put on a show for you. Your imagination gets to run wild once more. After being cut off by your analytical brain, it is now able to provide something to feed that, now resting analysis. Bring it on, it is now showtime. Everything that enters your mind is emphasized, or disguised. It is building up the cast, for your dreamscape. The shadows are milling around, trying to get your attention. Not so much your conscious, but your unconscious attention. They are vying for the lead, in the play to follow. When you close your eyes and open the curtain. The shadows will come out to perform their dance. They are directing your thoughts, and allowing the other actors their chance, to get in position for their big scene. They are ready to run away with your imagination. To take it to far away lands, and into exotic locations. The stage is now set and the cues are in order. You are ready to file into the theatre. The house lights are up for you to find your seat. Gather your confections, and settle into the seat. In this theatre, everyone sits front row and centre.

Amy talks about Brent's belated interest in the straight girls. Tanya understands his delay. She shares his desire, for this jewel before her. She is amazed, that he could ever see another. How could he see past Amy. One look had hooked her. She was only a child, but she saw something, more than all she had seen before and since. Anything Amy does, is as much as she would ever need. There is nothing else, to her. She can only imagine that Brent is bringing her here to get Amy's approval. Evelyn's approval is secondary. He wants to remain close to Amy. What else could he do? Why else would he come? He is a moth drawn to the brightness of Amy's flame.

In their room, they imagine the view from the proposed new window. Looking straight out over the lake, will make this room, the most desired room in the cottage. They had thoughts of a wrap around porch. I have to discourage that thought, for the immediate future. I do agree on the value of it.

They lay back, thinking of how far they've come. First as lovers, then as students, and last of builders. As women, they have made their mark in industry. They have done well in staying focussed on their goals. First to provide a retreat for the family. Then to train in building skills. Finally to assure a future home, for themselves. They even like the snow.

They find sleep, and in doing so, burst onto the scene of a remote cabin in the woods. The play being written, will now come to life. The cottage is there in the middle of winter. Wolves are howling and then are outside the house, panting as they search for an opening, a way in. They see themselves rising from the bed and clamouring to the wall with as much weight as two little women can make on a wood floor. The wolves back off a pace. They do not leave, until a horseman arrives firing a shot at the beasts. It is Brent, mounted on the horse outside. He bursts in the door and takes Amy in his arms, like a knight in shining armour. Then they see Amy disappear from his arms and in her place is the new girl. Petite and pretty, she sits in his arms and watches Amy in the arms of Tanya. The scene is mixing and roiling, the images and story. They are gone. Lost from view and far from hearing. The night continues, yet the play is over. The shadows are working on a new script. One that will bring out their emotions. One that will pull the mind out of the wood, and into the open, to see the shadows as they are. They find the shadows wearing the fur from the deer and goat.

In the daylight, the sunshine is sweeping across the lot, creeping in and crawling across the room. Opening their eyes to take it in. They each look upon their partner with satisfaction. They are there together, through it all. They lay there, enjoying the view of each other's eyes. Tanya's eyes are a steel gray-blue.

Amy's eyes are opalescent, changing from brown, through green to blue. They look like a cool fire flickering in the face of her goddess. Tanya knows the depth of those eyes. She has felt their pull, drawing her in deeply. She never fights it. She will give herself joyously. She would dive into those limpid pools of warm, tropical waters.

The work is beckoning. They are tempted to ignore the call, but know what they want to achieve will not happen without them. It is their view of this place that they want to inherit. If it had not been for Amy's retention of her past life memories, these two would be like any normal fifteen year olds. Amy's deep fear of her past life, is driving her to be more than she had ever dreamt, back then.

They have built the ladder and are finishing the first side of the railings. They were hoping to get more of that done before anyone came up. Faith is on her way, and the detour to work on the porch split their focus and neither are going to be done in time. Faith has both Christian and Briony, as well as Christian's girlfriend. Briony has been very good with her program, and is being rewarded with this trip to see the new theme park, we are building.

They decide to finish the railing today. It needs another coat of varnish to give it that deep clearcoat effect. It is a safety concern, as much as appearance. I hurt from the rough texture and no one likes a shard of wood stuck in their hands, or elsewhere. It will be still tacky when they arrive.

I had said earlier, the time it takes to get here, was about two and a half hours. I miscalculated. I was going by an earlier trip to the area. The driver had been motivated, at the time. It is about an hour longer. I don't feel so bad about my travel time now.

Once the girls have finished the porch and railings, they can do the floors. They want to have the basics, before they get to the finer things. They will be taking their reward time on the lake, after Faith arrives. Until then, they move on to get more of the porch done. It is to be a 5X10 foot space. It must be done before the season ends, or we won't be safe in the cottage this winter.

George and I will be able to come up, after my next appointment. I will have a larger window of time then. I go for that on Tuesday, and Marie would like to leave right after it.

When faith pulls into the lane, they see a black bear and her cub heading away from the cottage area, and out of the woods, to cross the road. While they appreciate the chance to see them, they are unnerved by the proximity to the camp. Faith steadies herself for the backlash she expects from her companions. They are talking about it, but don't seem to be ready to panic. The hilly drive, although shallow, gets more notice than the animals did. Complaints of queasy stomachs, are heard from more than one passenger. She turns the corner into our path to a chorus of oohs and aahs.

The hostesses hear the car, before they see it, and are already heading out, to welcome their guests. Offering warm hugs, they help carry stuff to the cottage. Faith has brought a few things from me, so that I will have more room, to fit the kitchen pieces in.

The visitors get to choose their accommodations, and surprise Faith, in picking the tents. After seeing the bears, they had not been afraid to be so accessible to them. They stow their luggage, in their choice of tents and head to the beach. Faith gets her kayak down to the water. Tanya puts the canoe in the water, while Amy brings armfuls of lifejackets. Out on the water, they look back to see the camp. It is a great feeling, to know that this awaits them, anytime they want it. Paddling down the lake, they see more wild life feeding on lush grasses. A family of deer perked up on their passing by. Faith mentions the bears and the girls are alarmed. They had not known and immediately, are concerned for their stock, tied near the woods at night. They were assured the bears were heading off, across the road. They will have to move the animals closer to the cottage, tonight. Faith had not seen the animals in camp, and asked about them.

Amy describes their pets, "We have a horse belonging to the vet. There is a goat that is from a client of the vet. Then we have a deer being rehabilitated."

"Wow, where do you keep them?"

"They're tethered on lines, or tied to trees, around the space between the lake and the woods."

"Wow, can we pet them?" Briony asks.

"Sure you can! We will go with you so that they won't be startled by you."

"Lets go see them now!"

"Does everyone want to go see them now?" It was unanimous, so they turned around and headed back. Amy wanted to check on them anyway, now that she heard of the bears in the area. They left the boats on the beach with the lifejackets inside.

She took them to see the goat first. It was glad for the attention. They petted the coarse coat, and felt the stubby horns. Living in the city doesn't give them much in the way of opportunities to pet animals like this. They turned to go to the deer next, and Christian gets butted from behind, the minute he turned his back. The goat gets to wrestle with him now. He grabs the horns and the goat twists its head and lunges at him. Christian pets it to settle it down. The minute he turns around again, brings another butt upon his. He walks on to see the deer, ignoring the kid.

The deer is amazing them. It doesn't shy away. It is too accustomed to people now. That may not be good, once it is released to the wild. It keeps munching on bushes, pausing to acknowledge the caressings of these strange animals, in funny looking fur. This is a real treat. A wild animal, so relaxed, standing so close, allowing them to touch and stroke it gently.

When they get to the horse, it is overwhelming them with its size. It is welcoming them, just as the other two had. As they stroke the huge animal, they hear someone approaching from behind them. It is Brent, with his new girlfriend, Lidia. Evelyn is with them. They join the group in stroking the horse. Introductions are passed around the, now large, group. Amy tells Brent about Faith's spotting of the bears crossing the road. He is as concerned as she was. He agrees that keeping them close to the house would be the best idea. The vet may be around soon to check on them and can assess the situation further.

Lidia is talking with Tanya, about how she had met Brent. The only similarity with Amy was her height. She was even shorter than Amy. It would make Amy feel, absolutely, tall. A good three inches shorter than Amy, she was very petite, not skinny at all, but slim. Everyone was towering above the new girl. Briony had just turned sixteen and was surprised to find out, Lidia was, not only the same age, but that she was born on the same day.

Evelyn was talking to Faith about the cottage life here. It is farther than her aunt's cottage, but Faith can get here anytime, and will, as much as possible.

The group migrates toward the cabin. Filing up the stairs and into the cottage. The builders are rewarded with more of the oohs and aahs, over the new ladder and railing. Crafts of all kinds are practiced in this family, and the level of talent is noticeable. This is a renewal and improvement, of Marie's early endeavours. They give them the fifty cent tour. Giving the railing a test, they recommend waiting until tomorrow, to look upstairs.

The boats are spotted on the beach, so Brent asks, if they want to go for a paddle, before cooking supper. That was agreed to and Brent went home to bring his canoe around to meet them on the beach.

Down on the beach, they are preparing for the ride. Lidia was surprised at the beach being there. It was more common on the lower lakes. "It was trucked in. We have this to add to it, but have to get something in to finish it." Amy said, pointing to the streak of sand, stretched out toward the animals.

Brent pulls up to the beach and hands two lifejackets to his mom. Lidia is too small for the ones he brought, but Amy brings out Bradley's vest. It fits perfectly. They are off down the lake. The girls are getting their reward and a large party to share it with. The lake is still flush with greenery, in the bright spring colours. It is July, and the life is in full swing here. Many of the cottages are occupied and others are out in their boats and canoes. They don't see the speedboats here, on this part of the lake. There are younger cottagers on the upper part, that like waterskiing and jet skiing. The older crowd at this end enjoy the peaceful, easy feeling, that comes with oars and paddles in the water. The channel between the upper and lower parts, has some rocky parts and is generally avoided by the power boaters. Only occasionally, fishermen will brave the straight. The resulting calm brings animals of all kinds down to the water's edge. As you pass by the other boaters, you have the occasion to chat and get to know your neighbours. The fishing here, is a closely guarded secret, by folks on both sides of the straight. The fish are larger and more calm. It gives the angler an advantage, but it is still a struggle to land the behemoths, that can be found here. That is one reason the bears come around, down along the river banks.

The tour of the lake is bliss for the harried city dwellers. Some may long to be aboard a powerboat, but this is something you only learn to enjoy by trying it. You feel the power in your arms and back, just as you will feel the pain there, when you are new to the experience. They are moving at a leisurely pace, so the pain will be avoided. Lidia and Christian's girlfriend, are the only newbies, on this trip. Landing on the beach is welcomed with the growling of more than one stomach. The life jackets are hung up near the house.

Brent goes to start the barbeque and Tanya retrieves the meat. Amy starts preparing the side dishes. Faith has brought some food and gets to preparing that. The rest go to visit the smaller animals. Lidia is very fond of the fawn. It seems to respond to her. Christian and his girlfriend are playing with the goat. Briony joins Lidia, and Evelyn goes in to help Amy. The horse takes no notice, of the group's preference, for the other stock. It is busy in such a way that it is relaxed. Everyone is doing something so far apart, it feels an idyllic scene.

Amy, Evelyn, Faith and Tanya, arrange the seating and set up tables around the fire pit. The planks on logs make the diners feel like the camp life is the one they want more often. Having the weekend to enjoy it, is exciting, for those from outside the area. The others, remember when it was just as exciting for them. The food is brought out and laid before the congregation. Brent stood, to offer prayer for the meal. Given the signal to eat, the plates were passed and emptied quickly. They consumed the meal with an urgency, that showed they had gone too long in preparing it. The suppliers, seeing their lengthy preparation dissolve into scraps, in very few minutes. They almost hesitated, to take the empty plates, for fear of losing a limb. Having only one child, Evelyn was the most surprised. Amy, having seen it in her previous life, in a family of mostly boys, was the least shocked by it. "It really is most common, Evelyn." Amy witnessed.

The diners that did not prepare the food, were enlisted to clean it all up. Those four were surprised at their assignments. Even Lidia, had to take part. Brent knew that his doing the grilling was a good move. Although he was a natural volunteer, when he stood to offer his hand at drying, was told to plant it, which he quickly did.

"You have to let others have a part in it. They are able and have received their reward, before hand." Evelyn advises her son. "You will have plenty of time to help Lidia, if she is attuned to sticking around."

Amy gave her an approving smile. Brent did like to jump in too quickly. It was the Sir Lancelot Syndrome. Too easily turned by a damsel in distress. When she learned that Lidia was only four foot ten, she quickly assessed the things she had seen. "I think I've grown!" and Tanya agreed. At long last, Amy had broken the five foot barrier. It was a monumental achievement for her. She felt like dancing on the tables, but knowing how loosely they were built, decided against it. All at the table congratulated her. Her sister had been towering over her so much, she didn't notice the difference. She was ready to advise Brent to marry Lidia. The girl that made her feel tall, she wanted to keep her around. Until now, only Bradley was shorter than she was. I congratulate her on her 'huge' achievement of growing an inch. 'It's all that fresh air.' I tell her.

After they had washed up the kids came over to join the group again. Amy got up with Brent, to get the fire started. She sat next to Lidia, and learned about her family, and how life had been, in this small town atmosphere. She asked how many other guys she had dated. She wasn't surprised to hear he was the first one. She heard about the guys in her class always harassing the girls with figures, and not even looking at her. She was glad she didn't have much of a figure. Amy told her, those guys weren't in her class at all. She asked about Brent and how they met. Lidia was just as nervous about him, as he seemed about her. She said she had to help in her dad's shop. She was usually in the office in the back. She had been called up front, to take someone's place, because they had gone home sick. Her dad had her in the back room, to keep her away from the guys. The ones that wouldn't look at her. He had seen these guys around town, and they were bothering the girls. When Brent came in, her dad introduced him, because Brent had helped some girls, they had been bothering. He got a great reputation because of that. Amy was happy for Brent, to get to meet someone like Lidia. She told her about Brent, staying by girls to keep guys like that away. She told Lidia, that he was her knight in shining armour too. He was her best friend, and she was happy that he met someone as good as she was. It was something she remembered, in my past, that made her decide, Lidia was the one for Brent, if he wanted her.

Brent came over after giving Amy enough time to grill Lidia. He sat down beside them and asked what they were talking about? They just said, "Boys." He knew what they meant.

I wondered, if there was something I could have done, to be more of the person that could have done that. Amy said that I was, but it wasn't always about, what I had done. It was the timing and expectations. When you get rewarded for being a creep. You become more of a creep. When you realize the mistake and try to fix it. You have to start from the beginning, not the middle. You can't take the spices out of soup. You have to make another pot. "I think, I understand." I had to say, "It's too bad, they couldn't find the problem sooner." I'm sitting alone at my desk, writing another book. Nobody hears my voice.

'It all worked out. Now you can help others, with what you've learned.'

"I might just do that." Still no one hears, but Amy.

Chapter Twenty Six

Outside the box

Faith and the kids had a wild time. The forest was an amazing playground for teenagers and a teenager at heart. Tanya and Amy joined in on the fun. They got some tips for the camp, from the other teens. They had seen it at another place. They weren't sure if they could get it to work with the distances. The kids had taken the animals for a walk, including the horse. Nobody knew how to ride bareback, and it wasn't their horse, so they just walked it around. Christian had climbed some of the trees, marked for the tree house, and zip line. None of the girls were going to try that. Most of those trees were pine. They were too rough and the pitch was everywhere. The main part of the tree house was to go in an oak. That is where the walkway would come from and that is where the sleeping rooms would be.

Amy saw Brent down by the cottage, and went down to see him. He thanked her for visiting with Lidia, and having them all over for supper. Lidia had thought that Amy had an interest in him. He wanted to ask, if he could tell her about their relationship, and her being gay. Amy was glad he asked. She also, wrote a note to Lidia, to tell her that. In it, she tells about her virtual marriage to Tanya, and that she was happy to see Brent with her.

That was the best they could do. It would be up to Lidia, whether she accepted it. It would also be up to Brent to help her believe it. Actions speak louder than words.

He said he would leave his canoe there if she needed an extra. He has his dad's boat and Evelyn, doesn't use them alone. He took off with a purpose. Amy smiled. She would love to have Lidia become a friend, but would be just as happy, if she was just interested in having Brent.

Only the lonely. It popped into our heads. It fit. A melancholy moment. Like she was watching a son, running off to propose to his girlfriend. 'How old were you in that past life?'

'Only twenty three. I had my Bachelor of Arts and I was fresh onto the working scene. I wanted to go back for my Masters. I can hardly see it now. The path I had planned to take. I wish I could remember. I might later. Can't you see it in my memory?'

'Right now, I can hardly see anything. I am drawing a blank.'

'Yes, I see. You're having an episode. Two more days, Dad. Two more days and you and Mom can bring up the kitchen. As you know, we're goofing off.'

'It's good to do that even when you are the boss.'

The natives are restless. They are acting like wild Indians. I wonder if that is something to be saying, in these days of political correctness. The kids certainly are acting like the Hollywood version of the old west. It is more descriptive of the middle east, and the up risings there. We only see what is aired. What ever the correct term would be, they are having a wild time. They are having pinecone fights. Christian started pelting the girls with pinecones, from the trees and he quickly ran out of cones. Now the girl are having their revenge. Four women throwing pinecones at one guy, who is busy trying to climb higher, into the thickly branched pine tree. He will be itching and sticking together for quite a long time.

This is what I was looking for, in a cottage. Long beaches are nice. Great Lake waves are fun, too. But having all this choice around you? This is it. We are still able to go to the sister's cottage. Taking long walks on the beach. But this, this is what I was looking for.

The fun had to come to an end, and it was nice, that Christian didn't fall from the tree. The women had enough and let him come down. Of course, once he hit the ground they plastered him with pinecones. He would have, if he only had a few seconds more. He would have done it to them. Armed with still more pinecones, they took him captive and brought him in, with hands tied behind his back. "Now," they said, "it has come to the end."

It was time to get ready to go. Amy stood guard over the prisoner, while the rest packed their things and Tanya packed Christian's things. They had some food. Christian was fed by his girlfriend. They wouldn't take the food from camp, only what they brought. They will untie him, once he is far from any pinecones. Faith puts her kayak back on the roof of the car. The girls load the rest. They give some hugs, hugs for triumph and hugs for goodbye. All in the car? Be back in a couple weeks. Yes. They drive out the lane. The scene is quiet. The hostesses reflect on the excitement they had had. They give each other a hug. A few tears are escaping. It is getting harder to let people go home, after their time here. They know there are more coming up. In just two more days, Mom and Dad, George and Connie, will all be here to have some more excitement. It is like my childhood memories of Gram's cottage. I never wanted to leave. I never wanted anyone to leave. There wasn't enough room for everybody, but I still didn't want them to leave.

The girls retire to their bedroom. It is time for a 'nap.'

Monday morning, and they are back at work. They won't get any money for this work unless they sell the place. This is investment. Investment in the futures market? In a way. Investment in a retirement fund? That too. Investment in the longevity of their relationship. Investment in the promise that I made Amy. The trust she has in me. They do get paid, in the hands on training. This is their internship. They will be able to do this to get through university. They are hoping to complete their course, on cottage renovation, by the end of the season. Today though, it is time to get back to work.

Eye on the prize? Yes sir. The other is on the job. The porch is going in today, they declare. They have laid the under framing. Now they lay out the joists and fasten them with hangers. They put up the rim joist, and fasten the joists to it with hangers. Amy reviews my memories. She is hoping that it is complete. It is not the same as learning from a qualified instructor. It is learning, second hand, from memories of TV shows, that may not even show the complete plan, or all the steps. Their deck is now ready to put in the spacer blocks. They are all cut and while Amy nails them in place with the framing nailer, Tanya tosses them to her. Planks are spread across the joists, to walk on. The job is going smoothly. She just has this nagging doubt.

I am no help to her, because I have less access to my memories than she does. I look up the drawings on the computer. 'The flashing over the ledger, to protect it from moisture in the joint by the wall.'

Tanya goes to find the flashing. They install the flashing. 'Anything else, Dad?'

'No, you're good to do the decking.' They start to plan out the deck boards. They lay down the boards simply. They don't need fancy up here. They start to fasten down the boards but hesitate. There is a confusion in my brain, that is messing up Amy's perception. It seems like the atmospheric distortion in radio and TV waves.

I am nodding off and recovering, to look at the images on the screen. I stop looking at the screen and tell them to lay out the thin plywood on top of the joists and under the flashing. We are going to enclose the tanks and the plywood will allow the rain to run off the deck and not drip through the decking boards.

They carefully lift the flashing to fit in the plywood. They then apply caulking along the tops of the framing lumber. They get the plywood and as they reach its size the slide it in and place it on its assigned spot. They have allowed for the overhang on the first piece. They work their way to the end of the deck and place the last piece. Now they have to make it fancy. With the plywood down, they need to allow for the water to run off the deck, and not get trapped on top of the plywood. They figure out the pattern and start cutting. It is on an angle starting in the middle and flowing out on opposites toward each end. While they do that I lay down to calm my thoughts and recover. They are doing well and I don't want to disturb Amy right now.

They finally finish the deck boards. It is reward time. The stairs are next and they want clear heads. This is a step I have clear memories of doing myself. First things first. They get out on the lake in their canoe and troll fishing lines on either side of them. They have clipped the rods into the frame of the canoe, in a way that they will act as outriggers. It doesn't take long to get a bite. They let the canoe coast as they grab the rods. Tanya's line has got one on and as she fights her fish, Amy is pulling in her line. As Amy's line gets close, she gets a fish on. Now they have a fight on both sides of the boat. Amy pushes the net, so they can both reach it. Tanya has nearly got her fish up close. Amy's fish is already there. Amy's is a Pike. They go quiet and don't fight until you get them in the boat. Amy nets her Pike and dumps it on the floor of the canoe. She passes the net to Tanya, but her hands are full. Her catch is a real fighter. By the way it is diving and passing under the canoe, she thinks it's a Smallmouth Bass. She has got it close but is all over the place. Amy leaves her fish, and gets the net ready for Tanya's fish to get back on the starboard side. It just peeks around and Amy dips the net in and pulls out a very nice four pound Bass. Pound for pound, they are the fish, with the most fight in them. They each tend to their catch and get the hooks free. They stow their rods and put the fish on their string. They hang the chain over the side and get ready the basket to put them in. Everything is out of the way, so the fish are hoisted back in the boat and into the basket. The Pike starts its fight all over again, but with the basket closed it is fighting in vain. They continue the paddle up the lake. Reaching the end, they turn and head for home. It looks like there will be fish for dinner and breakfast.

At home, they put the fish in the fish cooler. Some fresh water goes in to keep them alive and fresh until they are ready to clean them. I get a vision of what the girls may look like in fifty years, in this same scenario. Amy is not amused at first, but seeing it gave her pause. I could be right and that may not be a bad thing.

They check on their livestock of the four legged kind. The animals are good so they take them for a walk around the yard. They walk the horse separately, so as not to overtax themselves. Getting them back on their tethers, they brush their coats. Time to clean those fish. The Bass is relatively easy to fillet, but the Pike has a lot of bones that are hard to get out. They just clean the Pike and barbeque it. When it is done, they can get the bones out easier, but carefully.

I make arrangements to have a bobcat at the cottage for Wednesday. While the cupboards are installed, I will be able to get the sand, onto the beach. I have a good feeling about my sight in the left eye. I can see clearly. It almost makes the pain worthwhile.

The stair stringers have been put on and are alongside the filter troughs. The steps go on easily. The railing and roof are yet to do. They bring the deck post bases. They aren't pretty, but they do the job well. Next the posts go in and are cut to the proper height. Collar ties go on the posts. The roof will sit on top of these. They are slipping along freely. The roof is up and the railing will go on tomorrow. They are just putting the tools away for the day when they hear Brent's car pull in. They look up to see, Lidia is with him.

Brent and Lidia, walk over to the porch and she thanks Amy for the note. She had never met anyone that was gay, and never even considered, that someone that she knew would be gay. That is something you don't hear about, in this neck of the woods. She wasn't a social person, due to being overlooked, by most of the people in her school. She had no real friends, outside of the family. She enjoyed talking with her, at the fireside. She sounded like anybody else she had known. She never thought, that she, would have a gay friend, but she thinks she has one now.

Amy invites them in and gets the door for them. Tanya is making tea. They don't have a filter on their water line yet. So they boil the water to drink, if they don't have bottled water. If they're boil it, they may as well have tea. Their guests take a seat by the stairs.

Lidia rubs her hand along the railing. "It's so beautiful. It's like a fairytale cottage might have."

"Thank you. It's from some pictures my dad had saved on Pinterest. He loves the cedar log homes' furniture and appointments. So we, decided to put them in. It is a break from the plain old reno jobs here."

"Where did you get them from?"

"We made them, from wood we got after the storm."

"Where did you get the ladder from?"

"We made it too." Amy smiled.

Brent spoke up, "They've done almost all of the work on this cottage. The tearing out of the old stuff. Putting in new subfloors, wiring, plumbing and everything else that's been done here." He couldn't hide his pride.

"That's amazing. How long did it take?"

"We are just about to start our fifth month of working here. We bought it almost two years ago. We only work during the summer, and the few times we could, or had to be here."

"What do you mean, had to?"

"We had to come up here for the court case."

Brent adds, "They were the girls that were harassed in my store."

"So, you knew them before?"

Amy offers, "We went to school together. I've known Brent for a few years now. When I told him I was gay, he watched out for me and kept the other guys from hitting on me."

"Why would you do that?" she looked at him accusingly.

"I had a crush on her. I was her stalker, until she asked me to walk with her instead of behind her. She said her dad wouldn't allow her to date until she was thirty five. I didn't want her to be harassed, by the guys in the school, after she told me she was gay. I hung around to look like her boyfriend, so they would leave her alone."

"It worked too." Amy added.

"So is she your ex-girlfriend?"

"I've never had a girlfriend. But if I did have one, it would have been her."

Tanya spoke up now, "I was her girlfriend at the time and ever since. He never had a chance."

"Are you two living here?"

"No, we work here and stay here. We wouldn't really call it living here until we get our kitchen in." Tanya said plainly. Tanya's voice had changed a lot since the day Amy came to visit. It is no longer a soft little squeak, but a powerful, mid-toned voice. She is loud and proud.

"And you bought this?"

"My dad bought it, after two summers of camping and looking. We are going to be added to the deed when we turn eighteen." Amy said.

"Wow. That's cool. You have done a great job."

Brent nudges her, "Check out the bathroom. They did it with Amy's brother-in-law."

Lidia gets up and walks into the bathroom. "Wow! That is beautiful! You do an amazing job!"

"It was our first time and Brad started us off and supervised the whole thing."

"How long did it take?"

"A whole two days."

"That's incredible!"

"Thanks. We're learning as we go. Tomorrow, Mom and Dad, are coming up with their friends to install the kitchen cupboards that his friend made. We will be doing as much of that as we can. When we retire here, we want to know every inch of it. If something breaks, we could fix it."

"That's amazing. How long before you turn eighteen?"

"Two and a half years." Amy answered.

"Get out! You're kidding me! You're younger than me?! You look at least seventeen!" Lidia has lived a sheltered life out here. "I knew I was small, but I didn't know I was that far behind."

"I developed very early. I looked like this before I got to high school."

"What year are you in high school?"

"Oh, I've graduated this year. I'm going to Waterloo University in the fall."

"Wow, brainy, built, and beautiful. Triple threat." Lidia was feeling a bit left behind. "What school are you in, Tanya?"

"Grade ten, high school."

"I feel better now. I'm still in high school too. I was afraid, you were a triple threat too."

"Thank you, Lidia!"

"What do you two do out here at night?" Lidia is looking for a TV, or a radio.

It's Tanya that fields this one, "We usually sit by the fire and then, we go to bed, a-n-d sleep. We work all day. Except to fish, or canoe the lake. It's too nice and quite, here, to have any noise on. If we were at home we would do all that stuff, TV, stereo, Xbox. Here we love the peacefulness."

"Do you get many animals around the cottage?"

Amy says, "We use to. In the winter there are the wolves and a bear, or two. In the summer, they stay away for the most part. Although, my sister, Faith, saw two bears leave our woods to cross the road."

"Doesn't that scare you?"

"It bothered me about the bears, because we have a goat, a deer and a horse, on loan to us, and we didn't want them harmed." Amy explained. "We aren't too afraid, because we have our kitty cats."

"Cats!? Cats will protect you from bears?"

"These ones will. Won't they, Brent?" Amy teased.

"Oh yeah, they'll scare that mama bear as much as the cub." Brent chuckled.

Amy told her, "Brent was scared by them, the first time he saw them."

"What kind of cats will scare a bear?" She was intrigued.

"Mountain Lions and Panthers."

"You have a cougar?"

"No, but we have its South American cousin, the Panther. Two of them."

"Really!? You have two panthers?"

307

"Yup," Tanya quipped.

"Where are they?" she looked nervously around the cottage.

"They're in the loft, but we should have them near the tents." Amy says, "Come on, take a look." She went to the ladder and climbed up. She sat between the 'pets' and stroked them, as Lidia peered over the floor of the loft.

Tanya turned on the sound-track. She watched Lidia jump and nearly fell down the stairs, but Brent was there to catch her. "They're statues." Brent told her. He didn't laugh, and neither did the girls. Lidia would feel bad enough without being laughed at. Brent hugged her close. She settled down. "They use them to scare off guys, like those jerks, and animals, like the bears, wolves and raccoons. Amy's dad brought them here to protect them and the cottage. They work pretty well. Don't they?"

"Y-yeah, they do." she was shaking. "Why didn't you laugh at me?"

"You were going to feel bad enough as it was." Amy calmed her. "We don't want to be jerks. You couldn't believe us, so you had to see. Nothing else for it."

"Well, thanks for not laughing."

"Are you okay now?" Brent murmured in her ear. She nodded. She looked at him. He was still holding her in his protective hug. She felt she had to give him a tender kiss, long and soft. He smiled and returned the kiss.

"Alright, get a room." now they laughed at Tanya's bark.

"You guys are nice, I feel like you like me. I feel accepted here. Thank you for being nice."

Tanya gave her a pat on the shoulder. "You're welcome. Thank you for not being judgemental."

"Why? What do you mean?"

"That, is what we mean. You didn't even think, it was worth being judgemental about. That we are lesbians." Tanya emoted.

"Is that what gay means? Oh, ewww!" Lidia smiled. "I don't think I have the right to judge someone I don't know. I hardly know what it is like to be a lesbian. How can I say it is wrong?"

"You can come here anytime. You can even bring him with you." Tanya said resting a hand on her shoulder.

Brent clutches her shoulders gently from behind. "It's getting late. I better take you home."

Tanya and Amy look at each other. Then they look at him. "Does your armour ever get rusty?"

He grins back at them. "Not anymore. Since I stopped crying inside it."

Amy coughs, "Aww, that's sad."

Their guests smiled and said good night. They left out the front over the new deck. "Nice work girls."

"Thanks." They climbed down behind them and went to get the animals. Their menagerie is getting quite accustomed to them. They come to meet them, and nuzzle them, affectionately. The girls stroke the coats and rub them down a bit. "Maybe we should put stalls in the barn." Tanya suggests.

I hear that and weigh in. 'You would have to be living there, full time.' Amy shares my comment.

Tanya complains, "He can hear ME now!"

"When you talk to me, he does."

"Well tell him we need some water, or a filter for the taps."

"He said, okay." They cracked up.

In the morning, they have the bass, they caught yesterday. They cook it in lemon juice and olive oil. Seasoning with a dash of pepper. Serving it with tea. A very simple existence here. They are fit, happy, busy, and together. They could stay here like this. It is a better way to live. Lots of company. Peace and quiet. One problem, they need to be able to keep it paid for, and supplied. Tanya barks, "Spoil sport!"

They get the trim under the porch decking up and put in the railing. The lumber supplies are holding out, but should be topped up. 'I will get more, when I am up there.' Once done the porch, they go in to measure up the other railing, for the loft. They get out there to the stock pile. They can take the animals for a walk, and look for more branches. They bring all three pets with them. They are used to the animals and the animals are used to them. They stroll through the woods and down to the road. Turning around they see some dark shapes, back in the trees. The horse gets agitated but doesn't run. The shapes stop and change direction. The shapes are going to go around them, and give them a wide berth. The horse's head is straight up and level. The girls don't move. They have a feeling, they stand a better chance, staying and keeping the animals calm. They watch as the shapes get closer to the sunlight. It was the mama bear and her cub. Tragedy averted. They continue their walk, still looking for branches to add to the woodpile.

I am finished my appointment and we head for home. We get some food on the way home. We get home and knock on the door, next to us. George is there and they are all set. They are just finishing the cooler packing. Their truck and trailer, along with my van, are holding the complete kitchen. We are on the road soon and the traffic is light. It is the best time of day, to go past Toronto. It would only be lighter during the night hours. Our old eyes won't work that way anymore.

The teens have put their charges on the tethers. They are going through the pile of branches. When they have a good candidate, they strip it and hang it up to dry. When they feel they have enough, they test fit them. Once they have enough to fit, they apply glue and tack them together with a brad nailer. Then they start to apply the coating. It will take several coats to get it right. They have now finished their goal for the day, and head off to the canoe. Lifejackets on, fishing rods clipped into the gunwales. They stick the fish cooler in the boat, and shove off. They have a pail for their bait. Out on the water, they toss out the lures. Just like yesterday, there is one on each side. They don't get far. They stop paddling and coast as Amy pulls in her line, Tanya is fighting her fish. This one likes to run and can. Her line is whizzing off the reel. She gives the pole a yank and it stops. She starts reeling it in. It is fighting still, like it was trying to spit that thing out. Fed up with that, it takes off again. She lets it run for a while and then gives another good yank. She starts to reel in, in earnest. Pulling the rod back and then cranking it in. Alternating, one to the other, she pulls it to the surface. Amy quickly jabs the net down and scoops up the fish. It was just about to go for another run. That helped her net it. It dove right down into the net. This big pickerel was one tough fish. It would have got away on the next dive. The hook was just about torn loose. It hadn't fully hooked the jaw. He likely, would have died after a fight like that. They put some water into the fish cooler. They pull out the knife and carefully gut him. The guts go in the pail and the fish in the cooler. They paddle out to the centre of the lake. They take some entrails and bait their hooks. They toss in the hooks with some sinkers on the line. They start trolling, cutting close along the points of the bays' entrances. They are close, but still in deeper water. Tanya has the hit again. It feels like a snag, but the line keeps moving ahead of them. Tanya reefs back to set the hook. The fish just jostles, but continues its course. They shudder, to think of what it was they hooked into, this time. Tanya is reeling in as hard as she can. That just makes the canoe go faster. Amy remembers her line and cranks it in. Tanya sees something under the water. It is huge. It comes up like a submarine, at speed. It looks like an alligator. It is a Muskie. Like the Pike, it is a member of the same family, as the Gar, and the Barracuda. It looks like it's a log. An alligator-log. How are they going to land that. Tanya is still reeling in. They are going to be coming along side. Amy has the net, and the extra-long, needle-nosed, pliers. She is going to try to slip the hook out, or net the beast and wrestle it into the boat. At any point, if it starts to go wrong. Tanya will cut the line and Amy will drop the net. It is tied to the boat, and can be pulled back in after the fish shakes it loose. All of their equipment is attached in some way to the canoe. Before she moves in, she pulls out her camera, and takes the picture of it. She looks at the jaw and it is nowhere in sight. This big guy swallowed the hook. She drops the pliers into the boat and slips the net over the brute's head. Tanya drops her rod back in the boat and grabs the net from Amy. Amy, in turn grabbed the lunker's tail and they heaved it up into the boat. It landed, wedged between the cooler and the wall of the canoe. They slipped some bungee chords, from one side of the boat to the other. They spun that canoe around and headed for home.

"Holy crap, Marie. The girls were fishing and caught a humungous Muskie. They got it in the boat and are heading back to the cottage. From what I can tell, it is close to five feet long."

They slide up on the beach. Jump out of the boat and pull the canoe all the way off of the sand. They see the vet checking the animals. Tanya calls him over. He heads right to them. When he gets close, she points into the canoe. He comes up and looks in. "Holy Mary, Mother of God. How did you get that in there?"

Tanya says, "I caught it and we both yanked it into the boat. It swallowed the hook and towed us along the lake."

"What bait did you use?"

"Pickerel guts." Tanya said.

"Well, why don't we measure it and weigh it?"

"Sure!" Tanya was getting excited. The vet got some scales from his truck.

"Here, let's see what he weighs." The vet stuck a hook into its gill and lifted it out of the boat. "58 lbs. and seven ounces. Here, use my tape. Measure around its thickest point."

"30 and a half inches, and.... 59 inches long. Amy get a picture of the doctor and I with the fish."

"Now, can you two hold it up like this. I have to verify your measurements." He took the tape measure and put it around Tanya. "Oops. The fish, the fish. You are right at thirty and five eighths inches. The length is fifty nine and one sixteenths inches. That, my girls, is a world record fish. What are you going to do with it?"

"We can't get the hook out of it. It was caught on the other end of the lake. We don't want to throw it back if it will just die. What should we do?"

"I can get the hook out. If the fish dies, it won't be because you caught it and let it go too late. It will die eventually. Everything does. You could release it, eat it, or stuff and mount it. Taking this guy out of the lake at his size, will help the other fish live longer." He laid out their options. "What were you hoping to catch?"

"Lake Trout. Where can we get it mounted?"

"I have a friend that can mount it for you. Would you like me to call him?"

"Yes, please." She had just answered when she heard someone driving up the lane. She sees Amy going to meet them.

"Okay, I'll call him. What can I take him in?"

"This fish cooler," she opens it and lifts out the pickerel.

Amy and the rest of us are hurrying over to see this monumental occasion. We get there just before they were going to lift it into the cooler. We talked about it and congratulated Tanya. We then helped to heft him into the cooler. Then we carried the cooler to the vet's truck. They had a bunch of pictures of it. We started walking around the property and telling the stories. We showed Connie and George the different accommodations, then asked them to choose where they would like to be sleeping tonight. Then we went into the cottage and see what was done in there. They are aghast at the ladder and railing. They check into the bathroom and loved it too. Nobody visits, who isn't amazed at the beauty of the work. All of our kids are remarkable, and two of their best fans, are here with us today.

George quickly measured the space, to set his mind at ease about the fit of the cupboards. Connie chose one of the cottage rooms. Amy changed the sheets on it and they gave us the other room. We moved all the furniture, out of the main room. The trucks were then unloaded. Cupboards were sorted out by location. We measured and marked where things on the wall were, so that we didn't bury anything. Before we installed anything, we reviewed all the requirements. We looked to see where we could maximize the space. We took the kick plates off and measured for drawers. They will be like the trundle beds. They'll be on rollers and not attached to the sides. This will give us space for many things that are only used occasionally, to free up space for things used often. George and I will go over this at home. We will try to find some ultrathin rollers, or bearings, to utilize the space in these drawers better.

George shows the girls how to install the cabinets. He arranged them in the order to be installed. Then the girls and I tried our hand at it. As is usual, I could only do the one, before being relegated to the sidelines. We watched the girls, with their enthusiasm and nimble fingers. They took very little time to finish the first half of the lower cabinets. George pointed out the points of concern on the other side, and let them go to town.

I feel useless in some ways. Amy reassures me that I am still strong for short durations. My weight can be an asset, when moving heavy things, like cars. I am, also, a memory bank for her, and her personal video system and communication network. She is such a good girl, for building up the old guy.

George gave us room for a large double sink. It is one I found a good deal on. It is the kind that sit in the cupboard front, sticking slightly forward. The farm house type, some call it. While the girls finish the cabinets, George and I set the sink in place, under the window. Tanya gets in the cabinet, under the sink, to hook up the plumbing. She has a longer reach, and can get her slim fingers up behind the sink, and still move them. Amy is done her job, and gets George, to show her the finer points, of hanging his upper cabinets. She gets up on the ladder and they set the height they would like them to be. Amy doesn't mind using a stool, or stepladder, to reach things up there, but Marie does. We have the stove going in by the back door. The fridge is near the front door. The wood stove is in the space in the middle of the room toward the front door, with a stone barrier around it. The chimney goes up and out the old vent opening. We had to cut out some rot from nests there and that made the opening right for the stovepipe. The stone will keep people from backing into the hot stove. Sitting in the middle space, allows the air to circulate around it and use every bit of it. We put a sleeve around the pipe that will utilize the heat from the pipe and push it out into the room.

This kitchen flew together. We stopped for the night after Tanya finish the plumbing. We all got out on the lake for a paddle. Amy and Tanya used Brent's canoe and the rest of us were in ours. We saw the spot at the other end of the lake, where the girls caught the muskie. We showed the channel to the other half of the lake, and viewed the wildlife on and off shore. The moose was back. Mama bear and her cub were up the lake a ways. Loons and herons, beaver and muskrat, deer and a fox, all lined the space along the lake for us. We got back and walked the animals. The goat was going back to its owner soon. They found a home for it. We tethered the stock near the cabin, and enjoyed a fire. The night was early for most of us but I still needed to wait. They were all asleep in the house, when I came in. I had gone for a walk in the woods along my rope. My sight is better. The little problem that remains, is miniscule compared to what it was. I still need my rope in the woods. I don't relish the thought of becoming disoriented out here. The worst that would happen with the ropes there, is that I would follow it all night, until I could see something familiar. I also need reading glasses, still.

In the morning the girls finished the upper cabinets, while we walked in the woods. Connie agreed, the rope is a good thing for someone like me.

I said to her, "I know now, my life could end at the end of a rope."

Marie hits my arm, where she knows it will hurt longer, and yells, "Stop saying things like that! He always does that."

They laughed and I clung onto my arm.

Chapter Twenty Seven

A New Ball Game

The kitchen was finished. We celebrated the event. They have done everything they have been shown and have done it well. We went for the reward ride in the canoes. The girls were trolling again. They hardly get going fast and they have a bite. It's Tanya's turn to pull in her line. Amy is fighting hard, with this one. This fish is all over the place. We have drifted to a stop, not far from them. Amy is pulling so hard, my arms are tired and weakening. I feel that as I grow weaker, she grows stronger. As I tire, she is more alert. It is similar to the Dorian Gray phenomenon. Instead of youth and a picture, it's strength and stamina, from person to person. The fish jumps on the opposite side of the boat. She swings around with the rod, to get on the same side. She's reeling fast as she does. It dives and soon pops up on the other side, again. It didn't jump this time. She sticks the rod down into the water, as she cranks it in. She pulls it up and leans back, as the rod and the fish come out of the water and over the boat. She brings it down inside the craft. Tanya grabs the fish and sticks it in the cooler. She dumps a bucket of water in too.

"Lunch!" Amy shouts to us, and they throw their lines in again.

"How big was it?" George asked Tanya.

"About four pounds." she replied.

I hear engines behind us. I crane to see. It is the Bobcat. I apologize and turn the canoe back to camp. "I just have to take delivery of it, and we can come back out."

"That's alright, Tom. We don't have to go back out. I think I'm done." George still has time when the energy is just not enough. Like me, it is something he just has to watch for, and take care of. The treatments were so hard on him. He had heard me describe the feeling, years before, and recognized it for what I had said. Sometimes, you listen to the experiences they have suffered. It may be that you are being sent this message, as a warning of things to come.

"No problem, a nap is a good reward."

"You said it, buddy."

We slide up on the beach and pour out of the canoe. I go to the driver and they go inside. I get the machine down to the sand, and start moving the pile, onto the beach. It is a lot of sand, but it doesn't seem so, after it is spread out. The girls come back and after getting the cooler out, they pull both canoes out of the way. They grab the cooler and go to the porch. Pulling out the two good sized bass, they take them inside, to try out the new kitchen countertop. They have cleaned them out in the lake. Just like before, they cleaned them and this time, just dumped the entrails in the lake, to feed the big fish, and keep them in the area. I shut it down, when I am called for lunch. When I come in, they are waiting for me. I sit right down and toast to the new kitchen, and the hands that made it. We have the bass, with fries, and scrambled eggs. The stove was put through its paces.

We never lack for a good meal up at camp. We try to eat healthy up here, but this time we had to celebrate the new appliances and prep area. We will use basins in the sink, and toss the wash water and rinse water, out on the plants around the cabin. Reducing the load on the system is still a good practice. Even with, the recycling of the wash water, to the toilet. We still can do more.

The team goes out for a walk with the animals. I get back to sanding that beach. I am going to need another load. This machine is a fun little piece to use. I've operated heavy loaders and bulldozers, as well as small farm sized ones, and this is more fun than any of those. When I get to the end of the pile, I tip the bucket and grade the pile remnants and beach flat. I call for another load of sand, and two loads of stone. They promise to deliver tomorrow. I am glad I bought this machine. Amy tells me that Connie and George are going back in the morning. I expected they might. I run the Bobcat up into the trees, and slip a cover over the cab. I walk toward them as Amy directs me. They are enjoying the animals. The goat is being picked up today. This afternoon. The days here are so different from home. The time is irrelevant here, at least in our camp. An hour away, it is more like home time. They have schedules. People try to fit more into it, or make what's in it, stretch out to fill it. Here we do and then not. At home there are lists, if someone would write them down. I hear the lists echoing and forget half, or more, until the echo is back. Marie knows the list and will tell me. But I have so bad a memory, remember, Marie? I think she might, too. I am upon them and enjoy the conversation, that Amy silently interprets for me.

George wants to see what I have planned. We split away and walk back through the woods. I point out the marked trees, explain the colour code and describe the upcoming adventure, into the above ground level, living and entertainment. He enjoys my whimsy and imagination. He has some ideas, and gets into the mood of this type of play. We see things through our childhood selves. We skip back decades of maturation and in our case, it takes nanoseconds. It is as if we had never left. Aint it the truth. Our aging bodies are trying to get our attention, but we were infected fifty, or so, years ago, by Walt Disney's Imagineering, and we have rejected the treatments against it. If it isn't fun, don't build it.

"George, when the grandkids were here, and didn't know about the plans I have. They looked around and said, 'this place is awesome.' Imagine what they will say when it is done."

I took him inside, where we could rest, and look over the plans we drew. I pointed out the new windows and doors for the bedrooms. I told about the plans for a balcony. I showed him a new idea, I just planned, for a net between the porch and the balcony. It is modelled after a picture of a resort in the tropics. The net will be of thick, soft rope. It will likely have to be replaced, every few years. That will be the price I would have to pay, for a simple indulgence. We agree on the plans, naturally, and he gives me some pointers, on how to make it happen.

The women walk in the door, and I ask, "Did you get all of that, Amy?"

"Every word and picture."

Marie demands, "What are you up to now?"

"Just home improvements, Marie. Just home improvements."

She does not look amused. She doesn't share our visions. "When are they coming to pick up that machine?"

"They're not. I have three loads coming tomorrow, and I will be needing that to distribute them."

"How much sand do we need?"

"Only one. There are two loads of stone coming for the driveway and the new tile bed I will likely have to put in. Any left over will go for the foundation of the barn."

"Have you heard from the township, about that?"

"Not yet. I will not hold my breath. Governments at all levels, like to make you wait. Especially, if there is a chance, you will drop it. It won't be dropped by me."

"Where is that going to fit in?" George asks.

"Oh, I'm sorry! I didn't show you that. That is going to be beautiful. It goes right over there." I say showing him out the back door. "Right near the trees, by the edge of that hill. It will be a garage in the bottom, a workshop on the second floor, and on the end, we will have a two storey greatroom. A big natural stone fireplace will be at the end. There may be a couple bedrooms, a bathroom, and a kitchen. It will be able to turn into a rental, with just changing the zoning, or whatever you need, to do that."

"That would look great. You'll have lots of room here for all kinds of people."

"It will be for Amy to run after we've gone. She has put the most effort, with Tanya, to build it. So, it will go to her. The others can still visit, but she will own it. She will have built almost every part of it."

"That will help them get settled after college is done." Connie said.

322

"She will also inherit my models and all of that stuff. She and I worked on it together, and it will go nicely into the loft of the workshop."

"Great! She can take it all now, if she wants." Marie grants.

"Marie, we haven't built the barn, and I will still be using it." I stated firmly.

Amy looks at Marie and frowns. George and I sit down to rest some more. I, a little more urgently, than he. Amy tells me, to just let it go. It is all arranged. No one needs to know. I offer drinks and Amy fills the orders. It was just a call to say, I need one. Even as I say this, I feel that I need two. Amy fills one, deep and dark. Tanya will turn sixteen, next month, and Amy, in November. Yet, here they are bartending like pros. Yes, I know what you're thinking, and no. They aren't drinking while up here alone. In fact, if they did try this stuff? It would discourage them from wanting more. They aren't even into coffee. They tried it, don't like it. They don't go in for overpowering tastes.

Talk changes direction, with the advent of drinks. The menu is in question. I know the teens have got it covered, but I don't say a thing. Amy goes to the fridge and taking something out, hands it to Tanya. She goes out the back door. Amy pulls out more containers and starts preparing. Marie is talking to Connie about what she would like. Connie sees the action going on and says, "I'll have what they're making."

Marie looks around at Amy, busy at the counter. She shrugs her shoulders and suggests a short walk. As they leave, Amy tells me what Marie is going to talk to Connie about. I just say, that we all need our sounding boards. Connie will listen and remind Marie, that she hasn't had to do the work up here, and it would not have been done, at all, if it wasn't for Amy and Tanya. George and I are just resting. I must put up the hammocks, before I go back again. George would not have been able to lay out in the sun, so I should have a shelter to move them to, when he and I are up here again. I will need it anyway. The downside of having the pine forest, is the drippings of sap and the humidity, held in there. Another thing the tarps help fix.

Tanya is barbequing some steaks that Evelyn picked up for them. There is little fat and no spices. Marie has her reflux issues, and George's diet has been cautious ever since his stem cell transplant. It is better to let everyone, add their own spices, to their own tastes. Amy is making two of Marie's famous salad recipes. She is also making a wonderful desert, that Grace had made, the first year she stayed with her. It was started yesterday. The meal is going to be fabulous.

The steaks are done, and are on the way in. Tanya calls out to say that dinner is ready. The two women turn to come back to the cabin.

Dinner is served out on the round table, that Marie had mistakenly bought, for our trailer. The scale is much better here. The sage is burning in a brass pot in the middle of the table. A wide array of seating is available, and each person chooses their own. I am on a hefty wood log round. I leave the view of the lake, for our guests. The appetites grow rapidly, as the food comes into view. Some already on the table and some coming down the stairs, on platters borne by the hostesses. All adversities are forgotten, in view of the feast. The spice choices are offered for each to choose.

Some foods affect different people different ways. This one was lovely and the conversation, lively. It was a feast for the ears, eyes, and palate. It lasted longer, as the talk grew livelier.

The tastes were to each person, which made it a hit all around. The wine was served, and probably aided in the conversations. When the desert was served, they were astounded. Connie stated outright, that the legacy of taste, was certainly being passed down, from mother to daughters, in this family.

After dinner, the cleanup was quick. Leftovers were nonexistent. We sat around the fire, adjacent to the dinner table. Off to the right of us, Brent's car was pulling in. He and Lidia got out and approached with an envelope held high in the air, above his head.

"Your response from the planning office. It just came." He handed it to me and I opened it then.

"They have approved the plans for the barn. We can go ahead and start construction as soon as I submit the fee and pick up my permits."

A chorus of, "Congratulations!" filled the night air.

"How much is this going to cost?" Marie looks straight at me.

"About one tenth of the value it will be when I finish it. Plus, it will give comfort, that the other accommodations here, have not."

"Yes, but how much?"

"Seventy five million dollars."

"What!?"

"We have yet to figure the cost out. The pad, is all that will be done, at first. The pole structure, will come next. Then the straw walls. It will be done as the funds become available. We will not go into debt on this project. It may move the entire family here, at some point. For vacations and celebrations. It will mean this will be a year round cottage of proper proportions. It can spawn an industry. It will certainly, be a worthwhile reason, to keep going through Toronto. It will be a family hub for generations to come, with Amy and Tanya as our hostesses. What is going to be costly, is the solar equipment to be installed. It will pay for itself and fund the future constructions we are planning. It is going on the cottage. When the barn roof goes up. It will go on it as well. It will mean running power cables, underground, to the poles out on the road."

"When were you going to tell me about this?"

"I have already told you, several times. You never want to discuss the future plans, until you have the money. You tuned me out and continue to do that. The only way you get the money for things, is to plan for them, and talk about them. Just like saving for the trip to Cuba, every year. We talk about it. We put a plan into action. We save for it. And then, we pay for it. I have to do all the planning with Amy, because you never listen to me. It is this place and my writing, that is providing for the extras in our future. The pension cuts from the company, and the government, is being replaced by the plans, you don't want to talk about. So, surprise!"

"I don't remember you telling me about any of this."

"That's because, you are so good, at the things you do, to tune me out. You will not have to worry about it. We have it all under control. Just sit back and enjoy the ride. There won't be anything demanded of you. Your participation is purely voluntary, like everyone else."

"So, we can still afford to go to Cuba, in February?"

"Most definitely!" I bow to her. "And to the cottage on Lake Huron, too."

"When are we going there? I didn't think we booked it."

"We didn't. But, we can go on any week she has left open, if you want to go there."

"I'll have to talk with Nan. I thought we would be coming here."

"We can. I was just offering you the choice."

"Oh, okay, I wasn't sure. I thought we were just going to come here."

"We still can."

"Okay, I'll talk to Nan then."

"Well, we're going off to bed. We have that long drive in the morning. Goodnight." Connie says while standing up to go.

"Goodnight." George echoes.

"Alright, goodnight." we all say in return.

Marie says, "I think I'll go to bed now too. I'm just going to read for a while."

"Okay Kitten. I'm going to talk with the girls a bit. Goodnight." I turn to talk with the girls after Marie leaves. "I hope you two are still okay with the arrangements here."

"Oh yeah, these two are visiting and we can do what we want. There is more than enough money left. We're good. When will you get started on the pit for the foundation?"

"Right after I spread the sand on the beach, tomorrow. I'll pull out those trees by the site. I can use them, like the family trees in the cedar log homes on TV. I might need to rig something that will make it work with 'Little Joe' over there."

The four of them asked, "Who's 'Little Joe'?"

"The Bobcat. After my little buddy, Joey, the cat."

"Ah, that makes sense." Amy says aloud.

"Brent are you still happy with the arrangements?"

"As long as it's okay with Lidia."

Lidia looks at him queerly. "What about me? What arrangements?"

"Us coming here, to check on the girls and getting things for them, when he's not here."

"Oh, okay. Sure. I thought we were just visiting."

"We were but it was also for their protection. They don't have any way of getting around. So I help them."

"Good. I'm okay with that. That is why I thought you two had had a relationship. Romantic."

"Oh. I would have, if she was straight."

"Is there anything else we can do?" Lidia asks.

"Only what the girls need." I say. "Brent, I need some rebar. Do you have it?"

"Not in my department. I'll have to ask the manager. I can find out where to get it for you. I'll let you know tomorrow night."

"Great. I'll do the beach and spread out the stone for the driveway and new septic bed. Then I'll try to take down those trees. This is getting too exciting. I hope I don't blow a fuse."

Chapter Twenty Eight

Treebeard Walks Again

I left Brent and the girls and wandered over to the tree line. It ran across the ridge of hills, that were more or less, covered by trees and scrub brush. The brush was hit or miss, along the line. The trailer sat on the highest of the tree line hills. It had trees down the front a bit. The tent decks were displacing the scrub brush. The trees were around the back. The barn will sit between the trailer's hill and the lane. The second biggest, tree line, hill is just behind the building site. As I stand looking over the scene, I feel an arm go around my waist, or a little below it. Amy was revisiting a scene from my memory. My dad, standing at the gate, looking out over the back forty. He was having one of his last cigarettes for the day. He would stand there silently, contemplating his existence, for all I know. He never said anything. He was six-two. Lean and lanky. Here I am. Barely five-ten. Ruggedly obese. That's the best way I can say that. I was nine or ten at that time. Slim, so much so, that my ribs looked like ski jumps. I wouldn't fill out, until I met

Marie. That is to the best of my knowledge. Amy is short, but not too big around. Actually, she has an amazing figure, for her age. One that fathers' are both proud of, and afraid of, for what will be chasing that figure. I am close to all my daughters. Sons are different. They seem to have to set the boundaries. Rewrite the rules. My dad was dead before we got to that stage. I was so glad to have a second chance, with my father-in-law, that we skipped over that. Now Amy and I are occupying each other's head. We are there, wherever we are, and tonight I am glad she has her arm around my hips. Well not all the way around.

"Dad, sometimes you are so full of it, to the others. Then, other times, you are this big, block, of mush. You can do this, Dad. You and Little Joe can move that mountain you're forming in that brain of yours. It smells nice out here tonight. So, if you're full of it, you haven't dropped any out here."

"You are so sweet. Stubby."

"Hey!"

"How is your mom's head now?"

"She's trying not to think of it. You didn't get mad this time. So, that was good. She just doesn't like it when you show her up to be, what she is. She is her mother's daughter. She doesn't like that and it is starting to be obvious to her. And you know, she hates that."

"Is it safe to go in?"

"As safe as it will ever be."

"Goodnight, Amy."

"Goodnight, Dad." she turned to watch as I walked away, as if, toward my doom. She hopes to avoid the things girls dislike about their mothers. It is the parents' curse. It is universal. Unavoidable. She shudders.

'I felt that like an earthquake. It was as if all the daughters of the world, were thinking the same thing, at the same time.'

I walked into a darkened room. I left to get ready for bed and when I returned, the room was lit. She was sitting up, waiting for me. "I'm sorry." she said, "I didn't mean to ignore you. It seems like a waste of time, thinking of things we can't get."

"We may not be able to get them one day, but on another, we might. So our plans don't come through for us this time, or that. If we keep making them, we will find a way, to make them come through for us. Disappointment is the fuel, that feeds the fire under us, that will keep us going."

"I don't like having to do those things. I just want to go places, that we can afford."

"Doing that, will mean, that one day, we won't be able to go to the grocery store."

"Why do you say things like that?"

"Because it's true. We have to do something more than some, but less than others. We are doing now, more than I ever dreamed of, before. Now, I am dreaming of it and we are doing it. If you don't like the way we're going. You'll just have to get out of the way. We are going, and we are going there, for you."

"I don't want to talk about it anymore." she lay down and turned off her light.

I turned on mine and started reading my book. There is no use, what-so-ever, to continue talking.

In the morning, the whole household was up, to see our guests leave for home. I hope they got more sleep than I did. They drive around the cabin, and out the back, before heading up, and out the driveway. They are down the road and gone before the truck with the sand pulls in. Amy signals him down to where the first load was put. He does as he is directed and spreads the sand over the same lines. He circles the building and stops by our van. "Where would you like me to put the stone loads?"

"Right where your truck sits right now."

"Okay, just sign here. I'll be back as fast as I can get loaded."

"Okay, see you then." Amy says.

Two and a half hours later, there he is. He pulls in toward the Young's, and backs down to dump the load. "Sign here. Same place next time?"

"Right in front of it."

He nods and races back down the lane. He is back in an hour and a half. He follows the same procedure. Dumps the load, pulls ahead and jumps out of the cab. "No line-up this time. Sign here. It's paid for." Amy gives him a generous tip. "Thanks," he said, "I appreciate it." He climbs back into the cab and races down the lane again.

By this time, I am becoming operable, after my nap and some rest. Amy and Tanya are going to get ready to put down the flooring. I get a call from Brent. They don't carry rebar, but he found someone who does. He gives me the number and I thank him. I am ready to eat and they have left some food wrapped up, in the microwave. I check to see if it's warm, and it is good enough. I eat and then head out and get on Li'l Joe. When I feel up to it, I drive Li'l Joe down to spread out the sand. Amy tells me, that Marie is in the trailer, cleaning. I have a ball moving the sand. It nearly feels like a toy.

Marie asks Amy where they have been sleeping? She thinks the question. Amy excuses herself and goes to tell her, it was in the nylon tent. She hurries back to Tanya. Amy tells me that, 'Mom is think asking me things.'

Tanya is getting flustered with the pieces of flooring. Amy switches with her and Tanya hands her the pieces. They struggle with it and eventually finish the first room. It had the trap door in it. Marie is finished cleaning the trailer and tents. I am grading the beach. It now extends out to where the sand was dumped. There is room enough for a lounge to be set there and still get around the canoes. As soon as I finish the grading, I tell Amy, I'm ready to go, and they all come down, to get the canoes in the water. They are really taken with the size of the beach, Marie especially. They take off their shoes and walk on the fresh sand. It's not quite the same as the beach sand on Lake Erie, or Huron. But it will do. The kids can play in it. It will take some time before the soil overtakes it, as it did the old sand. It will do nicely. The sand nearly hi-jacked the canoe trip down the lake. Breaking the spell, we slipped our canoe into the water. The other one was left on the beach. We are not fishing today, just paddling. We have brought our repellent, in case we want to brave the channel. It is an ominous sky. The clouds are threatening to interrupt, just getting to the end of our lake. We need to get the exercise and a little rain won't hurt, if I can get back before being soaked. I get infections easily, and just getting a slight cold can bring one on. We have four at the paddles, so we can get to speed fairly quick. The sky is mainly overcast and the water is dark. The bottom is not as easily seen today. The animals are ready for the coming storm. You see none of the usual fauna. They have all taken for cover. Half way down the lake, though, we decide that it is time, we took shelter too. The canoe is swung around and we make the most concerted effort, we have ever done, to date. The scenery is used mostly, for a gauge of our progress. Landmarks to offset questionable depth perception. We are traveling very well, as evidenced by the wake we are creating. We have a long and wide vessel to project through the darkening waters, and we are displacing a good volume of water. The beach is now visible and we are approaching at a now, tremendous rate, for our mode of travel. We don't slow up, but slide back, to lift the bow out of the depths. We slip onto the beach and are accepted well, by the soft pliable coating on shore. We come to a stop and disembark as quickly as our legs will lift us. Mine are not enough to get me up in this position. The girls haul me to my feet. Thinking back to the big storm we had earlier, we pull the canoes up to the cottage and bring the life jackets and paddles inside. The canoes are tied to the stairs. I must remember to put a rack on the side of the porch to hang the canoe from. I go to get Li'l Joe, up onto the hill. These are extreme measures for a rainstorm, but once bitten, twice shy. The deluge we had gotten previously, made us think and respect the power, the old lady can wield.

All is under control. We have made shelter in good time and await the show to begin. We can see the flashing start in the distance. The sky is dark, but not overly. The rumbling was muted and distant. The air is muggy. It seems to have been amplified, in the time we were away for our ride. It is getting quite close. We open all the windows to let the breezes come through. It is not working. The air has become still and quiet. There are more threatening shadows on the horizon. We watch from our chosen aperture. Picturing the storms advance, and imaging its affect on our landscape. The woods across the lake, once green are now gray with the loss of light. The advance is vigorous. The sky now black. It is deathly quiet. Neither a twig snap, nor a grass blade rubbing. The wind is starting. It sounds as if a torrent of rain, approaching in a solid wall. It hits our little shack as if, trying to bear its weight and carry it away. The sound is changing as the rain erupts on the scene. It is approaching as the wind was described. It is so thick, there are no images beyond it. A funnel appears and just as quickly is gone. Another much lower one swipes, as a plane buzzing the audience at an air show. Particles pelt the roof and walls. The rain hits and the structure groans under the force. Now inside the deluge, we can see the line of sky, against the lighter tone, of trees in full leaf, yet colourless to our eyes. A blast of sunlight breaks through from beside us, showing the full majesty of the forest colour. It lingers for a time and then, all is the bleak tone that beckoned it. We are locked in the essence of the storm. Our hearts pounding, our breath laboured, our eyes transfixed on the show beyond our panes. Marie breaks the bond and remembering the instructions, orders us into the space beneath us. It may be late and inadequate, but this is the safest bet in our flimsy dwelling. The rumbling of the show outside, seems to abate, as we enter the crypt. The insulated walls dull the volume and we will wait until it has all passed us by. When the sound stops, we can again venture in the open air. It is dank and dirty here. We are disgusted with the texture, coating the layer of plastic, covering the ground. Hush. It has stopped. We push open the hatch above us and peek into the room. It has gone and the sun is shining its best. You can hear the birds. We climb up and line up to take a shower.

I suggest we go for a swim instead and get our grime off in a more entertaining fashion. The idea has merits and three of us head out immediately to get back to nature in its most welcoming form. As we reach the beach, Marie has decided to join us and make it unanimous. The water is still and warm. No great waves to erode the shoreline. We stand in the water and rub our selves all over, to loosen the imagined crud, we felt in the crawlspace. Then we dive in and feel relieved to be here. This is life, of the kind we longed for. We have no body surfing, as in the Great Lakes. We have no towering waves that engulf you at the waters edge. We have ripples and little tiny peaks of choppy surface. The miniaturized version of its larger cousin. Peace and contentment, from surf sound free, nights.

Cleaner and relaxed we have to check for storm damage. The house had been spared, considering, we need a new roof. Looking at the trees by the shore, there are some branches down. We grab those and take them to the sorting area. We continue up to the trailer. Everything looks undamaged. No branches down around it, but looking up, we see the top of a pine had been torn off and had fallen into the branches below. It was hanging above the trailer tarp. We will have to climb the tree to tie a line to it. It will have to be drawn away from the trailer to fall nearby. The first tent is good, but the tarp had been pulled free, and needs to have some ropes replaced. The old canvas tent had had the poles inside slip and the tarp was sagging on it. We were in good shape. A walk through the woods, will give us some more branches down, I'm sure, but we need to check the Young's cottage, and make sure Evelyn is okay. We walk calmly and relaxed. We don't want to get her worried, by running over. Their cottage looks okay and we breathe easier. We are nearing the door, when she opens it to greet us. She had a scare from the violence of it. Nothing was wrong though. Just the thing to hear after one of those storms. She had called Brent at work, to let him know she was fine. We let her go and left to look for anything else to clean up.

"Couldn't you use that tractor to check these things?" Marie wondered.

"I'll save on fuel and get some exercise, checking it out on foot. I could stand, to lose a hundred pounds, but it didn't work. So I'll have to walk."

"I guess it would be good to take a hike around. Evelyn doesn't seem to have lost any trees, or even branches."

"It might not have been close enough, to her place. There might be more damage further into the bush here."

Amy wonders, "Should we split up to check a wider swath?"

"I don't think we need to do that, unless you want to."

"Yeah, we would like to walk alone for a while."

"Alright, you take the half way point and go to the ropes. Then go half way to the tree line and come back to the lane. We will go about three quarters of the way to the road and go to the ropes, and then come back along the road. Watch for falling branches. We will meet at the house." They agree to the plan and quicken their pace, to get some space between us. Marie would like to walk that fast, but she can't leave me behind. At least, not do it and get away without the guilt. Amy would see to it, that she feels the guilt for it. I try to go quickly. I just can't keep the pace that she likes.

"We will just be getting to the spot to turn in, and they will be at the ropes already."

"Marie, think of the relaxing feeling, then it won't feel like work. I need to go slow enough to see what I want to see. I want to get limbs, as soon as I can, after the breakage. I can cut it better and it will give me a stronger piece."

"Okay, I'll look for those things. I can see them better, I guess."

"Most assuredly." I would like to go and get Li'l Joe, and cruise around in it. I want to get my exercise. I need to lose at least seventy pounds. If I give in, it will start a domino effect. I will do what I want and not what I must. My diabetes will get out of control, I could lose one, or both of my legs, my eyes, and my wife. That is suicidal. I'll walk, thank you.

The teens do get to the ropes fast. They may not have seen it all. They need to look carefully to see the treetops. The trees are thickly spaced. It may only take a breeze to bring these branches down. They are caught by the weakest branches. As we go along, Amy and I start planning the barn build levels, and how these branches and treetops will fit in. We envision the cedar log homes and hope that recreating that in pine, would be good enough. It is easy to see what others do and drool all over it. But to take that and make it your own, is the trick that takes an industrious and creative mind. I can handle the creative, but can she handle the industrious, enough to pull it together. She thinks, the three of us can do it. I would need to be only in key areas. She has faith in us. She can see my vision and can figure a way. Concessions will have to be made. Pine is a far cry from the Western Red Cedar. Or, is it? It isn't as impervious to bugs as cedar. Amy found a good sized Christmas tree, broken from a treetop. I have her stick it in moist ground, so it will reroot. Marie shows me a large tree down, leaning against another. Down by the road we have several trees down and broken. I will be coming back down with Li'l Joe, and dragging these up to the sorting pile. I need a chainsaw. After we clean up what we can, I need to see Brent about a chainsaw. I have used one before, but it wasn't my strong suit. Grace and her brood will be down next weekend. Brad can help me learn about the chainsaw. Amy saw that we were going to be awhile, so they went back to start bringing in their finds. They took the extension ladder and rope. While we brought our smaller finds up the lane, they were going for the large piece over the trailer tarp. They just want to get the rope around it, to attach it to Li'l Joe. We set the wood at the sorting spot. Marie goes to the facilities and I jump on Joe. He starts right away, so I go to the girls to get that rope tied to Joe.

"That is brilliant!" Amy had climbed the ladder into the tree. It was too far to reach the objective. So, she took the top half of the ladder, anchored it to a sturdy branch and with the rope, she lowered the top of the ladder, to rest against another tree. This formed a bridge that she could walk across, and tie the end of the same rope, to the broken piece. Then walking back, she looped the rope over the branch above her, and threw down the rope for Li'l Joe. I tied the rope to Joe's draw pin and slowly pulled away. Tanya was watching Amy. Amy was watching the load. I was watching Tanya. The ladder boom, started to lift and then the load started to move. The pivoting anchor point, was doing well. When the load was free, Amy signalled to stop. Tanya relayed the signal and I stopped. We had to include Tanya, because it was a view, that we didn't have. Amy pushed the boom out over an empty place, and holding it there, she signalled to lower the lift. I let Joe roll backwards. The load was descending well, until I ran out of room. Tanya and I loosened the rope and lowered the load until it touched down at the foot of our tree. Amy came scrambling down the tree to the ladder bottom and then down to us. "Excellent rigging, for a first timer. We can go to the other spots and use the same ingenuity to take care of them. Amy, get Mom to bring the van to the end of the lane. Tanya, you tie the ladders to Joe and jump on."

Tanya and I got to the leaning tree and started to work out a solution. Marie and Amy drove down in my van. Amy has her drive right up to where I was. Marie would have rather parked on the side of the road. "It's a legal prospective. Parked here on our land, we are dealing with our land issues. Out there, we would be encroaching on crown land. If our tree falls onto crown land, we can retrieve it, but we don't want it too close to blocking the road."

We put the extension ladder together again and place it against the tree being leaned on, from the other side. Tanya climbs up to tie the rope to the top of the fallen tree. We tie the other end to Joe. Once everyone is clear of the lift and swing zones, I slowly pull forward on the lift. The tree starts to move, it looks like it is going to follow me as I pull it. No, it has somewhere else to go. It wants to swing around sideways. I pull faster to draw it away from some young trees. I was just fast enough to keep the young trees. It is laid out flat now. I drag the whole tree down the lane to our sorting spot, and beyond. Untying it I head back to the women. Evelyn stopped me and said, she could use a machine like this.

"What would you like me to do for you?"

"I was looking in our woods and there are several trees that need trimming and hauling out of there."

"Okay, I'll come by once we are finished at the road. Okay?"

"Okay."

I got down to the girls and pulled up to the van. They showed me some other trees leaning. I drove over to see them, but they were on the other side of the ropes. I turned to come back and met them. "They're on the wrong side of the rope."

"It looks like your ropes were moved." Tanya said.

"I'll have to get the survey from the van." Tanya ran to get it for me. She brought it back and showed the marker. I got out and walked over with her to the marker. There was a wooden stake with red paint on it, and an iron rod driven down into the ground. "You're right Tanya. I'll have to move the ropes back." She took off to where she saw the deviation from the path. She then, retied the ropes along the trees, straight down to the marker. That put the other leaning trees on our side of the line. We proceeded to do the same to those trees. It bothered me that I would have to remove three healthy trees to make room for the barn foundation. I had based my proposals on that site. I will have to look at other options. We finished the day dragging four full trees, that had fallen against other trees, back to the camp. The sorting area is getting very full.

"We have to find good straight pieces from the broken branches and others good for features. Any that aren't good for building will go for firewood. All of the building logs will have to be stripped of bark and branches that can be resorted. Watch out for pieces that give you ideas that we have considered yet. We all have a stake in this build. Anyone can submit suggestions for a certain piece, before moving on with the processing. Okay, let's get started. I'm going over to help Evelyn, at her place."

I drove Joe over to see what she had in mind. Seeing me coming, she ran out to meet me. She waved me around to the back of the house. Coming out the back door she walked through some tall ornamental grasses. I tried to fit through the same opening she had used. At least there is a gateway there. I saw her down a short slope. She was pointing to the stream. I shut Joe off and climbed down to see what she was thinking. She said she needed a bridge there. "How big a bridge?"

"Four feet wide, and high enough to get where this slope isn't to steep. I want a trail through the woods and back, to give me a place to walk for exercise."

"Do you want it to meander? Up and down, in and out, this way and that?"

"Yes that is exactly what I want."

"When would you like it by?"

"When ever you have time." She shrugged. "I have relatives coming this fall. It would be nice to have it ready for them to see."

I think of my own projects and what needs to be a priority. I rub my hands over my face as I try to concentrate. "I will need to get my foundation in for the barn yet. It needs to set over winter. I might be able to do it then. I'll have Marie, go with you to mark out the path for me to follow. She has a good artistic analyzing eye. After she does that, I can make changes if I have to, because of different regulations." I went to get Marie. I backed Joe out of there, and went looking for her. As I got around the house she was there.

"Amy said you wanted to see me,"

"Yes Evelyn wants a trail back there through the woods. Go with her with some spray paint and mark the route she wants. I'll go get the foundation dug out."

"Okay. Where is she?"

"Around back and through the pampas grasses."

"Do you have some paint?"

I hand her some spray cans of paint, from inside Li'l Joe. I drive back over to start preparing the site for digging.

Marie and Evelyn begin talking about the path she wants to walk. She wants a bridge across this low stream. Its banks are too steep and she would love, to just have this entrance to her wonderland trail. Marie marks the low point of the easement, where the bridge should start. They walk along the streams edge, to get to a more accessible crossing point. While they walk,

Evelyn remembers the strolls through here. She recalls the things that drew them back here time and again. He had promised to build a bridge for her, in that spot. Something had always come up, to keep him from getting it done. Marie recalls the many things, I had promised, where things would always come up. The things we have set up, for others to do for us. If we want them done we have to do them for ourselves. She said that she didn't mind so much, because she was always the thing that would come up. She would give him more and more things to do, that he could never get it all done. The day he died, he was going out to start building that bridge. Something came up.

She wants it built for him now, as a memorial. "To the memory of 'My Mighty Joe Young'." she said.

They got around to the other side and back opposite the marked area. She marked the edge of the drop, on that side. They walked the path she wanted to take, and Marie marked the way as they went along. They came to a promontory rock. From that point they could view the lake, both upper and lower. They could see the course of the river winding its merry way. The only thing they could not see, was the paved road, in either direction. This was 'Magic Point' to us, we were cut off from the scars of man. They would come here everyday and sit on the rock.

"Would you like a bench here to sit on. Something natural looking, or of natural material?" Marie suggested.

"Oh, that would be lovely. Could you?" she beamed.

"If nothing comes up." Marie joked, "Yes, we will do that."

They continued walking and talking and marking their path. They came to a karst. They looked into the cave below. "Brent and Joe would go down there exploring and said it was amazing, but treacherous. They stopped going after they nearly fell through a crevasse. They called it 'nap crevasse' because of the sudden drop off." Marie was making a mental note of the details. As she would make the notes, Amy was writing them down. She and Brent would help the project get done.

While they were charting the job for Evelyn, I was carving out the base for the foundation of the barn. The basic shape was halfway there, and I remembered, the trees needed to be taken out, to protect the roots. I was all set to get that done. I was not going to be able to do this with my Li'l Joe. I would roll down the slope after the tree. I gathered some rubber straps I had saved for protecting trees, when I would have to winch the truck out of a ditch. I wrapped the rubber around the tree and cinched it on with some ratcheting tie-down straps. I got the tow chains from the van and hooked them around the trunk of the tree. Hooking the chains to Joe, I gently pulled the tree. Tanya was my safety man and would signal me when the tree was starting to move easily. At that point, I would have to pull to the side and get out of the drop zone with Li'l Joe protecting my way. Sure! I can hardly walk let alone run. If you're not living life on the edge, you're taking up too much room. That's what the boy's at work would say. I get the signal to stop. I get out of the Bobcat to see the trees root ball is free from the slope and is sliding, upright. Honestly!? Did anyone see that coming. The point it's at now, will make it a wild card. The cottage is just out of range, which means there is no more room to slide. The power line is in imminent danger. The trailer is threatened. I need to change the height of the contact point and pull it over toward the woods. Putting it back from whence it came. The soil that collapsed behind it, will keep it from sliding and force the bottom, out from under the trunk. This time I will be protected, by the height of the hill, between the tree and myself.

I am being laughed at. Amy could not keep from laughing at the tree sliding away from the hill. The soil of that particular hill, is very rich sandy loam. There is no clay in it. It is literally crumbling away. That means, we will need a retaining wall. Either that, or the hill is sloped back at a shallow angle. I may have to consult with the town on that. Most of the hills are silt deposits from glacier retreat. This hill, could have been a garden compost heap, from a historical homestead. Forest reclaiming the area, would thrive in this soil. I decide to leave the other trees along that line and build around them. In the space this tree will leave, I will put a path, sloping the hill up on a slight grade, and having a door for ATVs to access. I will go ahead with extricating this tree and make do with what we have already got.

Marie and Evelyn come over to see the reason, a tree was walking to the lake. They had just got back in time to see the treetop moving perfectly erect. Amy let me know that they had some erotic suppositions on the subject. They ask why I don't leave it there, and build around it.

"You would have a permanent Christmas tree through your greatroom roof." I test her. "Knocking down the walking tree, it is."

"How are you going to use these whole trees, you have here beside the cottage?" Marie challenges me.

"I will rent a crane, and lift them in place."

"Oh, this is not going to be good." she is not sure, about the size of project, we have here.

Evelyn calms her, saying, "Give him a chance. He has a vivid imagination and enough nerve to see it through. Hopefully you won't need the insurance company."

I reattach the chains and add ropes to give me a safer distance to work with. I pull the tree back to the hill and as the root ball crumbles further, it lays smoothly and gently down into the trough it made. We celebrate a plan 'B' victory. We reattach the chains and cladding near the root ball and over the cage of the Bobcat, to attach to the ends of the bucket. The bucket is in the fully raised position. Again, I gently take up the slack and hitting the limit of slack, I move carefully forward and the tree slides along behind. Not wanting to tempt fate, I keep moving in a wide loop around the cabin and back to the other side. I did it. I half expected the Bobcat's hydraulics to fail, or the bucket to rip open.

I tore up a lot of the scrub brush, that filled the floodplain. Animals will be around tonight, smelling that fresh turned soil smell. Raccoons, skunks, and others, will want to get at those creatures, whose homes we have disturbed. I get out and talk to the older women about the work that has to be done at the Young's place.

Chapter Twenty Nine

Dedicated

I was apprised of the details in the project for Evelyn. For as long as she will live, it will be part of Joe's legacy. I need to take it up with Brent. We can source out materials and decide on a plan of attack. This will be his and he will want to have a hand in it. The bridge is of concern. The depth of the ravine is fairly substantial, for anyone to fall in.

Brent and Lidia have come in to visit the girls. I take a bit of his time, to discuss what his mother, has requested. He likes the plans, and will look at coming up with the items we will need. I go for a walk in the evening shadows, with Marie. Her visit with Brent's mom, made her think of the things, that she wants me to do. We talk about Joe Young. We discuss the things he had put off. We talk about my excuses and his. They sounded identical to her. I was beginning to think, that I had just stepped in something, very unpleasant. I told her that with my memory being sharp as it isn't, I had to regret not doing somethings and rejoice in others. I usually found out there was a flaw in my plan and my abilities. She said that it was sometimes, a good thing, that I didn't get to do some things. She told me that Joe was going to do that bridge just as he died. He was going to get started on it. I feel that, she is afraid, that I won't survive long, trying to do everything she wants. I hope I don't put that much pressure on myself, to do it all. I do not want to shy away from things, for that reason alone. I hope to do things for her, and myself, for as long as I can.

It starts to rain, so the kids are forced inside. Marie and I go to one of the tents, and lie in bed, and put aside the thoughts of loss, and make thoughts of possibilities, fill our minds. We do celebrate that we are together, and that we can. The night is pushing us, to remember the camping days, and nights. The skunk routing around in the add-a-room. The raccoon having a tug-of-war with a friend over a pie. We are glad we have the camp. Stepping into the old tent, or the trailer, brings back the days when we were young. We cuddle up for the night.

When we opened our eyes in the morning, the rain was still at it. Thank God it was just a gentle rainfall. It was gloomy and uninspiring. We cuddled up and enjoyed a day off. Marie wonders what the girls are up to. I don't jump at that bait. I just hold her. We are far from the figures, we had as teens. We're far from whom we were, as teens. We enact the feelings we had. Memories so deep and engraved in our memory. We are as one, the envelopment of our love so deeply felt, so deeply longed for. We turn to the times long ago, that drove us and enabled us. The warmth of the flesh. The pace of the heartbeat. The sensitive touch that carried the fingerprints to the brain and sent shivers of delight through our frames. The hopefulness that we had then, to be allowed to be uninterrupted. The hopefulness now to be fortified in our purpose. Memory filled surroundings to suggest the ability is still there. The hopefulness that we can be deceived. The movements once made by youth in our skin, are mimicked by the present occupants. The fullness of our bodies compete with slight rays of dwindling hope. It is secured. Although not taking us to the centre of the universe, it is well received and welcomed, as payment for the things, that take us apart, to put us together. We lay in our embrasure, keeping all we have attained and placing these, in the days of wonder museum. We are not as we were, but more than we will be.

Amy and Tanya tried to stay in bed. They tried to arouse romantic moments, but strain within their union, has taken that from them. Every paradise has its poisons. In the world of land and sea, as well as the land of flesh and feelings. Jealousy has reared its ugly head. Was it momentary madness? Or, was it deep seeded resentment? To await the decision, they are filling their morning with blood and sweat, and avoid the tears. A rift in the paradisiacal pairing. Will there be a cure, an antidote for the poison of this paradise.

They are installing the second room's flooring. They struggled with the first, and they were on good terms then. The tension in the room has reached a contained level, near the saturation point. Will it dissolve, or boil over? Amy cuts the pieces and hands them to Tanya for her to install. It is as mechanical as they can make it. Tanya is fitting with force to vent her feelings. Amy is handling her part with equal detachment. Bang and slap, fit and snap. It moves on methodically. No emotion is showing now. It seems to be included in the force on the floor. The problems from their previous effort is missing today. Tanya whips out her hand. Amy slaps in the piece. Tanya fits it in place and snaps it home.

Amy is hit with each reach of the hand. Tanya's hand reddens with each slap of the floor piece. It is gaining momentum, and I am feeling every blow to Amy's side. The routine is defusing the tension and the girls are trying to stifle their pain and a laugh at the same time. The situation fails when Tanya's aim fell a little too high and I felt the pain as if I had the anatomy to provide it. Amy fell back with pain and a burst of laughter. Tanya erupts into laughter as she comes to comfort the wounded. Marie asks me what is wrong as I clutch my chest. "Tanya hit Amy, a bit too hard." I say, as my eyes fill with water. Marie joins the laugh fest, and Amy tells Tanya, about my ailment. The laughter hurts as much as it helps. Their spat is disarmed and they signify it with some caring moments. Marie rubs my chest for me, so I return the favour. All-round a good outcome. The rain is still falling in a gentle constant. "We can't get anything done, lying in bed like this." I said.

"What are you going to do in the rain?" Marie challenged me.

"Have sex in bed. It's better than just laying here." I am slammed with a pillow across my face. "Okay, pillow fight it is."

In the cottage, the indiscretion is forgotten. It was mainly imagined as it was. Production continued, for the finished look and feel, of smooth and clean floors. The difficulty they had the previous day, was overcome. Progress was getting them excited again. They get the euphoric feeling, from seeing your efforts take on the shape, you have been trying to obtain. The finished form is in sight. It will be their place. It is from the pioneering spirit, they saw in their studies. How are they going to feel, about leaving in the fall? Living apart, not even in the same city. They have to stop thinking about that and concentrate on the job at hand.

The day is nearly done, we feel like John and Yoko, lying in bed all night and day. The rain has stopped now, so we can leave our nest, and venture into the wet grasses and shrubs. Our pets have gone home. The vet took the deer to release her, and the horse's stall was vacated and ready for him to come back. The landscape has been altered drastically, by the huge walking pine. As I dragged it through the field, it uprooted many of the remaining bushes, not cropped by the grazers. There is no reason to go mucking about with Li'l Joe. I would like to have my breakfast, but since it is supper time. That is what we will settle on. Amy has shown me, that they are on a roll, and will continue, until the job is done.

Marie and I make dinner in the trailer. Hot dogs are a staple for lunches most days at home. Hamburgers are the menu tonight, to change the tastes. I do the barbequing, while Marie prepares the toppings and salads. I raise the tarp to allow the breezes to cool the space. I put family sized juice bottles, on the end of tent poles, and push the tarp up with them. It looks like a circus tent in miniature. We serve the workers at the job site, and clear it up for them, while they return to the job.

We decide to sleep in the tent again, so as not to disturb their surge. They work on until the cottage main floors are done. They realize that they have worked half way through the night. The loft floor is all that is left to do inside. They go to their room and collapse. In the morning, we let them sleep.

When I am up to walking, Marie joins me in exploring Evelyn's woods. She meets us and gets excited with our plans for tackling her walk.

Chapter Thirty

A Widow's Walk

We comb the Young's forest, looking for things to use in building the bridge and bench. We're looking for something to accent the connection with the property. A newly fallen tree could give enough for both projects. Branches could be used like the railing for the ladder, in our place. We would be satisfied with a log for a bench to put on that promontory rock. We find some large rocks loose enough to lift. I will come around with Li'l Joe to collect them. Marie marks a tree near them to help us find them again. For nearly an hour, we have found only rocks and old rotted trees. One newly fallen tree, was rotting as it stood and was useless for our purposes. We were getting discouraged. I told Evelyn, that we can get some from our wood stores. I know she would want something found of her place. We finally come to one that was damaged, but still stood. It can be taken down and provide all we need, from the bench, to the decking on the bridge. Marie marks it and we keep going, trying to find something already down.

We came up empty for fallen trees, but we have what we needed. I was surprised that that storm had not done more damage here. Those funnel clouds seemed close to the treetops.

Marie's sister was camping in this region, years ago. She was cooking breakfast in her dining tent, as a storm approached and the next thing she knew, she was standing in the open air. The wind had plucked her tent from around her and carried it off. She was not even hurt by any debris. It was just gone.

After returning to our camp, I gather up some things to help do the work at Evelyn's. I called Brent to give him the length of the span. He has to go to Peterborough to get it and won't have the time until the following week. That will give us time to get the other material collected. I ask him to check for equipment rentals, and tell him what we need.

Amy is up and telling us, there is food waiting. Tanya had been up and got it started. She had to wake Amy. We have to celebrate the flooring completion, with them. Achievement in any part of your life should be celebrated when you have gone beyond being comfortable. Stretching your abilities, standing up against your own reluctance, is something you should, at least, reward, if only by yourself.

We will be ready now, for Grace and her crew, to visit us this weekend. Then I go back home, for more appointments, and getting chores done there. We won't get too much done until the equipment is here, so we can enjoy a holiday.

I recall seeing an illustration of a bridge being built over the type of terrain this is. Amy is drawing up the vision for me. Although I have good long term memory, holding that in the forefront of my consciousness, requires short term memory. With Amy's talent, I will not have to search my memory for it, again.

Learning to live with this blessed curse, is difficult, but it can be done. It will drive you crazy, but it has its merits.

For the base of the bridge, we must plant two four foot 12X12s, one set back three quarters of the one below, on both sides. We need to place one end of the beams in the setback of the 12X12s and lowering it, cantilevered, down onto the matching space on the other side. The beams will then be joined, by the deck boards. We will be cutting the deck boards, from that one tree we have to cut down. We will also cut a seat, from that same tree, to place on the promontory rock. As I develop the idea in my head, Amy is drawing the plan. The picture is forming from my imagination, faster than I can think the words. As fast as my description of the picture is, Amy's drawing is faster. If I was to say the words aloud, it would look as if I was describing her picture, and not my thoughts. We will bore holes to hammer rods through the 12X12s and that, plus the beams between them should hold the bridge solid. Forcing rain water onto the bridge in grooves and emptying through drains, midspan, will minimize the erosion around the base. Now that she has the drawing, she can help Brent to plan for the construction. He can get the logs cut and we can put it together when I return.

That was the extent of our work for today. The canoes are ready on the beach, and we are to go fishing. Our freezer drawer is empty. Amy and Tanya's talent for catching fish is going to fill it for us. We are all going out to record the action. We will see how they do, under the scrutiny of the camera's lens.

We start out with the anglers in front, so we can record the play by play action and their techniques. They have the rods at the ready, as before. One goes out one side, while the other goes the other way. There is a longer time until the first bite, than before. It isn't too long. The rod dips and the paddles stop. They coast, ready to set the hook. The line starts to play out. Amy is reeling in the other line. Tanya pulls up on the rod and feels the tension strengthen. The fight is on. It is a bass. They seem to like this part of the lake. The girls catch more bass in this area, than any other. The fight is fierce. She enjoys the test of her grip and arm strength. It is like holding onto a drill, that is binding in the hard knot of the wood. She brings it in close and it takes off, for any structure it can find. The closest is the canoe, and it is a game of cat and mouse. Tanya is as fast as it is. It is no sooner under the boat, then the rod is there waiting. She has it close, and there is Amy with the quick and accurate dip of the net. The fight is over. The fish doesn't clue in on that, though. It is squirming, as they raise it up, for the folks at home. The camera has caught the fight and the finish. Next, the fish is gutted and its entrails are to be used for bait. The bass goes into the cooler.

The hooks are baited and the lines are set. Canoes are moving again. Marie is the videographer. She has the steady hand and the keen eye. The rods dip and the paddles stop. The lines are playing out fast. The rods are both in play this time. A test for both angler and cameraman. I paddle back to give Marie room, to get the wider view. Both girls are struggling. Amy has another bass on, while Tanya, seems to have a pickerel. Both fish are strong fighters and both girls are up for it. They swing around in their seats. They aren't about to stand, even in this wide bodied canoe. Amy tries to keep her bass away from Tanya's line. She fights it down as close to the stern as she can manage. She has the net near her, but will be hard pressed to get hold of it. Her only hope is to help the fish jump and swing it into the boat. She is as agile as the bass is. Tanya's fight is strong and away from the boat still.

Amy is getting the bass in close and is ready to move at her first opening in the struggle. It gets in against the hull and is beating at its side, drumming the hull, as if announcing the move. Amy jerks the rod up and into the boat comes the fish. Tanya has got the fight closer and Amy's freedom, to help her net the pickerel, is timely. She is ready to make her move. Tanya has got to get the fight closer to the boat. The fish struggles and out goes the line. Tanya gives it a bit of room and then puts the pressure on again. This is surely, tiring the fish, because it is tiring the fisherman. Tanya gets it back in range. It is much slower in the turns and lighter in the run. Is it playing the player? She gets it closer, but needs to pull it back more, for Amy's net. It tries to make another run. Tanya swings in her seat and forces it to turn. It makes its lunge right into the waiting net. They have done it. Two strong fighters in the water, met the two strong fighters in the canoe. The girls rest and shake out the tension from their arms. This is it. The fishing is done for the day. They weren't taken on a cruise this time. They had to give all they had. All the fishing up to now, has been in preparation for this fight. That is the feeling in both their minds. Their strength recovered, they hold up the catch for the camera. They gut the fish there in the boat, and offer the contents, to feed the remaining fish. It will show what can be taken without getting a hook, and set the stage for the next act.

The fish are in the cooler, and we can set paddles to the water once more, for a leisurely float around the near end of our lake. It is a very relaxed pace. The teenagers are not up to making a wake anymore. We are prepared to offer a line to tow them back, if necessary. We see them hesitating in their strokes and ask them if we can go back to the cottage, please. They feign reluctance, but capitulate. We get turned in the right direction.

There is someone on shore, waving. It's our friendly neighbourhood veterinarian. As we pull up to the beach, he tells us the muskie is here. Hooray, from the four of us. Marie isn't aware, that it is stuffed and mounted, for the cottage wall. We show our catch and offer him one for his visit. He declines, respectfully. We go to his truck and there it is. That record size fish, laying in the back of the truck. It did not break the record, but matched it. Someone in Michigan, had already caught a fish that size. It is a rarity, just the same. One of the largest ever recorded.

Marie is in awe. "What are you going to do with that?"

"It will go on the wall in the cottage, in wait, until the barn is built. Then it will be hung over the greatroom mantle. It is a great honour for the girls, to be able to say, 'we caught that,' and we have to give them that."

"Alright, but it looks hideous."

"It should. It is one of the largest freshwater carnivores. A relative of the barracuda."

"I'm glad we aren't having it at home." Marie grumbles.

"So are we." Amy says, "It fits here. It gives the cottage the definitive identifier. A great big monster. That, will make the kids choose to sleep in the trailer and tents."

Marie laughs.

"See there is the silver lining." I say.

I pay the doctor for getting it done for us. We heft it out of the truck, and lug it up into the cottage. At five feet long, it is a humungous job to place it. Amy and Tanya go to collect my thought's suggestion. They come back with the extension ladder and take it apart. They set it up over the cupboards. There are five of us to get it hung up. Amy gets up to mark the studs' locations.

I drill holes at their width, through the mounting board. The doctor and I get on the ladder. Amy is concentrating with me on the steadiness of my footing, Tanya, with her light frame and height gets on the counter. They hand the fish up and Tanya drives in the mounting screws. Her agility gets it done fast. We ease up on our grip and the monster is hung, by the chimney with care. Tanya drills two more holes at the bottom, and drives in two more screws. We all get back, to look at it, and all agree. It is one, ugly, monster fish.

The teens go out carting the ladder. They return with the cooler and their fish. They open the cooler, and look at their catch, and then up on the wall. They look at each other and then at us. "I think we've had enough of fish for a while." They say together.

"I'm on it." I get out to the van and head out to town. The vet is gone when I get back. I bring in my catch. Some steaks, burgers and hot dogs, to barbeque, and an extra large pizza.

Marie has processed the fish and they are safely in the freezer. I mix up some drinks. A large pitcher of Pina Coladas, for me and my ladies. I decant the drinks and add the rum to Marie's and to mine. I toast the girls accomplishments, both in the sport of fishing and in construction. We sit in our log chairs on our replenished sandy beach, and look out over the quiet peaceful waters of our lake. I feel a spray of sand, on the back of my neck and turn around, to see one of the plants, buried when I spread the sand, has popped up out of the blanket of sand. All is as it should be. Nature claiming its own.

Brent's car pulls in and he and Lidia, come to set a seat next to us.

"Your early." I say looking at my watchless arm.

"I got the day off and went to see about that equipment. They didn't have one of the saws, but I got the address of someone that has it. I have to get a trailer, to have the logs loaded and taken up there. I'll need your van to get the trailer, if I can borrow it, please?"

"When do you need it for?"

"Whenever we can get at the tree and get it cut up for the job."

"I will be gone for a week and a half. I have doctors' appointments for my eye. I have to get a phleb, and then we will be back up here, by the Friday. We're going back on Sunday, when Grace and the family goes home."

"We can do it then, then. I'll need your expertise to set it all up."

"Amy's got that. The plans. The knowledge." I say.

"I think we will need all the hands we can get for that job." He worries about Amy's safety.

"Okay. We will set it all up for then."

Amy says, at my bidding, "Come on into the kitchen you two. I've got something to show you."

The four teens go inside, "Holy Toledo!" Brent shouts. "That is a monster!"

"The vet brought it by. It took five of us to get it up there." Tanya said.

"That will give you nightmares!" Lidia peeps. "Why would you want that?"

"Tanya and I caught it, in this lake. It's our merit badge. It is a record size. We matched a world record."

"Wow, I don't think that would be enough, to make me put it on a wall." Lidia is annoyingly frank sometimes.

"You know, I think that is bigger than Lidia." Brent says, holding her up to compare.

"What are you doing?" she screeched.

"Comparing trophies." Brent says, proudly.

"I am not a trophy." she complains.

Tanya mutters, "That's for sure." Lidia missed that.

They take that to file out to get a fire going in the pit. Tanya goes to get the wood and takes the long way around. She is not fond of Lidia, by any means. She takes her time, to get away from her. Amy's friendship with Brent will keep her ever present among them. Nothing she can do about that. She takes as much firewood as she can carry, but puts most of it back. She'll need an excuse to get away from her again. When she gets back, the only space is between Amy and Lidia. 'Great' she thought to herself, with a bit aimed at Lidia. Lidia looked at her as if she heard. She sat down with more force than she wanted. She had her sulk on. It is going to be a long night, if it's only five minutes.

Amy could read her thoughts almost as ours. Tanya's are from experience and constant togetherness. I begin to think that there is more of a psychic connection there. Amy loves Tanya, but has trouble with the moods sometimes. She doesn't blame her for disliking Lidia. She is one girl that she would love, to be able to avoid.

Brent is quiet. I think he knows what the girls are thinking. He peeks over at Lidia occasionally. If she caught him, he would smile sweetly. Marie has no psychic thought, but can plainly see, what is happening in front of her. She would like to see it lighten up some. She knows Brent is going to find his life strained with Lidia. She saw her mother say things like that and there was an edge in relations with her. It is difficult with someone you love! Being together under strain like that, has got to be more than she could see anyone wanting. She thought to herself, 'She better be good in bed, or wealthy, because there isn't much else going for her.

Amy could not help a burst of laughter. She had to excuse herself and leave. Tanya follows. "What was that from?" Tanya demanded.

"Mom, she was thinking that Lidia better be good in bed, or wealthy, because she doesn't have anything else going for her." They both laughed so hard they were in tears.

Lidia was looking in their direction and back at Brent, alternately. Marie and I are watching and waiting for her to say something. When the girls came back, Lidia asked them, "What was all that about?!"

"Nothing important. It's been a long day and I just got distracted and thought of something from long ago. I just couldn't help myself. I could just as easily have burst into tears."

'Oh, that was smooth!' I thought to her. 'Take a bow for that act.' She faced me and bowed.

Brent was getting more uncomfortable, than he could stand. "I'm sorry. I'm pretty tired too. I think I should take Lidia home. Goodnight everyone."

"Goodnight." We all returned.

"Goodnight." Lidia snapped.

They went to the car without another word. They got in and drove away. Brent pulled over down the lane before they got to the road. They talked about what was bothering him. He told her about the deep connection he felt with the family. He felt she was too opinionated and frank for the relationship, to go on without hurting the people he loved. He would like her to try not being so forthright with her comments. She sensed her vulnerability and fawned on him, begging his pardon and his forgiveness. He was sullen. She pleaded and got more amorous than she had ever been before. They continued beyond his judgement.

We had heard the car stop, and wondered what was wrong. Amy had guessed correctly, why they stopped. She also was correct in her estimate of Lidia's response. "I think he is going to find out, Mom."

"Find out what?" Marie asked innocently.

"If she's good in bed." as she said it we all fell over laughing.

"Is that what you were laughing at?" Marie asked.

"Yes." Tanya replied.

"You know, I hear what you think!" Amy stated.

"I forget now and then. It's not something that I expect."

"It's a good thing Lidia can't read minds." Tanya says.

We talk about her foibles at length, sitting around the fire. The dark is starting to envelop us. The fire is fed and we talk some more on other topics. Then we hear the car start again. Tanya says, "I think Brent owes us a thank you. I wonder if he stops by to give it?" Another round of laughs. We keep talking and laughing about a number of things. It is quite late when lights flash over our way and a car pulls to a stop. Brent gets out and walks over. "Hi folks, I'm sorry Lidia was that way. I told her she needs to be more considerate and less open about her thoughts." He says.

"You're welcome." Tanya says to him.

"What?"

"You're welcome. You did get laid didn't you?"

"Tanya! Not like that. That's like she would say it." Amy scolds her. "I'm sorry Brent, but we couldn't help notice the length of time you talked. You do look like you know what she's talking about."

"She was very apologetic. Very apologetic." he trails off with a smirk. "I think she will be better behaved, next time."

"So. Is she your first?" Tanya asks.

"Tanya, you're talking like her." Amy scolds again, "Well?" she says to Brent, with eyes raised and lashes flashing.

Brent's face went beet red. He turned and stepped off, then turned back. "Yes!"

Amy smiles and says gently, "Well, you 'are' welcome."

Brent thought to himself, but was understood by all of us. 'I wish it was you.'

"Come on, sit and talk some more." Amy said. He joined us sitting next to Tanya. The conversation stayed lively. We talked long after the fire went out.

A flashlight came floating across the space to the laneway. Evelyn's voice was heard faintly. "I thought I would find you here."

"Pull up a stump, Ev." I beckoned.

"Are you pulling an all-nighter?" She asked.

"Not intentionally." I replied.

"It's two in the morning, Tom." she scolded lightly.

Marie spoke, "I guess it's time for bed."

"I'll drive you home, Mom." Brent said, "Goodnight."

"Goodnight." was echoed. They all turned in.

Later inside, Tanya snuggled down in bed and turned to Amy and said, "I was thinking she needed that. I was tempted to tell her."

"Who?"

"Lidia. I was going to tell her to go get..."

"I'm glad you left it up to her to decide." Amy laughed.

In the morning, The mood was light. There was no work planned for the day. I looked out and saw Li'l Joe sitting there, and thought I would like to get something done with it. I sat down to breakfast with them and they all looked a bit goofy. "What is up with everyone!?"

Tanya answered, "Brent wasn't the only one."

"Huh?" Marie looked at her. "Oh!"

"Pipe down and eat your breakfast." I demanded. I guess I was too busy to notice.

I started to clear off the foundation bed. I'll have to get Brad to help me map out the footings. I will get someone else to come to make the forms and pour the footings. They may as well do the foundation and then we can takeover. Amy and I both feel, that we can step away from that job. I'll clear off the site and get ready to hand it over to the pros.

Marie and the girls go out for a paddle, while I'm playing with Joe. We never know when Grace will come up. They aren't against getting an early start and it depends on the baby they have at the time, and Brad's job schedule. Brent comes to see me, and gets me off the task at hand. We discuss the change in the plans, for the bridge. We set out the timeline and agree on what each of us can do. I list off the things we already have and what we still need. Brad is bringing a chainsaw and we can get the tree down before I go home. We make one change and that is the width of the bridge, from four feet to eight feet. He leaves and I get back to work. The girls are at the far end of the lake, watching wildlife on our side, and water-skiers, on the other. Brent and Lidia come over and get his canoe. They head down to meet the girls. I see them leave and warn Amy. Marie is with them, and she would not want to be in the middle of anything. Brent approaches the other canoe and he and Lidia wave a greeting. When they stop, Lidia apologizes to all of them for her attitude last night. She ended it there and didn't try to expound on it further. The girls accept the apology, as it is, and don't try to communicate, any more than that. A real mess of attitudes are convening in the tippiest of crafts, in the middle of a lake. The wildlife are watching them now. You wonder what might be going through their minds. No, I will not volunteer for that comparison. Ask Dr. Doolittle.

I work fast and even with the Bobcat. I scrape the dirt away until it is firm and undisturbed. I have just put Joe away, when I see the van pull off the road. Brad and Grace are here. I have given the notice to Amy, and they are heading back. Lidia has asked Brent, how they knew someone was there from that far away. He just said, "Bluetooth." Lidia was looking to see the device in Amy's ear. Her hair was down and covering her ears. It really doesn't matter what you say to some people. Nobody hears it, the first time anyway. He's beginning to think she needs another scolding, or is he in need of another fawning.

The kids are to carry their own stuff to the tents, or trailer, which ever they prefer. I help with some things.

"Where is everybody?" Grace asks.

"Canoeing." I reply.

The cooler goes in the cottage and I follow. They assume I am hungry. I open the door for them and wait for their response. "Good Lord! Where did you get that?" Grace demands.

"Amy and Tanya caught it and the vet took it to a friend, to have it stuffed and mounted."

"What are you talking about?" Brad asks. Grace points and he sees it. "Oh! I didn't even see that."

"It is a match to the world record holder."

"I believe it." Brad says.

"Holy Cow! That's big." Grace is awed by the horrendous monster. "Mom let you put it up there?"

"I did." Marie said as she came inside. "It goes in the barn, when it is done."

"It should!" Grace says.

"Over the mantle in the greatroom." I insist. I am starting to get an anxiety attack. I sit right down and relax. It is confrontation this time. I may miss getting things done with Brad.

Amy walks in and says, "Don't worry, Dad. I'll tell him everything." She brushes my hair.

Brent and Lidia come in, and Brad says, "Whose kid is this? Yours?" he asks Brent.

"She's my girlfriend. She's sixteen and small for her age." Brent says tersely.

"Sorry, I didn't know." Brad apologized.

Lidia looks at them both. She doesn't like what's been said, but doesn't want to upset Brent. Amy is holding her hand over her mouth, afraid to respond. Brent accepts the apology and doesn't make anymore of it. If she hadn't been acting like that the day before, he might have done more. As it was, she was not going to make him get worked up, any further.

Amy and Tanya greet the nieces outside. She heard what was happening inside and didn't want to get involved in it. "Where have you decided to sleep?"

"Jo is in the canvas tent, and I'm in the other one. The rest are in the trailer." Jayme says quickly.

"Would you like it in the same tent if there were twin beds, instead of queen size?" Amy wondered if that was why they chose separate tents.

Jo answered first, "I like the big bed. I'm kinda scared alone, but I don't want to share."

"I wouldn't mind a twin bed, but I like the queen size better. It's a little scary, but I can manage." Jayme adds her choice.

"We can give you an animal to guard your tents for you. Not even a bear would go near you with these pets outside."

"Wait, there are bears up here?" Jo says, startled.

"They come to the river to fish farther down. They don't come up here with the cats here." Tanya tells them.

"Okay, I'd like one." Jo says, "What kind of cat?"

"Didn't you see them before?"

"I'd like one. How many do you have?" Jayme calls out.

"They are panthers and we have two. They are statues. We have sound tracks for them. They growl." Amy details.

"Did you show them to us before?" Jo asks.

"I can't remember. Oh, Papa and your dad are bringing them out."

"Wait, how do you know that?" Jo asks.

"I know everything. Remember?"

"She can read Papa's mind."

"That's freaky." says Jo.

"Tell me about it." says Amy.

Brad and I come out of the cottage, carrying the statues. We take them and set them by the tents.

"Coo-o-ol." Jayme likes these statues. "Where did you get these?"

"I ordered them online." I tell her. "Which one would you like?"

"I want that one." said Jayme, pointing at the crouching cat.

"Good, 'cause I like that one." Jo says, pointing to the strutting panther.

"The crouching one goes down at the nylon tent and this one goes here." I tell their father.

"How did you know?" Jo asks me.

"I know everything." I say, to mimic Amy.

"Papa, so, you can read her mind?" Jayme asks me.

"Only when it's light out. After dark I listen to her mind."

"Ha ha, Papa, that's so funny." Jayme mocks me.

Brent and Lidia sneak up behind us. "Ah, we're going to get going. Bye."

"Bye, Brent. Bye, Lidia." we say, looking around at them.

Amy and Tanya walk them to their car. They don't talk they just walk along. At the car, they say goodbye again. It is very uneasy. They watch them drive away. "What is going on with them?" Tanya asks.

"I don't know. I was afraid he was going to say they were getting married." Amy was seriously scared of Lidia getting control over him.

"Maybe he wanted to have to get mad at her again. So he could get laid!" Tanya teased.

"Hey, maybe! That would make more sense than wanting to marry her!" They both laughed at that thought.

Grace and Marie are setting out food, and Amy calls to the rest of us to come and get it. Grace hears her call and turning to Marie, says, "That would drive me crazy. Her knowing what you're doing all the time."

"I don't notice it as much as Dad does." Marie tells her, "She knows what I am thinking, but I don't get that from her. She and Dad have a lot of trouble with it."

"It's handy sometimes, but it would freak me out when it goes on and on. Can't they turn it off?"

"She and I had a real argument about that. No, they don't get a break from it. She even said it could drive her to kill him. But it won't, they care deeply for each other. He is probably the one person alive who can stand up to it with her. She's like you. She dotes on him sometimes, like you do."

"Do I dote on him?"

"Yes, Grace, you do."

"Where are we going to seat everyone?"

"Amy's got it ready out the front here by the lake."

"How did you know that?!" She stares at Marie.

"She always sets it up out there." She grins.

"Oh gosh! You were freaking me out!" Grace picks up some stuff to take out. She is just getting to the door and Tanya opens it. "You don't have that too, do you?"

Tanya laughs, "No, Amy told me to get the door."

"You guys are freaking, kidding me!?"

"Every chance we get." Amy smiles sweetly.

Marie and Grace are setting out the food and Tanya calls down, "Should I bring the baby?"

"I was going to bring her out last, but sure." Grace says and heads back for more food.

Marie brings the rest, as Amy hands out the cutlery. She is keeping the dishes under the filter trough. They have a sink to wash them, by the filter. They have a portable water heater, to heat the water out of the hose. It is rain water and heats up faster, than the water from the river. At least it seems that way. It could be just, that we are feeling the remoteness and it's effect on our expectations. Although, when we get a large group up here, it doesn't feel remote. We have our own village here. The feast is on and it is so much better tasting, with family here to share it with.

"Who would like to go fishing tomorrow?" Amy asks, looking from side to side at the whole group. No takers. "How about canoeing?"

Jo and Jayme wave their hands in favour. Bradley does too, after his sisters do. The baby waves her hands out, too. "Yeah, I bet you do!" Grace says to her and wipes all the food off her face.

After dinner, I get Brad to look at the barn's foundation site. "I would let them do the whole thing. It's one less headache for you. Get the biggest company in the area, and ask around. Get some estimates, and call some of their customers. You've got relatives here, don't you? Call them and get their input. That's going to be a big job for you, and I don't think the girls are ready to take this on. You don't want to pinch pennies on this part. That's what I recommend."

"Good. That's what we decided. Come on, I've got another job I'm doing for my neighbour. I want you to look at it."

"Is that the kid who was here today?"

"His mother, mainly. Her husband died of an aneurism last year."

"Oh, yeah. I remember that."

"Well he died just as he was getting ready to do this job for her."

"What's it paying? If you don't mind my asking?"

"Nada. I'm just supplying some help for her son and my Bobcat and tools. Some knowledge and finesse."

"You have a Bobcat? When did you get a Bobcat?"

"A few days ago. This place needs a machine that can get in through the tight spaces and is compact. Not so much of a target for thieves."

"Why not a small tractor with a mower, snow blower, and frontend loader."

"I didn't find one available for the price. I don't want to be cutting lawns out here. I can get something like that, if I see one come up for sale cheap enough. I was going to spread that stone out along the driveway, but thought, until I get the foundation ready to be built, I would spread it over the foundation site. We can park up there. Easy to get in and easy to get out."

"That would be a good idea. It'll compact the base too."

We walk around the house and through the pampas grass gateway. "There. A bridge across here. Two 12X12s on either end, staggered, with holes bored and rods driven through them. Beams across, with wood planking, cut from a tree off of their lot. Grooves down the side like ditches in the decking, to have water runoff come down there and through drain holes in the middle over the stream. Hopefully, it will keep the erosion from happening at the bases. It won't last forever. It should do, for quite a while."

"Sounds good, Father." Brad is thinking and looking for the drawbacks. I don't want him to find any, unless there is something to find. "How wide?"

"Eight feet."

"Railings?"

"We'll see what we can think of when we get there. Brent has really helped us a lot in getting our place done and watching out for the girls while we were at home. I want to think of something appropriate for them."

"When do you plan to start?"

"I want to use that chainsaw you brought, to fell the tree, and cut it into eight foot lengths. Then get them over to the laneway for Brent to load on the trailer he's renting."

"When are you going to start building it?"

"When I get back from home, in two weeks."

"I'll think about it for a bit and let you know if I can find any bugs in the plans. Wait, bugs?"

"We'll use a layer of pressure treated lumber underneath the top deck."

"Why bother with the top layer, then?"

"Nostalgia. It is wood from their forest."

"Water between the deck layers?"

"I'll put a lath strip every foot, lengthwise. A quarter inch spacing between each of the lower deck boards. No spacing between the upper decking boards and pitch sealant between them. We'll seal the boards before laying them. No cuts on the lower decking. Sealing the screw holes."

"Sounds like a lot of work for a bridge like this."

"It will be dedicated to her husband's memory."

"Sounds good, Father."

"We can start whenever you are ready. Mom will show you the tree. We will also need a length of whatever is left to make into a bench for her to sit at the top of her hill over there."

"Okay, Father, I will get right on that in the morning."

We walked back to our place and I showed him Li'l Joe. "We need to get you a pet, Dad. I don't care what Mom thinks. You'll be naming the trees next."

"They are out by the fire, Amy says. She says they have dessert for us, too."

"Well what are we walking around out here for?"

The fireside chat was a favourite of ours at camp, when the older three were young. We got some group camping after some years. Then we tapered off, when it was just us. We didn't have the fires at camp as much. We were starting to grow up. I am glad we got that stopped. We said we would like a cottage on the beachfront. Just, so we could have fires on the beach. Now that we have our beach all done, we can move the fire pit to the beach. We will have to dig down to clear out plants and roots in the future pit site. Buried plants can carry the fire underground several feet away. When we get the plants out of the area, we need to build an enclosure that doesn't burn. We can use stones, concrete, a steel ring, or an old tire rim. We have an old bent up tire rim. I'll lay it with the shallow side down. I have some iron rods that I make a square with and place the rim on top of it. This will allow air to get under the fire to feed it. I put a metal disc in the middle of the rim to build the fire on. That is my project for the day. While the tree is being cut up. After I build the fire pit, I get in the Bobcat and start off to bring the logs to the lane. I loop a chain around the bucket. We lay out the chain in front of it. The log is then rolled onto the chain and it is brought up to link onto the rest of it on top of the bucket. We carry the logs quickly, with that method. All the women were out to help, and took any job we had available. Once I showed them, how I wanted to hook up the logs, I could stay in the drivers seat. We were very efficient in the time and moves we made. It was using all the available women. We had one log left that was only seven feet. We used that one to make the bench. I marked off the cut lines and gave the angles to cut at. Brad did the cuts for me and I removed the piece once it was free. I divided the scrap piece with a line down its length. Brad made the cut. We moved the three pieces, to the promontory rock. I placed the first half of the scrap pieces, on the rock, to let the bench roll against it. I then rolled the bench into place. Then I stuck the other scrap piece, into the space in front. We knocked the wedge shaped pieces, tight into the space and the bench was ready to be tested. Brad and I, sat down on it and the angles were perfect. We used the chainsaw, to polish the seat smooth. A drain line was cut on the ends, for water to drain easily. We got Evelyn up to the rock, to check out her new bench.

"It is perfect! Thank you so much! Now I can sit out here and look at the view and remember Joe. I can even show my grandchildren. If I get any."

"I'll give you grandkids, Mom." Brent says as he comes up the hill, alone. "I just have to find the right girl."

"Brent, what about Lidia?" Evelyn pressed him.

"I don't think Lidia is the right girl, for me, to marry."

"Why not?"

"I can't stand her negativity and her blatant mannerisms."

"You'll find someone, sometime soon." She smoothed his hair as he sat down in the bench.

He looked up at me and thanked me. He got up and walked away toward the cottage. We started away to our place.

"Wait! You are all invited for a meal at my place. I've already prepared it." Evelyn called to us all.

We joined her for a great meal. There was enough food to feed an army. As we weren't quite an army, we couldn't be expected to finish it all, but we did leave enough, for chipmunks and squirrels. We invited them to come, to our inaugural fire, in the new fire pit.

The new pit was prepared and ready to go when we got there. Once everyone had a seat, I struck the match and set the pit ablaze. The talk began a trek, into the years gone by. Remembering friends and family, that didn't get to see their grandchildren. We remembered the soldiers, that never got to see their own children. We remembered the disasters and the terrorism targets. Then we changed direction and talked about the good times and the people that volunteer for schools, churches, hospitals, and charitable institutions. We were about to get on a different topic, when it started to spit. We gathered our things, said goodnight to our guests and headed for beds in the various directions.

The rain, even gentle, delays working on the foundation pad. We don't want the Bobcat digging up the soil with ruts and gouges. I am likely to find that Amy has taught herself, how to use the machine. She knows the basics, from paying attention when I am driving it. Knowing how, and doing it right, are two different things, when using these vehicles. She does have the room to practise. It took a few minutes for me to learn each new machine, once I learned, on one. She can get used to it, by piling the stone into neater piles. As long as she practises away from the build site, she will become good at it. She can watch the tutorial in my mind. She just has to move slowly and with caution. More caution than I used, when I was a beginner. She sees the things I did wrong. She has the patience to avoid those mistakes. She is adept at learning new tools and mediums. She draws the feel of the objects as they affect me. The pressure I need to apply, is something that she feels from my experiences.

I really don't understand it all. It's like the pressure exerted on me is exerting on her. We have never tried to develop this connection. Psycho-kinesis, or telekinesis, external pressure felt by the mind, and exerting pressure from the mind on objects, not physically in contact. It is two sides of the same coin. We feel the things felt by the other, but can we move objects with our minds? We should explore this portion of the dynamics, we have already enjoyed. The best way to learn something mechanical, or physical, is to do it. We feel each other's feelings, psycho-kinesis. Do we have the power to move objects, mentally, telekinesis? They have been used as interchangeable titles. Are they? Or, are they specific to their applications? The yin and yang? Inward vs. outward? How is it, that we have the connection? In what way, are these feelings limited? If I imagine a cooling breeze, coming to cool me, when I am hot. I feel it come and affect me as desired. If I knew these limitations were not applicable to us. We could move objects remotely, with only a thought. Some people have exhibited this power, whether fact or fiction. I feel the need, suddenly, to pursue this bent in the terminology. I am lying in bed now, and trying to decide, how much failure I am willing to take, in this test. How much success, as well. Is it a fear of failure? Or, is it a fear of success?

The rain is steady, but light. It may only affect the top layer of soil. That would dry soon enough, for us to get out there and work. I am sleepy now, goodnight.

The morning finds the ground quite wet, although the rain had stopped. After listening to my talk with Brad, Amy gets acquainted with Li'l Joe. She looks over the controls. She pauses to picture me using it. Now she is ready to go. Her first time driving any motor vehicle. She carefully drives the Bobcat around to see its stopping distance. She tests the responsiveness of the steering. She works the controls for the bucket. She sees some brush she would like to push back. She approaches and lowers her bucket, as it hits, she pushes the control down to the float position. She scrapes back the brush and then scoops it up to drop it in the sorting area. Now to practise on the stone piles. She will pile them into one big pile. Tanya is watching her manipulate, that tough little machine. She wants Amy all the more. But she would also like to learn to drive it. She's been spotted. Amy waves her over. She sways up to the tractor, if she was going to get one wish, she might get the other. She has a long skirt hanging on her hips, just for this effect. The hips exaggerates the move and the long flimsy skirt delivers the show. Amy leans forward to kiss her girl. Then she tells her to change into her shorts and boots and come learn to drive. This just knocked her down and picked her back up. She ran in to change her clothes.

The rest of the camp are looking around for treasure. Grace and her girls are rock hounds. Every time they are near the beaches or rocky terrain, they hunt for rocks. Any kind of rock will do to start, but they are really on the lookout for precious and semiprecious gemstones. The whole family does craftwork of all kinds. So this would be just the beginning of the process. Marie is with them. Brad is with the baby. They like to nap together at the cottage. I am in bed semiconscious. I awoke with the Bobcat starting up and just lie still, to rest from the nights sleep. I hear my cell phone ringing. I fumble with it but answer in time. It's Nicholas, they have been in Gananoque, and would like to see the cottage. I gave him directions and said that I will meet him at the end of the lane, in the van.

I get up and dressed, and go out to find Marie. I see them down by the river where the rocks form a large protective wall against erosion. I wave to her to come to meet me. I keep walking and of course she doesn't. I get to where my voice will be heard. "Nicholas and the family are coming."

"Coming where? Here?" she gets like that.

"Yes, he just called. They're in Gananoque. I'm going down to wait at the end of the lane."

"Okay, I'll be up in a bit. We've just found something here."

I head over to get in the van. I have to plough out of the spot I'm in. Amy and I have left a ridge behind the cars. I have no trouble, since I have had years of raucous driving habits. I drive down the lane and wait at the end. I get out and find a log to sit on. I rolled it against the truck and sat down leaning back against the grill of the van. I hear the Bobcat coming down the lane. Tanya is driving with Amy sitting uncomfortably beside her.

"We came for the log you found." Shouted Amy. I got up and rolled it up to the bucket. Tanya hoisted the load up, so she can see over it. They turned Lil Joe, and drove back to camp. Amy is finding that loader is a hoot and a half. Amy tells me they are getting ready a meal for the newcomers. Knowing the visitors, I know it will be vegetarian. I have been there for an hour and then some. I finally see their car approaching. I stand up and wave, and as they see me, they slow down to turn in. I get in the van and drive in, after them. When they parked and got their things out, I suggested choosing their sleeping quarters. They say they aren't going to stay, but I know they would like to. It looks like a huge construction site, which it is, but you have to put up with it, to get the place you want.

I have Amy park the Bobcat, and come to greet her brother and sister-in-law, and see her nephew.

Marie and the others are on their way. They are studying things that they have in their hands. Their attention was drawn to us, so they quickened their pace. Tanya and Amy arrived first and reached out for Oscar. He returned their reach. Reluctantly, Nicholas handed his son to Amy. I offered them a tour and they accepted.

Nick wondered, "What are you building?"

"A barn, workshop, and greatroom, with another couple rooms for more guests."

"How can you afford all this?"

"I have been writing books and they have been selling, plus our pensions. We scrounge for materials. We help our neighbours and they help us. Tanya and Amy do most of the work, while I do some. Mainly, I am a repository of information and ideas."

"So you've been using child labour?" he accuses.

"Not only, child labour, but they don't get paid, either."

"Dad, that's against the law. You can't force kids to work for you, for nothing."

"Well I don't force them. They can't be stopped. Their pay, for all this work is their names on the deed. When they come of age. I bought the place and they developed it. When it is done, we can have separate living quarters. You and all the family will have a voting interest in it. You can come and use it anytime you want. You don't even need to call ahead, providing you take the rooms that are available."

"So Amy and Tanya, own this whole place with you?"

"Yes, they do. Watch."

I pinch my arm hard, and Amy hollers at me, "Ow, what did you do that for?"

"To illustrate to your brother, how close you are to me." I look toward Nick.

"What happened there?"

"Have you heard of the Corsican brothers?"

"Yes, why?"

"Amy is my biological daughter, created to share this bond with me. I have told you before, but like most people, you disregarded that. Don't feel bad though. Most everyone in the family did too. God created Amy out of our flesh. She was our daughter before the adoption. We are joined together, for the rest of our life. Mom and I can get a divorce, to separate us. Amy and I cannot be separated, by anything but death."

"Why would you want to divorce Mom?"

"I don't. That is how we can be separated. It's not going to happen, but that is an option for us, that Amy and I do not have. Remember when I asked if you believe in miracles, and you said 'no'. Well meet a miracle." Amy was down at the beach with her little nephew and Tanya. She turned and lifted her T-shirt to show Nick her missing navel.

"How did she know to do that?"

"She feels, hears, sees, smells, tastes, and knows, everything I know, smell, taste, feel, and see. We are very similar to the Corsican phenomenon. She works, I get tired from her effort."

"That is impossible."

"Improbable, not impossible." I change the subject, "Were you on the Thousand Island Cruise?"

"Yes we were. Oscar had a great time."

"C'mon, I'll show you the facilities. You should be in need of them by now." We went up the back stairs and stepped into the main room. They were awed by its condition. "They do good work, don't they?" I showed them the rooms, while I led them to the washroom. When I opened the bathroom door, I watched their eyes grow. "Brad and the girls did this."

"Jo and Jayme?"

"Tanya and Amy."

"I better get Oscar."

"I'll have Amy bring him in." I don't move. They see Amy look up at the house and pick up Oscar to bring him in. She walks in and hands him to Nick, whose eyes are stretched as wide as they could be.

I remember telling the kids, when they were little, that they always need to be told three times, before they would do anything. It is still that way. You need to tell anybody, anything, three times, at least, before they will know, or understand, what you are saying. I have told many people over and over, about Amy, and they still act like it is the first they've heard of it.

As we spend more and more time here together, I seem to be living in Amy's world, more than she in mine. I do get involved with my thoughts and drift away from those around me. It is not that way with Amy. I am drawn out of my thoughts and into her life. I go willingly. I accomplish so much through her. I would be lost without her. As she grows in our relationship, she learns to go about living as if I was just a mole on her back. She knows I'm there, but thinks little of me.

"Dad. You are being unfair with me. I don't think of you as a mole on my back! You're more like, a zit on my face! I'm kidding. I love you Dad, but I have a life to live, just like Nick, Faith, and Grace. We can't be all about you, all the time. I do have more compatible interests with you. More than they do, but I am building a future with Tanya. I have to desensitise my connection to you a little. Don't worry, you will always be part of me. Seriously, always!'

We gather for another meal on the plank table, outside. The stump chairs are fun, more than comfortable. If we run short? We cut another from our log pile.

After the meal we get ready to go. I have an appointment. Nick has his work. Brad has his work and the rest move with us, out of habit. An invitation to stay for the week is extended to all of the followers. They can be returned to their regularly scheduled programming after this brief week of vacation. It stops them in their tracks. The wheels are turning in their heads. A time without the usual. Less stress on those that will go to work. A bonding time with family. Like summer camp. Literally, like summer camp. Amy and Tanya will be camp leaders. Faith will be up next weekend. Exit plans are being delayed.

Remember when you were young, and an opportunity like this, came along? You just about held your breath, or begged anxiously, to be allowed to stay. Your parents were really put on the spot. They wanted to let you. They had to be realistic. It had to be reasonable. They needed to have someone responsible to oversee it. Either cheers, or jeers, would follow the verdict.

"What's it going to be, people? The suspense is, like hardening arteries, killing us!"

Aww. It's too bad. They all have things to do. Jobs, classes, appointments.

WAIT!

They could call in sick. They do need to have a vacation. They could change their appointments.

"Yes, they can stay!" Brad will ride back with Marie and I, in our car. Nick and his family go home. The rest stay. Grace will be the voice of reason. Faith and her kids will be coming next weekend. Then they will all go home, on the next Sunday.

Marie and I will be back on the Wednesday, after they go. The car's loaded up and ready to go. Goodbyes are said and hugs are given. The drivers pull out and the vacationers start thinking of things to do.

They all go next door to be introduced to Evelyn and Brent. Brent was remembered by the girls. They walk around back to see the bridge site. They take a hike through the woods on both sides of the lane. Evelyn is closer to Grace's age than ours. They get along well. Brent takes an interest in Jo and Jayme. It looks like he will be coming more often. Evelyn thinks he is looking to get married soon. Grace says that her girls aren't thinking about that yet. They want to finish university first. Amy hears that and surprises everyone including me when she dropped the bombshell, and said that she was second guessing going to university. I don't mention it until we get home. Amy is now saying she would like an apprenticeship, in carpentry, plumbing and electrical. Now what do I tell Marie.

In the week we were away, Tanya and Amy took turns spreading the stone across the barn area. They took the kids out canoeing. Grace's girls moved into the trailer with her. The panther statues and soundtracks were moved closer to the trailer. Amy and Tanya were alone in the cabin. They behaved well in front of their guests.

In bed at night, they felt, more than ever, that they were lost. The world is, suddenly, so far away. They have so much company, and yet, they feel small, in spite of their accomplishments. There is so much life to go through and it is now looming over their heads. Amy, is about to enter an adult realm. In spite of the, readily called upon, memories of her past life. She feels more the child than ever before. Tanya was always buoyed by Amy's towering strength. Now, she feels dwarfed by it and so much the little girl she was, when they met. She feels bravado, that she had shown these last three years, has gone missing within the woods that surround them. They cower in their bed, not afraid of the dark, but of the light, which will prove them to be the frauds they feel they are. When they look at each other, they don't see the confident lover. They see the frightened little girl, hiding under the blankets. They hold each other close. They feel more of the tiny fifteen year olds. Playing at life in the real world. The pink peg they are picking, still has significant meaning. It means they have been riding on a dream, that is about to crash. I am aware of their plight. I see the shaking blankets. I feel the fear. I try to steel up Amy's confidence. This, they should have realised long ago. They have performed well above what I would have seen for them. They have lasted through the crush phase, the first love phase and have planned realistic lives and courses of action. They have acted years above themselves. This night is an overcorrection for them. They climbed too high, too fast. They aren't going to crash. They need to turn on the lights to view the feats of inward ability. It is being hidden from them. It is being masked by the fears and the dark. Amy gets my message, at last. She turns and switches on the light, by her bedside. She looks at the room, the floor that caused them to doubt themselves. The kitchen outside their door, is reassuring her that she was able and could follow instruction to accomplish more. She looks at the frightened face looking up at her. She is restored. She turns out the light, takes Tanya in her arms and celebrates their life together.

If your life is gloom and doom, just turn on the light. Look for the things that buoy your spirits and see your possibilities. Stop the spiral before it starts. Being diagnosed with clinical depression, is not telling you to keep up doom and gloom. It's a wake up call, to start looking at the beauty around you. The hopeful people nearby, are to feed your hunger for a better outcome. If there are no positive people? Get some!

Morning has everyone up and ready to do something. Grace comes in to feed the baby. Soon after, you hear the boy. Bradley is nattering at his sisters. Amy starts getting breakfast ready. Tanya is still preening, but will be at her side in a moment. "How do you want your eggs?" Usually a good question to ask at the cottage, but not today. "Pancakes?" Yes, we have a starting place. Tanya and Amy work so hard and get out for exercise regularly. They don't get much call for weight watching yet. Well, except for keeping it on. They eat well in the mornings and cruise for the rest of the day. They do up a load of pancakes, and offer some fresh fruit to top it off. Another suggestion that goes unanswered. Butter and syrup it is. She gets the fruit and yogurt for Tanya and herself. That helps raise interest from Grace, as she is free to get something for herself.

With the meal out of the way, they get started at planning the day. Amy wants to get some work done and visit. She offers to go canoeing or walking the woods with them. They ask her to go fishing with them. They heard how they get fishing done quickly here. They like that. Sitting around and waiting for a bite, isn't exciting to these ones.

So, out come the rods and reels, lifejackets and paddles. Into the canoes they get. Spectators ride in one canoe, while the participants ride in the other. The cooler and bucket are in the middle with Amy. Jo is in front. Tanya is in the stern. The rods are set out each side, with Amy baiting, netting and gutting the catch. They will change participants at the other end of the lake.

They are out in the deep with rods deployed and paddling the course that is usual for them. They follow the drop offs and troll by the structures. The first bite is on Jo's line. "Stop paddling." Amy calls. Tanya reels in her line. Jo is a bit overwhelmed by the sudden action, and fumbles with the rod. "Just hold the rod while it takes some line. Now pull up sharply to set the hook and start to reel in to keep the line taut. That's it. Is it pulling?" Amy is coaching.

"No it just feels heavy." Jo answers.

"Just reel it in and be prepared for it to kick up and run. You just keep the line taut and coming in. It might just be waiting to give a good fight. Or it will fight once we get it in the boat." She sees the fish nearing the boat. It just floats right up to the side of the boat. Amy nets it and now it decides it should put up resistance. A bit too late for that. Amy holds up the fish for Jo and the rest to see. She pulls the lure free and guts the fish as is their normal routine. Jo chokes at the sight but manages to keep her breakfast. Amy baits her hook and Tanya's too. They cast out again and start paddling. The choking wasn't confined to their boat. The spectators had to hold their food back.

They are moving at a good speed. They don't get too fast with paddling the canoes. They are fast enough, to get the attention of the hunting fish. The next bite is on Jo's line again. "Stop paddling. Beginner's luck. Do what you did before. Let it take some line and then pull up to set the hook and reel it in."

Grace was proud of Jo, for sticking with it. She didn't think she would.

Jo sets the hook as she is told and there is an explosion of activity on the line. The fish is like the wobbling wheel of the grocery cart, and pulling away down into the depths. "Pull back and reel in. Not too hard. Let the line play but keep the tension on it. When it slows down, then you pull back farther and reel in as you let the rod go forward again. You keep that up until it takes another run. Keep reeling it in. You are doing great, Jo." The fight is tiring the novice angler. Her arms are tired, but still strong. She gets it near enough to see the image way below. A flash of its tail and she nearly drops the rod. She hangs on. She plays it as she was told. Sometimes they can find some shelter and snap the line. This isn't the day for it. She gets the fish in close enough and it is in Amy's net. A nice sized pickerel to keep the pike company in the cooler. "Great job, Jo!"

She is happy she did it but wants to pass the job on to Jayme. For this they pull up to the shore and the two sisters switch canoes. Back on the water, Jayme is anxious to perform as well. Her bait is on and the lines are back in the water. They don't get a chance to move far when Jayme's hook is taken. "Stop paddling. Wait for it to take some line." Nothing happened. They give it some time and nothing. Amy takes the rod and pulls gently with no response. She twists the rod from side to side and works the hook free. "It was just caught on something. We'll try again." They get out a little farther and in go the lines. They are moving along for a while before Tanya's line gets a bite. "Stop paddling and reel in your line Jayme."

"How come?"

"You don't want to get your line tangled with Tanya's, while she is fighting her fish."

"Oh, I see." she reels in her line and turns to watch Tanya fight the fish. This one is wobbling too. It isn't the same though. It is a fighter but it's different. She fights it for quite awhile. It is a surprise to see the barbs on its mouth. They hadn't caught a catfish before. It was tough and full of fight. They netted it and threw it in with the others. Back on the move the lines are in again. They are getting nearer the channel to the other half of the lake. The activity on it is busy. The line on Jayme's rod went taut and then, limp.

"Reel in your line, Jayme. I think you lost your bait." She did as she was told, and sure enough, the hook was bare. "Your bail was closed the tension was tight and the fish ripped the bait off and got away. I'll just put more bait on. Now turn this so it is loose and cast the line out. Then set your rod in place." She followed the instructions well and got back to paddling. Tanya pulled in her line. She thought she should check the bait. It was still there and as she cast the line out, Jayme's line started playing out. Tanya pulled her line back in, as Amy talked Jayme through the fight. The fishing was giving them some good entertainment.

When Jayme's catch was netted, she didn't want to keep it. "I'm not going to eat it. Will it be okay if I let it go?"

"Sure! You can hold it up and we'll take your picture, and then you can release it." They took the picture and she placed the fish back in the water and held it until it swam away.

"It won't die will it?" Jayme asked.

"No. It wasn't putting up a big fight, at least not for long. It should be good to catch again someday."

She was finished with fishing and offered to let someone else try it. Bradley wanted to but he wanted to stay with Mom. Amy passed the rod over to him, and told him what to do. He had his own ideas of how he should fish, but Grace talked him into following his aunt's advice. It was a struggle just to get close enough to net the fish, when he got it close enough to see it. They had to come so close to the other canoe. He was able to get his picture taken with a fish that he caught by himself. He let his fish go back as well. They came back with six fish at the end of their cruise. Considering they didn't want to eat fish, the catch would last them a good long time.

Since I left my van there, Brent used it to bring a trailer around to get the logs loaded, while they were fishing. He managed to get it loaded alone. When he came back for a second load, the canoes had returned. He got Tanya and Jayme to help him load the trailer and said he would be back for the rest shortly.

Amy and Jo finished cleaning the fish, and took the pail out, to empty the innards into the lake, for the fish to get. There was nothing left to attract the bears and other critters. They put some of the fish in the freezer and made the catfish ready for lunch. They also had something the non-fish-eaters could have.

Brent was back as the food was on the table, so was persuaded to join them. After lunch, Jo and Amy helped him load up and sent him on his way. Tanya and Jayme cleaned up the dishes. Grace liked the arrangements for cleaning and storing the dishes outside. "It really makes you clean up after yourself, to keep the animals from coming around." Tanya expressed her concerns about the nighttime visitors. "It keeps the more durable dishes, where there are more chance of breakage."

Brent returned once more. This time with a load of lumber. Everyone gets to help with the unloading at the Young's cottage. After the trailer is empty, Evelyn brings out a dessert she made for the helpers. It was a good thing I wasn't there this time. Brent said, he will get the big timbers for the span, in the morning, and the rest of the lumber in the afternoon. They plan to be ready for when he gets back. The Bobcat will be used for the first load, and they can take a long break, between the loads. The heart wood of the logs they took out, are to be used for the seats of the deck span.

Amy's experience this summer and last, is confusing her plans for her education. She loves the construction, but is able to get a less physically demanding career, if she would stick to her initial plans. We haven't tried to influence her directly. We have thought about, what our life experiences have gotten us. Our limited education, with our struggle to keep paying for the essentials. We are constantly robbing Peter, to pay Paul. We just make sure, they don't talk to each other. As we review our situation, and that of our other children, we are keeping Amy's thoughts moving in that general area. We aren't trying to confront her. We are just highlighting the rewards and penalties. She is aware of what we are doing. She realises that it is for her benefit and a form of nonconfrontational arguments. We are gradually moving forward in our achieving our goals. There is the inchworm effect taking place, including where we have to stop and see, if this direction is the right one. She is seeing Nicholas' struggle is on a higher plane than ours, and for different goals. His life had not been free of disadvantages. It is his disadvantage, that is turned into an advantage. Faith has had her setbacks. She also has the struggle that is closer to ours. Like us, she has people there to help, on the level she needs. Grace has made everything look as if it is effortless on one hand, and extremely tiring on the other. She and Brad have worked together consistently. It is this effort shared, that has made it all look so like the cornucopia. The empty cup, that overflows into many other lives. Doing what needs to be done. We all are doing it with such differing results.

The week of having so much company, is helping to get the couple to see into the future. There is no crystal ball. It is the furor that reveals the peace. It has turned the cottage camp into an anthill. They recognise the participants' contributions, and the result of the influx of disorder, to help them think straight. They were working at one thing after another and methodically moving along. This week the methodical, is lost to the entrepreneurial. It is showing how the equipment is not always, something you can see, or touch.

Faith arrives and is happy to get back to this wonderful playground. She comes with her family in tow. The camp is swelling to its most useful point. So many of the family are here and there is room for them to have privacy and togetherness. There is a willingness to cooperate and sacrifice. The plans evolve to give every member, both a job, and the full experience of camp life. They have the freedom to try new things they had never thought of.

The group falls under Amy's directions to begin building the bridge. They line up the crews and dig in, to use all the plans we had thought out, before I left. The bridge construction is under way. The niches are hewn from the ravine edges. The timbers lowered by pulleys and ropes. There are barriers between the wood and the ground. It has all been sealed by the painting team, brushing the coating to make each piece resistant to water, bugs and moulds. The boring of the supports for the beams, is done by Brent. After sealant is poured through the holes, the rods are hammered in, to lock the ends together. The beams, which formed the uprights of the crane, are now lowered slowly across the gap. They are pivoting on the end, that will become the home of the entrance, to the trail network. It is as if the boom of the crane, is being lowered to pick up a load, in the chasm below. The top of the boom is now closing in on the other support. This is a tricky point. If the tension is not maintained, the load could slip and fall into the crevasse. If the tension is too much, it could swing around and trap anyone on the sides, that are waiting to guide the boom into the slot. They have ropes to keep the latter from happening and they must drop them, if the boom should fall. No one person has any experience in this type of work. They are like the pioneers. They have one rope hanging from the boom with a weight to keep the balance. It will also be used, to lift it back out of the ravine, should it fall. The ends meet. The fit is made, and the boom is lowered into its seat. One huge beam has made it home. One more is ready to follow suit. Tanya is the intrepid Bobcat operator. She is watching every movement Amy makes. She is alert to the dangers, and the life, that is depending on her, to keep a steady hold on the situation. Amy is putting as much thought, into ways to keep them all safe, and get the job done well, as she possibly can. She is reviewing the detailed long term memories from my brain. I could never recall it in as much intricacy as she can. She is using her mind as the processor and mine as the hard-drive. There is no computer as quick and versatile as the human mind. Let us all hope this one is as accurate as the mechanical ones. The second beam is readied and all is set to drop the second, main piece of the bridge span, in place. All hands are in place. Briony is watching the baby for Grace, as she gets in to help make this piece find its way, as well as its sister. The difference here, is that the first beam, was already in its job as the boom, and therefore, it had already been set in its pivotal point. This job is a stretch for the little Bobcat. It wasn't equipped to be used like this. It was being used like the settlers used their animals. So the group of emotionally charged teenagers, with the adults, as prepared as they were, ready to find this project's desired end. The beam is now in position, and the intensity of the first, is doubled for this one. The boom is being lowered and is finding its way gently, toward the crew on the other side. The lip of the end is very close to the slipping point. The top of the boom is now touching and being coaxed into the slot. It is ready to be set in place. They have done it. I can breathe again as all of them are. It is sitting in its permanent location, and it is as protected as any wood structure could be.

They take their leave of the worksite, to celebrate, with a meal fit for the hunger that will devour it. Evelyn has it laid out and in no time at all, the crews are getting at it.

I tell Marie what took place and she finds it incredible, that they would even try to do that, without us. I help her to understand that we would, probably be a liability, if we were there.

They all had so much fun there, doing as much as they could think of doing. The feeling of entitlement for a job well done, gave them the freedom to enjoy the life they had. When the weekend was over, they were well worn out. They left for home reluctantly. Our return would be at the end of the week.

Chapter Thirty One

All Decked Out

The weather had been good when the beams were placed. It did not cooperate the remainder of that week. A massive low had taken over the skies and although it wasn't fierce, it was persistent. The rain was oppressive to the mood of the cottagers. Many gave up and left for home, only to find the same thing there. Brent was working and was just happy to be there. No use being off, for weather like this. Evelyn was busying herself in her craftwork. The girls were out spreading the stone, since they had left a good starting point prepared, for continuing the job. They were glad to have the bathtub in the cottage. After a wet workday, that was their reward. They shared a hot bath and let the heat, replenish the hopefulness, the rain was washing away.

We drove up in the rain. Knowing we were on our way, got the girls going, planning a welcome that would make the wet drive, feel worthwhile. They cooked up a meal and got a fire built inside. They left the lighting of the fire, until Amy saw us getting close. She watched, as she saw us approaching the laneway. The meal will be ready by the time we were all in the cottage. "Good news! The weather front is almost done! It is supposed to clear up overnight." Marie announced as she approached the girls.

"We missed you so much." Tanya said.

"You have done a great job, while we were away." I encouraged them. "We can get some little things done now. The zip-line, we can put that up. We can put the barn on hold. Next year, we can do that. We have to help finish the bridge and then do the tree house. How did you like my ideas for the bridge railings?" I asked Tanya.

"You know I haven't told her yet."

"Why not? Don't you like them? I didn't get any feedback on it."

"Brent wanted to do that, and I wanted to let him." Amy told me. "You've already done your share. Let him do something."

"Alright, I can do that." She knows that I felt disappointed about it. She also knew I was able to let it go. I know what it's like, with somebody telling you what you should do. They wouldn't do it themselves, yet they are certain that you should. Besides, I have my own place to do. "We need some more tent decks. A large one for Grace's tent and another for Faith's."

"It's pickerel, Mom." Amy answers Marie's unspoken query. "Jo caught it."

"Amy?" Marie warns her. "You know that creeps me out."

"I'm sorry. I hear it as if it was spoken. So, when are they coming?"

"Amy!" she was quite perturbed by this habit Amy has. "They will be coming tomorrow. Aunt Nan still has a job. I get the feeling you are doing that on purpose."

"Your thoughts are all over the place. I can only try to get it straight if you can. You are thinking in snippets. You have to know what is going together, before I can get the clear picture."

"I know. There is a lot that's bothering me. I worry too much."

"Yes you do, Mom. You have got to let people run their own lives. As for us, we will get by. Your friends have been looking for greener pastures, all their lives. At least they are still in the same province, in the same country, on the same side of the ocean. You'll get together. Faith has a determined soul. She won't let other peoples thoughts rule her life. She is super strong, in will, as well as in body. Grace and Brad are watching out for her and she won't pull them down. If we have to sell this place? We can sell it and start over. Dad has given me a great education, even if he can't access his own thoughts. We got the bridge made. He did that. Getting Li'l Joe up on blocks and anchored to those oak trees, was the best idea. Using the wheels to hoist the loads? I was amazed. We could have got the second piece on differently, but the crane setup was already in place. He can get things done with help. We're still going to be here for you. So you see? Don't worry so much."

"I guess I let things get to me. That's the way I've always been."

"Look at Dad. He doesn't worry. He trusts that God will give him the inspiration to fix anything, or even start again."

"He gets lost trying to find where he put things."

"He's sixty five. It happens to you, too. Not as often, but he doesn't worry, until he has to." Amy is my champion. She has helped me find things. Bringing the memories out for me to find them. She also plays games with my mind, too. She helps to confuse me, for fun.

Tanya is tired of all the talk. "Are we going to do something, or what? Who wants to play a game?"

"Yes. Let's play a game." Marie is tired of the talk, also. "What do you want to play?"

We played games for several hours. Finally tiring of that, we got ready for bed and read our books. I out last them all, being still awake at three. There is something about constant anything. You get adjusted to it, and it becomes your way of life. The insomnia, the pain, even the transient pain. After so many years, it is like one of the family. The one you wish would move out. The black sheep.

We wake up to sunshine. Weather experts get it right once in a while. It is chilly, for the beginning of August. It is supposed to warm up this afternoon. Nan and Jim will be coming this afternoon. We know that will happen. They have so many cottages to go to now. They don't even have to keep them up. I had to get my own. I wanted it this way. We can tent, trailer and cottage, in the same place. There is also my sister's place.

Amy and I walk over the place to look for things that have possibilities. Rocks and trees, in the right place can make the scene. The angles of the branches, show their potential for tree houses, or bridge terminals. We need a launch point for the zip line. We have to have a safe avenue, for it to run through. How to end it as well. We take some notes and pick up some elements. The more natural elements we have, the better the thrill of the experience. It is time to make this place shine. We are also buying time for the funds to reach the bank account. Having the woods here, was a big bonus. The most valuable things a property can have are trees and water. Trees feed the soil and the soul. Water provides sustenance, entertainment, and tranquility. In this property, we have a gold mine of both. The forest brings a privacy screen against the outside world. It brings the wildlife to help us feel more alive and part of this earth. It gives us building material and fuel. We finish the tour of our place at the site of our future barn. Where the foundation is to go, we have a stone bed. Where the 'walking pine' was dragged away, it forms a ramp down to the waters level. Its former space forms a ramp into the woods. A third entrance comes in from the laneway. The new septic system will be just at the bottom of the first ramp. It will be filled in to bring a more accessible route to the house.

Tanya and Marie are coming to join us. They don't have the advantage, or disadvantage, of seeing where we are, until they can see us in person. Together we go to visit Evelyn. Brent has been working since the bridge base went in. It is the civic holiday weekend. It will be busy in his department. The sun is up and so are the cottagers. DIY projects are facing some cottage owners. Getting something different to enjoy up here, is bringing in some more shoppers. We talk with Evelyn for a bit, then walk with her across the bridge beam. It is a little scary, but we are up for an adventure. Once the bridge is done, we can grade her trail for her. We walk up to the bench. There is enough room for three to sit if you squeeze in. It's perfect for two to sit and cuddle, looking out over the landscape. The bench will last for some time, but when it goes, it will feed the earth and not pollute it. We walk on. We try to see the markings, Marie left to show the path. Some were overgrown already, but still visible, once you see the next, and can figure out which tree it is on. We saunter along, picking up sticks and push their ends into the ground, to further mark the trail. We make our way along and back again to the cottage. She is very pleased with the way the trail is looking. Marie is thinking that we, should have a definite pathway, through our section of woods. Amy and I agree, and plan that for a birthday gift to her. She will not expect it, as nothing was actually said. Amy heard her thoughts and relayed them to me. There is something else to do this month. We will have to avoid walking with her in the woods, once we begin work on it.

Back at base camp, we get some assignments handed out. Tanya helps Marie to fashion a circular staircase, to put around the trunk of the tree, that will host the tree house and start the elevated bridgeway. Amy and I start setting up the course of the zip line. It is late afternoon, when we hear Jim's truck coming in. The truck being here, means he brought some building scraps. Treasures! We leave the jobs and go to meet them. He has some nice remnants for us. Nan says they would like to stay in the old canvas tent. Grace had told her about the beds and they wanted to get the old camping feeling, but with the comfort we have now. The canvas tent is ancient. The polypropylene floor, had long ago rotted away. It was replaced with a canvas tarp, sewed into the tent walls. There were chairs to relax on, under the oversized tarps, that covered all the shelters. We carried their things to their choice of abode.

Another car pulls in beside Jim's truck. It's Faith! She is alone this time. Grace wasn't coming up, so Faith decided to go by herself. Her kids are with their father, this weekend. We help her with her things. The kayak, paddles and luggage. She is going to stay in the nylon tent. We tell her about putting up a deck for her tent. I suggest having it up in the trees. That gets her excited. After setting the guests up, we go to prepare for supper.

'We have good meals and good talks, good paddles and good walks. The chosen spirits to face the day, help God take our breath away.' Our recharge time is here for Jim and I. We will see how the camp compares with our Great Lakes sessions.

The marsh is reaching out into the lake. This is what they call a dying lake. It will gradually fill in with reeds and other bog plants, leaves from the woods and the annual death of the water plants will add to the soil and give the new growth a fertile bed to grow in. The lake is dying by adding more life to it. If we fill in the marshes, we kill off the life it holds. It will add growth elsewhere. If we dredge it up? It might come back, but we risk losing the fish it attracts. The oxygenating plants are gone and the lake will be truly dead. Tread lightly. Be a part of the cure. We talk of this as we talk of our religious feelings. We should not force our will on people, or the planet. Our food comes from nature, so we must feed nature.

Jim likes to go snorkelling. Amy and Tanya try it with him. If there is any parasite in the water, Jim finds it. Or, should I say, it finds Jim. If it does it will limit their visits with us. The rest of us get into the boats. Faith has her kayak and Nan joins Marie and I in our canoe. We are going for a nature cruise. We go in where we have seen the wildlife feeding. We go right up close to the beaver lodge. Nan says she'll have to warn Jim about the possible parasites from this. I say I'll have Amy tell him now, and also about the leaches by the marshy area. When she relays the message, they take off out over the deeper water. We see an elk, in one of the bays. This is the first elk I've seen in the wild. It looks up to check us out. He is probably thinking, 'Huh, I've seen too many of them before.' The mama bear and her cub are down near the channel. They look up at us and watch what we are up to. They soon decide to go someplace else. They move on into the woods. Some turtles pop their heads up near the channel, in by the reeds. A crane flies up over the lake around where we saw the elk. We head back, because the nights are coming earlier now and we have just about overstayed our daylight. It is so energizing to see such diverse animals. Up ahead, some geese fly across the lake, above the treetops. The snorkelers are back on shore now talking about the things they saw. Leaches and other nasties aside, Jim likes this lake. We glide up onto the sand and climb out to solid ground. Sitting in canoes will likely, never be completely comfortable, but what a peaceful ride. It is worth the cramped up joints complaining to you, when you get out.

Amy leaves to get the fire pit going. We hear from Jim about what they saw. He turns to Nan and tells her about the beavers in the lake. She laughs and tells him about asking Amy, to tell him that. Oh, was all he could say to that. He was excited to watch the fish below him. "There was all kinds. Everywhere you looked was fish. It is deep out there. How deep would you say this lake is, Tom?"

"This end is about sixty feet in the middle there. The other end is closer to ninety."

"That's what I was figuring too. No wonder the two catch so many fish. They are everywhere boy. I'm surprised there isn't more people fishing here. Your neighbour here, Joe must have caught some good fish when he was here. Man, I tell ya, they are all over."

We sat down to enjoy the fire and get away from the bugs. "That's the first time I've been bit here." Jim reports.

"We didn't get to the fire early enough."

"How much of that stuff do you go through?"

"One or two bundles a week, I think. We have it growing here now. We heard about some stuff to have in your garden. It will keep critters away, except for skunks, because it smells like skunk. There's another thing to keep slugs out. I'll have to get Amy to write you a list."

We sit exchanging tips and trivia, until the stars can be seen overhead. It is the ritual. Things to learn and laugh at. It keeps your heart pumping, someone said. Yes, it lifts your spirits. Helps you belong somewhere. We let the fire burn out. A semi early night tonight. The tenters take the sage pot with them, to set upwind of them. It is warmer now then it was all day. At least they won't get a chill like they would have had last night.

I took Jim over to see the bridge, as it was. We talked about how they did it. He asked me, why they didn't do it this way. I told him, the choices they had available at the time, were limited to the pioneer methods, I had seen on documentaries. I described the crane they rigged up. "Holy cow!" he said, "That's resourceful. That's neat!" I told him about my grandfather having to do that, on the mud roads, he had to haul on. "They could have done it different, but it would have been just as risky." He liked the lumber that was to be used on the deck. Like the pioneer settlers would have had. It's nice to see ways of using things like that.

Evelyn came out to chat and meet Jim. Joe had told her about him. They talked about things as only Jim can. I tend to step back and let him go, when he has someone to talk to. I have trouble thinking of things. I just watch the master.

Back at our place, there was something they wanted us to do, and when they asked Amy where we were, she told them, that Uncle Jim was talking to the neighbour. Nan said "Well forget it. They won't be back for hours."

"What do you need? I could do it." Amy offered. They said what they wanted and she went ahead and took care of it. There isn't much that she wouldn't try. If a man can do it, she could too. She would just do it differently. If it was something too tough for her, you would find it hard to get anyone to do it. She is like her sister Faith, that way. That reminds me, I wanted to have Faith, show me how to use that router, of mine. Amy laughs at me. She'll show me.

The afternoon is wearing on. Brent is coming home from work. Evelyn says she has to get supper ready and Jim takes the cue to let her go. When Brent gets out of the car, Jim has a few words with him, until he gets the call to help her inside. Jim thinks she is a great talker.

We walk in the door of the cottage and Nan says, "Well, she finally stopped talking, did she?"

Jim said, "Man, that woman can talk!" He has to laugh. He knows they wouldn't believe that. Evelyn will talk, but she won't interrupt a visitor.

Nan tells him, about the job they had for him, and that Amy did it. "I'm sorry. Thank you, Amy. You should have called us." Well you would need to have someone else with him, besides me. I'm like Evelyn. I can't just interrupt someone unless it's an emergency. Even then, like my brother, he hurt his arm at work and went to report it to his boss. His boss was talking to his supervisor. It wasn't until the supervisor saw the blood dripping from his arm, that he told the other man, "I think this man would like to tell you something." Both my brothers are like that, and I am too. I know if I collapse, someone might take notice. I guess we respect the other people's right to have their say. We learn more from listening. Not that I would remember it.

Amy suggested that food might have been ready. 'Like I said, an emergency.'

Putting up some bits of the projects, was fine with Jim. He was on holiday from being retired. He might bring his grandkids up, and our projects would give them loads of fun. The staircase was coming along fine. The platforms need to be put up without damaging the tree. We are to tackle that job, today. Amy, Jim and I are handling that, with Li'l Joe's help. We get the inner frame built and have the supporting pieces ready. We put a clamp on the trunk of the tree and raise the frame up with the Bobcat. Our extension ladder sections, go up underneath the frame. The supporting lumber is fitted in place and fastened solidly. Cross pieces go on top of the clamp to form a square base and more supports are attached to the other two sides. Now we fill in the centre of the frame, with removable panels. This will keep the little ones feet, from falling through. Jim is working off of the bucket. Amy and I are on the ground to ladder detail. Our communication is silent between us and only vocal with Jim. He is holding and levelling the platform. Whatever we need, is passed without a word. It seems very eerie to Jim. We call him for a level reading and follow his directions. When it is solid and ready for the next steps, we let Jim down to walk around and shake the arms to limber up.

Jim is the same age as me. We are both fifty years older than Amy and Tanya.

Faith, Tanya and our wives, have put together the sections of the stairs. Now we will all work together to attach the stairs to the platform. The extension is back together and placed against the spot where the stairs will be joined at the top. Amy is up on the ladder while Jim and the framing beams go up in the bucket. I will stay on the machine out of the way. The first beams are nailed to have a lip on top and bottom to anchor the inner frame to the platform frame. The opposite side is done the same way. Now the others start assembling the stair sections. Some temporary posts hold the first piece while they bring in the next. I lower Jim to let him take the top of the second section. Amy is on the ladder to hold the other side. They have the layers fitting like a puzzle piece. It is propped up and nailed. Jim and Amy get up on the platform to attach the top section. I raise it up with the Bobcat with the ladder in sections again help Faith and Tanya to get to the joining spot. It is fixed in place and ready to be bolted together. The stairs are clad with pieces of wood, cut from the logs we were squaring off, for posts to prop up the outer frame. The bark clad stairs have a more woodland elf presence. When we have finished the stairs, we are wishing we had had this, when we were kids.

The work was over for the day and we could pursue any interest we wanted. Faith is to go back home tonight, for work in the morning. She heads out in the kayak, with the teens along side, in the canoe. Us old folks, take a walk down along the river. We have not been down here since last year. The river moves slowly at first. The rapids start about twenty minutes along. They make it seem odd. The slow of the upper river and the fast paced waters below. We climb down a rocky slope and continue our trek, until we get to the falls.

"I thought you rode your trike down here. How could you do that?" Marie demanded.

"I took the portage. It is very gradual that way." I responded.

"Why didn't we go that way?"

"You wanted to follow the river."

"How far away is the portage?" Jim asks.

"It is about ten minutes that way. It is pretty rough going to get to it. It joins the river beyond the bend in the river below the falls." I described the difficult scenery we would have to go through. "I thought you wanted to see the exciting part of the river."

They decided to go back the way we came. We got our exercise on this route. Apparently, they wanted to go to the store. Who knew?

We got back and had a meal with Faith, so she could be on the road, when she was ready. She asked if that platform, would be for her tent. I said hers could be higher up, than that. It was fifteen feet above the ground, this one. She thought that height, would be enough for her. I tell her I will figure something out. She looks at Amy to get reassurance. Amy nods her agreement.

We do some work on the tree house, while Jim is there to help, but every other day. The other days we would go hiking, or paddling. Jim didn't get any rash from the lake, so he would go snorkelling with Amy and Tanya. We went through the channel and down to the marina. It wasn't too bad there during the week. Traffic was light.

Tanya's birthday is coming up and so are the moms. They will be arriving next weekend. Jim and Nan will be leaving today. We have not much time for reflecting on sadness here, when friends and family go home. We get on to doing the next job. While we have them, we enjoy them. Once in a while, we get lingering on the void they leave. We welcome them to come at any time. Even if it is just to say, 'Hi, how are you?', to stay a night, or a week.

Jim and I are up on the platform. We walked up together, to test the strength of our stairs. They passed the test. We expected to end up in a woodpile after taking out the temporary support posts. We added more trunk clamps, to reach under the steps in a couple places. Amy was prepared to send in the team to rescue us. They are relaxing at the beach. Jim points out some spots to tie into, on the neighbouring trees. No work today, just talk. They had a good week here. We had some rain at night, mostly. It was warm. Nobody went to the hospital. Those are good things. We did some work and had some fun.

We've seen some visitors next door. Glad to see they have company. Brent has one more year until he graduates. Evelyn is alone most days.

There is so much missing here, that we are glad of it. Noise is mostly natural, birds, bugs and animals. The trees swallow up a lot of the sound we make. Li'l Joe and the compressors, are the noisiest. No powerboats bother to come here. There is so much space between the cottages here. It is only a matter of time, before this side of the lake is discovered.

Amy and I have learned to handle our arrangement. Her usual pains are hardly as bad as the IBS that I have had for years. I give her more than she has been able to give me, in the pain department. She is more careful than I am, even when she takes on the toughest tasks. Tanya is always at hand to help. I have my chores to do, but they are mostly things that have been cleared by Amy, to avoid more pain for her.

We have the first platform complete and will be putting on the structure for the kids to get inside. We need to put the first bridge across to the next tree. They will be rope bridges, with steel cables tucked out of sight, to give it some longevity.

The Bobcat lifts the supplies to us, but the work is done from the ladders and the platform. I feel almost useless, for the most work is done, while I can only watch. They get going right after breakfast. Normally, it's Amy and Tanya doing the work. Marie helps, when they need an extra pair of hands. If that is not enough, they wait for me to be ready. The landings are scaled down versions of the first platform. They have no trouble following the plans we get, from different sources. They marry them up to handle our own needs. They love that they are doing the work, with only occasional help from the guys.

We have tried to use the psychokinetic trait to move things. The most we have been able to do is to stretch our reach, the same as anyone else could. I'm not saying that it isn't possible. We just haven't been able to do it. We keep trying though. Nothing ventured, nothing gained. I have had some success with something similar. I was on the highway, approaching a line of cars and thinking that I need them to move, and the whole line moved aside at once and let me pass on by. Coincidence? Maybe.

As the week draws near the end, we have finished the first landing and bridge. The moms will want to help. They get excited when Tanya tells them about the work here. This is a real adventure for our guests, whomever they are. Marie is going home to bring her friends up, to have a holiday. She really misses them. They get together whenever we go back home. She will go back when the moms do, then drive her friends up and back, and then drive her car here. It will be their first time here.

Tanya's birthday celebration has begun with the arrival of 'the moms'. Millicent and Brenda have been missing her, with all her summers spent up here. She is turning sixteen. Once a mousy little girl, she is now a confident, beautiful, young woman. Tall to begin with, she now stands five foot nine. Amy was put off by her lack of physical growth. She is now a towering, five foot three. She is happy for that much, and that she grew more than Tanya did. They have only had one spat, in their nearly four years together. Marie and I were together for four years, before we were married. We had plenty of fights in that time, and after as well. We have to ask them for their secret to frictionless coexistence. I still have the feeling I got, in their only fight. It wasn't quite as bad as being kicked in the groin, but it felt similar in my chest. Amy always laughs at that memory. Being back handed in the chest, was what ended the fight. They both roared with laughter, as Amy clutched her chest and said, 'Oooh, my dad is feeling this.' It even gets me laughing.

Tanya takes her moms on a tour of the jobs she has been busy doing this summer. When they get to the elevated platforms and rope bridge, they had to climb it and cross the bridge. "It's like being in Neverland!" They beg her to have them help do more. She agrees, knowing that was our plan all along.

While they are on the tour, Amy is leading us in preparing a surprise for Tanya. We are decorating their room to look like the hollowed tree trunk in Neverland. We brought a lantern with a fairy figurine to be her Tinkerbelle. There were wall panels hidden in the crawlspace below their room. Moss was hanging from the walls and ceiling. The floor was covered with panels that were also hidden below. Pictures of the 'lost boys' were stuck on the walls. Although they loved their jobs up here, it was work. This will add some fun to their off hours.

Tanya took them to see the 'bridge on the river, why?' as she had called it. They talked with Evelyn for a time, and then the four of them, went across the beam, and up to see the bench on the hill. They admired the view and started back.

We were all finished, before they returned. Amy went down to meet them. Marie and I got the food set out for dinner. Amy brought them around to the lakeside table. Candle lanterns were lit around the area, hanging on poles and placed on the table. Tanya had no notion of this being arranged. Amy sat her down at the head of the table, in a chair she had made for her. We took our places on both sides. Amy served Tanya and then the moms. She sat at the opposite end to look at her for the meal. We ate, and talked about the tour, she had given her moms. The meal was one of her favourites. After the meal, Amy brought out a cake she had made and decorated. She was given presents and after they were opened, Amy took her to see her room. We hurried in ahead of them to catch her reaction. Of course the tears started to flow. I couldn't help it, I get emotional. Luckily, the females were too busy wiping their own eyes, to notice me. On the bedside table, Amy had placed a crocodile alarm clock. Amy whispered to Tanya, "and tonight, I'm gonna poke-your-hontas, Tiger Lily."

We had a beautiful sunset, and as we sat around the campfire, an array of tiny lights lit up on the tree house bridge. "There, when we walk the bridge to the sleeping platforms, we will have them to guide us." I said.

"Won't they keep you up?" Brenda asked.

"No, that's what the bridge is for." I quipped.

Marie said, "They aren't very bright, up close."

"They look smarter from farther away." I finished.

Millicent asked, "Who are you, Henny Youngman?"

"No, Funny Oldman." I answered.

"You wish." Marie chided.

"And she gets all the laughs." I poke at her.

Chapter Thirty Two

See You In September

The moms were up with Marie and the girls, and out to help work on the tree bridges. Amy led the detail and they followed the same plan, as for the first landing. This one was further into the forest. The rope bridge was the same. This network will go along, deep into the woods. The sleep platforms will be set up on the oak and maple trees. The landings will be on the pines and other conifers. The ground beneath the trees, is soft, covered with rotting leaves and needles. When they take a break from building, they walk along the route underneath the bridges, looking for rocks, that work their way up through the soil. It's not unusual for a rock, to lift some of the tree roots, as they come up under them. We gather them up, when we find them, to use on the stone hearth of the greatroom. Now if you fall from the walkway, you have a better chance of getting off easy.

When I join the party, early or late, I take Amy's place and the work moves faster. She continues to call the shots, but she can be up there working with them. I, pretty much, am a safety man, as well as the hard drive of the Amy computer. It is disheartening at times, not being in on the building. They just told me, a dozen or more concussions, are too many. The next one could end it for me. I told some friends, I was trying to overcome my fear of heights. They suggested that I was going about it the wrong way. Let's face it, gravity works. I had a vision for my headstone. 'Tom Wrent, this way he went.' with an arrow point down. I kill me.

Marie is wanting to stop expanding the walkway. She thinks like an adult. I still think like a kid. There is never enough places to have fun. If we go on far enough, the kids will get tired enough, with out doing the whole route, each day. If we stop too soon, they will get bored of it. I'm talking, kids my age, too. Wait until we get the zip line in. It should, really, go all the way to the lake. Marie shakes her head, side to side. The rest nod their heads, up and down. It's funny, because they are all behind her. The straight girl, is the only one, that wants to grow up.

They go back to work and she goes to sit on the beach. I sit down beside her. "It won't likely reach the lake, but it will go as far as we can make it. It has to be worth it. It's for holidays, not a kid's birthday party. Family will come for this. Friends will come for this. Strangers will want to come for this."

"Why does it always have to be out of control?"

"Because at work everyday, is under someone else's control. I know, I don't work, but I did once. Thirty six years of working for someone else. I'm not dead yet." I get up to go back to do what I can. She gets up to come with me. Amy tells them what I said and that she's coming. They cheer for us.

"Aren't you going to put up railings?" Marie asks.

"Yes we are. I don't know what to use yet. If we make it too safe, they won't be as careful. I could put up netting under the whole thing. And what would they do? They would jump into it. Even if it was supposed to collapse and let them down easy. They would try to do something else that is crazy, and I haven't thought of it yet."

"You have to make it safe." Marie insists.

"I have to make it scary. Scare the hell out of them. They will be too scared, to do something stupid. The nets and glass panels are good for us, but what about the birds. They will break their little necks, for our safety. They need to be safe too."

Amy tells us to, "Make the driftwood railing. It will be scary. And let the parents go through first and then they will tell the kids."

"You think? They might do something stupid and set an example." I laugh.

We do as Amy suggests. At the foot of the stairs, we put up a sign that says, "Enter at your own risk!" painted in dried blood red, with runs of paint. We will put up skeletons, hanging from the rope bridges. And my skulls at the foot of the stairs. The skulls for post caps. Yes, that's the ticket. I knew they would go somewhere. Halloween all summer long.

Amy is getting in the mood. She tells the others what is on my mind and all but Marie loves it. It will be like Treasure Island and Pirates of the Caribbean.

The crew leaves the walkway after finishing the bridge they were doing and start preparing the railings for the platforms and landings. Down to the wood sorting pile. Everyone takes a hand at pulling the best branches, for getting the look we want. We strip some and soak them in the lake. A day or two will do it.

Others we strip only parts of and leave them ragged. Some long straight ones are perfect for pickets. The pieces are starting to shape up. It feels like listening to music as it builds and forms. It resonates and reverberates, and gets down into your soul. It fills you with an energy that takes control of you. You move and sway to the rhythm and the melody. I fall into the space, where the whole world is not. I feel the creativity taking me, controlling me. I am no longer who I am. I am carried into the stories we are miming with these stage props. I see the original characters taking shape and moving through the scenes as if they had been there, and long to be there again. They are pleading with me to go on, and give them back their world. Pleading with me to use the gifts we have and form their lives again, in the minds of anyone that comes to see this and experience the magic of the mind.

Amy and Marie place their hands on me and gently bring me back. I look at each of them in turn. They rub my shoulders and back and get me to sit down. They thought I was getting ready to check out. I let them care for me. Amy knows what I saw and she can make it real for me. They bring me some food and drink. Marie places a wet rag on my head. They think the sun had got me. I don't know, maybe they're right. I can't really tell if I am back yet. It was a beautiful place. It was nice to see my old friends. I enjoy getting away. I don't mind leaving my body to fend for itself. What did it do for me? I would gladly move to another, if I could. Maybe I can. I haven't tried it yet. I have had the chance. But, how do you know which one to pick. They may be just like me. If I could talk to their soul and ask what it's like in there. Maybe they would like to see how other bodies feel. Maybe they would like to be an empath. It's alright if you like that sort of thing. Maybe they already are an empath and just want to change the view. Amy is calling me. I know she is there. I can find her if she just keeps calling me. It is darkening in here. Have I gone into a tunnel? Am I coming back out of it? I was here once before. I cried that time. I'm not afraid of it this time. Maybe I have faced my fear of close spaces, like tunnels. Marie was with me the last time I was here. The rest aren't here. I can't feel them or hear them. They were talking and laughing until they found that I was stuck in the tunnel. I had company when I went last time. They took the same bus. Only my part of the bus, went into the tunnel. I can't remember how I got out of the tunnel. I didn't even see how I got into the tunnel. I was on the floor. Crawling. Crawling and rolling. I hated that tunnel. I am okay with this tunnel. I feel safe in this tunnel. I see a light. There is a light in the end of this tunnel. It looks familiar. It looks like someone is there waiting for me. Oh, it's just a mirror. It's me at the end of the tunnel. I guess I got out again. Maybe this tunnel, is a funnel, to help me get back in, the right way. It is a long one. I'm getting tired of trying to get there. It is so slow in here. It is like I am trying to walk through molasses, or grease. There is another light coming in. It looks like a person. They are going to help me. They are pulling my arm. I am getting out of the grease. It is still sticking to me. It makes me feel heavy. There are more lights coming. It is more people. They are pushing me and pulling me. It feels like they dropped me. They are pushing me around and around. Where are they going with me? Hey, let me go. You're making me dizzy. I feel sick at my stomach. I don't know these people. I can't see anyone I know here. I've seen this place before, or one like it. There are more lights. Don't shine those at me. It hurts my eyes. One of those people is trying to talk to me. I have no clue, what she is trying to say. Hey, I know her, that other one, that is behind the talking one. It's Marie. Hi, Marie. What are they doing with me? Where am I? Why don't you answer me? Now what? I can't hear Marie. She's trying to say something to me. Why don't they speak up? Are they doing that trick I do with Marie, when I just mouth the words, when she asks me what I've said? It's not funny! Stop it. Why don't you say something out loud? I should have stayed in the tunnel. Marie is crying. She just kissed my forehead and left. Wait! Take me with you! I don't like this anymore. Let me go! I'm just going to close my eyes. I don't want to see this anymore. They're shaking me again. Leave me alone. Alright I'll open my eyes. Quit shaking me and quit mouthing all the words. Amy is still with me. I hear her. She isn't with me. She is still in my mind. 'I can hear you, Amy. Why can't I hear them?'

'You're sick again. Something happened to you at the sorting pile. You just stood there going back and forth. You had a strange look.'

'I was in a trance. I was hearing music and I saw Long John Silver and Captain Jack Sparrow. They were pleading with me to do the railing like we were going to. Then I felt you and Mom holding me and sitting me down. It went black like I was in a tunnel.'

'I felt you and heard something, but it wasn't clear what you were doing. It was like you were away from your body. I couldn't get you to respond. I can see what you saw. I can't feel anything from that time.'

'I wasn't there. I was gone from my physical body. I could feel nothing from it.'

'I'll tell them what happened.' she said.

'Don't! They shouldn't know about you!'

'They already do. Mom and I told them. They would have operated just to see what was wrong. I couldn't let them do that. It might have kept you from getting back in. They might have severed the connection between you and your body.'

'I was looking for someone to trade with me.'

Amy told the doctor what had happened. That I had left my body. That I was ready to let go of it. Trade it with another soul. They couldn't figure what had caused it. She told them that it was not the first time. She told them that I was an empath. She told them about the last time, when I couldn't get back in. She told them my long history. She told them everything about me. She told them, that she can communicate with me now. She told them, that I can't hear them, or anyone else, but her. She told them, that I can't use my voice. She told them what my body is like, right now.

They were incredulous. They had never heard of this before, in the real world. It was like something out of the movies. Science fiction. How could they believe this. They ask Amy, how she could expect them to accept this fairy story. She gave them the only physical sign, that said they were different. She showed her ears, and when they laughed that off, she lifted her shirt to reveal her missing navel. They had more cause for pause, now. They touched her and pressing firmly, realised there was no sign of there ever being a depression, or an umbilical cord. No structure beneath the skin what-so-ever. Alright, they will accept her as what she says she is. How can they, now, help her father. Give him a sedative and check him in the morning, but check his vitals through the night, without waking him. They would do as she suggested. They left strict orders about this procedure and that it must be followed to the letter. They were to allow him to wake up, on his own.

The morning found me waking about eleven, as is usual. I sat up and looked around to understand where I was. A head was stuck through the door. When they saw me up, they came in to check my vitals. They called the doctor. They asked me the usual questions to see if I knew who I was, and what I was doing here. "I know who I am, but I could not hazard to self diagnose. I am Thomas Orville Wrent. I was brought in for being awol."

"What do you mean, awol? Are you in the military?"

"No, I was having an out of body vacation. Just a short one. I was inspired."

"Do you do this often?"

"Now and then. More often now than before."

"Why do you think you were out of your body?"

"It was either that or I was out of my mind. I could see my body as I was being brought back. It was in the light at the end of a long tunnel. Then there were more lights, that were people. They were helping me back down the tunnel. I know I was out of my body, because there was no pain anymore."

"What do you mean, no pain? Were you in pain? Where was the pain?"

"I'm always in pain. It is everywhere. Some constant. Some transient. I have fibromyalgia, diabetes II, haemochromatosis, arthritis, and other 'itises.'"

"How long have you had this pain?"

"A little under six feet. Almost all my life, from when I can remember."

A doctor comes in the room, with some others, and the nurse told him what I had been saying. He repeated the questioning, while he poked and prodded, asking if it hurt there, while I was trying to answer the first questions. He was probably trying to see, if I could repeat the answers, while responding to other stimuli. He must be a specialist. No bedside manner. He didn't seem to take note of anything I was saying. He turned to the others and assigned them some tasks. Those that were assigned left the room. He told me he was going to do some tests to try to determined what caused the blackout. I told him it wasn't a blackout. It was a step out. He took no notice. The nurse that had been questioning me, said that I had a sense of humour, so I didn't seem to be affected much. She said I was sitting up, when she came in the room. He told me not to sit up, or try to get up. He told me to lie still, and they will run the tests.

Amy had been listening to what was going on, in our peculiar way. She was telling Marie how I was. That calmed Marie. "Why does he do things like that?" she asked. Amy explained how it started. She could see it happening and everything that went on, until I past a certain point. After that, she said, that was where she lost me and got scared. I heard her telling the story. I didn't interrupt her. She said it could have started after having the falls. There were some that point toward concussions as a place that could bring on a number of psychic phenomenon. Clairvoyance, psycho kinesis.

"Isn't that what you have with him?"

"Yes but that was not from a fall. He did have some other things, that could have resulted from the falls. It is hard to say. The memories that I share with him, are those that he was able to record, and eventually, form in the long term memory. I can't access anything that his brain didn't perceive."

"So you can't tell them what started this?"

"No. I can tell them, when he started having these, 'vacations,' as he calls them."

"Could you tell them, so they can figure out where to look?"

"I did, and it doesn't necessarily point to the cause. It may just tell them where to look in his history. I can tell them some things, but the unrecorded events, are more likely to hold the answers."

"How long are they going to have to keep him here?"

"It will take a few days. Maybe more. They have that incident from last year that they will concentrate on, for now. You can go and have your friends up, and that will help you cope, and pass the time. He is alright. There is nothing going on that hasn't been going on before. They are not likely to find anything new. They might and I will always be in touch with him. If anything happens, I will know it first, before they do. You can have the girls up, without any testosterone, in the way."

Marie laughs slightly. "How can I concentrate on driving, with him in here?"

"You know you can. That is what gets you through the traffic. You are focussed when you are driving. You won't be alone, until after you take the girls home. I will know what is happening with you, too. Everywhere you go, I am in you head. Hope that doesn't freak you out."

"It doesn't. Not now. It's reassuring."

"I'll see if we can go in to see him and then we can go home. We can get busy and keep the workforce on track."

They let them come to see me. Marie was feeling better, until she started to leave. I was alright. They might find something they missed before. I don't care too much about that. I was tempted to say Arnold's line, from Kindergarten Cop. 'It's not a tumour.' but that wouldn't help Marie. Amy agrees that, that would be very inappropriate. They left and I just went for a stroll, in my mind. Hope I don't get out of the body again, but what are you supposed to do, when you're stuck in hospital? I don't even have my phone.

Amy got Marie busy, with putting up the railings. She drew pictures of what it is supposed to look like. Marie got the branches from the lake and placed them in the sun to bake. They put up the pickets at the ends of each of the bridges. This should clue anybody in, that there is an open space near. They fit the pickets, which were the sturdiest of the poles, into holes in the platforms and bolted them to the frame beneath. More contorted poles were used as the upper and lower railings. The shorter pieces fit as pickets on a fence would. It didn't take the long to put it all together. It looked great and they felt so much more safe, when they were working on the next section.

Amy asked, "Mom, aren't you glad that your husband is almost as smart as you?"

"I think, Tom is smarter than I am."

"Oh, of course he is. He married you didn't he?"

"Thank you, Amy."

"Dad wanted me to say that. He knew what you would say."

"Of course he did. He's going to write it that way in his book anyway."

They accomplished much more, than Marie would have wanted, in the time the moms were there to help. Our wood sorting area was nearly bare, save for the trees. Marie loved that. "Everywhere he goes, he has a mess, waiting for him to do something with." She is so glad to see it go. "What are we supposed to do with the rest of it?"

Amy answered, "We have some things in the main cottage to do. The rest is for the barn. After that, he has some projects, we are going to work on together."

"So this will never be gone?" Marie held a hand to her forehead.

"It will be gone from here. It will be stacked up behind the barn."

"That's a relief. Then we can get this area looking like someone lives here."

"This area will be filled in, in a way."

"What is he planning for it, now?"

"It will be a dry watercourse to drain the runoff away from the cottage and down toward the river. It will fill with water in the spring and be dry the rest of the year. We're going to fill it with rocks and bushes and small trees. There will be a bridge over it."

"How long has he been planning that?"

"About twenty seconds. Just long enough for me to tell you."

"So he's doing well?" she perks up.

"Yes, he is on cruise control, he says, and just letting them do all their tests. He said there is one test, that he won't let them do. An autopsy."

"Why does he say those things?"

"If he can say those things, he is showing that he doesn't let them worry him."

"But it worries me."

Three moms will go back in two cars, and five will come back in a truck. Marie did the banking, while she was at home. She had to change all my appointments, from up here. Her friends were glad to see her. They talked nonstop all the way up. They wondered what the place would look like, when they saw her turn into the laneway. But when they got into the driveway and saw the view, they were simply awed. Just the sound of escaping sighs filled the air. That was only seconds though. They had lots still to say. Unloading their effects, gave them time to notice much of the features.

"It looks like Disneyland down there. The grandkids would love that." said Crystal.

"We just finished that, before I left." Marie said, almost proudly.

"Whose idea was that?" asked Dee.

"Tom and Amy decided on that, and everybody piled on. Our last guests, Tanya's parents, spent the whole time up here working on it."

"It's like a wilderness B&B." said Dee.

"Are we camping?" Heather asked, disgusted with the idea.

"Yes and no. We have two bedrooms in the cottage, and a loft. There is a log ladder to the loft. There are two tents with queen size beds, our trailer, with a double, a king, and a three quarter bed, and an add-a-room with another queen size bed. We have a proper bathroom in the cottage, and a composting toilet and solar shower for the campers area." Marie is listing. "We will also have sleeping rooms in the tree fort thing."

"Where will we be staying?" Heather asked.

"I'll show you the rooms and then we will make the choices. They call it glamping, when you have the tents done up like we have. It's a popular thing in Europe and some places over here. We will look at the tents first."

"Glamping? I hope it's not cramping." one of them said, probably Heather.

They walked down to the end of the row of decks, and looked in on the nylon tent first. As they climbed the stairs, they got a scare, and nearly fell over themselves. "Don't worry. They're statues, to scare off animals. They have a sound track to make it convincing." Marie said, laughing at the faces they showed. She walked up to trigger the sound.

Pat jumped back and looking at the others, as she slipped out a laugh. "That's amazing. Very clever."

"You said 'they'. Where are the others?" Crystal asked looking around. "I hope there aren't any real ones checking them out."

"The other one is at the next tent. Come in and see what this one is like." she said, holding open the door flap.

"Are there animals like this around? I wouldn't want to run into one." Crystal asked, while waiting to look inside.

"There is a mama bear and her cub, that seem to be afraid of us. There are moose, elk, deer, beaver, and some really beautiful birds." said Tanya from behind them. Marie was put off by her openness. She was worried, they wouldn't want to stay.

"Are there any big cats like this one?" Crystal asked.

"We have never seen, or heard any cougars. No one around here has warned us of any. There aren't any of these. These are panthers from South America and Africa, I think." Tanya said, hoping to redeem herself in Marie's eyes.

"Oh, this is lovely. This is clamping, is it?" Heather is known for her adlib words, either natural, or by design.

"Glamping, glamorous camping." Tanya pointed out. She had not met Heather before. She wasn't sure of what she was like. She may learn in the morning. I will leave it for the girls to experience first hand, although Amy, has just learned, from the memory that has flashed through my eyes. She clamps her hand to her mouth, to stifle a squeal. Tanya didn't notice. She will see as I have suggested.

They move on to the canvas tent. As they climb the stairs, they see the other cat. Only Pat is startled this time, and she has to laugh. "Oh, it's a different one." Crystal states.

"Yes, Tom didn't want two the same, or it wouldn't be as affective. The growl is different on this one making it more effective." Marie explained.

"I like the lounge areas, by the tents" Crystal declares. "This is so much different, from the other cottage."

"That's one of the reasons for that walkway, up in the trees. They are going to put in a zip line, from the trees toward the lake."

"What's a zip line?" Dee asks.

"It's a cable that you hang from and slide down. They have them in wilderness areas, to give you the feeling that you're a bird, flying through the trees and rocky places. They have them at amusement parks too." Marie was excited about that.

"This is nice, Marie." Pat says, looking into the tent. "It's like the old style tents."

"Yes, that was our second tent. Tom never throws anything out."

"He only keeps things that have a purpose, or value. He just sees value, in almost everything." Amy defended me.

They move on to the trailer and then the house. They were familiar with the trailer. They had seen it many times, when they visited us at the beach, on Long Point. They hadn't seen the addition on the back. Down at the cottage, they were amazed at the finishes. They loved the rustic ladder, but didn't see themselves, climbing up there to sleep. "We'll take the loft and someone can use our room." Amy offered.

"Thank you, Amy. I have an idea, who would love to use that one." Marie said, amused by the thought. "Here's the first bedroom. The basic one. And here we have, Amy and Tanya's room."

"This is perfect for you, Heather." Crystal asserted. Marie agreed.

"Oh yes, this is my style. This will be perfect. Now, where is my Indian friend?"

They roared. That was awhile ago. "He met someone else, Heather." Marie told her. That would have been a hoot, to have 'him' back. That would have been too much. "I will take the loft, if you girls would want to take one of the tents."

Tanya said, first, "Yes, that would be nice. We would keep anyone else, that wanted the tents, company." Amy agreed.

Dee opened, "I'll double up with Heather." Crystal and Pat, said that they would share. Marie was not surprised, at all, that they would choose to double up, rather than going the glamping route. Heather was easy to sleep with, Marie had told me. She lays down, closes her eyes, and doesn't move until morning. I'll take her word for it.

Amy was right, the doctors are all over the reason for my stay, last year. MRIs, EEGs, X-rays, they are doing them and redoing them. Ultrasounds, they have got me coated with gel. I had them go ahead and shave my head. I didn't want anything in their way. It was too warm in the hospital, anyway. I only have Amy visiting me, and that is by telepathy. She is always here and lets me know all the grizzly details of the women's holiday, as they happen. Tanya had walked into the cottage, just as Heather greeted the day. Talk about the education! She is never going to be the same. She will not tell a soul, anything, about the things they are to witness. It was quite a different image of Marie, that she saw here. They do know how to party. They are rarely out of control, that means, they did it all on purpose. They are ladylike, that means, in the broadest sense of the word. The stories I could tell, could get me in trouble, big time. They have connections. I feel blessed to have this little hideaway to come to. It's like a spa, one where they shove needles in you. It is fortunate, that there are few neighbours, that can see you here, or hear you. They have invited Evelyn to join them. She naively accepted. Amy had prior knowledge of the activities, at their women's weekends. She did not warn Tanya about any of them. I am very glad I have her. At times like these, I live through her. I am able to walk in her steps, breathe the clean air through her nostrils, and feel the gentle touch of human hands. I don't dwell on these things. I just enjoy the connectedness.

Marie asks Amy, to sit with her, and help her to talk with me. She closes her eyes, and talks as if I am saying the words. It reminds me of the scene in Ghost. Amy tries to keep herself out of the scene. We just talk to each other. We don't go through anything more than that. It keeps Marie sane, until she comes to visit in person.

The women take a walk through the woods. They ask about the ropes, still tied to the trees. They think it is a good idea. They didn't realise that I had had so much trouble seeing. Marie said she hadn't either. As much as I told her, she still didn't know, because she tuned me out. I hope she still thinks, that that was a good idea, after I'm gone. Will it change anything? I sincerely doubt it.

They get up in the walkway through the trees. It is an awesome feeling up there. I especially love it, because, of my

427

vertigo. The thrill is more enhanced, than without it. They love the platforms, where they can congregate and point out scenes of interest. The bridges scare them, but they enjoy it, with everyone close by.

Tanya was trying to mate them up, in her mind. When she told Amy, she heard that Dee's late husband, had jokingly called the get togethers, lesbian weekends. It was another dynamic, that kept us all together.

It was a fun filled week. Many laughs. Many plans made. They loved our place here, but they also loved the Huron cottage. Marie told them about the barn that would have living quarters as well. It is better, but takes nothing away, from Lake Huron, or Lake Erie. Marie agrees. Amy wonders, if she should make a plan, to buy this place outright, to free me up, to get a place on the Great Lakes.

Marie is all set to take the ladies home. She will come back, with either Faith, or Grace. She had planned on bringing her car up, but changed her mind, when I was sent to hospital. She is afraid, that they will take away my licence. I am too.

I am virtually, a basket case. That is what I may be travelling in. I will be trussed up, in a suit of modern armour. This time hadn't been a fall, but they think it was because of a fall. They think that I am at the brink of a stroke. They are trying to err on the side of caution. I may be banned from flying, even. They are not giving me much of an existence. How will I be able to exercise? Swimming is my only choice now. Even then, I will have to wear a lifejacket in the pool. Will I be advised, to refrain from bending forward, to minimise the pressure in my brain? Our waterbed is out. I will even have to be careful, of how I excrete waste. How bad is that. Blowing my nose. Is that next?

Will I be using things to control all my bodily functions. Will I be banned from going up, or down the stairs? What about the elevators? Is that next? They go up too fast, so I can't use them?

I can see some dolt saying, 'Boy, look at Tom Wrent. He's got it made. Never has to do anything. They wait on him, hand and foot.' I would be afraid to eat, in case I gained weight and lose my legs to diabetes. What kind of a life is that?

Hold everything. Stop this pity party. It hasn't happened yet. They are still poking and prodding. They have no decision made at all, yet. Don't go putting yourself in a hole, until they bring the casket.

It is a good idea to set aside driving. You've been doing that for some time now. You can do that. Do one thing more, on your own. Quit planning the trouble. It is very good at handling its own affairs. Focus on the good things in life, that you still enjoy. If they bring in restrictions, handle that then.

Grace and the girls bring Marie back up. They come to the hospital to visit me, before going on, to the camp. I know I have Amy there all the time. It still feels better to have someone know, that someone cares about you, enough to come in. It is depressing, when they look at you with pity. Grace and the girls stay for two nights. Brad and Bradley are at his mom's place for the same two days.

The elevated walk gets the attention, right away. The kids get up there and before long, they have Grace up with them. Marie asks their opinion on the zip line idea. They agree, it would be awesome. Amy calls down to them. She is perched in a tree with Tanya, while attaching the anchor braces for the zip line. They're coming down to affix the anchors at the other end. Tanya drops a rope down and ties it off at the top.

The sight of the girls climbing down the ladders with their tool belts full, is outstanding for the onlookers. "You look like real construction workers." someone calls to them.

"That's because we are. We actually built ninety five percent of the cottage, decks, and this walkway in the trees. So we are actual, real, construction workers. We just don't get paid for it." Tanya shouted back.

"Papa isn't paying you?" asked Jo.

"We're interns to an invisible boss. How can an invisible boss pay you? With invisible money?" Tanya reasons.

"He's not invisible. He's just not here." Amy argues.

"He never tells us what to do, when he is here."

"He doesn't need to with me here. I tell us what to do. He wouldn't be able to form the ideas into words. The memories are beyond his recall abilities." Amy is my defender. She won't let anyone, get away with deriding me, in any way.

"We want to have this done, for when he comes out of hospital." Tanya announces.

"He won't be allowed to ride it." Marie tells them.

"We know, but you can and we can. He can experience it, through Amy." Tanya justifies it.

"You totally, got that right! E=MC squared." Amy tells her.

"Will you stop quoting from TV shows?" Tanya complains.

"It's a family thing." Jo says. "We all do it."

They walk with Amy, to where she is looking at having the lower terminal. She wants to put it up, near the lake and the stand of trees there.

"How are you paying for this?" Marie demands.

"Millicent and Mom, are buying it. They want to give it, to thank you, for having me and them stay here." Tanya said proudly.

"Wow! Thank them very much. It looks expensive."

"It is, but the cheaper version looked unsafe. They went to a place that installs commercial equipment, for parks. They are coming to put it in. We are just placing these pieces to show them where they have to put it." said Tanya. "They want you, to have them back. So they wanted to do this, for you."

"They don't need to do that." Marie objected, "They can come back anytime."

"They are quite well-off. They can afford this and much more." it was Tanya's turn to object. "They will want to ride this, when they come back."

Amy speaks up now, "Mom, just accept it and let it go. There is no logical argument against it. If you decide to sell the place? They will buy it for Tanya."

"Okay. No more objections from me." Marie promised.

Amy says, "Dad always says, 'If you stand by a table long enough, someone will put food on it.' Let's have some supper."

Chapter Thirty Three

Back To It All

I hope this doesn't become an annual thing. Two years in a row, I spend the end of summer in a hospital, in Peterborough. I have nothing against the city. I would like to see some more of it, than its hospitals.

Ontario is one of the most beautiful provinces in Canada. I feel blessed to be born and raised here. I just wish the winters, didn't come so soon. It's not here yet, but the nights are getting too cool for their own good, and mine. I am going home and I don't mean the cottage. They are taking me there for the night, and then, it is off to the city. Tanya has high school starting soon. Amy has to get ready to head off to college. We will be back to the cottage now and then. I will have to catch up on my banking and my doctors' appointments.

I will miss our Miss, when she is at school. I will have her in my head all the time. I can see her face when she looks in the mirror. I can hear her voice clearly. It's like the hospital. I will miss seeing her coming in the door, everyday. I will miss Tanya, being with her. I will miss her being there to defend me. She will turn sixteen, after Halloween. There is going to be a lot of things to miss, just as with the other three. Empty nest, take two.

I am not to drive, longer than twenty minutes. I have to have my trike fixed. This old one needs its bearings repacked and a new chain. It will take awhile for them to get it back to me. I will be relying on Marie's good temper, to drive me to appointments. She doesn't like going to places, when it has nothing to do with her. If she gets sick, I help take care of her. When I get sick, I take care of me. She tells me that, she never wanted to be a nurse. Well, I never wanted to be ignored. Deal with it.

Having my sight again is very nice. I can work on those fine details, on my models. I can reach for something, and it will be there. I can put paint on without missing the surface. Life is good.

Amy has been through frosh week that has been the start of so much of the university life. It was comparatively quiet. Amy kept a low profile. She hates it when I say that, because of her height. She did keep well away from groups. She has taken back her baggy clothes, from high school. Other girls were trying to get noticed. Amy was trying to be missed. It didn't help when someone pointed out her age. Her roommate was eighteen, a pretty girl, taller than Brent. She was six foot two. She was having much more trouble, trying to go unnoticed. She dare not wear a scarf in winter. They would be calling her the flag pole. As odd as they looked together, they got along famously. Her name was Sarah. She said her brother's friends would say, 'Sarah taller girl in the country?' She laughed, when she saw Amy changing. 'That's a trick I could never pull off.' Amy didn't even try, to suggest, what Sarah could disguise herself with. She was too nice, to tease at all. They shared some classes. They had some similar goals. They talked like they grew up together. Amy had to remind herself that she was in an exclusive relationship. It was hard. She didn't even know what Sarah's orientation was. She didn't ask. There was no use sticking that iron, in the fire. If she doesn't know she can let it go. She hopes.

'You're fickle.' I told her.

'I know, I want so many.'

'Three, that is so many?'

'Maybe not to you.'

They went out to movies, to miss the drinking crowd. Amy was unable to get away from her sweet smell. 'Move over one and put your snacks between you.' I suggested. She did and it helped at some shows. They would just have to skip the popular ones. The worst thing about it was, when she would concentrate on Tanya, she would want Sarah, all the more.

Sarah was from the Thunder Bay area. Amy remembers that area, from her past life. They talked about the places they both knew. Sarah seemed to find it odd, when they talked of one place, Amy described it as brand new. Sarah knows, that it has seen better days, much better. Then Amy told her about the horse drawn carts, that were still delivering to houses and businesses. Sarah asked Amy how she could have seen those things. Amy realised what she had done. She decided, to let Sarah in on her remembering the past life, so clearly, that she could mistake it for the present.

I was concerned, that the familiarity she shared with someone, would cause her to divulge other secrets. She promised to watch out for that.

Sarah asked her for more of her past life memories. She was interested in how it fell within the bounds of her studies. She thought she could do a paper on it. She asked how her life had ended. Amy said she had gone to college, in another city. Her parents had moved before the war. Her dad's job had moved and they went with it. The war was on in Europe, and he enlisted when the call came. Her mom went to work for his boss, to keep his position open. She learned to do his job well. Her brothers had enlisted along with their father. Amy had started college, and the steady income, kept her there. She told about the fights. She didn't mention that she was gay. She didn't mention that, it was Nazi sympathisers, that were stirring up the hate, for gays. She told about the brutality of the murder, and how she was, when she was found. As she was waiting for her body to be discovered, she had seen her mother's pain. She couldn't hear things, but she could see. There was no pain for her. It had stopped somewhere during the beating. Well after they had raped her. She had likely slipped into a coma. It was merciful. They wouldn't let her mother see the body. Just the clothing that had been left hanging off the body. When they had found it, they thought it was an animal, that someone had tried to put clothes on, before butchering it. They knew what they had, when they saw the bone structure of a hand, that was dangling from an arm. They verified it, in an autopsy.

Sarah knew she would have trouble, writing that story. She had become so emotionally invested in it.

Amy's sharing of her story, held the friends fast. Sarah had no attraction to Amy, in any way other than a close friendship. Amy could feel it, and soon lost the sexual urges, she had thought she had, for her tall friend. She did ask to try her perfume. At least she could get that, out of the investment she had made. Amy was not surprised, when Sarah, had been approached by a modelling agency, through the school. She was sure, that she would not be noticed, for that métier.

Amy found she would be happy in this place. Her professors were easy to follow, and respect. There had been a lot of interest in the course, so only the most promising students with high academic profiles were admitted. This made the grading higher, but the involvement of her classmates, livelier. She enjoyed the atmosphere, when they gathered to discuss, points of interest.

When we arrived to get her, for her birthday celebration. She had mounds of emotion about the course and life in general. Tanya wasn't sure what was happening here. She was afraid, that Amy had fallen in love, with someone. Amy found a chance to take the idea, out of her lover's mind.

On the way home, both girls were discussing the advent of driving classes. When I was asked what vehicle I could supply her with, I told her 'Li'l Joe'. "Great, then I could pick up guys." We all knew that was going nowhere.